A VENETIAN MOON

by

Bill Rogers

C A T O N

First Published December 2013
by Caton Books

First Edition

Published by Caton Books
www.catonbooks.com

ISBN: 978-1-909856-08-0

Cover Design by Dragonfruit
Design & Layout: Commercial Campaigns

In the moonlight which is always sad,
as the light of the sun itself is, as the light called
human life is, at its coming and its going.

Nel chiaro di luna che è sempre triste, come è la luce
del sole stesso, come e la luce chiamata la vita
umana, al suo arrivo e alla sua partenza.

Charles Dickens – A Tale of Two Cities

Chapter 1

As dusk fell, the last rays of the sun crept across the lagoon, dappling gentle waves that lapped the quay, burnishing the palazzo roofs and church spires with tints of gold and misty rose. The city, which by day had been a magical, bustling place, now cloaked itself in an altogether more mysterious, mystical mantle.

Kate reached out, and placed her hand over his.

'Thank you,' she said.

Caton turned to look at her, and smiled.

'What for?'

'For this. For marrying me.' She patted the increasingly evident bump in her tummy. 'For everything.'

He raised his glass in salute.

'I should be thanking you.'

'What for?'

'For saving me.'

Her brow furrowed.

'What from?'

'Myself.'

The flickering light from the candle in the glass at the centre of the table cast shadows in the hollows of his face. It was difficult to tell if he was serious.

'It was a lovely surprise,' she said. 'Venice for our honeymoon. And the Orient Express.'

He followed her gaze across the water, beyond the

statuesque San Giorgio Maggiore and the Campanile in Piazza San Marco, to where the minaret-topped domes of the Byzantine Basilica peered above the red-tiled roofs of the Palazza Ducale.

'I was fifteen when I first came here,' he said. 'A school visit. It blew me away. I promised myself I'd come back. You were the first person I really wanted to share it with.'

The waiter appeared from nowhere to clear away their dessert plates.

'*Avete finito, signore, signora?*'

'*Si, grazie,*' Caton replied. '*Tutto è stato delizioso.*'

The waiter smiled and gave a quarter bow.

'*Di niente,*' he said. '*Caffè? Decaffeinato? Forse un digestivo?*'

'Kate?' said Caton.

'I'm fine,' she replied.

'No, *grazie,*' Caton told him. '*Abbiamo finito. È stato perfetto.*'

The waiter bowed, and left.

'I bet you didn't learn that when you were fifteen,' she said.

'More or less,' he told her. 'I studied Italian while I was at MGS. Since then I've had a few opportunities to practise it at Europol conferences.'

'With seductive Italian beauties, no doubt!'

Behind her laugh he sensed the tiniest hint of insecurity.

'Only if you count middle-aged, overweight, chain-smoking men, squeezed into belted uniforms bristling with medals.'

The sun finally dipped below the horizon. The moon slid, as though by some unspoken agreement, from behind a cloud. A full moon, tinged pink from the afterglow, with large blue-grey patches the size of continents.

He curled his fingers around hers, raised her to her feet, and led her to the water's edge.

They stood there, drinking in the view, until the wind off the Dolomites began to whip up waves in the lagoon. Kate shivered. Caton placed his arm around her shoulders and pulled her close. They turned away, towards the ancient floodlit church of San Clemente. Clothed in gold, ochre and white, it glowed like a beacon on this tiny island.

'Let's have a peek inside while they're making the coffee,' she said. 'They only open it once a week, or for special occasions, like weddings and christenings.'

They were standing in the central aisle when a woman's scream pierced the silence.

'Stay here,' said Caton, already moving in the direction from whence it came.

'No chance!' She hitched up her dress and hurried after him.

The scream was replaced by a frantic cry.

'*Aiuto! Aiutami!*'

They followed the sound of sobbing, behind the church and across a stone-walled courtyard abutting the hotel kitchens. A narrow passage at the far side led onto the lagoon. Framed in the archway was the shadowy form of a woman. She turned at their approach, her hand to her mouth. He saw at once that she was young. Sixteen or seventeen, perhaps.

'What's the matter?' said Caton. '*Qual è il problema?*'

She stepped aside, her back pressed against the damp stone wall. Wordlessly she pointed down at the narrow channel of water ahead of her.

In the half-light of the moon Caton could just make out the shape of a human body, spread-eagled, face down, floating listlessly back and forth with the ebb and flow of the water as it lapped into the confined

7

space, hit the stone steps and washed back out again.

'*È morto?*' asked the girl.

The body was distended. Bloated from days in the sea. Longer, perhaps.

'Yes,' said Caton. 'I'm afraid he is.'

She seemed not to have understood.

'*Sì,*' he said. '*È morto.*'

Kate put her arm around the girl, felt her shudder, and hugged her gently.

'Come on,' she said. 'There's nothing you can do.'

She led the girl carefully along the narrow path and out into the courtyard. Two doors had opened from the kitchens, flooding the courtyard with beams of artificial light. Three men in blue aprons, two of them with matching caps, hurried towards them. One held a cleaver.

'Maria, *che cosa c'è? Perché hai urlarto?*' said the tallest of them, his height exaggerated by the chef's white toque.

'*C'è un cadavere!*' she replied, emboldened by their presence. She pointed behind her. '*Nel riello. Nel ingresso del canale!*'

The two sous-chefs set off towards the inlet where the body lay.

Worried that the man with the cleaver might panic when confronted by Tom in the dark confined space, Kate shouted after them.

'My husband is there!'

The chef took the girl by the hand.

'*Stai bene?*'

'*Sì,*' she replied. '*Ora sì.*'

She turned to Kate, and gave a wan smile.

'Thank you,' she said in halting English.

He led her away towards the huddle of kitchen workers that had spilled out into the courtyard. Kate turned, and hurried back to Tom.

She found him in the archway of the passage. He was holding up his warrant card, explaining, she assumed, why it was best they didn't go any further. With nothing to fear from a dead body, the two men were plainly keen to have a look for themselves. When it was clear that he would not step aside, they retraced their steps, muttering as they went.

'Come on,' she said. 'It's not our problem. And I'm getting cold out here.'

'You go,' he told her. 'I'll just make sure someone from the hotel keeps this area secure, and then I'll come.'

'What are you afraid of?' she retorted. 'That he's going to swim back out to sea?'

She instantly regretted it.

'I know I'm being petty,' she said, 'but it is cold, and it is none of our business. And it *is* supposed to be our honeymoon, for God's sake.'

'I know,' he began.

'*Signore!*'

The hotel manager hurried towards them. At his side was a taller, heavy-built man in a black puffer jacket and shiny black trousers.

'*Signore, signora,*' panted the manager as he joined them. 'I am sorry. This is a terrible thing to happen.'

'No need to apologise,' said Caton. 'I don't suppose this is your fault.'

'*Dio no!*' the man exclaimed, Caton's attempt at humour lost in translation and the gravity of the moment.

He waved his colleague forward.

'This is Paulo Mancini, our Head of Security. He will take over now.'

'He does know not to touch the body, or let anyone else in there, until the police arrive?'

'I speak English, *signore,*' said the man without

9

rancour. 'And of course I will guard the body. It is best if you leave now.'

'Amen to that,' said Kate, grabbing Caton's sleeve and pulling him away before he changed his mind.

'Goodnight, Mr Caton, Mrs Caton,' the manager called after them. 'And thank you for your help.'

Chapter 2

'You didn't need to do that, Kate,' Caton told her. 'I was coming.'

'Better safe than sorry.' She tightened her grip on his arm, and took his hand in hers. 'This will be something to tell the children when they ask where we spent our honeymoon.'

'Mmm,' he replied.

'That was nice, him calling us Mr and Mrs Caton. I'm getting used to that.'

'Mmm.'

She tried again.

'You're sure you don't mind me keeping my maiden name for work?'

'Sorry?'

She stopped, and punched him lightly with her free hand.

'Let it go, Tom. This has nothing to do with you. It's out of your jurisdiction.'

He had the sense to look chastened.

'I know, I'm sorry. Force of habit. But it's still someone's life snuffed out. Family and friends, wondering where he is, what's happened to him.'

'Not for much longer. The Italian police will identify him and contact them. Their job, not yours.'

She hugged him. He put his arm around her shoulder and pulled her gently into his chest. They began walking towards the hotel entrance.

'I was asking if you minded me keeping my maiden name for work?' she said.

'Of course I don't mind. I always liked Webb, it suits you.'

Although his face was in shadow, she could tell that he was grinning.

'I hope that's a compliment.'

'Course it is. Anyway, we both know you'd keep using it whether I approved or not.'

He let go of her hand and bounded up the first flight of steps into the hotel lobby. He turned, and called to her.

'Hurry up, Spider, your victim awaits.'

Caton emerged from the cavernous bathroom to find her standing at the window. The only light came from a single bedside lamp. The curtains were still drawn back, and she was staring down the tree-lined drive that led to the landing stage. The satin nightie clung, accentuating her sensuous curves. With the rest of her body in shadow, the pale light from the moon formed an aureole around her auburn hair, like the halo on the statue of the Blessed Virgin in the church of San Clemente where they had stood less than an hour ago. He had an overwhelming desire to take her in his arms and tell her yet again how much he loved her, how fortunate he felt to be loved by her, and that he would always keep her safe.

She heard him approach. She felt his arms encircle her, his hands enfolding the space where their unborn baby slept. She rested her face against his. They stood there in silence, both knowing that any words would be superfluous, inadequate, would break the spell.

She turned, found his lips with hers and kissed him, lightly at first, and then with a passion that took him by surprise. Still locked in her embrace, Caton found the cord and drew the curtains behind them.

Outside, in the lagoon, a sleek white and blue launch with POLIZIA emblazoned on the side docked at the landing stage, its flashing blue lights strobing the trees and the stone-paved drive until they were extinguished, and the dark returned.

'I can't sleep, not tonight.'

Kate sat up and switched on her bedside lamp. Relieved not to have to lie there pretending, Caton did the same. Always after making love they would fall into a deep untroubled sleep. But tonight was far from normal. It was a rare human being, he reflected, even with the frequent exposure to death the two of them experienced in their respective jobs, that could just switch off after seeing the body of a victim of a tragic accident or heinous crime. Anything was preferable to lying in the dark with that image imprinted on the retina like a negative hanging in a photographer's darkroom.

He fired up his Kindle and prepared to read. While he was waiting, he looked across at the book she was holding. She saw him craning his head, and angled it so that he could see the title: *The Evil That Men Do. FBI Profiler Roy Hazelwood's Journey into the Minds of Sexual Predators.*

'So much for not bringing your work on holiday,' he said. 'It's hardly bedtime reading, is it?'

'You can talk. What was it you were reading on the train coming down here?'

She lay the book down and scribed virtual speech marks with the index finger of each hand.

'*Caminada – the Crime Buster. His own incredible story.*'

'Only because The Alternatives have chosen it as

book of the month. And he *was* an Italian Mancunian.'

She picked up her book and turned over the page.

'I hope you're intending on being there this time,' she said. 'You've missed the last two meetings. You used to enjoy it. And it means I'll be able to get on with some work without having to feel guilty.'

'I didn't choose not to go. Corpses cropped up, in case you've forgotten. A bit like tonight.' He pointed to her book. 'Anyway, what's your excuse?'

'Stewart Baker and I have been asked by SOCA to prepare a comparison of the FBI ViCAP programme Hazelwood developed, and the Royal Canadian Mounted Police ViCLAS handbook.'

The most recent violent crime linkage analysis widely used by national police forces. He used it all the time. As did Kate in her work as a Home Office profiler.

'*Our* ViCLAS?'

'Mmm. Apparently, the National Crime Agency are hoping to refine it in time for their launch in October.'

'Isn't that just a bit of public relations?'

'Not if we can come up with some significant improvements. Regardless of whether or not we can, I have to do a presentation for the Serious Crime Analysis Section at the end of September.'

'Hence the rush?'

'Precisely. Now, why don't you read your book and let me finish this? Then I can get back to some lighter reading.'

'Such as?'

She reached across to her bedside table, picked up the other book lying there and held it up for him to see: *And the Mountains Echoed*.

'Khaled Hosseini's latest,' he said. 'I want to read that.'

'You can,' she told him, putting it down and

shifting her position so that her back was towards him. 'When I've finished it. Which will be sooner, the less you keep distracting me.'

Half an hour later, Kate yawned, put the book on top of the one by Hosseini and switched out her light.

'Night, night,' she said, turning onto her side, pulling the single top sheet up to her neck and snuggling down.

Caton dimmed the display on his eReader and switched it to night-time reading. He persevered for another half an hour, but the hoped for drowsiness evaded him. Giving up, he shut the Kindle down, placed it on his side table and lay there in the dark, listening to Kate's gentle breathing and the muted sound of a Scops owl in the branches of a maritime pine out on the Lido. Occasionally he thought he heard voices, low and indistinct, and found himself imagining the comings and goings at the landing stage, newly erected floodlights in the kitchen courtyard, and ghostly white figures crouching in the archway of the narrow inlet. Eventually, exhaustion overtook him, and he slept.

Chapter 3

'Another coffee?' said Caton.

They had almost finished their breakfast in the enchanting fifteenth-century cloister, with its ancient well at the centre, pairs of marbled columns along the perimeter, and fruiting peach and pomegranate trees.

'Why not?' Kate replied. 'Our water taxi's not due till 11.30.'

Caton twisted in his chair to catch the waiter's eye. Instead, he found himself staring directly at the hotel manager on the top of the steps leading from the breakfast room. At his side were two uniformed police officers. A man and a woman.

'Here we go,' he said.

On cue, the manager spotted them, spoke to the male officer, and led them down the steps and across the courtyard.

'*Signore, e Signora Caton,*' he said in a hushed apologetic tone. 'I apologise for disturbing your breakfast.' He shook his head sadly. '*Soprattutto dopo la notte scorsa.*'

Caton nodded graciously. *Especially after last night.* The stress of events, he realised, had left the man confused as to whether he should be speaking Italian or English. More so since he had an audience consisting of both.

'*Ma, Il Commissario vuole parlare a voi* … err … he

16

wishes to speak with you before you leave today.'

'Of course,' said Caton, rising from his seat.

The manager stepped smartly to the side, leaving Caton and the male officer face-to-face.

The commissario was a head shorter, and some years older, than Caton. Approaching fifty, perhaps, his hair was prematurely silvered. He was compact rather than svelte, but still elegant in his peak cap, navy-blue jacket and tie, crisp white shirt and smartly creased light-blue trousers with a narrow purple-red stripe along the side seam. He wore epaulets on which were a three-tiered castle, a single star and a small emblem like a cobra's head, all of them in gold. He took off his cap and tucked it beneath his arm.

'Umberto Bonifati, *Commissario Capo* of the *Polizia Di Stato*,' he said, offering his right hand.

'Tom Caton,' he replied.

They appraised each other.

The policeman had intelligent blue-grey eyes. Eyes that would miss nothing. They reminded Caton of the painting of the white tiger on the wall of Ying Zheng Xiong in his office high up in the Beetham Tower.

Caton introduced Kate, and watched as she took his hand and blushed almost imperceptibly as the policeman half bowed, his eyes firmly fixed on hers.

He straightened up, and waved his companion forward.

'I present Sovrintendente Catarina Volpe,' he said.

It was Caton's turn to be discomforted. She was in her early thirties, slim, with a perfectly oval face, inquisitive dark-brown eyes and matching hair to her shoulders. She wore a tailored jacket and skirt. In black shoes, with three-inch heels more suited to the office than the flagstone streets and waterborne Venetian transport, she was marginally shorter than himself. He sensed Bonifati's amused smile and Kate's glare as he took the hand she proffered. It was firm and cool, despite the heat.

'*Piacere di conoscerti,*' she said, her lips curling into an amused smile.

'*Spero di si,*' he replied.

Her smile broadened, and he heard the commissario chuckling to himself.

'Would you like to sit down?' said Caton. 'We were just about to have a coffee.'

Bonifati glanced around the other tables. Seeing that they were either empty or far enough away for their conversation to remain private, he moved to the chair on Kate's right.

'Thank you,' he said, sitting down.

Caton pulled out the chair next to him for the sovrintendente, and waited until she was seated.

The manager stepped forward.

'Would you all like a coffee? *Caffè*?' he asked nervously.

'A caffè latte for me, please,' said Kate.

'*Cappuccino scuro,*' said the sovrintendente.

'*Anch'io,*' said Caton.

'Commissario?' said the manager. '*Un corretto forse?*'

Bonifati nodded indulgently. As though reluctantly bowing to pressure.

'*Perfetto,*' he said.

It reminded Caton of someone else who loved to start his day with a coffee 'corrected' with a slug of grappa.

Bonifati caught him smiling.

'I say something amusing?' he said.

'Not really,' Caton replied. 'It just reminded me of someone. An imaginary person.'

Bonifati was intrigued. And persistent. He leant forward.

'*Una persona immaginaria*?'

Caton had dug himself a hole, and it was too late to stop digging. He wondered how Bonifati would take it.

'Commissario Brunetti,' he explained. 'From the novels by Donna Leon?'

The policeman sat back in his chair and began to laugh loudly. Heads turned on the tables in the far corner of the courtyard.

'Guido!' he said. 'You were expecting Guido Brunetti and Lieutenant Scarpe to turn up, and instead you get me and Sovrintendente Volpe.' He laughed again. '*Che spasso!*'

Then he explained it all in rapid Italian for his assistant's benefit. She smiled thinly and shrugged her shoulders. It was clearly not such a hoot for her.

'I understood her novels were not available in Italian,' said Caton. 'Something about not wanting to attract the displeasure of her neighbours here in Venice?'

'I am more Dante than *novelli Giallo*,' said Bonifati. '*Perche*, is … how you call it – busman holiday?'

'A busman's holiday.'

'But these I like. You are correct that they are only now in *Italiano*. I relate to Guido Brunetti. He is…' He searched for the words. '*Ammirevole, onesto, simpatico…*'

'Admirable, honest, likeable,' Caton translated for Kate.

'Not all of my colleagues would agree,' continued the commissario. He chuckled. 'Mainly the ones who find the stories uncomfortably close to the truth.'

'Giallo?' said Kate.

'Because,' Caton explained, 'in the 1930s a series of mystery crime novels called *Il Giallo Mondadori* was published in yellow covers. The name stuck.'

The waiter arrived and served their coffees.

The commissario took a sip, nodded his head in approval and set the cup down. He wiped a thin smear of coffee from his upper lip, took a small notebook from his jacket pocket, and looked across the table at Caton.

'Unfortunately, Chief Inspector, we are here about a real-life mystery,' he said. He saw the flicker in Caton's eyes and nodded. 'You were asked to show your passports at reception. No need to ask why you are here.'

He turned to Kate.

'Congratulations on your marriage. I hope you will both be very happy.'

It sounded rehearsed, but genuine.

'Thank you,' she replied. 'Though we were not expecting to find a body.'

He nodded thoughtfully. 'But it was not *you* that found the body.'

'A girl,' said Caton.

'Valentina Moro. *Un apprendista.*'

'An apprentice?' said Caton.

Bonifati nodded.

'She says that you said…' He pretended to consult his notes. '*È morto.* He is dead.'

He looked up and regarded Caton closely.

'How did you know it was a man?'

'The corpse had short hair, a large frame, even allowing for the fact that it was bloated. It was wearing a jacket and trousers, and one heavy black shoe. It was a reasonable assumption.'

The policeman processed the information, shrugged and made a sound like a grunt that Caton took for grudging acceptance.

He looked at his notes again.

'Did you form a view on how he may have died?'

'It was impossible to tell,' Caton replied. 'It was dark. He was on his front. There was no way of knowing if he had been hit on the head, shot, stabbed, strangled, poisoned.'

Bonifati looked up and stared at him. His pupils widened.

'But you assume that he was killed. That this was not *un accidente*. Why is that?'

'He had what looked like rope around one of his wrists, and the opposite foot,' said Caton.

'You didn't mention that to me,' said Kate.

'You hadn't spotted it. I didn't see any point in mentioning it. Not at the time.'

'Nor since,' she muttered.

'Both arms,' said Bonifati.

'Sorry?' said Caton, wondering if he had misheard.

'*Both* arms,' the policeman repeated. 'And both legs. He had pieces of rope around...' He used his hands to demonstrate. '...*i polsi e le caviglie.*'

Caton nodded to show that he understood.

'The wrists and ankles. He was tied up before he was thrown in the sea?' he mused as he tried to imagine the various permutations.

'*Non esattamente.* There were bags attached to the ropes.'

'Bags?'

As he spoke, the commissario used his hands to give an indication of their size.

'One bag, each rope. The bags we use when the city floods. To protect our houses.'

'Sandbags,' said Kate.

He turned to her and smiled. 'Thank you, Mrs Caton.' He savoured the words. 'Sandbags.'

'But then he would not have floated to the surface,' said Caton.

'Ah, but they were not full of sand,' said Bonifati

dramatically. He paused for effect. 'The sand had been replaced … *con sale.*'

'With salt?'

'*Si, il sale che viene utilizzato sulle calle, e nelle piazze, in inverno.*'

Kate looked thoroughly confused.

'The salt they put on the streets and the squares in the winter,' said Caton. 'But why? Surely, when the salt dissolved, the body would rise to the surface.'

The policeman nodded in agreement. 'It is what they wanted to happen,' he said.

'How can you be sure?' Caton asked.

'Because the bags had been…' He made cutting movements with his hand.

'Slashed?' said Kate. 'They slashed the bags? Why? Surely the salt would dissolve naturally.'

Bonifati shrugged. 'Eventually. But the sea is already heavy with salt. Perhaps they want the body to be discovered soon.'

'You are sure they wanted it to be found?' said Caton.

'Oh yes.'

He flicked back through his notes and found the page he was looking for.

'This was on all of the bags.'

He pushed the notebook across the table towards Caton. In the middle of the page was a crude representation of a euro sign in what he assumed must be permanent black marker. Caton showed it to Kate.

'Money bags,' she said. 'They wanted them to look like money bags.'

'It's a message,' said Caton, handing the notebook back.

'*Sì,*' said Bonifati. '*Un messaggio.*'

'The implication being that he had stolen money from the wrong people,' said Caton.

'*Forse,*' he replied with a shrug.

'Only perhaps?' said Caton.

The commissario closed his notebook and placed it back in his pocket. Then he took a mobile phone from his pocket, switched it on and flicked through several screens. He placed it in front of Caton. On the screen was a satellite image.

'We believe,' he said, 'that the body went into the water here.'

As he stabbed the screen with his index finger, his assistant gave a look of disapproval.

Caton bent closer. He could make out the end of the Giudecca Island, with the Cipriani Hotel at its tip, the island of San Giorgio Maggiore, the island of San Clemente, and the long strip of the Lido beyond. Bonifati's finger rested on a narrow channel of darker water between the Isola San Maggiore and the San Clemente.

'In the time of the Doges,' said the commissario, 'this is where *criminali condannati* were brought to die.'

'A place of execution for the condemned?' said Caton.

'*Esatto.*'

Kate shivered at the thought. 'The Mafia?' she said.

'*Mafioso?*' said Bonifati, dragging the phone back towards him and switching it off. He returned it to his pocket. '*Ci voliogno far credere cosi,*' he said, as much to himself as to the two of them.

He finished his coffee, pushed back his chair and stood up. His assistant followed his lead. She flicked her hair back over her shoulders and smoothed her jacket in a way that accentuated her curves. It looked mannered yet unconscious to Caton, until he realised that she was staring straight at him, gauging his reaction, with that same amused smile. Embarrassed, he looked away.

Bonifati half-turned towards her and made a curious gesture with the back of his hand, as though shooing a cat away. Her face expressionless, she moved away towards the well in the centre of the courtyard and leaned on it, watching them. Bonifati placed his hands on the table, leaned forward and lowered his voice conspiratorially.

'I tell you all this out of professional respect,' he said. 'I would prefer it remains our secret. Though the Questore…' He paused, struggling yet again to find the words. 'You have a saying … *perde come un setaccio*?'

'It loses like a … *setaccio*?' said Caton. 'I'm sorry, I don't know that word.'

Bonifati grimaced, held his hands out half a metre apart in front of him and began to jiggle them from side to side. Neither Caton nor Kate had the slightest idea what he was supposed to be doing. Sovrintendente Volpe, who had been watching with apparent amusement, came to join him and laconically mimed shovelling something into the space between his hands. Caton struggled to keep his face straight.

'I think it's supposed to be a sieve,' whispered Kate. 'Either that or he's driving a bus and she's his clippie.'

'A sieve!' said Caton. He took up the mime. 'The Questore leaks like a sieve?'

Bonifati stopped riddling. His assistant stepped back a pace. She made a clicking sound with her tongue that sounded like disapproval.

'*Esattamente*,' said the commissario, smoothing the sleeves of his jacket. 'Like a sieve.'

'You are not alone,' Caton told him.

The policeman nodded. 'I understand you have a plane to catch,' he said. 'I am sorry to have taken your time.'

He proffered his hand to Kate and Caton in turn, and then saluted.

'*Arrivederci, Signora* Caton, Chief Inspector,' he said.

'*Arrivederci*, Commissario,' Caton replied. '*E buona fortuna.*'

The policeman gave a wry smile. 'Good luck,' he said. '*La preghiera del poliziotto.* The policeman's prayer.'

They watched as Bonifati and his colleague disappeared into the hotel.

'What was it you said?' Kate asked. 'Middle-aged, overweight, chain-smoking men squeezed into belted uniforms bristling with medals?'

'That's how I remembered it,' he told her.

'Mmm. She's young to be a superintendent.'

'She isn't a superintendent. Sovrintendente equates to a sergeant in the UK. Something like that.'

'What did you say to her that caused such amusement?'

Caton looked puzzled.

'When you were introduced to her.'

'Oh, that. She said it was a pleasure to meet me, and I replied, "I hope so."'

She began to laugh.

'What?' he said.

'Tom Caton. She's almost young enough to be your daughter.'

'Rubbish,' he told her. 'Anyway, you've got it wrong. What I meant was that when the police turn up it's rarely for pleasure.'

'You're also a very bad liar,' she retorted. 'Not a good trait for a detective.'

He looked at his watch.

'We'd better get a move on. The water taxi will be here in less than an hour.'

He stood and set off towards the interior of the hotel. She hurried after him.

'And what was that he said when I asked if it was the Mafia?'

Caton waited for her to join him.

'I'm not sure I heard him correctly, but it sounded like, "That's what they would have us believe."'

'I wonder what he meant,' she said.

He took her hand. Together they entered the breakfast room and headed for the corridor that led to their staircase.

'I have no idea,' he said. 'I'm just glad it's his problem and not mine.'

Chapter 4

'Have you got your phone and your warrant card?'

Caton patted his pockets.

'We were only away a fortnight. It hasn't left me entirely brain dead.'

He took a final slurp of his second cup of tea and picked up his work bag.

'Are you planning on going in today?' he asked.

'I'm working from home,' Kate told him. 'Sifting through a batch of UCAS applicants. Looks like we're going to be over-subscribed again. Then I thought I might work on my PhD proposal.'

'You're definitely doing it then?'

'Our department head is under pressure to get everyone to doctorate standard. It affects the university's rating. Besides, it'll be something to do when I'm on maternity leave.'

'I thought you said you were planning to use the university crèche?'

'Not until I've used up my maternity leave. I'm not totally insane.'

He waited until he was halfway out of the door.

'Only partially then?'

The half-eaten slice of toast struck the back of the door, bounced off and landed butter side down. He stuck his head around the door jamb and grinned.

'So this is married life.'

As she reached for the teacup he withdrew his head, closed the door and headed for the stairwell with a spring in his step.

'How was the honeymoon, boss?'

Detective Inspector Holmes sat smirking on the corner of the desk.

'Fine. If you behave you may even get to see some of the photos.'

The grin broadened. 'Unexpurgated?'

Caton shook his head. 'You're incorrigible.'

'I assume that's a compliment?'

Holmes slid off the desk and made a play of brushing the back of his trousers with his hands.

'I don't think anyone's cleaned this place while you've been away.'

'Get me a drink and a couple of biscuits, Gordon,' said Caton, 'and I'll tell you what did happen in Venice. I promise, you're not going to believe it.'

'Sounds fishy to me,' said Holmes.

'Is that supposed to be a joke?'

'No, seriously, boss. Who'd go to all that trouble? Why not just stuff a wad of euro notes in his mouth and shoot him in the back of the head? That's what I'd do.'

'That's reassuring, coming from a senior detective.'

'It's what the Mafia would do, too,' he insisted.

'I know,' Caton admitted. 'I think that's what Commissario Bonifati was trying to say. Anyway, enough of this, what have you been up to?'

'I've been putting the finishing touches to the Janus investigation pre-trial notes. I've got three meetings lined up with the CPS this week, then we're off on holiday.'

'Of course you are. Where is it you're going?'

'Some place in Majorca. Porta Plensa?'

'Puerta Pollenca, up on the north coast of the island. I stayed on the Pine Walk some years ago.'

It had been during his brief relationship with Helen. It was almost certainly where Harry had been conceived.

'Great for a chill-out,' he said.

Holmes grimaced. 'I'd have been happy with a fortnight in Benidorm, so would the kids, but it was Marilyn's choice, and since she does all the arranging, what can you do?'

'Lie back and enjoy it,' Caton suggested.

He eyed the stack of papers piled high in his in-tray.

'What's happened while I've been away?'

'It's been quiet. Even the criminals have to have a holiday. Burglaries are up as usual, not that that's our problem.'

'Any category A or B suspicious deaths?'

'No. There have been two Cat Cs: a road death, which is a possible homicide or fail-to-stop that the Basic Command Unit has in hand, and a sudden unexpected infant death which the Cat C team at Chadderton is dealing with; and what looks like a drugs overdose. DS Stuart is on to that. Incidentally, she got word while you were away that she'd passed her Inspector's Board.'

Caton was delighted. Nobody in FMIT deserved it more.

'Not before time,' he said. 'I bet she's over the moon.'

Gordon shook his head and stood up.

'Not exactly,' he replied. 'I'll let her tell you why.'

Caton was a third of the way through his in-tray when there was knock on the panel partition that served as the doorway to his cubicle.

'Come!' he said.

DS Stuart appeared around the screen.

'Welcome back, sir,' she said. 'DI Holmes said you wanted to see me?'

He pushed back his chair.

'Jo,' he said. 'I gather congratulations are in order.'

He shook her hand, invited her to sit down and sat back down himself.

'I told you you'd sail through.'

'I wouldn't say it was that easy,' she replied. 'But I have you to thank for persuading me to go for it.'

'It would have been a tragic waste of talent if you hadn't. The force needs people like you in senior roles.'

If it had been anyone other than DCI Caton putting it that way she might have taken offence, but she knew that he was alluding to neither her gender nor her sexual orientation.

'Thank you, sir,' she said. 'Shame they don't take the same view up on the Fourth Floor.'

'What do you mean, Jo? Has someone said something to you?'

She shook her head. 'Not in that way. It's just no sooner than I'd been told the news, Detective Chief Superintendent Gates asked me up to her office. She was highly complimentary. Said what a great job I'd been doing. How I came out of the exams and the Board with flying colours.'

She drummed her fingers on the tabletop in sheer frustration.

'But then she said, "I'm sorry about this, DS Stuart, but I'm afraid in the current climate there is no imminent likelihood of promotion."'

So that was what Gordon had been on about. Caton felt gutted for her. He should have known. There had been an internal memo among the pile of papers that he'd just dealt with. Only it hadn't registered. Not in relation to DS Stuart.

'I'm sorry, Jo,' he said. 'I should have realised. I've just seen the memo. If it's any consolation, it's not personal. It's all down to the cuts they're having to make. It's only a matter of time.'

'Are you sure about that, sir?' She folded her arms. 'Only I'm not convinced it's just about the cuts.'

He had never seen her this angry.

'I'm not sure I follow.'

'I'm talking about what's been happening over the past eighteen months. Them hiring all these retired police officers, and people from other departments like Customs and Excise, and even the Audit Office, to work on Cat C investigations. There are rumours they're going to do the same for Cat B cases next.'

She was right of course. Not content with using retired officers to work on so-called cold cases, the powers that be had been recruiting larger teams of ex-officers, and civilians outside the force with investigative skills, to take on those homicides where the perpetrator had already been identified. Given that was the majority of cases involving murder or manslaughter, it left the remaining teams in FMIT, like his, to deal with the far fewer, more complex, cases.

'Well, that is one of the reasons,' he conceded.

'With respect, sir, the *main* reason. They can sweep up all these cases with just one DI supervising a large team of civilians, and a whole raft of cases, and they're all on pensions so they're saving a shed load of money. On that basis I could be retired myself before they get round to making me an inspector.'

He couldn't fault her logic, although he was aware that it was just as much a problem in the uniformed divisions. He'd even heard rumours that officers were being told they would have to retake their exams and go through the Board process all over again if too much time had passed before a vacancy came up. Looking at the miserable expression on her face, he decided not to share that little nugget of information.

'Tell me about the investigation you're dealing with,' he said, in the hope of lightening her mood.

'It's a tragic case,' she said. 'Young mother out on a hen night. There were six of them. Popping pills and drinking, as you do. She said she was going to the loo. When she didn't come back, one of her friends went looking for her. She was in one of the cubicles. Didn't respond to her friend hammering on the door. This friend climbs up on the seat of the adjacent cubicle, sees her slumped on the loo, panics, slips off the seat and bashes her head on the cistern. Blood everywhere. Fortunately, there's someone at the mirrors touching up her make-up. She raises the alarm. A bouncer smashes down the door. The first girl is unconscious. Paramedics on the scene, plus a couple of officers from the Saturday night TAG team. Girl number one arrests. They attempt CPR. Rush them both to hospital. Our victim is dead on arrival.'

'Bloody hell.' said Caton. 'Some hen night.'

'I know. The one who smashed her head was the bride. The dead girl was a single parent with two kids under the age of five.'

She pointed to his monitor screen.

'I can show you if you like, sir?'

He logged out, and scooted his chair to the side so that she could get to the keyboard. He marvelled at the speed with which her fingers flew over the keys as she logged in with her own password. He'd kept promising himself that he'd take a speed-typing course, but had never found the time. Now she was entering the case number. Then she clicked on the icon and stepped back.

'Here we go,' she said.

Chapter 5

Caton stared at the screen. Mandy Morgan stared back at him. Twenty-one years of age, going on thirty. It was a head and shoulders photo that looked as though it might have been taken for her passport, but rejected because of the smile. He had seen that smile on the faces of too many victims, living and dead. The lips telling one story, the eyes another. It made you want to weep.

'What had she been drinking?' he asked.

'What hadn't she? They front-loaded on alcopops at the bride-to-be's house, and then starting hammering the cocktails in one venue after another. Mojito was the favourite starter, but it seems after that they were following the hen night menu.'

'What's that?'

'Cocktails with a sexual connotation. Sex on the Beach, Harvey Wallbanger, Bride of Dracula, Manhattan, Blue Lagoon…'

'You've lost me,' he said, holding up his hand.

'I'm relieved to hear it, sir,' she said. 'Though I'd have thought you'd have tried at least one of them on your honeymoon.'

'Long Island Ice Tea, Vodka Martini and the obligatory Bellini in Harry's Bar was as far as we got. Looking at this, I can't say I'm sorry.'

'It wasn't the alcohol that killed her,' she said.

'Though it wasn't for want of trying.'

He looked back at the photograph.

'So what was it? Drugs?'

'The paramedics thought it might be ecstasy, or most likely one of those recently banned legal highs – Benzo Fury, NBOME, green Rolex, salvia.'

Caton nodded. It was a litany of names with which they were all too readily acquainted.

'Like those three who died here earlier in the year,' he said. 'What was it? A magimix bag of pills in assorted colours?'

'It was then; on this occasion the tox results say it was Fentanyl.'

'China White?'

'There was a case in America last week. A young girl fished out a used patch her grandmother had thrown into the waste bin, and stuck it on her stomach because she had tummy ache.'

'What happened?'

'She died. Difficult to believe, but apparently, it's a regular occurrence.'

Fentanyl. An opioid breakthrough pain reliever one hundred times more potent than morphine. A boon for cancer patients. What the hell were they doing peddling it for so-called recreational use? Caton knew it was a stupid question.

'Didn't I read something about Fentanyl and the Ukraine?' he said.

'It's an epidemic over there. There are now more deaths from China White overdoses – mainly self-injected – than road accidents.'

'Is that what happened to Mandy Morgan?'

'No. It seems she was offered a tab.'

'Do we know who sold it to her?'

'It wasn't sold. There was a guy giving them away.'

Promotional handouts. Just like a new brand of

chocolate. Only a thousand times more sinister, because this one little treat could get you hooked. Or killed.

'Was anyone else affected?'

'Not that we know of. Not yet. One of her friends took one, but she seems to be okay. One of our theories was that she might have been on some other medication that exacerbated the effect.'

Or, he reflected, hers could have been from a dodgy batch cut with something else.

'Wouldn't that show on her medical records?'

'Not if she bought the medication herself, or got it from someone else. As it happens, the tox results tell us that she'd ingested benzodiazepine the day before. Just long enough for some to remain in her system when she took the Fentanyl. Enough to slow her breathing to a level where it stopped altogether.'

Caton sat back in his chair, and steepled his fingers.

'So, an accidental overdose,' he said. 'Except we don't know if it was the Fentanyl alone or the combination of the two that killed her.'

'My bet is the Fentanyl. It's so dangerous, in the States the drug squads are warned to wear gloves if they suspect they may be handling it.'

'Either way,' he reflected, 'she was given a Class A drug that resulted in her death, either on its own, or in combination with the benzodiazepine.'

'I know what you're thinking,' she said. 'That supplying the drug was a criminal act, therefore the dealer has committed unlawful act manslaughter.'

He shook his head. 'Except that in taking that pill, Mandy Morgan acted in a free, voluntary and informed way, thus breaking the link of causation between her, and the lad that supplied the drug. Although I fail to see how it can be viewed as informed when she couldn't be sure what was in that pill, nor the effect it might have.'

'However,' she responded triumphantly, 'the supplier could be held to owe a duty of care to the person he supplied. He did not inform her of the potential risks, nor did he – as far as we can tell – seek help to remedy the situation that his action had caused. In which case he's guilty of gross negligence manslaughter.'

'Maybe he'd already left the club. Maybe he didn't know she'd collapsed.'

'Then not sticking round to make sure she was okay, and anyone else he supplied, that qualifies as a failure of his duty of care.'

'I can see how you sailed through your Inspector's Board,' he said. 'But you might have a difficult job convincing the Crown Prosecution Service.'

He looked again at the image on the screen.

'Either way, this is definitely one for us. If they're giving these pills away they must be looking to start supplying en masse, in which case we could end up with a string of Mandy Morgans. It's going to be a city-wide investigation. Potentially Force wide.'

Her face fell.

'I know what you're going to say, sir,' she said. 'It'll have to be you or a Detective Superintendent as Senior Investigating Officer.'

'I'm sorry, Jo' he said. 'But I'll make damn sure that you're my deputy SIO. You've passed your exams and the Board; how else are you going to get the experience?'

Her face lit up.

'Thank you, sir, but what about Gordon … I mean DI Holmes?'

'DI Holmes has two weeks' leave starting this Friday. And don't worry about the others. It's your turn, and my shout. You'll be fine. Better than fine. Trust me.'

Chapter 6

They started with the victim's mother.

The house was a smart Edwardian detached on the border between Chorlton and West Didsbury. There was a white Audi TT in the drive, alongside the Nissan Micra that probably belonged to the Family Liaison Officer. Nothing surprised Caton any more, but it was a long way from the stereotype most people might have in mind for the victim of a drug-fuelled death. It seemed that Mandy had been neither a celebrity nor a member of that mythical underclass that a certain right wing mid-market newspaper was always ranting on about.

Hannah Morgan answered the door herself. She had been told to expect them by the FLO, and ushered them straight into the larger reception room.

'Please sit down.' She indicated the sofa and waited for them to sit before lowering herself into one of the three voluminous armchairs.

Caton put her in her late forties. Fifty at the most. She had dressed as though ready for work: a dark-grey jacket and matching skirt, over a white silk blouse, and white shoes with a two-inch heel. He guessed it had been an unconscious decision, because she kept glancing anxiously at the two young children playing in the garden room at the end of the lounge.

In his experience, people in shock were often on autopilot. She caught him watching her.

'I decided not to go in today,' she explained. 'I couldn't find anyone to look after the children.'

She turned to DS Stuart, as though seeking an understanding ear from another woman.

'My sister lives in Australia, you see. She won't be here until tomorrow.'

She was hugging herself, and rocking slightly, back and forth. Without warning, she put her hands on the arms of the chair and levered herself up.

'God, I'm so sorry, I haven't offered you a drink.'

'You leave that to me, Hannah,' said DC Alan Norris from the doorway. 'What would you like, sir?'

'A mug of boiled water for me, please,' said Caton.

'I'll have tea please, Alan, milk no sugar,' DS Stuart told him.

'And your usual, Hannah?'

'Thank you, Alan,' she said, subsiding gratefully into her chair.

'He's wonderful,' she told them. 'I couldn't have managed without him.'

'Where's your husband, Mrs Morgan?' Caton asked.

She hugged herself, and started rocking.

'We separated. Six months ago. He's in the States. He's flying back today. Much good he'll be.' She sounded neither bitter nor regretful, simply resigned.

Caton glanced at DS Stuart. He was mentally kicking himself for not having checked before they arrived.

'I know this is really hard for you, Mrs Morgan,' said Joanne Stuart, getting them back on track, 'but we need to ask a few questions about Mandy. About her friends, her lifestyle. Is that alright?'

'Of course. You need to find out who … who did this … who killed my daughter.'

Her eyes began to well with tears.

'Is that what you think happened?' Joanne said.

Hannah Morgan pulled a damp handkerchief from out of one of the sleeves of her jacket, and dabbed at her eyes. She blew her nose, crumpled it up, thought about putting it back and then stuffed it into one of her side pockets instead.

'Of course,' she said, evidently puzzled by the question. 'Someone slipped something into her drink. How else could it have happened?'

There was a long pause while DS Stuart considered how best to respond.

'It wasn't something that could be put in a drink, Hannah,' she said. 'It was a pill. It wouldn't have dissolved. Certainly not straight away. She would have noticed it.'

'Not necessarily. Not if she was distracted, or had had one too many.'

They could both see that she was grasping at straws. Desperate to convince herself of her daughter's total innocence. Gently but firmly, DS Stuart pressed on. After all, it was going to come out at the inquest.

'We know that she was handed it some time before she was found unconscious.'

Hannah Morgan looked from one to the other, trying to work out what was being implied.

'Handed it? By whom?'

'A young man. Not known to her, or her friends. We think they were free samples, designed to drum up custom.'

Her hands gripped the arms of the chair. She shook her head violently from side to side. Part denial, part warding off a reality impossible to contemplate.

'No! No!' she cried. 'She wouldn't. Not Mandy. Not drugs. She'd never do drugs! Never!'

The Family Liaison Officer appeared with the tray

of drinks. He put it down on the coffee table, took an occasional chair from next to the sideboard and placed it next to Hannah Morgan's. He sat down.

'Don't upset yourself,' he said. 'There could be an alternative explanation.'

Caton frowned at him. It wasn't his job to help her face up to the truth, to cope with it maybe, but not to protect her from it.

'How frequently did Mandy drink alcohol, Mrs Morgan?' he asked.

She seized upon it.

'Not that often. At home, only with meals. She enjoyed herself when she went out with her friends at weekends.'

She looked to Alan Norris for support.

'They all do, don't they?'

To his credit, this time the detective constable remained non-committal.

'By *enjoyed herself*, I take it you mean she'd be under the influence when she came home?' said Caton.

'Well, tipsy I'd say. Yes, tipsy.'

'Only, on the night she died, Mandy had a level of alcohol in her blood that indicated she must have drunk in excess of twenty-one units of alcohol that evening.' He let it sink in. 'That's the equivalent of more than two and a half standard bottles of wine. More than the recommended maximum *weekly* level for a woman.'

'But they all do it, binge drink at the weekend?'

It started out like a plea, but there was a hint of desperation behind it. Her voice dropped a register.

'But that's not what killed her, is it?'

She turned to Alan Norris.

'You told me,' she said, 'that she'd been drugged. By that boy.'

He looked embarrassed, conscious that both Caton

and Stuart were hanging on his response.

'I said that Mandy had drugs in her system,' he corrected her. 'That according to the autopsy she died either of the drug itself, or from the combined effect of the drug and the alcohol she had drunk.'

Almost triumphantly, she turned back to face Caton.

'Either way, it was the drug that killed her, not the alcohol. The drug that boy gave her. If it wasn't for him she'd be alive today. My Mandy would still be alive.'

'I'm afraid that there were also traces of a benzodiazepine in Mandy's blood,' Caton told her. 'Indications are that it must have entered her system at least twenty-four hours earlier.'

Her face fell. 'Entered her system? I don't understand.'

'It comes in the form of a pill or capsule. She would have to have swallowed it or placed it under her tongue.'

She looked confused. 'B...but I don't understand. You said that boy slipped her a pill that evening. In the club. That's what killed her.'

'*Gave* her a pill,' Caton clarified. 'And you're right. We do believe that was what resulted in her death. But I'm afraid that we still need to establish if Mandy was a regular drug user. It may be that this young man was a contact of hers.'

'No! No!' she said. 'She did not do drugs! She promised me she would never do drugs.'

The silence hung in the air like a menacing cloud before a storm.

'Do you take any medication, Mrs Morgan?' Caton asked gently.

She looked up. Her eyes were damp and skittish, flitting from side to side as she tried to process the mass of information they had thrown at her.

'Medication?' she said.

'Anything the doctor may have prescribed for you?' said DS Stuart.

She reached in her pocket for the handkerchief, wiped her eyes and held it in both hands like a child's comforter.

'Ah ... since Mandy ... I haven't been able to sleep. The doctor gave me some pills. Sonata?'

'And before that? Did you have any prescriptions at all?' said Joanne Stuart.

'Umm. Not since ... umm ... well...' She looked up. 'When I found out about Jason, my husband, when he left me for ... that woman, I had panic attacks. I couldn't sleep. I was a mess. The doctor gave me something. Loraz–'

'Lorazepam?' said Caton.

She nodded. 'Lorazepam. That's it. But I stopped taking them months ago.'

'Do you still have any in the house?' he asked.

'Yes,' she said. 'I think so.'

'Where are they, Mrs Morgan?' said DS Stuart.

'In the bathroom, in the cabinet under the sink.'

Her forehead creased with puzzle lines. It still hadn't registered.

'Do you mind if DS Stuart takes a look?' said Caton.

They sat in the car and took stock. DS Stuart held up the packet in its sealed evidence bag.

'A high-potency quick-acting benzodiazepine of intermediate duration. Three months' supply, of which two months remain. You were right. It's too much of a coincidence.'

'We won't know that until we get the second set of tox results,' said Caton. 'But my bet is she was either popping them before she went out at the beginning of the weekend, or she was missing her father more than her mother realised.'

'Either way, it's not going to help her mother get over her death, is it, sir?'

'I don't suppose it will, though she has nothing to reproach herself for.'

'Try telling her that,' she said.

They sat in silence for a while, contemplating the senselessness of it all.

'How do you tell a mother her daughter as good as killed herself?' Caton said. 'Taking drugs that could have contained any manner of lethal substances. And there are tens of thousands of kids doing it every weekend.'

'Not just kids,' she reminded him. 'Sometimes I think we're fighting a losing battle.'

'Not a battle, a war,' he said. 'A war we're never going to win. It's just like cigarettes, and booze. You can educate people as much as you want, but in the end it's their choice.'

'It's a selfish choice,' she said. 'Did you see those two children? Little lost souls.'

'All addictions are essentially selfish; they can all be cured if the will is there.'

He started the engine.

'What made you choose Alan for the family liaison?'

She grinned. 'He was the only one who'd passed the training who wasn't on holiday. I did have my reservations with there being two infants in the house, but he seems to have come up trumps.'

'Now who's stereotyping?' he said with enough of a grin to let her know he was joking. 'And I've told you before, stop calling me sir. You can save that for when we're in public. Otherwise it's boss!'

She placed the packet in the glove compartment and gave a mock salute.

'Yes, boss!'

Chapter 7

Jade Jones was in the final stages of blow-drying a client. They agreed to wait. It wasn't too much of a hardship. This was a high-end salon. Classy magazines, and a selection of drinks. Nespresso coffee, high-end teabags, even a spritzer, or a glass of sparkling wine. Caton felt compelled to converse in a hushed voice.

'Tell me again,' he said. 'She knew Mandy Morgan how?'

DS Stuart put her latte glass down on the glass-topped coffee table.

'They were at school together. St Chrysostom's Primary, then The Barlow RC High. Mandy went on to the Xaverian Sixth Form College to do A Levels, Jade to Manchester College for Hair and Beauty Therapy.'

'Best friends then?'

'According to the mother.'

She looked around the salon, at least what they could see of it.

'She landed on her feet. One of the top salons in the city. I couldn't afford to come here. Neither could you.'

Caton decided not to reveal that Kate did. She'd always claimed it was one of her little treats.

'What are we talking about?' he said.

She pursed her lips.

'Depends. Fifty pounds for a style cut and blow, up to seventy-five plus for the top stylist. Another fifty quid if you want it coloured.'

'Bloody hell!' he said, more loudly than he'd intended.

The receptionist glanced up from her magazine and frowned. He mouthed an apology. She returned to her reading.

'Mind you,' said Joanne Stuart, 'it'll last up to eight weeks. We've got friends who have their hair permed, and then go for a wash and blow-dry every week. Probably costs them even more when you think about it.'

Either way, it dwarfed his miserly fifteen pounds every six weeks or so.

'You wanted to see me?'

A young woman hovered in the archway between the reception area and the salon. She was about five foot six, with a pale complexion. Beautifully conditioned blonde hair hugged her face, and fell to her shoulders. Her make-up looked natural and understated. She wore a fitted blouse over skinny jeans.

Caton stood.

'Jade Jones?' he said.

She nodded nervously. 'Is it about Mandy?'

'Yes. Is there somewhere private that we can talk?'

'Barry's in the office talking to the *Alterna Ten* sales rep,' said the receptionist, who had been listening intently.

'There's Caffè Nero,' said Jade. 'It's virtually next door, and there won't be many people in at this time.'

'So, let me get this straight,' said Caton. 'This was the fourth place you'd been that night. And you hadn't seen anyone selling or pushing drugs in any of them until then?'

'No.'

'And none of you had been taking drugs, not even popping the odd legal high?'

'No.'

She was upset and nervous. She'd even started biting the cuticles of the index finger on her right hand. Not a pretty habit for a hair and beauty technician. It was difficult to tell if she was lying or not.

'Listen, Jade,' he said, 'this isn't about getting you or your friends into trouble. It's about finding out what happened to Mandy, and preventing any more deaths from happening. You want to help us do that, don't you?'

She nodded.

'Good. So I'll ask you again. Had any of you been taking drugs, legal or otherwise, that night?'

'Yes.'

It was practically a whisper.

'Right, now we're getting somewhere,' he said.

'Who Jade? Who had been taking them?' asked Joanne Stuart, sensing the irritation in Caton's voice was not helping.

'Me,' she replied. 'Me and Kathy.'

'Kathy Carter, the bride-to-be,' said DS Stuart for Caton's sake.

Jade looked up.

'It was only Benzo Fury,' she said. 'Kathy got them off a friend. We only took one each. For a buzz.'

Caton sighed. *Only* Benzo Fury. A legal drug with lethal consequences. According to the weekly drugs update, in the previous month alone it had been responsible for a death at a rock concert, and for causing a normally respectable young woman to parade in the nude around a Tesco store down south, before karate-kicking in the head one of the police

47

officers who came to arrest her.

'Just because they're marketed as a legal substance, Jade,' said DS Stuart, 'it doesn't mean that they're safe to use. All it means is they haven't yet been declared illegal to possess or to use.'

Jade Jones looked both shocked and surprised.

'But they are legal, aren't they?'

'None of these supposedly legal highs have been tested properly,' Caton told her. 'Many of them contain chemicals that have never been used before. No one knows for sure what effect they might have on their own, let alone combined with alcohol.'

'All of them are likely to put you at risk in so many ways,' said Joanne Stuart. 'They can make you drowsy, paranoid, manically excitable, put you in a coma, even kill you.'

'At the very least they'll reduce your inhibitions far more than alcohol will,' added Caton. 'Not a nice state for a girl to get herself into. Anything could happen to her.'

His colleague gave him a disapproving look.

'Not just young women,' she said. 'Young men too.'

'When did you take them?' Caton asked.

'Before we set off. We'd had a couple of drinks at Kathy's as well.'

'And how did they make you feel?'

'A bit light-headed, and sick. I threw up in the loos in the first pub we called in.'

'And Kathy?'

'You'll have to ask her. She did go a bit daft, I s'pose. Tried to dance on the tables in the Moon Under Water, on Deansgate. Got us thrown out. It was only 9 o'clock. We'd hardly got started.'

Caton was wondering how far they could rely on their statements. It was bad enough that they'd been drinking heavily, without factoring in the drugs use.

'You're sure that Mandy hadn't taken anything else herself?'

'Yeh. She didn't really do drugs. She said her mother would have gone ballistic if she did.'

Caton exchanged a knowing glance with his colleague.

'But she definitely took one off this guy in the club?'

He turned to his DS.

'*Mayhem*,' she told him. 'In the Northern Quarter.'

'In *Mayhem*.'

'Yeh, definitely. We were all stood together then, near the bar. We'd just got a round in. He came over, asked if we wanted to try something special. Completely legal, completely safe, he said…' Her voice tailed off.

'What did he look like, this lad?'

'Normal. That's the thing, he looked completely normal.'

Caton had no idea what that meant.

'Can you describe him?' said DS Stuart.

'He was about five eight, slimmish, with shortish brown hair. He had a long-sleeved black shirt on. Brown jeans. Trainers. Could have been a student. That's what I thought anyway.'

'What made you think that?' said Caton.

'I don't know. Instinct, I suppose. He looked and sounded a bit more intelligent than the average. Like he didn't belong there. I remember thinking, I bet he's doing this to pay his way through Uni.'

It was a better description than he'd had from many a sober witness. But then it wasn't unusual for a girl to weigh a guy up in an instant. Even if she had been drinking. Instinct, she'd called it.

'And Mandy and Kathy were the only ones to take

a pill from him?'

'I said so, didn't I?'

'Why didn't you?'

She shrugged. 'I'd been sick once that night. I wasn't going to risk it again, was I?'

'Did Kathy take hers?'

She shook her head. Her hair wafted from side to side like a curtain, and then settled again perfectly. Caton could see how the cut made a difference.

'No,' she said. 'She made a big play of waiting till he'd moved on, and then throwing it into the middle of the dance floor.'

'Why did she do that?'

'I don't know,' she said miserably. 'You'll have to ask her.'

Chapter 8

'I hope you'll be gentle with her. She's been distraught ever since it happened.'

Mark Gayden, of Gayden Associates, stood in the doorway of his office. He was stocky, in a shiny grey suit, blue shirt, with a tie and matching handkerchief in the breast pocket. He had the air and appearance of a car dealer or an estate agent.

'I tried telling her not to come in. She's entitled to compassionate leave, and she's supposed to be getting married next weekend. She said she'd be worse off at home.' He shook his head and sighed. 'It's a terrible thing what happened to Mandy. None of us have really come to terms with it. Perhaps she's right. We're probably better dealing with it together than apart.'

He pulled the door to behind him, and left them sitting there while he went to fetch her.

'What is it she does exactly?' said Caton.

'She's just finished a law degree. She's training to be a solicitor.'

'And the victim, Mandy, also worked here?'

'As a legal executive. She came here straight after A Levels, instead of going to uni.'

'And what is it they do here exactly?'

DS Stuart folded her arms combatively.

'They're piss artists!'

'Come again?' he said, surprised by the vehemence

51

of her response.

'Personal Injury Solicitors,' she spelt it out.

'PIS. Piss artists.'

'That's a bit harsh,' he said. 'Not like you at all.'

'It's what Abbie called them,' she said. 'After she'd queried her last car insurance quote, they said most of the twenty-five per cent increase was down to increased claims due to crash-for-cash investigations. Now we've got these flash-for-cash scams all over the place. You can't tell me it's not down to these ambulance chasers encouraging everyone to claim for everything under the sun?'

She was right, of course. Criminals had moved on to flashing their lights at roundabouts and junctions to lure people into pulling out, then deliberately putting their foot on the gas and crashing into them. Net result, multiple claims for damages and whiplash against the innocent party's insurance company. And it wasn't just accident claims. One of the memos he'd just read warned about injudicious police use of the telescopic baton. Apparently, there had been ten times more formal complaints and claims for compensation over the use of the baton than with regard to the deployment of the taser. Simply responding to those complaints was using up thousands of officer hours filling in reports. Time spent away from front-line policing.

'Anyway, what is it with these rhyming names?' she said.

'You've lost me,' he replied.

'Mandy Morgan, Jade Jones, Kathy Carter. You couldn't make it up. It's like a High School Musical line-up.'

'Only with a tragic ending,' he said.

The door opened. Gayden held it as a young woman walked past him into the room.

'This is Kathy,' he said, looking over her shoulder. 'Do you want me to stay, love?'

She half turned.

'No thanks. I'll be alright, Mr Gayden, honest.'

'If you're sure.'

He closed the door behind him.

They had rearranged the chairs around a low table in the middle of the room. Caton stood, and invited her to take the remaining chair.

'I'm Detective Chief Inspector Caton,' he said once she was settled. 'And this is my colleague, Detective Sergeant Stuart.'

She nodded, and smiled wanly.

'Mr Gayden said you're here about Mandy.'

'That's right. I'm sorry to have to bother you at this time, given your impending marriage.'

'I understand,' she said.

'We've already spoken to Mrs Morgan, and to Jade Jones.'

'I know, Jade texted me.'

He and DS Stuart exchanged looks. The curse of the mobile phone. It was becoming impossible to stay a step ahead of witnesses in an investigation. She probably knew what questions they were going to ask her, had planned her responses, and compared them with those of her friend. So much for independent corroboration, if there was such a thing these days. It was probably already out there on their Facebook and Twitter accounts. Oh well, at least it was going to speed things up.

It turned out just as he had expected. Her account, from the moment they met at her house to the time they spent at *Mayhem* in the Northern Quarter, tallied exactly with that of her friend's. Right down to the description of the young man handing out the Fentanyl packed tablets.

'So why did you take one of those tablets and then throw it onto the dance floor?' he said.

'I felt sorry for him. He looked like one of those students you see handing out fliers in St Ann's Square. They get paid peanuts to distribute them. I always take those fliers too, and I throw them away.'

'You weren't tempted to try it yourself?'

'No way,' she said. 'I'm not that stupid. It could have had anything in it.'

Neither of them responded. Suddenly, the full import of what she had said hit her, and she burst into a flood of tears.

Chapter 9

Back in the Major Incident Room they found Detective Constable Jimmy Hulme going through the CCTV tapes he had finally retrieved from *Mayhem*.

'The owners insisted on a warrant,' he told them. 'Even then they faffed about for ages.'

'What was their problem?' asked DS Stuart.

'They muttered something about respecting their clients' right to privacy.'

'What did you say?' said Caton.

'I reminded them that this was potentially a murder enquiry, that they were neither doctors nor lawyers, and that the whole idea of having CCTV in the first place was to protect their clients' safety, not their reputations.'

'Nice one, Jimmy,' said Joanne Stuart.

DC Hulme had been with them less than six months, but Caton was warming to him. Okay, he had that irritating habit of parading his encyclopaedic knowledge of trivia, but he was shaping up well as a detective. And he'd been invaluable in their last major investigation.

'If you ask me,' DC Hulme continued, 'they were more worried about the fact that someone was peddling drugs in their club. It didn't take a genius for them to put two and two together regarding that and Mandy Morgan's death. It doesn't bode well for when their licence comes up for renewal.'

'If every club where drugs were being passed around was shut down, there wouldn't be any left in the country,' Caton reminded him.

'Research Statistics tell us that ninety-seven per cent of drugs present in the average night club have been brought there by the punters themselves, rather than by drug dealers,' Jimmy Hulme began.

'I bet the Drug Squad would love to know how they worked that out,' said DS Stuart. 'And what is an *average* night club anyway?'

'Don't encourage him,' said Caton.

He drew their attention back to the screen.

'Have you found anything?'

'So far, I've tracked the hen party the victim was with through two out of the three pubs we were told they visited that night, and the one club they went to immediately before they turned up at *Mayhem*.'

'Why only two out of the three pubs?'

'Because, in the other one the guy they laughingly refer to as Head of Security had changed over the tapes, but forgot to press the record button.'

Three out of four. That was about par for the course these days, Caton reflected. He had no idea why they hadn't all upgraded to the use of compact discs. Then they wouldn't have to change them as often. They could have a week's worth on one disc.

'Any sign of this lad handing out tablets?'

'No. Nor of any obvious dealing going on. There's some surreptitious passing of the odd tab or two, even some not so secretive. But it's just punters using and sharing what they brought in with them.'

'Hardly surprising,' said DS Stuart. 'What with CCTV, undercover police officers and marginally less bent doormen, these days what dealing there is will either have taken place outside or in the toilets.'

'Right,' said Caton. 'Show me what you've got from *Mayhem.*'

Each of them pulled up a chair on either side of DC Hulme. The three of them stared intently at the screen.

The club was smaller than Caton had expected. The lighting was generally punctuated by coloured lights strobing across the minimal dance floor on which a dozen or so girls were dancing. By comparison, the area around the bar and the open booths around the walls were packed.

'It's not exactly *The Haçienda*, or the *Twisted Wheel*, is it?' he said.

'That's how it is these days,' DS Stuart told him. 'It's more about bars with a dance floor than the other way round.'

'*Twisted Wheel*?' said Jimmy Hulme.

'Before your time,' said Joanne Stuart. 'We're talking icons here. I'm surprised they're not on your radar.'

'*The Haçienda*, obviously, but I've never heard of the other one.'

'Well, it doesn't matter now,' she said. 'They knocked it down in June to make way for another five-star hotel.'

'There!' said Caton pointing at the screen. 'That's them.'

Five girls done up to the nines in brightly coloured dresses that barely covered their bottoms, teetering on five-inch high-heeled platform shoes. They each had either a bottle or a cocktail glass in their hand. Two of them had handbags hanging over their free arm.

'No wonder they're not dancing,' he said. 'Why no fancy dress outfits?'

'Not cool any more,' pronounced DC Hulme.

'You an expert on hen nights too?' said Joanne

Stuart. 'You wouldn't want that spreading round the squad.'

'Where's the blushing bride?' said Caton.

They watched as the footage morphed between several camera positions.

'There!' said DC Hulme.

Kathy Carter tottered into shot. She had a clutch bag in one hand, and a long glass in the other. She stopped to sip her cocktail.

'Good job said,' said DS Stuart. 'The state she's in there's every chance she'll have spilt it all before she gets there.'

They watched as she joined her friends. They parted as she arrived. One of them threw her arm around her shoulders, causing her to lose her balance.

'There you go,' said Joanne Stuart, 'what did I tell you?'

The other members of the party backed away as half of the contents of the glass shot forwards. Some of it down the back of the man in front of her. He turned, feeling the back of his shirt. Running his hand down to where the liquid had landed.

'Is that him?' said Joanne Stuart.

Allowing for the heels that Kathy Carter was wearing it would put him at about five foot eight, five foot nine. He was slim, with short hair. What a barber would describe as a number five brush cut. He wore a dark long-sleeve open-neck shirt, a slightly lighter pair of jeans and trainers.

'He certainly seems to fit the description they gave us,' said Caton. 'It's a shame this isn't in colour.'

They watched as he smiled and shook his head. Obviously telling her not to worry about it. Then he reached into his pocket and took something out. Then he opened his palm, and the girls all craned forward to have a look.

'Can you pause that?' said Caton.

DC Hulme did just that, but it had overrun a second or two, and he had to run it back and try again. He zoomed in, but the lighting was simply not good enough. Plus Jade Jones's head was in the way. It was impossible to tell what the young man was showing them.

'Three guesses,' said Joanne Stuart.

'I saw that lad earlier on,' said Jimmy Hulme. 'I'm sure of it. In one of the other clubs. He caught my attention because he didn't seem to be with anyone. But I didn't see him approaching anyone, or offering anything.'

'Run it on,' said Caton. 'Let's see what happens next.'

Three of the girls stood tall, and turned away in a huddle.

'That leaves our victim, her best friend Jade, and her work colleague, Kathy, the bride-to-be,' Caton observed.

The young man appeared to be speaking earnestly to them. As though trying to convince them of something. Jade Jones shook her head, and raised her glass to her lips. Kathy Carter placed her clutch bag under her right armpit, and then put out her left hand.

'Here we go,' said DC Hulme. 'Caught in the act.'

They watched as he placed something in her palm. She raised her hand to her face and seemed to look closely at whatever was in it. Then she too had a drink.

'Did she take it?' said Joanne Stuart.

'No,' said Caton. 'Look, she's just closed her fingers over it.'

As she did so, Mandy Morgan held out her hand.

Caton would have given everything to be able to freeze the action. Tell her to give it back. Create a different ending. CCTV did that to you; it blurred your sense of past and present. Had you wanting to shout at the screen. He wasn't alone.

'Don't do it,' whispered DS Stuart. 'You silly, silly girl.'

But the tape carried on relentlessly. The young man placed something in her hand. Her hand seemed to go automatically to her mouth. He was already moving away, through the crush, towards the dance floor.

'I thought Kathy said she threw hers away,' said Caton.

The bride-to-be watched the young man skirt the dance floor, and veer off towards the toilets. Then she raised her left arm and made a throwing action in his direction.

'She did,' said DS Stuart. 'Thought better of it. It's a shame her friend didn't.' She shook her head. 'It's what tragedies are made of. A moment's stupidity.'

Chapter 10

The action on the rest of the tape unfolded just as they expected it would. They watched as one of the group, of Asian appearance, headed for the toilets.

'Aisha Nu'Puri,' DS Carter told them. 'She's the one who found her, and ended up in A&E herself.'

'She's broken the mould then,' observed Caton.

DC Hulme looked confused.

'Her name doesn't rhyme,' Caton told him.

DS Stuart patted the detective constable on the shoulder.

'I'll tell you later,' she said.

Two minutes elapsed, then another young woman came flying through the doors, one hand to her mouth, the other gesticulating wildly. Then all hell broke loose. Members of staff, including two of the bouncers, rushed into the toilets.

'Hold it there,' said Caton.

DC Hulme hit the pause button.

'There,' said Caton, stabbing the screen with his index finger. 'It's him again.'

The young man they had seen distributing free samples was standing by the door to the men's toilets.

'He's watching the action.'

'Do you think he knows what's going on?' said Joanne Stuart.

'Okay, Jimmy, let it run,' said Caton.

They watched as the paramedics arrived and disappeared into the toilets.

The young man moved slowly towards the centre of the dance floor, where the girl who had given the alarm was being comforted by friends. Her arms were flailing as she described what she had seen.

Two ambulance crews arrived with stretchers. A minute later, the two girls were whisked from the room.

The young man watched them go, then hurried towards the exit.

'He does now,' said Caton.

'Did you see the look on his face?' said Jimmy Hulme. 'He's scared witless.'

Joanne Stuart shook her head ruefully. 'So he should be,' she said.

Two officers from the Tactical Aid Unit arrived, one of them a woman officer.

'A fraction earlier, and they'd have had the place sealed off and caught him in the net,' muttered DC Hulme.

'Thanks, Jimmy,' said Caton. 'That'll do for now. You know what to do. Make three copies. Seal this one in an evidence bag. Give it to the collator.'

'Yes, boss,' he replied.

Ged, the office manager, waved to them. She was holding up her phone.

'DCI Caton, it's for you,' she said.

It was Alan Norris, the Family Liaison Officer.

'Mrs Morgan has just opened a bill addressed to her daughter,' he said. 'It's the phone bill for her mobile.'

'And?'

'There's been eight hundred quid's worth of calls made after she was pronounced dead.'

'Her phone's missing? No one told me that it was missing.'

'Apparently, no one noticed. Not even her mother.'

Caton didn't know whether he was more angry, or disappointed. Someone on his team should have noticed. There was no way she'd have gone out without her mobile.

'Eight hundred pounds?' he said. 'Where are they ringing, Mars?'

'Romania, sir. Five hours of calls alone on the night she died. The rest on the following day, when the bill was prepared.'

'Someone at the hospital?' said Caton.

'Unlikely. The phone wasn't among the personal effects logged in by the TAG team. I've checked with the paramedics and the ambulance crews. None of them claim to have noticed it. My guess is it fell on the floor in the loo. Maybe she was trying to call for help?'

'One of the staff, then.'

'Probably. They'll have flogged it on.'

'We should put a trace on it.'

'The company blocked it as soon as I explained the circumstances.'

'They can still trace it. Until the battery dies out. Get them to do it. Are they cancelling the bill?'

'No, sir. They say the mother's liable for her daughter's debt up until the point at which the phone was reported lost or stolen. Which it wasn't. Not till I told them.'

Caton despaired of the small print, and the small-minded people who kept you to it no matter what. Okay, they had a point. If people were careless with their phones and didn't even notice they were missing, the company could hardly be expected to pick up the entire bill. But this was different. The girl was dead.

'Remind them how it's going to look when the press find out,' he said. '*Heartless Phone Bosses Pursue*

Tragic Victim Beyond The Grave! That should do the trick.'

'I wouldn't bet on it,' said DC Norris. 'But I'll give it a go.'

'What did he want, boss?' said DS Stuart.

He told her.

'Shit!' she said. She was visibly embarrassed. 'I'm so sorry, boss; it's down to me.'

'No it isn't,' he told her. 'This wasn't your case, remember? Not till it was reclassified. Division dealt with it first.'

'But I should have spotted it wasn't among the list of her effects.'

'True,' he acknowledged. 'But don't beat yourself up over it. Save that for the big mistakes. We all make them sooner or later.'

'Do you want me to get her friends in to formally ID the lad in that video?' she said.

'Absolutely. And staff from the club. And use VIPER. I know it's only a formality, but the way the system works now, formal is the only way.'

'I thought the only way was Essex,' joked Gordon Holmes in passing.

They both ignored him.

'And let's get his picture circulated,' said Caton. 'See if he's known. Pubwatch and The Drugs Squad in particular, although he looks like a virgin to me. Speaking of the Drugs Squad, are they up to speed on this?'

'Yes, boss. I've been liaising with them since we got the autopsy results. I'm just waiting for their appointed officer to get in contact with me.'

'They should be cock-a-hoop at the moment,' he reflected. 'Drugs offences are down, and they've just had forty-five individuals convicted through Operation Cairo. Let's hope they move as fast on this.'

'It's in their interest,' she replied. 'The last thing they'll want is a string of drug-related deaths involving weekend revellers.'

'So long as it isn't DCI Lounds I have to work with,' she said.

DC Hulme joined them.

'Excuse me, boss,' he said. 'How many copies did you say?'

'Three.'

'I've had a thought,' said Joanne Stuart. 'If he is a student, he'll have a student card. For the libraries, the Students' Union, that kind of thing. It'll have his photo on it, and they'll have that on their system.'

'You'll be lucky,' said Jimmy Hulme.

She gave him a dirty look.

'I beg your pardon?'

'First off, they'll quote the Data Protection Act; secondly, have you any idea how many students there are in the city?'

'Surprise me,' she said.

He smirked. 'Eighty-seven thousand, four hundred and forty-one. That was in 2008. Bound to be more by now.'

'And you know this how?'

He held out his hand. It was holding a sheet of A4 on which were the numbers for each of the city's three universities.

'I looked it up just now. Thought you might be interested.'

He handed her the sheet, and headed back to his workstation.

'He's a cocky beggar,' she said. 'And a pain.'

'It's a good pain, though,' Caton told her. 'It pays to know the difference.'

Gordon Holmes called from across the room. He was waving a phone in one hand.

'Jo, there's a call for you on here. DCI Lounds. He wants a word.'

'What did I tell you?' said Caton.

As she stomped off to take it, Caton discovered he had a call of his own to field.

'It's Detective Chief Superintendent Gates,' said Ged, one hand masking the mouthpiece. 'She'd like to see you.'

'When?'

Ged grimaced. 'Right now.'

'Tell her I'll be straight up,' he said.

Chapter 11

'How is the Morgan investigation going?' she asked.

'Pretty well,' he told her. 'The autopsy was conclusive.'

'How did she die?'

'Respiratory collapse. The drug slowed her breathing. Her lungs stopped exchanging gases, so her body was starved of oxygen. Within five minutes her brain would have ceased functioning. When the paramedics got there it was too late to save her. She was pronounced dead on the way to hospital.'

'It was definitely the drug?'

'Definitely. The alcohol may have accelerated the process, but the drug was the decisive factor. According to the tox results, based on what was left in her system, it must have been at least double what is normally considered a fatal dose.'

'What about the person who supplied the drug?'

'We have him on video tape actually passing her the drug.'

'Is he identifiable from the tape?'

'Yes. DS Stuart is circulating a still image as we speak. The girls who were with the victim, and staff from the club, are being asked to confirm that it was him using a virtual identity parade.'

'I'm glad to see you're not taking any chances with this,' she observed.

He decided that she wasn't expecting a response, and waited as she shuffled some papers on the desk. He felt sure there was something going on, something she was building up to; he had no idea what it could be.

'There's a press conference at 2 p.m.,' she said. 'I want you to handle it. Take DS Stuart with you; it will do her good.'

'Yes, ma'am.'

It wasn't the press conference, he was sure of that.

'How is she doing by the way?' She was trying too hard to sound nonchalant.

'Very well, ma'am,' he replied. 'Well capable of managing it herself. She has passed her Inspector's Board, after all.'

She twiddled her biro distractedly between her fingers.

'Yes. Shame there aren't any vacancies in the offing. Still, the experience will stand her in good stead.'

She put the biro down on the blotter and looked up.

'This is an important case, Tom,' she said. 'The media are already talking of the danger of a deadly epidemic. A rash of drug-related deaths. The leader of the City Council has been on to the Chief, and the Police and Crime Commissioner. We need to nip this in the bud.'

'I'm well aware of that, ma'am,' he responded, determined to keep his cool. 'I appreciate their concern. When the dealers start giving it away, just to get people hooked, we know they've made a considerable investment in it. Probably got a steady supply, and a large amount of stock ready to flood the market. And to say that China White is lucrative is something of an understatement.'

She leaned forward, marking his every word.

'How so?'

68

'One gram of pure Fentanyl can apparently be cut into as many as seven thousand individual doses of street drugs. According to the Drugs Squad, the going rate on the street is £25 a time, in patch or tablet form.'

He watched her do the maths.

'That's over £175,000,' she said.

'According to them, a troy ounce of gold is currently worth around £825, and there are 31 grams in a troy ounce. That makes Fentanyl worth over five and a half thousand times more than its equivalent in gold.'

She shook her head in disbelief.

'Over a million pounds, for just six grams of a legal medicinal drug.'

'Used illegally,' he reminded her.

'Five grams is a heaped tablespoon,' she reflected. 'It beats having to use a container lorry, a yacht or a speedboat to smuggle your drugs into the country.'

She leaned back in her chair, picked up the biro and started doodling on the blotter.

'Speaking of the Drugs Squad, where are they in all of this?'

'We've kept them up to speed from the start,' he said. 'They've been carrying out their own enquiries on our behalf, and as soon as we were sure that it was organised drugs peddling I asked them to nominate a liaison officer to join the team.'

'And have they?'

He kept what he thought was a straight face, his voice neutral.

'It looks like it's going to be Detective Chief Inspector Lounds.'

She wasn't fooled.

'Dirty Dicky,' she said, looking up. 'I heard he'd been promoted.'

'Yes, ma'am.'

'I don't suppose you're best pleased?'

'Not really, ma'am. But I'll make it work.'

'Does that go for DI Holmes as well? They're not the best of friends, if I remember rightly.'

'No, ma'am, they're not. Fortunately, DI Holmes is off on leave. That's why DS Stuart is standing in as my deputy senior investigator.'

'Well,' she said, with the ghost of a smile, 'I think Dicky Lounds may find he's met his match in her. Speaking of which...' She dragged a thin brown Manila folder towards her with the index finger of her right hand, and flipped it open.

Here we go, Caton said to himself.

'How's Kate?'

It was the last thing he'd been expecting. It completely blindsided him.

'Erm, fine, thank you, ma'am,' he said. 'She's well, very well.'

'Good.' She began to scan the open page. 'I gather you speak a little Italian?'

'That's right, ma'am. Enough to get by.' He still couldn't see where this was leading.

'That explains it, I suppose.' Now she was sounding enigmatic.

He suddenly remembered how it had felt standing in the High Master's study back at MGS, when he and some other boys had been caught skiving off school to watch an Ashes Test at Old Trafford. He also recalled the school motto: *sapere aude*, dare to know; or, as some would have it, dare to be wise. He thought it wise on this occasion to let her tell him in her own time. She turned the page. It was a long wait. Finally, she looked up.

'It seems you had a bit of excitement while you were on your honeymoon, in Venice. In more ways than one?'

'Yes, ma'am.'

He was relieved that this was all it was. Unless there had been a complaint of some kind about the way he had handled the situation at the San Clemente Palace. He thought that unlikely. Unless he'd been accused of pretending to have authority he didn't have in those first minutes after the discovery of the body. The two sous-chefs, perhaps.

'Only it's come back to haunt you, I'm afraid,' she said, pointing to the file.

'I'm sorry, ma'am,' he said, 'I don't have the faintest idea what this is about.'

'That body you found…'

'I wasn't the one who found it,' he said.

She waved his comment away as though swatting a fly.

'That body you found was one of ours.'

Caton was stunned. 'Ours?'

'Mancunian,' she said. 'Born and bred. Well, born anyway. He was second-generation Italian. So, you could say he was Manc'alian.'

She seemed pleased with her little joke.

Caton barely registered it.

'The victim was from Manchester?'

'Out in Venice on a job. Worked for a travel firm based here in the city. It's all in here.

She closed the file and held it out for him to take.

'You can read it later,' she said. 'All you need to know is that the investigating magistrate – the Publicco Ministero I think it's called – has requested our assistance via Europol. Naturally we've said yes. Actually, both the Police and Crime Commissioner and the Chief Constable jumped at it. Probably hoping for a trip to Venice. Not that you heard me say that. Because of course they wouldn't. Though I can think of some that would.'

I'd stop digging if I were you, Caton thought.

'Anyway,' she continued, 'when I say *our* assistance, I mean *your* assistance, because they've asked for you. Their investigators arrive tomorrow. Manchester Airport at 11.55 a.m. Be nice if you were there to meet them.'

She sat back, folded her arms and regarded him closely. She raised her eyebrows.

'Must have made quite an impression, Tom.'

'But I can't possibly do it,' he said. 'Not till we've concluded this investigation. You said yourself how important it is.'

'Look, Tom,' she said with a tone that bordered on patronising, 'you've established what happened, where it happened, and how it happened. You've established the cause of death and the instrument of that death. You know who we are looking for. All you need is a name and an address. It's now down to bog-standard police work. You and I know that we'll have pulled him in before the week is up.'

'But what about the suppliers?' he said. 'And the threat to the rest of the punters out there?'

'That's down to the Drugs Squad,' she said. 'There's no way the CPS is going to try to lay charges beyond the person who actually gave her the tablet. Too messy, too tricky, too expensive, outcome uncertain. Let the Drugs Squad pursue them. The bigger picture, Tom. We'll wrap this one up tight as a drum, and deservedly take the credit for it.'

'So you're happy to let DS Stuart take over at this point?' he said.

She sat up straight, uncrossed her arms and placed them on the desk.

'I didn't say that.'

'Well, there's no one else,' he responded. 'DI Holmes is on leave. And I can't believe you'd bring in someone from one of the other teams.'

'There's DCI Lounds,' she said. 'He's part of the team now.'

Caton clenched his fists and bit his tongue. Had it been Martin Hadfield across the table he wouldn't have bothered to hold his temper in check.

'You don't mean that,' he said. 'For a start, he's not part of the Force Major Incident Team. Secondly, do you really want the Drugs Squad to take the credit for all the work we've done up to this point? And thirdly, it's Dirty Dicky Lounds we're talking about.'

He could see that one of those had hit a nerve, though he had no idea which.

'I still don't see any alternative,' she said.

Caton leaned forward, right on the edge of his seat.

'Make up DS Stuart to acting Detective Inspector for the duration of the investigation, then she'll have the rank this case deserves. Lounds remains in a liaison capacity only, and you can take a supervisory role, ma'am. I guarantee you won't need to involve yourself beyond receiving daily briefings from DS Stuart.'

As soon as she started to think about it, Caton knew that he had won.

'What about DCI Lounds?' she said. 'He won't like it.'

'Good,' he said. 'It's up to him.'

'It won't be easy to persuade Martin Hadfield, or the Head of Human Resources.'

'You're the Head of Serious Crime Division, ma'am,' he said.

She fixed him with the threatening look that in the past had been reserved for uncooperative suspects.

'Careful, Detective Chief Inspector,' she said.

Caton knew he had overstepped the mark. With the current obsession with managing the cuts, and the resultant policy on promotions, it would almost certainly have to go right to the top. All the more reason to go out on a limb. *In for a penny, in for a pound,* he told himself.

'Not only,' he said, 'is DS Stuart a bloody good detective, ma'am, who has proved herself over and over again, and was willing to put herself at mortal risk, but she is a woman who has had to overcome considerable hostility on account of her sexuality.'

He sat bolt upright in his chair and braced himself for the inevitable onslaught.

He watched the colour begin to mottle the skin on her neck. It was a faint but perceptible flush. Rarely seen. Rarely survived unscathed. She spoke quietly, slowly and with a steely tone.

'I hope, Detective Chief Inspector Caton,' she said, 'that you are not seeking to play the gender and sexual orientation cards?'

'Certainly not, ma'am,' he said with an impressive show of sincerity that fooled neither of them.

She studied him for a moment or two, and then turned her attention to her in-tray.

'We're done here, Detective Chief Inspector,' she said, without looking up.

Caton stood, and walked to the door. She spoke as he reached for the handle.

'One last thing before you go.'

'Yes, ma'am?'

'From now on, it's *boss*. I'd prefer it if you dropped the ma'am.'

'Certainly ma–, boss,' he said, wondering what that was all about.

'And don't forget the press briefing, along with your deputy. Two o'clock sharp in the Media Suite. And make sure DCI Lounds is there too.'

She lowered her head and pretended to be reading

the paper on the desk in front of her. When he didn't leave immediately, she made a shooing gesture with the back of her hand.

It reminded him of Commissario Umberto Bonifati.

He closed the door quietly behind him.

Chapter 12

'How was the press conference?'

Caton poured them both some water. He would have loved a glass of red with the bolognaise, but, since Kate was no longer drinking, it seemed selfish somehow. In any case, there would be plenty of opportunity later that evening if he did decide to go out.

'As you'd expect,' he told her, 'frustration that we weren't telling them everything; trying to hype up what we did give them; looking to sensationalise an individual tragedy.'

'But they've got a point,' she said, her fork suspended in mid-air, the roll of spaghetti starting to unwind, a dribble of tomato sauce splattering her bowl. 'If other people are given these tablets, there could be multiple tragedies.'

'Agreed. But do you really think they're going to carry on giving them out while the heat is on?'

She stabbed her fork in his direction.

'My point entirely. It's the press you're relying on to create that heat. The glare of publicity is what's going to keep the public safe, and help you get your man.'

Caton should have known it was pointless arguing with her. She had this knack of getting to the heart of a matter. Of saying what she knew he was really thinking. He wiped a smear of sauce from his lip and raised his glass.

'Touché.'

'Have you decided yet?' she asked.

'What?'

'If you're joining The Alternatives tonight?'

'I'm not sure. It's been a heavy day, and–'

'Stop making excuses,' she said. 'You're not supposed to be at the airport till midday. You can have a lie-in the morning. You deserve it.'

'I need to make sure DS Stuart gets a decent head start. DCI Lounds is bound to try to chuck his weight around.'

She waved her fork again.

'For someone who's supposed to be championing her, there's no way that you should be underestimating her. Anyway, I bet Helen Gates will leave Dirty Dicky in no doubt about who's in charge.'

'Even so…'

'Did the Chief Constable okay her promotion to Acting DI?'

'Yes.'

'And have you briefed her about how to handle DCI Lounds?'

'Yes.'

'And is she up to speed on the case?'

'Yes.'

'And do you trust her?'

'Of course.'

'Then let her do her job, Tom. Last thing she needs is you lurking in the background.'

'Does being pregnant have this effect on every woman?'

She put her fork down and folded her arms. Caton knew he was in trouble.

'Are you saying it's impossible for a woman to be

77

forthright, and assertive, without an extra dose of hormones?'

'It was only a joke,' he protested.

She frowned. 'You know where I stand on sexist jokers.'

He raised his hands in mock surrender.

'I'm sorry.'

'You will be,' she said menacingly.

'I think I will go out tonight,' he said. 'Just for an hour or so.'

She stood, and began to clear the plates.

'Make it two or three. It will give me a chance to catch up on some of the programmes I recorded while we were away.'

She turned in the archway through to the open-plan kitchen.

'And to plot my revenge.'

Chapter 13

'Look what the cat dragged in!' yelled Jamie.

The others turned to see.

There in the doorway stood Tom Caton. He was embarrassed to find that he was now the centre of attention for the entire room.

'Wonders will never cease,' said Craig, jumping to his feet.

'It's about bloody time, mate,' said Nick, pumping Caton's hand up and down.

'Your round, sailor!' simpered Jerome, grandstanding as ever.

Enveloped by this genuine warmth, accompanied by hugs and backslapping, Caton wondered why he had stayed away so long.

It was almost half an hour later before they'd brought Caton up to date with their news. Nick and Jamie were still playing football with Didsbury Beavers, Caton's former team, though Jamie was currently injured with a torn ligament. Nick had been promoted against all the odds, and was now a senior teacher at St Matthew's High. Craig had decided to put his encyclopaedic knowledge of literature to good use and had started to write a novel of his own. Jerome was working hard at being Jerome. He was now on the organising committee for Gay Pride, and had a new forever partner. His fifth in as many years, a management accountant with a big firm on King's Street. He punched the air.

'Max is the one!' he said. 'Kind, thoughtful, considerate.'

'He'd need to be,' said Jamie.

'No,' Jerome insisted. 'I've changed. I'm strictly a one-man gal.'

'And I'm the King of Siam,' said Craig, standing up to a chorus of approval and raising his empty glass. 'My round. Same again?'

He caught the eye of the taller of the lasses behind the bar.

'Same again, Jan!'

She shook her head in mock disapproval, but her smile said otherwise. He sat down again.

'That's the best thing about being regulars,' he said. 'Personal service.'

'Are you listening, Tom?' said Nick. '*Regulars.*'

'Alright,' Caton responded, 'you've had your fun. I thought this was a Book Club.'

'Don't tell me you actually read it?' said Craig. 'On your honeymoon! I thought you'd have had better things to do.'

'Give me a break,' said Caton.

'Is that what Kate said?' Jerome jibed.

Caton waited for the laughter to die down.

'Okay. '*Caminada: the Crime Buster*. Whose choice was that?'

'Mine,' said Jamie.

'I didn't have you down as an aficionado of the true crime genre, let alone the Victorian Underworld.'

'I'm not. It was Caminada I was interested in. I thought you would be too. One of Britain's most famous detectives, a Mancunian and an Italian to boot.'

'It was interesting,' Caton told him. 'Fascinating, to tell you the truth. I'm just surprised that it was your choice.'

Jamie twirled his glass, watching the beer swirl around, leaving a velvety smear around the surface. Cream of Manchester, they called it back in the Boddington's day.'

'I'm quarter Italian,' he said, taking them all by surprise.

'Why didn't you tell us before?' said Nick.

'No reason to. It's not as though I'm ashamed of the fact, quite the reverse; I'm proud of my heritage.' He swirled his glass again. 'My nonno's brother's name was Giacomo. I was named after him.'

'Nonno?' said Jerome.

'It's Italian for granddad,' Caton told him.

'And my nonna was Maria,' said Jamie. 'So strictly speaking I'm third-generation Italian. British Italian.'

'That explains why you talk so fast,' Craig observed.

They all laughed.

'Probably,' he agreed, with a lopsided smile. 'I'll tell you another thing you don't know about me. I'm an active member of the Manchester Italian Association. I even helped to organise the annual Italian Procession in June this year, from Ancoats into the city centre.'

'I saw it, on Albert Square, when it was passing the Town Hall,' declared Nick. 'I didn't see you.'

Jamie raised his glass and drank deeply. He put the glass down and wiped his mouth with the back of his hand.

'Well, I was there,' he said.

'Jamie Robins,' said Jerome. 'That doesn't sound very Italian.'

'Robino,' he replied. 'That was the family name.

My grandfather changed it to Robins during the war.'

'It must have been difficult for them during the war,' said Caton.

'Worse for those with Italian passports,' said Jamie quietly.

He stared into his glass as he spoke. They strained to hear him over the noise of the other drinkers.

'His brother, my father's uncle, hadn't been granted British citizenship at that point. He was interned, under appalling conditions, along with every other Italian male between the age of eighteen and seventy. In July the government decided to deport them to Newfoundland for the duration of the war.'

'Fair enoughski,' said Jerome.

The others glared at him. Craig kicked him under the table. Jamie seemed not to have noticed.

'They packed one thousand and sixteen internees, seven hundred and twelve of whom were Italian, on a converted liner, the SS Arandora Star. It had been converted as a troopship, painted grey and armed for self-defence.'

He paused and looked up.

'It should have been flying a Red Cross flag. It wasn't. Early in the morning of 2nd July, just to the north-west of the Hebrides, it was torpedoed by a German U-47 submarine, commanded by Lieutenant Commander Günther Prien, their foremost U-Boat ace.'

'Wasn't he the guy that torpedoed and sank the battleship HMS Royal Oak in Scapa Flow?' asked Craig.

'Shhh!' said Nick, Jerome and Tom in unison.

'He only had one torpedo left when he came across the Arandora Star that day, and that was supposedly faulty. Even so, thirty-five minutes later the ship had sunk, and eight hundred of those aboard had lost their lives. For weeks afterwards bodies washed up along the coast of Ireland, and the Hebrides. My father's uncle was one of those whose body was never recovered. According to an eyewitness, he broke his neck diving into the water. Apparently, he hit a piece of wreckage.'

He raised his glass to his lips, emptied it and put it gently back down on the table.

'His name was Giacomo.'

'Shit,' said Jerome.

'Bloody hell, mate,' said Nick.

Craig put his arm around his shoulder and patted his back affectionately.

'I'm sorry, Jamie,' said Caton. 'We had no idea.'

'That's alright,' he said. 'It was a long time ago. Way before I was born. But do you know what still gets to me?'

No one did.

'That it wasn't until five years ago, in Liverpool in 2008, that there was an official public commemoration of the sinking. And there has been no apology from successive governments for the way in which those men were treated, and put at risk.'

'That'll be the lawyers,' said 'Nick. 'Worried about claims for compensation.'

'Right then,' said Craig, determined to lift the mood. 'It's your round, Nick, and then let's get back to our friend Caminada.'

Over the next hour and a half they dissected the story that the former Detective Superintendent Caminada had committed to paper about his thirty years as a Manchester police officer.

Jerome had been delighted to discover that he and this real Sherlock Holmes shared the same Christian name. He also insisted that the detective must have been gay because he mentioned neither a wife nor children in his book. Craig disabused him.

'He married Amelia Wainhouse, at the Church of The Holy Name, on 19th December 1881,' he informed him. 'And their five children are buried together in the family grave in the Southern Cemetery. I checked.'

'Amy Winehouse!' declared Jerome. 'What an amazing coincidence.'

'*Wainhouse*, you plonker,' said Craig.

They argued at length about which was their favourite of the twenty cases detailed in the book. In the end they all agreed that the *Murder in a Four-wheeled Cab* was the most impressive display of observation, deduction and forensic examination.

'Bet you'd have been proud to pull that one off yourself, Tom?' said Nick.

Caton was inclined to agree. Whilst reading of Caminada's exploits – including the donning of disguises, and hiding inside a piano at the Free Trade Hall – he had wondered how on earth he himself would manage without the aid of modern forensic science.

His phone told him that he had a text. It was from Kate.

2 or 3 hrs I said!

The time on his BlackBerry was 11.47. He replied immediately.

On my way. XXX.

He drained his glass, pushed back his chair and stood.

'Thanks for a great evening, guys,' he said. 'Time to go.'

It was met with a chorus of ribald remarks and down-turned thumbs, suggestive of his being well and truly stuffed now that he was a married man. It was nothing less than he'd expected. Secretly, he found it comforting.

As he started down the stairs, Caton reflected that he had really missed these sessions. There was something about getting away from the often claustrophobic, almost incestuous nature, of his work environment. It did him good, he realised, to be with these normal people, with ordinary jobs, whose world did not revolve around serious criminality, domestic tragedy and senseless, wicked cruelty.

He stepped from the brightly lit interior of the Old Nag's Head onto Jacksons Row. He took a deep breath and exhaled, smiling to himself at the familiar taste and smell of the city. The tantalising aroma of nearby restaurants, the acrid scent of diesel fumes, a trace of woodsmoke from illicit stoves or a barbecue on one of the rooftop terraces. He listened to the muted sounds of laughter, clinking glasses, and general alcohol-fuelled camaraderie. There were the faint strains of a single saxophone. In his mind's eye he could see the guy standing at his favourite pitch outside Kendals, where Manchester's famous bag lady had slept for years until she disappeared as mysteriously as she had first appeared.

There were times, in the recent past, when Caton had felt he ought to move, to get away. To start anew with Kate and their unborn child. But it was, he knew, like a love affair, with its ups and downs, and spats, and making up. If familiarity really did breed contempt, it ought not to be only true of people, but of places too. He had plumbed the depths of this city, and witnessed incredible resilience, inventiveness and joyful expressions of civic pride. Like the rebuilding of the historic heart of the city after the IRA bomb, and that amazing summer of 2002 when the Commonwealth Games showed the city and her people in all its glory.

This wasn't Paris, Rome or Venice, but it was his. And it was home. Caton was sorry that he had ever doubted it.

He turned up his collar and headed – with as much of a spring in his step as four pints of bitter allowed – past the Reform Synagogue, towards the Central Library taxi rank.

Chapter 14

Caton had been tempted to pop into the petrol station on the airport campus, grab a coffee, park up at the side, and wait for Commissario Bonifati to text that they had left baggage collection and were heading for the Terminal 1 Arrivals pick-up point.

It was what he usually did. It saved having to park up and pay. It also obviated the possibility that he'd be told to move on from the designated pick-up area if his passengers got lost or held up.

But today was different. They were strangers in a foreign land. Fellow professionals. They deserved the courtesy of a proper meet and greet.

So here he was, in Terminal 1 Arrivals, scanning the screens for news of the 11.25 a.m. Jet 2 flight from Marco Polo, Tessara. Apparently, it was on time. He stood staring at the screen as it clicked through the changes. It was like watching paint dry, or, as his mother used to say, waiting for a kettle to boil. Five minutes later, at 12.55 p.m. precisely, it did.

It would be at least twenty minutes before they'd collected their baggage, so he decided to see if they let him have a mug of hot water at Café Select. It was a habit that he knew his colleagues thought of as some strange health fad, but he wasn't religious about it. He just liked to control the amount of caffeine he drank. It was a legacy of his years in uniform. Of the shift work, when he drank endless cups of coffee to keep awake on night duty and then found he couldn't get to sleep the next morning. In any case, he'd be having more than his fair share of coffee with these two, no doubt.

He had to smile as he watched them emerge from the tunnel-like corridor into the Arrivals Hall. Umberto Bonifati led the way, in a cream lightweight linen jacket over an open-neck white shirt and pale-blue linen slacks. On his feet he wore petrol-blue handcrafted loafers. In his left hand he carried a tan leather man bag. With his right he pulled along a medium-sized tan suitcase. He looked more like a very successful Mediterranean businessman than a police officer.

Behind him, towing a large black rolling suitcase over which was hung a red leather handbag, came Caterina Volpe. She wore a fitted white silk blouse and a black pencil skirt. Her heels were several inches taller now, exaggerating the difference in their heights. Her shoulder-length hair bounced from side to side as she moved. She reminded Caton of a model on a catwalk: erect, composed, almost arrogant, feet placed directly in front of each other so that her hips swayed seductively. He couldn't help noticing that her breasts seemed larger now that they had been released from the confines of her uniform.

Given the age difference, this was definitely a businessman and his PA combining work with pleasure. Or maybe a film director and his leading lady, in town for a premiere, or a dirty weekend. Either way, they stood out from the common herd in their sensible jeans and training shoes, and the handful of bargain break cheapskates wearing T-shirts over shorts. There was no mistaking La Bella Figura. He stepped forward and waved them over.

'*Benvenuti, Commissario, benvenuti, Sovrintendente*' he said. 'Welcome.'

They both smiled the universal smile of the weary traveller.

'May I take your case, *Sovrintendente*?' he asked.

She relinquished her grip, retrieved her handbag and stepped aside so that he could reach the handle.

'*Grazie*,' she said.

Kate would never have allowed him to, he reflected. She always insisted on managing her own case even though it was invariably the largest and heaviest.

'This way,' he told them. 'It's not far.'

They were on the M56 approaching Northenden. The commissario was in the front, his assistant in the back. The customary niceties about the flight, the on-board snack, and the weather, had been exhausted. Bonifati felt in his pocket for his cigarettes, and then thought better of it. He angled himself sideways so that he could see Caton's face.

'Please,' he said, 'from now on it is Umberto and Caterina. Or, if you must, Mr Bonifati and Miss Volpe.'

It sounded more like a slight rebuke than a friendly invitation. Caton glanced at him.

'While we are here, in England,' Bonifati continued, 'it is better that nobody knows we are *Polizia*, unless we tell them that we are.'

Caton nodded. It made sense.

The Italian detective grinned. 'And it is more friendly, no?'

He loosened his seat belt a little, holding it away from his jacket as though trying to protect its shape and texture.

'And one more request.'

Caton glanced at him again.

'Of course.'

'We try to speak English here if possible, please? It will be good for me I think.'

'Of course,' said Caton, though he wondered how Caterina Volpe would cope. 'When in Rome...'

'When in Rome, what?' said Bonifati.

Caton laughed. 'Sorry,' he said. 'It's a saying we have. A quote from St Augustine when he was living in Milan – *Cum Romanum venio, ieiuno Sabbato; cum hic sum, non ieiuno*: When I go to Rome, I fast on Saturday, when I'm here, I don't. It's about respecting the customs of another city or country.'

It was Bonifati's turn to laugh. It was the first time Caton had heard him do so. It was a gutsy laugh, like a prolonged chuckle.

'It is true,' he said. 'But not always so. Naples, for example. Do as they do?' He spread his hands. 'Rubbish in the street. Bodies in the rubbish. *Vedi Napoli e poi muori!*'

He started to laugh again, looking back over his shoulder to see if his colleague had got the joke. She stared fixedly out of the window.

See Naples and die; probably not the meaning the poet had given it.

'Your Latin, Tom, is as good as your Italian,' said Bonifati.

'Thank you,' said Caton. 'I had a classical education.'

He had hated it at the time, but was glad of it now.

They continued in silence towards the Princess Parkway, and along the corridor that led directly into the heart of the city. His two passengers stared out of the windows as the landscape changed from parkland, past comfortable suburban properties, the Victorian terraces, modern maisonettes and houses of

Moss Side and Hulme, and finally, the eclectic mix of industrial railway arches, canalside warehouses and gleaming high-rise flats and university buildings that was twenty-first century Manchester.

Instead of joining the Mancunian Way, Caton decided to carry straight on by the black-and-white frontage of The Briton's Protection, where he made a mental note to take them during their stay, and past the imposing Bridgewater Hall, home to the Halle and the BBC Phil when they were in town.

'*Che cosa è?*' said Bonifati, having forgotten his earlier request to try to stick to English.

He was pointing at the massive single-span glass dome of Manchester Central, the former Victorian railway station, now a conference centre.

Caton told him. What he didn't tell him was that this was the station where Ian Brady, the Moors Murderer, had met 17-year-old Edward Evans, his final victim, before beating him to death with an axe and burying his body on Saddleworth Moor.

He took them up Portland Street, pointing out Chinatown on the way, past Piccadilly Gardens, and out onto the ring road.

'I've booked you both into the Holiday Inn on Oldham Road,' he said. 'It's less than two minutes' walk from Police Headquarters. Two standard rooms, with king-size double beds. Breakfast included.' He glanced at his passenger. 'That was what you wanted?'

Bonifati grunted and nodded his head.

'Non-smoking, I'm afraid,' said Caton. 'But you can always smoke on the roof terrace. There are great views over the city, and the Pennine Hills.'

'Pennine Hills?' said Bonifati slowly. 'Like our Apennine Hills?'

Caton smiled. 'From the Celtic *pen*, meaning mountain or summit,' he said. 'Go back far enough and we are probably related.'

'Go back far enough,' said the Italian detective, committing the phrase to memory, 'and we are *all* related.'

Caton dropped them at the door. He checked that their rooms were ready, and left them to unpack and settle in. He promised to come back and give them a lift to Central Park HQ when they were ready. He wondered how long it would be before Bonifati set off the smoke alarm or, more worryingly, the sprinkler system. He also wondered what would happen when they discovered that their rooms were not only adjoining – all the hotel had left – but also had an interconnecting door. Would one of them choose to lock it? His money was on the enigmatic Caterina Volpe.

Chapter 15

'Very nice,' said Commissario Bonifati. 'Like a dish for TV.'

It was not the first time that Caton had heard someone make that connection with the magnificent sweeping canopy of the Transport Gateway station, but never put quite like that.

The even more impressive sculpture, The Seed, sitting as it did in the centre of the roundabout between the GMP Force Headquarters and the North Divisional building, drew a far more appropriate response from the seat in the back that Sovrintendente Volpe had made her own.

'*Buonissima*,' she said.

'You are very fortunate to work in a place like this,' said Bonifati.

'You're pretty fortunate yourselves,' Caton replied, pulling to a stop at the checkpoint for the car park.

He wound down the window, and held up his warrant card and pass.

'To work in one of the wonders of the world.'

The commissario laughed and turned to share the joke with his assistant. When he had finished translating, she gave a little snort of derision.

'Once, maybe. When it was ours,' said Bonifati. 'Now it belongs to the *turisti*. One million of them every year!'

Caton recalled the depressing sight of cruise liner after cruise liner passing through the Giudecca Canal, dwarfing the renaissance palaces on either side. Sacrilegious, Kate had called it.

'Pushing up prices,' Bonifati continued. It was becoming a rant and he slipped inevitably into his native Italian. '*Soffocando le piazze ei vicoli! Ristoranti che danno loro da mangiare merda!*'

Choking the squares and alleys. The restaurants giving them crap to eat. His assistant leant forward and gave him some more ammunition. As far as Caton could tell it was about a near miss between two cruise ships in the Lagoon earlier that month.

By the time they reached reception, his two passengers had covered foreigners buying up property, illegal immigrants tripling the crime rate, and the city sinking ever faster. They had barely drawn breath. It came as a relief when the vast and impressive glass and steel atrium finally distracted them from their domestic woes.

'This way,' he said, ushering them towards the lifts.

Caton gave them a quick tour of the Major Incident Room and introduced them to his team, more out of courtesy than anything else. They caused quite a stir. **Sovrintendente** Caterina Volpe in particular. The expressions on the face of the men ranged from slack-jawed admiration to outright lusting. Gordon Holmes was especially affected. Fawning came to mind. It was only the quick-witted intervention of Joanne Stuart that had prevented him from making a complete fool of himself.

Caton showed them into what passed for his own office space, and invited them to sit on the only two chairs available apart from his own task chair, which he pulled out from behind the desk. He pushed the desk right up against the partition to make a little more room and sat down.

'I'm sorry,' he said, 'but space is at a premium here.'

His guests were not the slightest bit bothered.

'No worry, Tom,' Bonifati told him. 'This place is a palazzo.'

He opened his man bag, took out a bulky loose-leaf Manila folder and placed it on the coffee table around which they sat. The front cover was blank but for a serial number. He flicked it open. On the first page the serial number was repeated, followed by what appeared to be a list of the officials involved in the case. As far as Caton could tell it included the Pubblico Ministero – the prosecutor whose role it was to investigate the case – and the Judiciary Police who assisted him. In many ways they were like the Crown Prosecution Service in the UK, but far more hands-on.

Bonifati nodded.

'Cesare Benedetti,' he said. 'You are lucky he is too busy to come. We are both lucky. A big trial has to be moved to Milano.' He shrugged. '*Interferenza.*'

Interference. Caton didn't need it spelling out.

On the next page was the serial number again, accompanying the words *Morte sospetta* in capitals and bold. Suspicious death. Beneath them was a name: Giovanni Richetti. It meant nothing to Caton. Nor did the photo on the next page.

It was a head shot, in colour. He was staring at the camera with a fixed expression that was neither happy nor sad, almost indifferent. Caton assumed that it was either a mugshot or had been taken from his passport. It showed a young Caucasian man of between twenty-five and thirty years of age. At a guess, IC2, Mediterranean European/Hispanic. Black hair, casually spiked with wax or oil. Dark curving eyebrows. Dark-brown eyes. A pronounced nose;

more Greek than Roman. A prominent chin. His face had a natural even tan.

Bonifati waited to see if Caton showed any sign of having recognised this man, then turned the page again. It showed the same image, but this time it was the victim's passport photo page.

Richetti, Giovanni, British Citizen. Born 26th December 1983. That made him twenty-nine. He had been right about the age. Place of birth: Manchester, England.

'Is he known to you?' asked Bonifati.

'No, Umberto, he's not. At least not to me. But I'll run him through the PNC and see if we have anything on him.'

Both of the Italian detectives looked quizzical.

'Pee En See?' said Bonifati, pronouncing it as though it was a series of words rather than initials.

Caton made a mental note to cut out the acronyms from now on. He explained about the databases: Names; Vehicles; Drivers; Stolen Property. How the names, or *nominals* as they were actually known, were of persons convicted or cautioned, arrested within the immediate past, wanted in connection with a crime, who had skipped bail, or who were Absent Without Leave from Her Majesty's Armed Forces. He didn't bother to explain the rest; he assumed they would know what data was collected on motor vehicles, their registered keepers, and on the close to fifty million drivers in the system.

'We have a similar system,' said Bonifati. 'Not as good. There are too many competing interests with needs of their own.' He paused and smiled to himself. 'And with interests to protect.'

Caton sympathised. The Home Office, and the Association of Chief Police Officers in particular, had at least managed to resist the pressure to over-complicate the PNC from the fifty plus organisations that had full or partial access to the data.

'I'd check him out right now,' said Caton, 'but it would mean accessing that.'

He pointed to his desk. The keyboard and the monitor were now out of reach.

'Can it wait until you've shown me the rest of it?'

Bonifati pointed to the photo.

'*Signore* Richetti is in no hurry,' he said.

The following four pages contained photos of the crime scene, and the forensic crime scene investigation report. There was nothing of real interest here for Caton, aside from the photos of the body when it had been retrieved. Now he could see the ropes fastened to his limbs, and the small sacks that were trailing from them. As for immediate perpetrator trace evidence, there was, unsurprisingly, none. The conclusion was self-evident. As Bonifati had first suspected, the body must have been placed in the water at some other point, and the currents, or the tidal flow – what little there was of it in the Lagoon – had deposited the victim on San Clemente Island.

Then followed the autopsy report, including more detailed photographs. The text was, in the main, way beyond Caton's ability to translate, but the photographs were self-evident. They showed the deep indentations around his wrists and ankles where the ropes had been tied. The weight of the bags full of salt, causing them to bite into the flesh.

The most shocking were the close-ups of his face. The nose and ears had all but disappeared, but there was no evidence of a clean cut in either case. Caton had seen this before. Had he been in any doubt, Bonifati was quick to confirm his suspicions. He made an up-and-down movement with his right hand and arm, like a snake, and then rapidly and repeatedly brought his fingers and thumb together.

'*Mordicchiato dai pesci,*' he said.

Caton nodded. 'He was nibbled by the fish.'

'*Si, e anche qui.*' said Sovrintendente Volpe.

Yes, and also here.

Caton was surprised to hear her voice. She had been remarkably quiet since they first arrived.

'*Per favore.*' She leant across him to point out, on the next photo, a series of random marks on the face and parts of the torso.

Despite the discolouration of the body, it was obvious that these too were bite marks consistent with the others. The majority were on the fingers and toes, but there were also some on the lower legs, back and chest, which suggested that some of the creatures at least had swum up his trouser legs, the sleeves of his jacket, and inside his shirt.

He could smell her perfume. Wayward strands of her hair brushed his cheek. It was a bizarre and uncomfortable juxtaposition, the combination of these photos, and this earthy female presence.

'*Moechee, e totanetti,*' she said.

'No, no, *anguee, e passariono,*' countered her colleague.

Caton leaned back as the two of them began to argue with each other across him. A light-hearted argument peppered with the names of creatures from the Lagoon. The first two he recognised as soft-shelled crab and tiny squid; he had no idea what the others were. Before he could ask, they had moved on to contesting the best way in which to accompany a *fritto di mare*. With shredded cabbage and radicchio salad, or with a squirt of lemon, and some bread.

He raised his hands like a referee in a boxing match. The two of them shrugged, and settled back in their seats. Caton turned the page.

The next photo was of the back of the victim's skull. An arrow pointed to a large depression on what Caton knew to be the right posterior fossa of the occipital bone, high up on the back of his head, on the right side. It had to have been caused either by a fall, or a blow of considerable force delivered by a right-handed person.

'The cause of death?' he asked.

Bonifati shook his head. 'No, he drown-ed. His...' He patted his chest.

'His lungs?'

'*Si*, his lungs had a little water.'

'Was this before or after he was dead?' said Caton.

'Before,' said the commissario, waving his arm as though delivering a blow. 'To make him unconscious.'

It made sense. A blow on the head to render him unconscious, so they could get him into a boat without alerting anyone. Tie the weighted bags to his limbs, and tip him over the side. The cold water was enough to bring him round. He would have fought to free himself and instinctively gasped for breath, thus inhaling some of the water before the natural reflexes caused his throat to spasm and closed down the airways. As he sank to the bottom of the Lagoon he would have begun to asphyxiate. Then he would have lost consciousness for the final time.

Caton turned the page. On the next two there were charts of the Lagoon between the mouth of the Grand Canal by St Mark's Square, and the Lido, the long, thin island that lay between Venice and the Adriatic Sea. San Clemente Island, where the body ended up, lay directly in the centre of both charts.

The channels through which the larger vessels plied, including the cruise liners, were marked in different shades of blue. Numbers marked the depths of these channels. Coloured lines indicated what

Caton took to be the prevailing currents. Bonifati stabbed the first chart in the centre of one of the channels that ran close by the Isola San Maggiore.

It was the place where Bonifati had said the Doges brought some of the condemned to die by drowning. Those who had not been dragged by a horse across the squares, and then hanged or drowned in a bucket in front of the judges in the very court itself.

The Italian detective traced a route along one of the currents, showing how the body might eventually have been carried to the island.

'It is only *una teoria*,' he said. He raised his eyebrows.

'Theory,' said Caton.

'A theory. But it is a good one.'

'How long from the time he was put in the water until he was found?'

Bonifati shrugged. '*Il Patologo*...?'

'The pathologist?'

'The pathologist says one, to one and a half weeks.' He grinned. 'We think eleven days exactly.'

'How can you be so sure?' said Caton.

Bonifati flipped the pages back to the first photo of the victim.

'Because Giovanni Richetti was reported missing exactly eleven days before he gave Valentina Moro, *l'apprendista*, a shock of her life.'

Chapter 16

The final section detailed everything that had been discovered about the victim. Rather than expecting Caton to struggle his way through it, Bonifati removed the final sheet and closed the folder. Using that sheet, which contained notes in English that he appeared to have committed to memory, but which he consulted whenever he was stuck, he began to give Caton a résumé.

'Richetti, the victim, worked for an English travel firm. He was in *Venetia* arranging packages with hotels and tour guides. On the morning of Tuesday the 10th of July, he failed to turn up for a meeting. The man he was to meet – a hotel manager – rang his office. They tried to contact him, and could not. The hotel said he had not slept in his bed the night before, or had breakfast. He did not return to his hotel that evening. He was reported missing the following morning.'

'The *Polizia* checked it out?' said Caton.

'Of course. His passport and travel pack with his airline tickets were still in the room security box.'

'The safe?'

'Yes. In the room. When he did not catch his plane…' He checked his notes. '…on the Thursday afternoon, he was officially identified as a missing person.'

'And?' said Caton.

Bonifati shrugged, and made one of those gestures with his hands that normally only a fellow Italian would understand. But the meaning was clear.

'There are many reasons why a person might want to disappear,' he said. 'The *Polizia di Frontiera* had no record of him having left the country. My colleagues waited to see if he might be one of the bodies that appear in the *Laguna*.'

'Do you have many?' said Caton, 'Bodies that appear in the Lagoon?'

Bonifati responded with his customary chuckle, and shared the joke with his assistant. Caterina Volpe snorted. It sounded decidedly unfeminine.

'*Molti molti*,' she said, staring unnervingly into Caton's eyes. '*Suicidi, incidenti, omicidi.*'

Suicides, accidents, murders.

'Just last month,' said her boss. 'In the Giudecca Canale, a woman. No head, one leg, with *una scarpone e...*' He raised his right leg, plonked his foot on the table and mimed what looked like a stiletto-heeled boot.

'*Un immigrato, Cinese illegale,*' added Caterina Volpe.

Bonifati gave her a look of irritation for having interrupted his flow.

'*Forse,*' he said. He turned to Caton. 'Is possible she was illegal. There are many hidden workers in the...' He tugged at his jacket. '*...fabbriche di vestiti.*'

'Clothing industry?'

Bonifati's English, Caton reflected, was getting better and better the more he used it, but this was still frustrating. Preferable, however, to having to dredge up his own half-remembered Italian.

He pictured the woman's body bobbing in the water. Her head and limbs severed by the propellers of passing vessels. Like the unfortunate Phil Ratten in the Manchester Ship Canal following the murder of the Premiership footballer, Okowu-Bello. If she was an illegal immigrant, working under slave-like conditions, her disappearance would remain a mystery. Her employers could hardly report her missing. Unlike Giovanni Richetti.

'You spoke to Richetti's contacts in Venice?' he said.

'Of course. That had nothing to tell us.' He shrugged. 'He was good at his work, *entusiasta*.'

'Enthusiastic.'

He nodded. 'Enthusiastic. He was not troubled. He had no enemies. It is a mystery.'

'When we were on the Isola San Clemente,' said Caton, 'and my wife asked if he could have been killed by the Mafia, you said something like, "Perhaps it's what they want us to believe." What did you mean?'

Bonifati put his notes down on the table and leaned back in his chair.

'Okay, it looks like an execution. The body is also meant to be discover-ed. The bags of salt, the euro thing. It is too much, too … *elabarato*.'

Caton knew what he meant. When a suspect began to embroider his answers, to give too much detail, it was a certainty that he was lying. It was also likely to prove his undoing.

'*Mafioso*,' Bonifati continued. 'When they want, you know, they shoot them in the street. Leave the body for all to see. Maybe cut off a tongue or a hand to make the point. Not this…' He waved his hand dismissively. '…*nonsenso*.'

'They were taking a risk, going to all this trouble to stage it like that,' said Caton.

'Not so much,' Bonifati replied. 'Everyone has a boat, or knows someone with a boat. They pick a time when the…' He waved his hands in front of his face as though parting a curtain. '…*bruma*?'

'Fog, mist?'

'*Si*, the fog is…'

'Dense.'

'And it is not a problem.'

'What about the police boats, the customs, the border patrols?'

Bonifati began to translate for his colleague's sake, but it was clear that she had understood. They were both grinning.

'*La polizia di acqua*,' said the commissario, '*detesto la bruma*.' He stopped himself, and reverted to English. 'They hate this fog. They stay in the Questura and have another coffee.'

'And the border police, the coastguard?'

'The *Guardia Costiera* are far out, in the *Laguna*,' said Bonifati.

'*Droga, immigrati clandestini*!' added Caterina Volpe with a force that took him by surprise. '*Meglio prendere i pesci grossi, prima di quelli piccoli*.'

Drugs, and illegals. Better to take the big fish first, before the little ones. Caton couldn't argue with that.

'We have a similar saying,' he told them. 'They have bigger fish to fry.'

'Very good,' said Bonifati. His eyes lit up. 'I like it. I remember that. *Pesci più grandi da friggere*. Bigger fish to fry.'

'So you found nothing in Venice that could explain his murder?' said Caton.

Bonifati shook his head. '*Niente*. The business appears to be, what do you say, clean?' He chuckled. 'Which in itself is suspicious. The answer must be here. It is why we are here.'

Just like the Chinatown case, Caton reflected, when he had had to travel out to Shanghai and venture up the Min River, deep into Fuzhou, to find the clues that would resolve the mystery. The Chinese police had been more helpful than he had expected. Now it was his turn to help a foreign force. Well, fellow Europeans, hardly foreign.

'Right,' he said, 'we'd better get started.'

He gave Douggie Wallace the victim's details and asked for everything he could find on him, his family and the family firm. In the meantime, he decided to take them to the canteen. He doubted that the food, let alone the coffee, would meet their exacting expectations. But then again, sending out for a pizza wasn't going to cut it either.

Chapter 17

'Here you go, boss,' said the crime intelligence analyst, handing him a sheet. 'I've sent you a copy on your computer. Not that it's a lot to go on.'

That was something of an understatement.

'The PNC check drew a blank' said Wallace. 'Giovanni Richetti had no police record. He had a clean driving licence, which was surprising given that he owned a ten-year-old Nissan Skyline. Popular with boy racers, horrendously expensive to insure. None of the family has form. Unless you count the fact that the mother had her car towed to the police pound because she'd parked in a newly identified traffic free zone. Her and hundreds of others. Her brother picked up three points for speeding on the Oldham Road. It hardly makes them the Corleone clan.'

'What about the family firm?' said Caton.

'Richetti Ltd. Loom Street. In the Ancoats Urban Village.'

'That's appropriate,' said Caton.

'Why's that?' asked Wallace.

'Because the whole of that area used to be known as Little Italy.'

'Little Italy?' said Commissario Bonifati, who had been struggling to follow the exchange.

'I'll explain in a minute, Umberto,' said Caton. 'Go on, Douggie, tell me about them.'

'Not a lot to tell. A family firm. They import Italian products and sell them wholesale. Established twenty years. Used to be run from their own house in Fallowfield. They're a small outfit, specialising in products from Valle D'Osta, Liguria, Lombardia, Veneto and Emilio Romagna.'

'All in the north,' said Caton.

'*Molto interessante*,' observed Bonifati. He saw the expression on Douggie Wallace's face and added, for his sake, 'Very interesting.'

'Decent turnover,' said Wallace. '£915,000 in the last financial year. But seventy-five per cent of that went on costs, including VAT and corporation tax.'

'They paid all of their taxes?' Bonifati sounded incredulous.

'According to HMRC they did. Their net profit was £228,750. There are five directors of the company, all family, all with an equal number of shares. That would give them just shy of £46,000 each before they paid the additional ten per cent of income tax due on dividends.'

'Hardly a fortune,' said Caton. 'Not worth killing for, even for the Mafia.'

He turned to the two Italians and brought them up to date. He slipped back into English every time he found himself struggling, but Bonifati at least seemed to understand.

'Don't underestimate the importance to the Mafia of small businesses,' he said. 'A lot of little bits of pasta make for a big meal.'

'Not that it's an issue for the Richetti family,' said Wallace.

'Why's that?' said Caton.

'Because Richetti Ltd is a signed-up member of the *Addiopizzo* Movement.'

'What the hell is that?' said Caton.

'You'd be better off asking Commissario Bonifati,' said Douggie Wallace. 'I've only just got my head round it.'

Caton turned to the Italian detective.

'Did you know about this, Umberto?'

The edges of the Italian detective's lips curled into a mischievous smile.

'Of course.'

'And when were you proposing to enlighten me?'

Bonifati's eyes widened, giving his face a look of quizzical innocence.

'*Enlighten*?' he said. 'If I knew what that meant, I might be able to give you an answer.'

Five minutes later, Caton understood. *Pizzo* was the name given to the money that the Mafia extorted from businesses in exchange for so-called protection. A practice that had existed as long as the Mafia itself, worth anywhere up to 40 billion euros a year. It also involved companies being forced to allow a member of the Mafia to become a sleeping partner, or the supplying of goods or services at a discount. Failure to comply led to bullying, threats and arson. *Addiopizzo* quite literally meant goodbye to the *pizzo*. No more paying the protection money.

The fight back had begun in Palermo itself, the heartland of the Mafia, although they had taken the practice of collecting *pizzo* way beyond Sicily, into the centre and parts of the north of the country. Not only the Mafia, but the other criminal organisations that had based themselves on the Cosa Nostra, such as the Ndrangheta from Calabria, and the Camorra born out of the slums of Naples.

'Are you saying that the practice of *pizzo* exists here, in Britain?' said Caton.

Bonifati chuckled again. 'You are saying it doesn't?'

You've got me there, thought Caton. He knew of

plenty of cases where home-grown crime gangs put the squeeze on small businesses, to the point of forcing out competitors. The provision of doormen in the pub and club trade for one, and the monopolies of gang masters in fruit picking for another. But paying protection money per se. That was now as rare as hens' teeth.

'I meant in relation to businesses run by Italians, and British Italians,' he said.

The commissario reached into his jacket pocket and began to take out a packet of cigarettes. He saw the look on Caton's face and reluctantly shoved them back inside. He folded the pocket flap neatly into place, and sighed.

'There are more than *duecentomila persone* in the United Kingdom,' he said, 'who speak *Italiano* as their *prima lingua. Venticinque mila* here in Manchester. Did you know that?'

Over two hundred thousand Italian-speaking persons in the UK, twenty-five thousand in Manchester. No, Caton didn't know that. Bonifati was not finished.

'In Manchester, *uno cento ventisei ristoranti e pizzerie,* and many, many businesses.'

He shrugged his now customary shrug.

'You think the Mafia is not here in your country, in your city?'

He sat back in his chair, muttered something incomprehensible to his assistant, and laughed.

Caton had known there were scores of Italian restaurants in Manchester, and had eaten in at least a dozen. And there was at least one pizzeria on every high street. But one hundred and twenty? Of course there would be organised crime involved somewhere down the line. At the very least in the laundering of money and the supply of cheap labour.

'So it is possible that the Mafia, or one of those other organisations, could have been involved in Richetti's murder,' he said, 'however unlikely it seems?'

'Of course,' the Italian detective replied. 'I did not say it was impossible.' He sniffed, like a person snorting coke. 'Just that it did not smell right.'

He pushed back his chair and stood up. Caterina Volpe followed his lead, as though they were tied at the hip. *Like a lapdog*, Caton thought.

'I need to smoke, Tom,' he said, 'or I am going to die. Where is it permitted in this...' He raised his to arms to form a semicircle. '...*boccia del pesce?*'

Caton had to smile. Fish bowl. He couldn't have put it better himself.

'Come on, Umberto,' he said. 'I'll show you.'

On the way out, Caton asked Ged to find out if the Richetti family were at home or at work. More specifically, if the mother and father were available.

'If they are, tell them I'd like to talk to them about their son, Giovanni.'

'Today, sir?'

'Today. If it isn't possible this afternoon, then this evening at their home. When you've found out, text me. I'll be outside with our visitors.'

Then he stopped at Douggie Wallace's desk.

'I want you to get on to the Serious and Organised Crime Agency,' he said, 'and find out everything they've got on Mafia-related crime in the UK, and here in the north-west in particular.'

'They'll want to know why we're interested,' said Wallace, stating the obvious.

'Tell them it's in connection with the murder of a British Italian citizen in Venice. If they want to know any more, they can contact me.'

The analyst looked dubious.

'It may take more than that,' he replied. 'SOCA are up to their eyes in their transition to the National Crime Agency. They're not in a giving frame of mind at the moment.'

'Do your best,' Caton told him.

As he headed for the door, he fired a parting shot.

'That's shorthand, Douggie, for get me that information.'

Chapter 18

The three of them were on the grassed area in front of the Fujitsu building. Caton and Bonifati were sitting on a concrete seat, the latter puffing away at his second cigarette. Caterina Volpe was stalking up and down like her namesake, the wolf.

Caton wasn't surprised. It must be a nightmare for her sitting there all day trying to follow a conversation in an alien language. Unable to join in, let alone exercise any real responsibility. It would have driven him mad.

His phone rang. It was Ged. They were in luck. The Richetti family were all at work. They were waiting for Caton to arrive.

He stood up.

'We're off,' he said.

Bonifati stubbed his cigarette out on the seat and lobbed the butt into the receptacle provided for that purpose.

'*Andiamo*!' he said for Caterina Volpe's benefit.

She muttered something Caton didn't quite catch, and stomped off as best she could in her high heels. She was having a bad day. Or maybe it was simply that every day she spent trailing behind Umberto was a bad day.

'This your car, Tom?' asked Bonifati as they fastened their seat belts.

'Yes. There are too few pool cars. Especially now, since the cuts. It's not unusual for officers to have to use public transport.'

'Us too,' Bonifati replied. 'Only in our case *vaporetti.*'

He shared a joke with his assistant, and then explained for Caton's sake.

'The *Polizia Di Stato* decided to get a car to chase the lunatic speeders on the mainland. So they got a Lamborghini Gallardo.' He laughed. '*Due cento miglia all'ora!*'

Caton wondered if he'd misheard. As he started the engine, he glanced across at his passenger.

'Two hundred miles an hour?'

Bonifati nodded enthusiastically. '*Si. Centosettanta euro.*'

He held up his fingers to emphasise the point.

Roughly one hundred and fifty thousand pounds sterling.

'A Seat Ibiza, not looking, drives out of a *distributore di benzina…*'

'Petrol station.'

'The policeman driver…' He waved his arms about, searching for the word.

'Swerved?' said Caton.

'And the Lamborghini is *completamente morto!*'

'A write-off?'

Bonifati started laughing again. Caton pictured the poor unfortunate driver of the police car. Still, it could have been worse. He could have killed a pedestrian.

'Is it far?' asked the commissario once he had recovered.

'Five minutes,' Caton replied. 'It's just down the road from your hotel.'

There was no parking outside the offices, but there were two marked bays free outside the church of St

Paul. The Italianate Romanesque style surprised and impressed both of the Italian detectives. Caterina Volpe stared at the towering campanile, and the basilica-like building beneath. It looked totally out of place among the predominantly red-brick Victorian buildings and former warehouses. English Heritage had recently begun to restore it.

'*Firenze*,' she said. '*Appartiene a Firenze.*'

It belongs in Florence. Caton smiled, it was what he had always thought.

'Builded by an Italian,' said Bonifati.

'An Englishman, actually,' Caton told him. 'It caused a stir at the time because it was the first Anglican church in what was a strong Roman Catholic area. I told you, this was Little Italy.'

He started to walk them back towards Loom Street.

'What was it like, this Little Italy?' said Bonifati.

'Thousands of immigrants from all over Italy moved into the terraces of former mill workers, alongside the existing Irish population. They whitewashed the walls of their cellars and made ice cream in them. They sold it from pushcarts and pony traps. There were knife grinders, barrel organ manufacturers and musical instrument makers. They made St Michael's, the nearest church, their own. Gradually the Irish moved away, up Oldham Road and Cheetham Hill. Ancoats must have looked and sounded like an Italian town.'

'Without the sunshine,' said Bonifati.

From the outside, the Richetti offices were like all the other newly regenerated former mill and warehouse buildings in the district, around which modernist apartment cubes in sheer white facing, or glass and steel, had now sprung up. The hundred-and-fifty-year-old bricks had been sandblasted. The windows replaced. The original stone paving cleaned and re-laid, a narrow strip of cobbles retained as a touch of heritage. A modest stainless-steel plaque gave the number of the property, the name – Richetti Limited. Italian Fine Food Importers and Wholesale Suppliers – and a logo, a red, green and sea-blue tricolour, in the middle of which was an orange circle with an orange cross in the centre.

Caton pressed the buzzer.

'I thought the Italian flag was green, white and red?' he said.

Bonifati shrugged.

'This is not the Italian flag,' he replied.

There was a buzz, followed by a click. Caton tried the door. It swung open.

They stepped into a small square tiled reception area that contained a single desk, three comfortable red chairs and a small potted palm. Ahead of them a door was open, and beyond it was a passageway that led to another door. To their right, a modern wood and glass staircase led up to the open-plan next level. A man appeared at the head of the stairs, and came down to greet them.

'I am Franco Richetti,' he said. 'Giovanni's father. The head of the family.'

He was taller than Caton. Six foot one or two. Taller than his son had been. Giovanni must have taken after his mother, Caton decided. He looked to be in his mid-fifties. If so, he had kept himself fit, either through work or exercise. Lean, was the word that sprang to mind. His hair, receding at the temples, was still black and shiny. He had worry lines on his forehead and at the corners of sad brown eyes. Caton wondered if they were a recent acquisition. Hardly surprising if they were.

'I am Detective Chief Inspector Tom Caton,' he said as he shook the man's hand. 'This is Commissario

Umberto Bonifati, and **Sovrintendente** Caterina Volpe, both of the *Polizia Di Stato*, in Venice. They are investigating the circumstances surrounding your son's death.'

Richetti acknowledged them with a nod, and turned to Caton.

'Circumstances?' he said bitterly. 'His murder, you mean.'

He seemed instantly to regret his outburst.

'I am sorry,' he said. 'I apologise. It is not your fault.'

'I understand,' said Caton. 'In your place I would feel the same.' He looked around him. 'Is there somewhere we can talk?'

'Of course, I apologise. Come this way, please.'

He led them up the stairs, along the wooden-floored mezzanine and through a set of double doors.

The room beyond was vast. Easily the depth of two houses. High wooden beams and trusses, supported in places by narrow steel columns, spoke of the original purpose of this building as a mill or warehouse. The walls were a mix of exposed brick and polished white surfaces. The floor was carpeted in blue. Natural light came from one long set of windows that looked out onto a small yard between this building and the next, and artificial light from spotlighting hung from long, thin aluminium tubes. The room had been subdivided by low dividing panels to provide for six workstations, what looked like a meeting area with a boardroom-style table, and a kitchen with a microwave, kettle, coffee machine, fridge-freezer, free-standing cupboards and a double sink.

The rest of the family were seated in the meeting area. They stood up as Franco Richetti led the policemen across the room. He introduced each of his family in turn.

First, his wife, Elena – a short, attractive woman with premature grey in her hair, and dark rings beneath eyes that glistened with tears. Then his mother, Maria – also short, but stocky, and with a fierce expression, a strong handshake and hair growing from a mole at the side of her mouth. Roberto, Franco's brother and therefore the victim's uncle was next – he was tall, very like his brother, but younger; late forties at a guess. His wife, Liona, had also been crying – she was the least Italian looking of them all, with pale skin, thin lips, slender nostrils and an elongated bridge that flattered her face; her eyes were a mixture of hazel and brown, and almost perfectly oval.

The last to be introduced was the victim's brother, Guido. He was tall, like his father. Over jeans, he wore a tight-fitted short-sleeved shirt that revealed strong, broad shoulders, a narrow waist and muscles on his arms that could only have come from a devotion to bodybuilding. His grip was intentionally strong, and his dark-brown eyes stared fiercely into Caton's. The phrase Italian stallion came to mind. Caton noted how the young man's expression changed as he held Caterina Volpe's hand a second longer than necessary. She too seemed to have softened. Was that a hint of a smile playing on her lips?

It was obvious that trying to interview them all together, and potentially in two languages, was a bad idea. It was agreed that **Sovrintendente** Volpe would start with the mother, then the daughter, and finally the nonna, Maria, and Commissario Bonifati with the father and the uncle. Caton was left with the son.

'Guido was the one who came to Venice to identify the body,' Bonifati had told him. 'So I have already questioned him. He was badly affected.'

Given the state of the body in the photos, Caton was not surprised.

It was fair enough. It was, after all, the Italians' investigation. He was only supposed to be assisting.

Chapter 19

'No,' Guido Richetti repeated, 'I know of no reason why anyone would want to kill my brother. He was a good guy, hardworking, fun. He had no enemies, believe me. No one knew him better than me.'

'Is it possible he kept any secrets from you?'

He shook his head vehemently.

'No. He wasn't capable of keeping a secret. He was the last person you would tell something you didn't want to get out.'

'But if it was his secret?'

'No! I've just told you. Never!'

He was angry. His fists clenched, the veins stood out on his biceps and pulsed on either side of his neck.

The tightness of his shirt wasn't helping. Caton wondered if he might suffer from roid rage. The mood swings and anger associated with excessive use of steroids. It was common among bodybuilders.

'Okay,' said Caton. 'Tell me about the last time you saw him.'

The young man appeared to calm down a little. His fists unclenched, he sat back in his chair.

'I drove him to the airport. We had a laugh in the car.'

'What about?'

'Nothing in particular. A mutual friend who'd just got ditched by his girlfriend.'

'And that was funny?'

He looked up.

'You don't know our friend, or his girlfriend. He was way out of his depth.'

'How was Giovanni when you left him?'

'Fine. Looking forward to the trip. He was confident about the deals. Looking forward to some decent food and wine, he said.' He smiled. 'And *belle raggaze.*'

Beautiful girls. Every salesman's dream away from home.

'Happy then?'

'Yeah, happy.'

'What about girlfriends?'

He looked confused. 'Girlfriends? What girlfriends?'

'Giovanni's. Did he have a girlfriend?'

He seemed to find that funny.

'Giovanni? He was never without a girl. Nothing steady. He liked to play the field.'

No surprise, Caton decided, if he was anything like his brother.

'So who was his girlfriend at the time?'

He shook his head in disbelief.

'Have you been listening to a word I've said?' He spelled it out slowly, as though speaking to someone with severe learning difficulties.

'He played the field. He didn't do girlfriends, only girls.'

'So you don't have a name?'

He threw his head back, and clenched his fists again.

'Mother of God! You're not going to catch them, are you? The bastards who killed Giovanni?'

'We will. But we need your help, you and the rest of your family.'

He sat bolt upright on the edge of his seat. His fists were balled now. He thrust his head closer to Caton. His pupils were dilated. When he spoke, Caton could smell garlic and anger on his breath.

'You think one of his girls did that to him? Followed him to Italy? Knocked him senseless? Tied him up? Drowned him? You must be even more stupid than you look!'

Caton decided it was a waste of time. At least until he'd calmed down.

'Thank you,' he said. 'You've been really helpful.'

Somehow he managed not to sound sarcastic. Not that it would have mattered. Guido Richetti had stopped listening.

Before they left, the father, Franco, insisted on showing them the equally vast storeroom and distribution centre down on the ground floor at the rear of the building. It was an Aladdin's Cave of products from all over northern Italy.

There were cans and bottles of extra virgin oil from their home region of Liguria, bottles of Balsamico, canned tomatoes, egg pasta, pasta flour, herbs, spices and sauces. There were packs of antipasti, salami and Italian charcuterie. There were shelves piled high with Panettone and Pandoro cake, Biscotti, Torrone and sealed packs of coffee. There were even pasta-making machines.

At the end of the tour he took them down into a cellar stacked high with bottles of wine. Umberto Bonifati picked up a bottle of Amarone and began to caress it. Caterina Volpe studied the label on a Brunello Di Montalcino. As though on cue, Franco urged the three of them to each choose a bottle.

'*Piacere*,' he said. '*Complimenti della casa.*'

Politely, but firmly, Caton declined. He noted the disappointment on the faces of his Italian colleagues, and felt a tinge of guilt as they slid the bottles back into the racks. This far from home, with no one ever likely to know, or care, it was a wholly understandable temptation. But this was how corruption started. A pint and a sandwich on the house, in a pub on night duty; complimentary breakfasts every early shift; tickets for a Premiership game; a free bet on a dead cert. He'd seen it all. The slippery slope.

They promised to do their best, took their leave and walked back to the car.

Caton told them how he'd got on with the son. Caterina Volpe, through Umberto, recounted her experience with the women of the family.

None of them had been forthcoming. Their tears and sadness had appeared genuine. They all told the same story. Giovanni was a good boy. He was never in any trouble. He had no enemies. He loved his work. Recently he had been even happier than usual. They did not know why. The impression she got was that they were holding back. That they were frightened of something. She had no idea what.

The conversations between Umberto Bonifati, the father, and the uncle had apparently yielded almost identical results.

'Did you ask them about the Addiopizzo issue?' said Caton.

Bonifati shrugged. 'Of course. But they said it was not an issue. It had nothing to do with Giovanni's death.'

'How could they be so sure?'

'I asked that too. They said it had never been a problem. They had never been approached by any *criminale*, or *malvivente*. That was the point of Addiopizzo. Of the sign on the door. Tell them they waste their time, they don't bother you.'

'As simple as that?' said Caton.

The commissario shrugged. '*Evidentemente.*'

Caton was sceptical. If only it was as easy as putting a sign in your window saying *No Cold Callers; No Fliers*. Not that that seemed to work.

'What sign on the door?' he asked.

'The flag of Liguria, with the *cerchio* in the middle.' He described a circle with the forefinger of his right hand.

The orange circle. Now that he thought about it there had been something written in black on one of the cross members. Too small for him to read without making the effort. So that was the Addiopizzo sign. A bit like the so-called Da Pinchi Code: the chalk symbols flagging up potential targets that criminals had been leaving on walls, gateposts and even kerbs, in Salford and across the UK. Only in reverse.

'He didn't work for the family firm,' said Caton as he unlocked the doors and opened the rear passenger one for Caterina Volpe. 'Did they tell you why that was?'

'He was headstrong. Ambitious. He thought he could do better. I got the *impressione* that he felt he was...' He struggled to find the words. '*All'ombra del fratello.*'

'In his brother's shadow.'

'*Si.*'

Bonifati got in the car and fastened his seat belt.

'How did the rest of the family take that?'

'Okay. The father described it as *amichevole*. Friendly?'

Caton nodded and started the engine.

'Amicable,' he said.

'He got a job with...' Bonifati consulted his notes. His notebook was almost identical to the one Caton used. 'Magical Italian Tours. Based here in Manchester, with agents in Venice, Rome, Naples.'

Caton started the engine and pulled away from the kerb.

'What did he do exactly?'

'He helped them to build and maintain their website, using his experience of the Richetti Ltd online business. He was also an *organizzatore*.'

'A fixer?'

'He visited the hotels, the agents in *Italia*, and he checked out the local guides for…'

'Quality control?' said Caton.

Bonifati thought about it, then nodded.

'Quite an important role, then. Making himself indispensable.'

The word was virtually identical in Italian, as were so many words. It was one of the reasons that Caton had enjoyed learning the language, and taken to it so quickly.

Bonifati grunted his agreement.

As they turned onto Oldham Road he twisted in his seat and said something to his assistant. Her reply was short and sweet.

'*Lo pensavo anch'io.*'

I thought so too.

Bonifati turned back and adjusted his seat belt.

'I got the *impressione*,' he said, 'there was something worrying them. Something they were not telling. Sovrintendente Volpe thought this too.'

Sovrintendente, Caton noted. Still not Caterina.

'Worried?' he said.

The Italian detective thought about it for a moment.

'*Spaventato*,' he said.

Caton looked in his rear-view mirror. In the back seat Caterina Volpe nodded her agreement.

Frightened. Given the way in which Guido Richetti had died, Caton was not surprised.

'It's too late to visit Magical Italian Tours today, Umberto,' he said. 'Why don't I drop you off at your hotel? Then maybe we could meet up for dinner? There are some really good Italian restaurants in the city.'

'*E la signora* Caton?' said Bonifati. 'Will she come too?'

'Not this time. She has a faculty meeting, and she's trying to get as much work done as she can before she goes on maternity leave. Clearing the decks.'

'Clearing the decks?'

'It's a naval expression. Clearing the decks of a boat to prepare for battle.'

The commissario translated for Caterina Volpe. In his mirror Caton saw her toss her head and sniff the air. It was a curiously feline gesture. Fitting for someone with wolf as a surname.

'*Molto appropriato*,' she said.

Very appropriate. Caton wondered if she was referring to Kate's situation, this case, or something entirely different. He pulled up outside the hotel.

'Here we are,' he said. 'Shall we say 8 o'clock? I'll pick you both up at 7.30.'

'*Alle otto*,' confirmed Bonifati as he exited the car.

'*A più tardi, Signora* Volpe,' said Caton to her back as she sashayed towards the reception.

She raised her hand in a gesture that could as easily have been a dismissal as an acknowledgement. If she'd said anything at all it was drowned out by the rush-hour traffic streaming up Oldham Road.

Umberto Bonifati turned, looked at Caton, raised his eyebrows and shrugged.

It was a *what can you do* sort of gesture. Caton sympathised. He was glad, for so many reasons, that Caterina Volpe was not on his team.

Chapter 20

San Carlo was packed. They had five minutes to wait while their table was prepared. They waited by the bar.

Umberto Bonifati was amazed.

'*Una serata di Lunedi*!' he exclaimed. 'All these people, on a Monday?'

'It's like this every evening,' Caton told him. 'Welcome to Manchester, Umberto.'

He pointed to a table away on the right-hand side to which Caterina Volpe's eyes had already been drawn.

'That's half the Man United team,' he said. 'And over there, for good measure...' He pointed to the opposite side of the room. '...are a couple of Man City players with their partners. Monday is a popular night for footballers. One of the few they can let their hair down.'

'They always come here?'

'Here, and San Rocco, and Puccini's in Swinton. And any time now they'll be flocking to George's – Ryan Giggs' new restaurant in Worsley. I told you, you're spoilt for choice.'

The Italian looked doubtful.

'I hope they have good taste,' he said. 'In my experience the best food come in *trattoria e osteria*.'

Caton could see the padrone coming to tell them that their table was ready.

'You're about to find out,' he said.

Caterina Volpe chose the seat that gave her the best view of the United players, and tutted when her boss chose the seat immediately opposite her, partly obscuring her view. Caton suspected that Umberto had done it on purpose.

From the outset there appeared to be an unspoken agreement not to talk about the case. Umberto in particular would have had difficulty finding the time to talk about anything, so engrossed was he in his Marinata Di Verdure Alla Griglia – chargrilled aubergines, courgettes and peppers marinated in fresh mint, extra virgin oil, garlic and chilli, served with buffalo mozzarella and parsley, followed by a Venetian favourite, Fegato Di Vitello Alla Veneziana – calf's liver with polenta, in an onion and Madeira wine sauce.

Caterina chose a single dish of Risotto Agli Scampi, made with a white wine, cream and tomato sauce, which took her as long to eat as did Umberto his first two courses.

Caton started with scallops in white wine and garlic on sautéed spinach, and followed it with one of his favourites, Garganelli Salsiccia e Porcini – egg pasta with spicy sausage, porcini mushroom and a light tomato sauce.

The gaps between courses were filled by the drinking of wine, and gentle banter about the merits of the various teams in the Premiership and the Italian Serie A respectively, and Manchester City and Juventus in particular. Caterina, it turned out, had once, but no longer, supported Udinese. Caton assumed that was because it was the nearest one to Venice. Umberto took great delight in revealing that the real reason was that she had gone out for a brief spell with one of their players before she discovered that he was married. At which point, Caterina had declared that she needed the women's restroom, and had disappeared in a quite dramatic huff.

Her route took her past the table full of footballers, who made no secret of their admiration. On her way back they even managed to persuade her to stop, and one of them appeared to be trying to get her to give him her phone number. She dismissed him with a coolness that greatly amused the rest of the players. Caton was also amused by the way that the haughty expression on her face said one thing as she returned to her seat, and the sway of her hips quite another.

She passed on dessert. Umberto and Caton shared a selection of Italian cheeses.

'Well?' said Caton as they relaxed with a coffee.

'Not bad,' said Umberto.

Caterina Volpe shrugged, and waggled her head from side to side.

Caton judged that an outright success. About as good as it got. Neither of them was going to admit it, but compared with the food that most of the restaurants in Venice served up this had been exceptional. With twenty-seven chefs in the kitchen, all Italian trained and all handpicked, it was hardly surprising.

'Can I ask you a question, Umberto?' he said. 'It's about your investigation.'

'Go ahead,' he replied. He chuckled. 'So long as it does not spoil my digestion.'

'The Mafia. Are you looking for any possible connections between them and Giovanni's murder?'

'Of course. For a number of reasons.' He counted them off on his fingers. 'Because the *Pubblico Ministero* sees the *Mafioso* everywhere he looks, and it is a way of making a name for himself. That's what you say? Making a name for himself.'

Chapter 21

When Caton called to pick them up in the morning, he was told to go straight up.

'Mr Bonifati is expecting you,' said the receptionist. 'Would you like breakfast sending up too?'

Caton didn't. Not after last night. A cup of tea, some cranberry juice, and a bowl of porridge had more than sufficed.

The door was open. He assumed the receptionist must have rung to say that he was on his way. He knocked, and entered.

Umberto was not alone. The two of them were sitting either side of an occasional table. Between them a tray was piled high with toast, pastries and croissants. On the desk another tray held two cafetières of coffee, a jug of milk and some sugars. They were both at the tail-end of a Full English Breakfast, each of which would have served a family of four.

Umberto's breakfast companion was a stranger to Caton. In his mid-forties, he had short blonde hair, and was wearing a navy-blue pinstriped suit and a crisp white shirt. He could easily have been a banker, an officer in the Forces. Something about him said police, or the intelligence services. Special Branch, perhaps.

The Italian waved to Caton with his knife.

'Tom, come join us. Pour a coffee, have...' He

130

'That's what we say, Umberto.'

'*Bene.*' He touched another finger. 'Because if we do not, it will be said we did not do our job. And because his family do this Addiopizzo thing.'

'But you don't believe it was them?'

Umberto shrugged. 'I don't know. Who is this *them* anyway? It could be any of three, four, five different groups people call the *Mafioso*.'

'But if it is, the answer is likely to be back in Venice.'

He shrugged again. '*Forse.* Perhaps. But maybe it starts here.'

'So have you got any information on Mafia-style organisations over here in the UK?

Umberto laughed.

'Any?' he said.

He leaned forward conspiratorially, and lowered his voice.

'Plenty. I show you tomorrow.'

He leaned back in his chair and signalled t' waiter for another coffee.

'Tom,' he said, 'you want one too? A b' maybe?'

'No, thanks,'

Caton didn't know how they did it caffeine, and still fresh as a daisy in the m gestured towards the bed. '*Pasticcioti.*'

Caton politely declined both, moved the tray, and sat on the end of the bed.

'This is Malcolm,' said Bonifati as he speared a piece of sausage and dipped it into the yolk of an egg.

'Malcolm Haigh,' said the man, half-turning in his seat, and sending Caton an uncommitted smile. 'I prefer Mal. I'm with SOCA. Serious Crime Directorate.'

Not a bad guess then. Simon Levi's team in the Serious and Organised Crime Agency. At least it wasn't Simon himself.

'How's Barbara Bryce getting on?' said Caton, establishing his credentials from the outset.

'Our Deputy Director?'

If he was surprised that Caton knew her, he didn't show it.

'Fine. Word is she's in the running for Deputy in the National Crime Agency when it's finally up and running in October.'

'And Simon?'

This time he raised his eyebrows.

'You know Simon?'

Clearly he hadn't done his homework. The last time his boss and Caton had met had been way beyond acrimonious. They had almost come to blows.

'He's on secondment with the NCA team at the moment, helping to plan the transition.'

That explains it, thought Caton. *But God help us all if Levi is helping to set up Britain's answer to the FBI.*

'What exactly are you doing here, Mal?' he asked.

The agent wiped his plate with a slice of toast, took a bite and then moved his chair round so that he was facing Caton.

'Same as you, Tom,' he said. 'Providing assistance to our Italian cousins.' He took another bite and began to chew slowly.

'How exactly?'

'The *Direttore Generale degli affari penali...*' began Bonifati.

'That's the Director General of the Criminal Division at the Ministry of Justice. Their *numero uno* Mafia hunter,' said the agent.

'...sent a file on the *Mafioso* in your country to Mal's boss.'

'So you *do* think there's a link with the murder of Giovanni Richetti?'

The Italian detective wiped his mouth on his napkin, took a slurp of coffee, and eased his chair back.

'*Ho detto che era possibile,*' he said.

'He says it's possible,' said Mal Haigh.

'Actually,' Caton told him, 'what Umberto said was, "I did say that it was possible."'

The agent smiled. 'You speak Italian, Tom? Thank God for that, because I don't.'

Caton was warming to him. At least he wasn't arrogant and paranoid like Simon Levi.

'We've been pulling together all the information held by different forces on the activity of all sorts of foreign criminal organisations, not just the Mafia,' said Haigh. 'The Nigerians, Yardies, Russians, Eastern Europeans, Former Soviet States, the Turks. We've even got a special team working on the Bulgarians and the Romanians in anticipation of the explosion of activity we expect, with the lifting of the right to work restrictions this coming January.'

'Unless Teresa May gets her way.'

'Saying's one thing, doing's another,' said Haigh.

Umberto Bonifati looked confused.

'*Facile da dire, difficile da fare,*' said Caton.

It wasn't exact, but it did the job. Bonifati smiled, and nodded.

'*E' politica,*' he said. 'That's politics.'

'As far as the Mafia are concerned,' said the agent, 'they've managed to stay off our radar more than most of the other groups. Partly because their presence here is more about laundering money from their Italian enterprises than setting up criminal organisations.'

'How are they doing that?'

'In the main, by buying up property, especially in London.'

Just like the scores of other criminal and corrupt organisations from all over Europe and the Middle East, forcing up the value of property in the capital.

'Also, by investing in Italian businesses over here. Pizzeria, restaurants, clothing and fashion outlets. The money goes in dirty as investment, and comes out clean as profits and capital assets.'

'Are you saying they aren't involved in any illegal activity?'

'Far from it. The Ndrangheta are active in gambling, just like the Parisii clan from Puglia. The Camorra is into trafficking drugs that have come into Italy from Africa, then across Europe to the UK. Both they and the Cosa Nostra are distributing fake designer goods. And I'm not just talking about the guys that approach you with a car full of flashy suits on the motorway services car parks.'

It had happened twice to Caton. Once at Hilton Park, and once at Corley. The story was the same. They'd just been to a trade fair at the Birmingham NEC, and didn't want to have to take the suits all the way to Milan. On both occasions he'd let the Motorway Police know. Not that they'd seemed surprised, or particularly interested.

'And all of them,' Haigh continued, 'use these fair isles of ours as places to hide out when the Criminal Division of Justice gets too close. Especially in this neck of the woods for some reason we haven't figured out.'

Caton knew exactly what he was referring to. In the past twelve months four Italian gangsters had been discovered living long term undercover. Two in Scotland, one in Lancashire not far from Chorley, and the other right here, in Middleton, just five miles north of where they were at this moment in time. Two of them even had British names and identity, with English wives and British-born children.

'But they are not yet in our top-ten most wanted organised crime groups. We have enough on our plate with all of these emerging crime syndicates; the last thing we need is for the Italian gangs to up the ante.'

'Is that likely?'

'Let me put this into context,' said Haigh. 'The Ndrangheta alone boasts of an annual turnover of more than forty-three *billion* euros. Can you imagine how many houses that's going to buy? The net turnover of the three of them – the Cosa Nostra, Camorra and Ndrangheta – is around two hundred and fifty *billion* euros a year. Their total assets are estimated at over eight hundred billion euros. Given they don't pay any tax, that makes them the three largest, most profitable businesses in Italy. And the best connected. They've blown up or machine-gunned over thirty judges, and scores of magistrates and policemen. On their own turf, in the south of Italy, between them they've killed over ten thousand people in just thirty years. Can you imagine what would happen if they had a turf war over here?'

Caton could. It would certainly put into the shade the Doddington versus Gooch spat of the 1980s and 1990s that had led to Manchester being given the labels Gunchester, and Britain's Bronx.

'So you see, Tom, we're not taking any chances. The Organised Crime Group Mapping Team are going to collate the information Umberto's bosses have sent us. Then we're going to shake them up a bit. See if we can't unearth a few more of them that have gone to ground over here. Give them the message that they're not welcome, and that this isn't going to be the safe haven they thought it was.'

Caton knew where this was coming from. The National Crime Agency had as one of its primary aims the pursuit and disruption of organised crime. If they could pull this off it would make a great headline for their launch in a little under a month's time.

'I can see that,' he said, looking at the Italian. 'But I thought, Umberto, that you didn't have this down as a Mafia-style killing?'

Bonifati shifted uncomfortably in his seat, and folded his arms.

'One can never be certain in this world, Tom,' he said.

Caton had a pretty good idea what was going on. It suited the Italian Criminal Division at the Ministry of Justice to link this murder with the Mafia, simply to get the NCA involved in winkling out the fugitive *Mafioso* they desperately wanted behind bars.

'It's not as if they haven't been known to pull some bizarre stunts when making an example of those who cross them,' Mal Haigh pointed out. 'Umberto was telling me how the Camorra tied a man to a chair on the beach, and then proceeded to force-feed him mud and sand.'

Caton was still not convinced.

'Are you coming with us, Mal?' he said. 'To visit Richetti's place of work?'

'No,' said the agent, getting to his feet. 'You're the one riding shotgun on this case, Tom. I was just clarifying a few things with Umberto. We, at the Agency, are looking at the bigger picture.'

Bonifati laughed. 'He has bigger fish to fry, Tom,' he said.

Caton opened the door for the NCA agent and found Caterina Volpe standing there, her hand raised as though ready to knock. Mal Haigh stepped aside to let her in. Her expression morphed from surprise to suspicion. The agent followed her progress across the room with rather more than professional interest.

'Have a nice day, Tom,' Haigh said, with an exaggerated wink as he stepped into the corridor.

Caton closed the door.

'*Chi è stato, Commissario*?' asked Caterina Volpe. She sounded distinctly miffed.

'*Nessuno importante,*' Bonifati replied.

No one important. It was obvious that it was a lie.

'*Nessuno importante*?' She snorted, and tossed her head in disgust.

This time she reminded Caton of a wild filly. He wondered why Bonifati had lied, and if he was storing up more trouble for himself than it was worth.

Chapter 22

The offices of Magical Italian Tours were situated over an Italian Pizzeria in Bridge Street. Entered by a separate side door, in glass and aluminium, they had a pretence of style, undermined by the smell of garlic and baked dough. They consisted of a single large room, at the rear of which was a smaller room behind a waist-high stud wall, above which was a glass partition. Someone didn't trust his office staff.

There were stands along the length of the left-hand side of the room holding various travel brochures. On the two facing walls were posters depicting popular Italian tourist destinations, most if not all of which Caton had visited at one time or another.

Two sofas, a coffee table, a drinks machine and a water dispenser looked to be an informal area for browsing and consultation, probably doubling as a staff restroom.

There were three workstations in the room, each supported by a small bank of filing cabinets, a phone, a computer screen and a keyboard. Two of them were occupied. The woman seated at the nearest of the desks rose to meet them.

Short, in her early fifties, a little overweight, she had a round face and hair dyed an unnatural shade of red. They had deliberately not made an appointment, and there was confusion and a hint of concern on her face even before they had introduced themselves. Had she been expecting someone else?

'How may I help you?' she asked, looking at each of them in turn.

'I am Detective Inspector Tom Caton, Greater Manchester Police. This is Commissario Umberto Bonifati, and his colleague Sovrintendente Caterina Volpe...'

He paused, and noted the relief that seemed to flood her face as he finished his sentence.

'...of the *Polizia Di Stato*, in Venice.'

It was the name *Venice* that seemed to have triggered her relief.

'Ahh,' she said, releasing, in a sigh, the breath she had been holding. 'You are here about Giovanni?'

'Yes,' said Caton. 'Commissario Bonifati is investigating your colleague's murder.'

'Poor Giovanni,' she said, shaking her head sadly, and looking over at the young woman seated at the second workstation, who shook her own head in sympathetic accord.

They both looked genuinely sorry, not that that meant anything.

'And you are?' said Caton.

'Oh, I'm sorry.' She sounded flustered. 'I am Teresa Borbone, the office manager.'

The door at the far end of the room opened, and a tall, thin man emerged. He was in his late forties, and had a slight limp as he came towards them.

Teresa Borbone gabbled an introduction, which he took in his stride. He extended his right hand.

'Arturo Santagata, Managing Director,' he said. 'You'd better come through to my office.'

As they walked the length of the room, Bonifati tugged at Caton's sleeve.

'You ask the questions, Tom. Okay?'

Caton stared at his companion, but could tell nothing from his poker face.

'Okay,' he said. 'Chip in when you're ready.'

Bonifati frowned. 'Chip in?'

'Forget it,' said Caton, standing back to let Caterina Volpe enter first.

Santagata saw them seated, and then checked what they would like to drink.

'Genuine Italian coffee beans,' he said. 'Our owner sources it himself.'

Unsurprisingly both Bonifati and Caterina Volpe accepted readily, if a little sceptically. Caton decided it wouldn't hurt this early in the day, and made it three.

'Teresa, four coffees, milk on the side,' ordered Santagata.

From where he was sitting Caton observed the face that the office manager pulled, and the speed with which she passed the task on to her colleague.

'It's a tragedy,' said Santagata as he closed the door, and took his seat behind the desk. 'Giovanni of all people.'

It was obvious that he wanted to talk, and they were all experienced enough to know that it was best to let him. He loosened his tie, and then placed his hands face down on the desk.

'He was a fine young man. Charming, personable, hardworking. Always happy, never an argument or a cross word. When he came to us for a job, I had my suspicions. Why would he leave a successful family firm like Richetti's? But he convinced me with his words, and within days of starting here he proved himself with his actions. The girls loved working with him. The customers liked him. He worked miracles with the hotels, the coach firms and the guides. And he was fantastic with computers. He streamlined our systems, and fixed any blips we had with the hardware.'

Caton thought the victim was beginning to sound just a little too good to be true. In his experience, nobody was that perfect. Nor did they swan into an established business, make changes and not rub any of the existing staff up the wrong way. Speaking of which, given that Teresa Borbone was older than Santagata himself, she hardly qualified as a girl, unlike the other one. As though on cue, there was a knock on the door, which immediately opened and was held back by the office manager to enable her colleague to enter with a tray of drinks.

'Thank you, Janice,' he said. 'Just leave it on the desk, and we'll help ourselves.'

As Janice leaned over the table, Caton couldn't help admiring the combination of her fitted ivory satin shirt with the black tailored trousers. Smart, yet ideally suited to her age, which he put at early twenties, she made her manager look positively frumpy in her grey suit. Bonifati was equally impressed, and Caton registered the look of disapproval and mild disgust on Caterina Volpe's face at her colleague's unashamed ogling.

'Where were we?' asked Santagata when the drinks had been distributed, and the door closed.

'You were telling us what an amazing worker Giovanni Richetti was,' said Caton. 'Quite a find?'

The Managing Director nodded, and blew across the surface of his coffee.

'Yes, indeed. Indispensable.'

'How did he find out about the job?'

'We hadn't advertised. I just happened to mention to a friend that I really needed someone to pick up that side of the business, because it was getting too much for me to do on my own. He mentioned it to his friend, who was a friend of Giovanni. You know how it is.'

Caton did.

'What was it that he did exactly? What was the nature of his job?'

Santagata put his cup and saucer down, leaned back in his chair and swivelled slowly from side to side as he answered. It irritated the hell out of Caton.

'Good question. Let me explain. We arrange mainly select group tours to the most popular tourist spots in northern Italy. The girls handle the bookings, online and face-to-face. I manage the marketing, advertising and the financial side of the business.'

'In what way are your tours select?' said Caton.

'Top hotels, at discounted prices, luxury coach travel, at discounted prices. Good restaurants.'

'At discounted prices,' said Umberto Bonifati with a mischievous smile.

Santagata stopped swivelling and stared at the Italian detective as though he had forgotten that he was there. Caton couldn't help being amused, but secretly wished that his colleague would save his tactical blindsiding for a more appropriate moment.

'Yes,' said the Managing Director. 'And we also take our groups to less well-known venues; secret places that most tourists don't have access to.'

'Such as?'

'Private palazzos with special art collections; specialist museums; hidden gardens; Roman and Etruscan remains behind the facade of medieval and modern houses. That sort of thing.'

'Right,' said Caton, who was fast becoming tired of the marketing spiel. 'And Giovanni Richetti did what exactly?'

'He negotiated access to all of these places. He negotiated discounts wherever he could. And he recruited, vetted and, where necessary, trained our representatives who accompanied the tours.'

'*E le guide che fanno visitare alle gente le case, i giardini e i musei?*' said Umberto Bonifati, so quickly that Caton only just caught it.

Santagata did not.

'I'm sorry,' he said, 'could you repeat that? My Italian is a little rusty.'

Bonifati did so. So slowly that it was almost embarrassing.

'Right.' Santagata was visibly annoyed, and it showed in his voice. 'Yes, and sometimes the guides who showed people around the houses, museums and gardens.'

Caton waited to see if his colleague had a follow-up question. When it was clear that he did not, he pressed on.

'Were there any particular deals that he was doing on his last trip?' he said.

Santagata reached down to his right, opened a desk drawer and took out a sheet of paper. He pushed his cup to one side and slid the sheet across the desk.

'I anticipated your question,' he said. 'This is a list of the appointments he had that I knew about. None of them are new ones, or particularly problematic.'

Caton studied the list and then passed it on to Bonifati, who scanned it and passed it in turn to Caterina Volpe.

'You said, *that I knew about*,' said Caton. 'What did you mean by that?'

Santagata pursed his lips and steepled his fingers.

'Giovanni was enthusiastic, keen to impress. He often used his initiative to improve things. To find new opportunities.'

'But he would always tell you about these?'

'Of course. Eventually. When the deal was ready to be done. The changes ready to be made.'

'Could *Signor* Richetti,' said Umberto Bonifati, 'have been making deals behind your back?'

Santagata's initial expression was one of surprise. As though the idea had never occurred to him. He seemed about to make an instinctive response. His lips parted, and his tongue prepared to form the word. Caton waited for the no, or never, to emerge. Then his lips came together, his brow furrowed and he stared at the desk. When he looked up, it was with a shake of the head.

'Making deals behind our backs? No,' he said forcefully. 'It is unthinkable. Not him.'

Caton made a mental checklist: repeating the question; mannered tone; formal construct; distancing himself from the subject; not to mention the cluster of telltale behaviours that had characterised this interview. The man was lying. Either that, or he was pretending to lie.

'Is anyone interested in buying this business?' asked the commissario.

This time Santagata's surprise was genuine.

'No.'

'Or wanting to buy into this business?' Bonifati persisted.

The Managing Director looked at each of them in turn, as though seeking clarification.

'I don't understand.'

'It's a simple question, Mr Santagata,' said Caton.

'No,' he replied, folding his arms. 'But I don't see what difference it would make if someone had.'

Caton was distracted for a moment by Caterina Volpe shaking her head. It was only a slight movement, accentuated by the sway of her hair.

'Don't be naive, Mr Santagata,' he said. 'Your employee has been brutally murdered, and cruelly disposed of, in a manner intended to send a message to someone. Commissario Bonifati and his colleague would be failing in their duty if they did not pursue every possible motive in this case.'

Santagata shrugged his shoulders and slid his cup and saucer away from him. It sat like a tiny barrier between the two of them.

'I see that,' he said. 'But I'm sorry, the answer is still no. We have never been approached by anyone.'

'You are the Managing Director of Magical Italian Tours?' said Bonifati, slowly pronouncing each word in turn.

'Yes.'

'Mmm,' the Italian responded. 'Is this then what you call a *Limited* company?'

'Exactly.'

'Mmm. Could you then tell us please, who are the other directors?'

Santagata was showing increasing signs of irritation.

'Of course,' he snapped. 'There are two others besides myself: Teresa Borbone, and her uncle.'

'Mmm,' said the Italian detective. 'And what percentage of...' He looked to Caton. '*Azione*?'

'Shares,' Caton told him.

'*Shares* does each of you have?'

'I hold forty-five per cent,' said Santagata. 'As does Teresa. We were founder members of the firm.'

'And her uncle?' said Bonifati.

Santagata shifted uneasily in his seat.

'Just ten per cent,' he said.

'Mmm,' said Umberto Bonifati.

Chapter 23

'He was lying,' said Caton as they stepped out onto Bridge Street.

'Of course he was,' replied Bonifati. 'The question is why? Because of Richetti, or because of the business?'

'Or both.'

'*Si*, or both.'

'Did you notice the office manager Teresa Borbone's unease when we walked in?' said Caton. 'I had the impression that it was you two that worried her. Your both being so obviously Italian.'

Bonifati arched his eyebrows.

'You think next time we should disguise ourselves as English? With bowler hats and an umbrella? Or maybe a T-shirt and dirty jeans?'

Caton tried to picture it. Neither of them could carry it off. Too much *bella figura* hardwired into their very being.

'Why did you switch to Italian, Umberto, when you were speaking to Santagata? And why at that point?'

'Because I wanted to know how good his Italian actually is. And because in my experience the Mafia often has a lot to do with deciding who can guide in certain places, and who cannot. And also in arranging these discounts he was talking about.'

'You think Richetti may have ruffled a few feathers? Blundered into a Mafia monopoly?'

The Italian shrugged and raised his hands skywards.

'Who knows?' he said.

It was becoming his favourite English expression.

'Do you think they may have Mafia connections?'

'Almost every Italian firm has a Mafia connection, whether they know it or not. My guess is that there is nothing at this end, in Manchester. The key will be in these deals they make. They may not pay *pizzo* for protection, but they will pay for these supposed discounts, and this privileged access he talks about to these secret places. Nobody gets access to anything without paying a price.'

Caton realised that the two of them had been walking briskly, and Caterina Volpe was lagging behind. He stopped to give her a chance to catch up.

'Let me ask you, Tom,' said Bonifati. 'When you are in Italy, and you pay cash for a meal or coffee, or a gift in a shop, do you check the receipt?'

'I always check the bill.'

'Ah, to see if you are charged the right amount. But do you check the receipt?'

'Not if the bill is correct, and the change is right.'

'You throw it away, or leave it behind?'

'I suppose so.'

'Then one time in five you are helping Mafioso…' He windmilled his arms in a disconcerting fashion. *'Pulire il loro denaro sporco!'*

To clean their dirty money.

'To launder money,' said Caton.

'To launder money.' Bonifati repeated the phrase, making a mental note. 'Next time, I suggest you check,' he said. 'Maybe there is a bottle of grappa, or a piece of jewellery you did not buy, written there. A magical sale to explain to the authorities money got by other means.'

'Such as theft, extortion, drug dealing, forgery, graft,' said Caton.

The Italian smiled. 'So you see, you are ... what do you say? *Accessorio* of the crime?'

'An accessory to the crime.'

'Bonifati laughed, and clapped his hands together.

'*Esatto*! Maybe I arrest you?'

They started walking again.

Caton wondered what he would do if he did spot such a scam. Point it out to the sales assistant? Complain? To what purpose? Report it to the police, who would almost certainly already know? Probably not. Too much trouble. He would shake his head and move on. Just like most Italians presumably did. Or did they only try it on with the tourists? And if they were inflating their sales to explain away dirty money, that meant they would be paying tax on the proceeds of crime. He stopped himself right there. Don't be silly. What tax? Wasn't that one of the reasons their economy was in such a parlous state?

He was brought back to reality by a sudden outburst. They had reached the car. The commissario and his assistant were standing on the passenger side, facing each other. Caterina Volpe, hands on hips, legs apart, was directing a torrent of words at her colleague. Umberto stood, arms folded, with a frown on his face. He began to give as good as he got.

It was all too fast, furious and colloquial for Caton, but he had the impression that the Sovrintendente had finally cracked. Her patience had been strained beyond breaking point. Frankly, he was not surprised. She had been expected to follow them around like a sheep. To sit silently through interviews, with the sole exception of the opportunity to question the women members of the Richetti clan. Even then, Umberto seemed to have barely registered the feedback she had given. The final straw must have been walking in at the end of that meeting with Mal Haigh. Knowing that she had been deliberately excluded. Knowing that her boss was lying to her.

Caton could tell there was no point in trying to intervene. He unlocked the car doors, climbed in and waited until the two of them fell silent. Both of their doors opened simultaneously, and they got in. Her door slammed shut. Her boss made a point of closing his with infinite care. The two of them sat in uneasy silence. Caton sensed the heat of her body, and the unpleasant aroma of sweat and perfume. Bonifati lowered his window, and rested his elbow casually on the ledge.

Caton held up his BlackBerry.

'I'm going to ring the office to get my intelligence officer to see what he can find on Mr Borbone,' he said.

He began to repeat himself in Italian for Caterina Volpe's benefit, but Bonifati placed a hand on his arm to stop him, and then, deliberately slowly, translated it himself, as one might for a child. If Umberto hadn't been pushing his luck before, Caton reflected, he certainly was now. He'd better check that communicating door was locked before he went to sleep, or he could have another murder to investigate.

Caton signalled right and turned off Prestbury Road. He drove slowly along Withinlee Ridge, trying to spot a number on any one of the stone pillars that acted as gateposts for the mansions set away from the road, down drives wide enough for two 4x4s to pass one another.

'Very nice,' said Umberto Bonifati. '*Molto impressionante.*'

'Footballers' alley,' Caton told them. 'Also known as the orange tan belt.'

'Orange tan?'

'Footballers' wives.' He patted the side of his face.

'Ah,' said Bonifati. 'Must be from all the holidays in sunny Italy? On the beach while their husbands get beat by *le squadre di calcio Italiane*.' He drummed the names off on the fascia with his fingers. *'Roma, Napoli, Juventus, Internationale, Lazio, AC Milano.'*

He began to laugh at his own joke. It was becoming another annoying habit of his.

'Not always,' said Caton, secretly conceding that it was most of the time. 'This is it,' he said.

He pulled up outside the entrance to a large mansion, partly shrouded by an impressive assortment of oak, birch, and pine on the broad front lawn. They stared through the car windows, trying to envisage the kind of money that would buy a lifestyle like this.

'You're looking at three million pounds, or three and a half million euros for a six-bedroom place up here,' he told them. 'This is considerably larger than that.'

'Cosa fa, Signor Borbone?' said Caterina Volpe, taking them both by surprise.

What does he do?

'Apart from having a ten per cent stake in Italian Mystery Tours?' said Caton. 'Quite a lot, as it happens.'

He held up his tablet to which Douggie Wallace had emailed a surprising amount of information gleaned in less than ten minutes.

'He owns fifteen restaurants in the region, two pizzeria chains, and various properties, here and abroad.'

'And only ten per cent of Magical Italian Tours,' observed Bonifati drily.

'Taken together with his niece Teresa's forty-five per cent, that gives the Borbones the controlling share,' Caton pointed out.

'Even so,' the Italian responded, 'I am thinking there must be a reason why he bothers himself with a little firm like this.'

'You said it yourself, every little counts. The individual and the pizza places are hardly big business, I would have thought, until you add them all up.'

'*E quindici ristoranti,*' said a voice from the back of the car.'

Caton turned and smiled at her.

'Exactly, Caterina,' he said. '*E grande affari*. That *is* big business.'

Bonifati sniffed dismissively.

'It does not make him the *Capo dei Capi* of Manchester,' he said. 'Where was he born?'

'In Crumpsall Hospital, here in Manchester. But his parents were both Italian. He has dual citizenship.'

Bonifati chuckled. 'I wonder,' he said, 'where he pays his taxes?' He relayed the conversation to his colleague, then asked Caton, 'Where in Italy were his parents born?'

'I don't know. But they currently live in a place called L'Aquila.'

'In Abruzzo,' said Bonifati. 'Very nice.'

Caton consulted his tablet.

'His full name is Salvatore Vincenzo Borbone,' he told them. 'Here in Manchester he is known as *Signor* Turi. Short for Salvatore, apparently.'

Bonifati laughed.

He translated for Caterina Volpe, who also seemed to find it amusing, but was not inclined to give her boss the satisfaction of showing it.

'It has another meaning, too,' said Bonifati to Caton. 'It comes from the verb *turare*. Do you know it?'

'No,' said Caton. 'I thought it was *tuppare*?'

'Also true,' Bonifati replied. 'But *turi* is from *turare*, which means to plug. Can you think of another meaning of this phrase, Tom? To plug?'

Caton could think of several. From American gangsters 'plugging' each other during the Prohibition, right up to 'pulling the plug' on someone on life support. He couldn't wait to meet *Signor* Salvatore Borbone.

'There is one other thing,' he said. 'With the single exception of Magical Italian Tours, everything else that *Signor* Borbone is purported to own is in fact owned by Cupello Holdings. Registered Office, an address in Cocullo, in Abruzzo.'

Bonifati shrugged his shoulders and turned to look at his colleague. In the rear-view mirror Caton watched as she also shrugged, and shook her head.

'There are two directors of Cuppello Holdings,' he told them. 'Salvatore Vincenzo Borbone, and a Pietro Alrigo Scibelli. The Company Secretary is one Teresa Borbone.'

'Mmm,' said Bonifati, rubbing his chin in a manner that disturbingly reminded Caton of DI Holmes.

'The rest of it stretches my Italian,' said Caton.

'*Dare mi,*' said Bonifati, stretching out his hand.

Caton passed him the tablet, and watched as he scrolled through the company information. From time to time the Italian detective pursed his lips, frowned, chuckled, even grunted. Finally, he handed the tablet back.

'In each of the last two years Cuppello Holdings makes a 2.7 million euro net profit, on a turnover of 47 million euro,' he said.

Caton did the maths in his head.

'That's approximately six per cent profit,' he said. 'That doesn't sound like a very good margin.

'*Esatto,*' said the commissario, nodding his head. 'But there is at least *one* reason.'

'Which is?'

'Cuppello Holdings each year has to repay part of a...' He windmilled his arms in what had become a habitual gesture. '...*un legame finanziario.*'

Caton looked blank. Bonifati tried again.

'A loan, for a long time.'

'A long-term loan? Like a debenture? From whom?'

The Italian smiled. 'Another company, registered in the city of Catania, in Sicilia. My guess is that *Signor* Scibelli is also a director of this company.'

'Huh!' exclaimed Caterina Volpe.

'You said *at least one reason*,' said Caton.

Bonifati spread his arms out wide and tilted his head on one side. It reminded Caton of a priest inviting a response from his congregation.

'Come on, Tom,' he said. '*Cosa ne pensi?*'

What do you think?

Caton knew exactly what both of them were thinking. High turnover and low net profit meant inflated costs. Dirty money lent to a business whose profits and costs were both inflated. Loans repaid and corporation tax obligations met, in Italy, rather than here in the UK. It had Mafia written all over it.

Chapter 24

'Call me Turi,' he said. 'Everyone does.'

Caton felt Umberto Bonifati's shoulder quiver where it brushed against his arm. He wasn't the only one struggling to maintain his composure and to keep his face straight.

Tall, thick set, and bald-headed, Salvatore Borbone was the embodiment of a plug. There were traces of dark hair above ears that appeared to have been squashed flat against an oval skull. His head sank into his shoulders, without the support of a neck. Hooded eyes, the colour of black chocolate, were set either side of a Roman nose. His mouth was full, his lower lip crafted to hold a cigar in place. His skin was dark. His overall appearance more Greek than Italian. His smile was welcoming, his stare inflexible; it was as though he was looking deep into their souls.

'Please, come into the den,' he said, leading them towards a large wooden door off to the right of the imposing entrance hall.

Twice the size of Caton and Kate's apartment, it was home to a desk, two sofas, two armchairs, a bar and a white mirror-finished grand piano.

Borbone stood beside one of the armchairs and invited them to sit opposite him. He remained standing until they were seated. His eyes were drawn, as all men's were, to Caterina Volpe's faultless legs. She waited for his gaze to move up and across her body, until their eyes locked. Then slowly, deliberately, and in what seemed to Caton to be an exaggeratedly demure manner, she crossed her legs at the ankle.

Borbone smiled in response. It was the smile of a man who relished a challenge. A smile that revealed artificially whitened teeth that against his olive complexion might easily have given the impression of a clown. In his case the effect was strangely sinister. Caterina Volpe was the first to lower her eyes. Their host smiled again, relaxed back, and rested his hands on the arms of the chair.

Caton couldn't help noticing that Borbone's feet were flat on the floor, and his upper and lower legs formed a perfect right angle. The chair had been custom-designed to fit his stature. The sofa on which Caton and Bonifati sat, and the chair occupied by Sovrintendente Volpe, were of a standard size, and significantly lower. He found himself wondering what else might have been customised in this mansion, including the red Ferrari parked in the drive. He had no idea what model it was. Gordon Holmes would have known.

'I will save you the trouble of informing me of the reason for your visit,' Borbone was saying. 'Arturo Santagata rang to tell me all about your visit to the office.'

He watched in amusement as the three police officers exchanged glances.

'Surely that doesn't come as a surprise?' he said. 'Arturo and I are partners, after all.'

'Partners?' said Caton.

'Fellow directors.'

He tapped his fingers up and down on the arms of the chair. Perhaps he was a pianist after all.

'Much the same thing.' He smiled that smile again. 'I hope it was not a problem, Arturo filling me in as it were? After all, it's not as though we are under investigation, is it?'

'Commissario Bonifati and Sovrintendente Volpe are simply trying to establish the facts surrounding Guido's visit to Italy,' Caton replied, deftly avoiding a direct answer to the question.

'But *we* are not under investigation, surely?' Borbone insisted, like an angler playing with a fish on his line.

'At this time,' said the commissario, stepping in, 'we are investigating the murder of an employee of your company. Nobody is under investigation...' He paused theatrically. '...at this time.'

Borbone regarded him with fresh interest, as though discovering potential he had not expected.

'You speak English, Commissario?' he said. It sounded condescending, and his expression confirmed that this was exactly what he intended. 'I had assumed that we might have to engage in our *lingua madre.*'

Bonifati raised his eyebrows. 'And why would you assume that?' he said. 'Because I am a simple policeman?'

'No, no! Certainly not. Were you an *Agente di Polizia Municipale* then I might possibly have made such an assumption, but a Commissario of the *Polizia Di Stato*? Never.'

All this without a flicker of emotion, or a telltale gesture. Caton thought it closer to mockery than sarcasm.

'I see you have good knowledge of the Italian police forces,' said Bonifati calmly. 'Do you spend a lot of time in Italy?'

There was an almost imperceptible shift in

Borbone's demeanour. A slight tension appeared in his shoulders. His upper eyelids closed ever so slightly. His fingers gripped the arms of the chair.

'My time is divided almost equally between here and Italy,' he said. 'And before you ask, since I have dual nationality – British by birth, and Italian by heritage – and have homes in both countries, my tax responsibilities were determined under the UK/Italy Double Tax Convention to be where my vital interests lie. Namely, in Italy.'

'That was not the reason for my question,' said the commissario, opening and raising his hands to show that he had nothing to hide. 'I was interested. Being polite.'

'I'm glad to hear it,' Borbone replied.

'But since you mention it, Turi,' said the Italian detective, 'what are these *vital interests*?'

For a moment Caton thought that their host might be about to get to his feet and throw them out. Not that they could have stopped him.

Borbone's hands relaxed. He settled back in his chair and smiled that lizard smile. He was going to humour them. He's one of life's chameleons, Caton decided.

'Property,' said Borbone. 'And businesses. Too many to mention. But I'm sure your colleagues at the *Agenzia Delle Entrate* could let you have a list more quickly than me.'

Borbone and Bonifati locked eyes, like rutting stags. Except that neither of them was hoping to impress the only woman in the room. There was something going on here from which Caton felt excluded.

The detective grunted. '*Allora*,' he said. 'I will ask them.'

'How well did you know the deceased?' said Caton.

Borbone turned to look at him.

'Only a little. I was introduced to him a few years ago, and saw him several times on the rare occasions that I visited the office.'

'You aren't hands-on as a director then?'

'Hands-on? Why should I be? I am not a manager. I leave that to Arturo, and Teresa. My role is simply to give my opinions at meetings of the directors.'

'How often would that be?'

He smiled as though Caton had cracked a joke.

'Formally, once a year when the accounts are published and signed off.'

'And informally?'

'Now and then. A phone call here, an email there. Arturo did tell you that I have only a ten per cent share?'

'Why is that, Mr Borbone? Such a tiny investment in a small business, especially when you have so many others to worry about.'

His lips curled in amusement.

'I never worry about my business concerns. But I suspect that you know why I decided to invest in MIT. To support my niece, Teresa. She and Arturo were the founders of the firm. They needed a little extra capital. I was happy to provide it.'

'And *Signora* Teresa, where did she get her capital from?' said Umberto Bonifati.

Borbone replied without looking at him. 'Signorina Borbone, she is *una vedova*. A widow. And, as to her capital, you will have to ask her.'

'How did her husband die?' asked Bonifati.

'In an accident.'

He made a play of looking at his watch.

'Now, unless you have a question to ask me that *does* have a bearing on the death of Giovanni Richetti, I will have to ask you to leave. I have some business to attend to.'

He gripped the arms of the chair, and levered himself forward.

'Just a few, and then we'll be on our way,' Caton said.

He was as frustrated as their host by the way the conversation appeared to have been hijacked by a totally different agenda on Umberto's part.

'Very well,' said Borbone. 'Two minutes. Then we all have to leave.'

'Did you have any idea of the nature of Giovanni Richetti's last visit to Italy?'

'None whatsoever. I didn't even know that he was due there. As I said, I have very little to do with the business, and nothing at all to do with its day-to-day operations.'

'What was your reaction when you heard that he was missing?'

He appeared to think about it.

'I believe that Teresa told me when they had not heard from him for over a week.'

'What did you think?'

He shrugged. 'What was I to think? A young man, abroad, on his own. Maybe he was taking a little time off. Maybe he'd found a woman to spend some time with?'

'That would have been out of character, by all accounts.'

'If you say so. I told you, I barely knew him.'

'And when you learned of his death, of how he died, what did you think then?'

'I was saddened for his family. Concerned for the firm. They had lost a good employee. In circumstances that were bad for the image of the business.'

'In what way exactly?'

He looked genuinely surprised, but Caton had already decided that it was impossible to tell when he was telling the truth.

'Would you entrust yourself to a travel company that was incapable of protecting its own employees?'

'Do you think it possible that organised crime was involved?'

Salvatore Borbone's expression never changed. It was so immobile, so mask-like, that for Caton it was a massive tell. Whatever the man was thinking, he was determined not to let it show.

'The thought had never crossed my mind,' he said.

'Bastardo bugiardo!'

'I wouldn't know about the first bit,' said Caton, 'but I grant you, he's an accomplished liar. *One may smile and smile, yet be a villain.'*

'Hamlet, Prince of Denmark,' said Bonifati. 'Regarding his Uncle Claudius. Another *bastardo*.'

'Donna Leon *and* Shakespeare,' said Caton. 'I'm impressed, Umberto.'

'Shakespeare knows his villains,' replied Bonifati. 'Because he was an Italian. To be precise, Sicilian.'

Caton had heard it all before. Just a year ago, instead of choosing a book to review, The Alternatives had discussed the claim at length, and with great deal of passion. The research carried out by a professor from Palermo was compelling, but not quite convincing enough. Michelangelo Florio Crollalanza had been born in Messina to a doctor and a noblewoman. His parents fled the Holy Inquisition. They changed their names to Shakespeare, the English equivalent of Crollalanza. The father once owned a house built by a Venetian who then murdered his wife in a jealous rage. The Venetian's name was Othello. Crollalanza's writing in the Sicilian dialect included sayings found in Shakespeare plays. One of his stories was even titled *Tanto Traffico per Niente*, translatable as

Much Ado About Nothing. And to cap it all, the young Michelangelo Florio Crollalanza, while travelling in Europe, allegedly fell in love with a young girl called Giulietta. When her family refused to allow him to court her, she committed suicide.

'You know this I think?' said Umberto, who had been watching Caton with an amused smile.

'And Dante Alighieri was a Welshman named Daniel Abergele,' said Caton, laughing it off. '*Il Divina Commedia* was originally called *How Green Is My Valley*.'

'Okay, we swap you Dante for Shakespeare.'

'Seriously though, Umberto,' said Caton, 'what was Borbone's reference to the Italian Revenue Agency all about?'

'Last year the Agency gave another agency the job to collect the local taxes from four hundred councils. To nobody's surprise the boss of the agency, and four of his staff, kept one hundred million euros for themselves.'

'A hundred million? How did they expect to get away with that?'

He shrugged. 'Who knows? They spent it all on yachts, private planes, holidays and parties. *Idioti stupidi!*'

'Perhaps they thought that if it was okay for their prime minister, it was okay for them.

Bonifati roared with laughter, and translated for his colleague.

Caterina Volpe nodded sullenly, and shrugged. It was the most explicit expression of the phrase *whatever*, that Caton had ever seen.

'So Borbone was winding you up?' he said.

'Winding me up?'

'Trying to annoy you.'

'He succeeded! But we'll see who is laughing when

I get the *Direzione Investigativa Antimafia* on to him.'

'He's not known to them already?'

'He is not on the list of *sospetti* they gave me. Doesn't mean anything.' He shrugged again. 'We'll see.'

Caton unlocked the car, and opened the rear door for Caterina Volpe to get in.

'That was interesting about Teresa Borbone's husband dying in an accident,' he said.

The commissario nodded sagely. 'Like I say, we'll see.'

Caton heard Bonifati's colleague mutter something in Italian as she ducked into the car. He could have sworn it was something like: *Forse è caduto in un canale.*

Perhaps he fell into a canal.

So, the beautiful sovrintendente had more of a sense of humour than he would have guessed, and a much better understanding of the English language than he had been led to believe.

He fastened his seat belt, started the engine and headed down the drive.

Chapter 25

Caton dropped them off at their hotel and then made the mistake of popping back to the Incident Room to clear his in-tray. The second he walked into the room he found himself cornered by DS Stuart.

'Boss,' she said as she hurried across to him. 'We've got him!'

'The dealer?'

'He's in Interview Room Two. We've just finalised our interview strategy. You can sit in if you like?'

She was understandably excited, and justifiably pleased with herself.

'No thanks, Jo,' he said. 'This one's yours. Well done.'

'Please, boss, I'd welcome your opinion. You can watch from the observation room.'

Caton looked at the clock on the wall. Kate wouldn't be back home for another hour. He could always come in early to work on his in-tray.

'Go on then. Just let me grab a drink, and you can brief me on the way down.'

'We still hadn't got a name or a possible ID from the CCTV images and the e-fits,' she told him. 'But I felt certain he must be a student at one of the unis. So I went to check out their database for the Manchester Student Card. All the students have to have one to access the libraries.'

It had been card based rather than digital in his day, but the principle was the same.

'They told me I'd have to ask the Information Compliance Manager. But I probably still wouldn't get it without a warrant.'

'Data protection,' he said.

'Anyway, as I was leaving, one of the librarians followed me out. "Can I have look?" she says. Then she nods her head. "Yes, I'm pretty sure it's him. I can't remember his name, but he must be studying Economics. That's what he comes in here for. He was in three days ago. In the morning, quite early." So that was it. I checked with the Faculty, and got his details. We went round to his student flat, and there he was. He caved in straight away. It was all I could do to get him to listen to my caution. He just wanted to tell us everything. I had to make him save it for the interview room.'

'Great work, Jo,' he said. 'A lot of people are going to be extremely relieved. The Chief Constable, Police and Crime Commissioner, Head of Crime, the Drug Squad, the Leader of the Council, not to mention tens of thousands of club goers and their parents.'

'And Mandy Morgan's parents,' she said.

'Them above all.'

'He was in a right mess when we arrested him. He had a load of bruises on his face, and a cut mouth. When he was searched in the Custody Suite it was evident he had other injuries too. The police surgeon says he's been badly beaten. Almost certainly has a couple of broken ribs, and heavy bruising to his abdomen and lower back consistent with kidney punches.'

'Just so long as he doesn't try to make out that it was you that was heavy-handed.'

'No chance of that,' she said, grinning. 'I got

statements from two of the students that share his communal kitchen. They claim he's been like that for over twenty-four hours. They nearly called the police themselves, but he wouldn't let them.'

They had reached the corridor that held two of the interview rooms and the observation room sandwiched between them. Detective Chief Inspector Lounds was standing outside Interview Room Two.

'Go for it, Jo,' said Caton. He leant closer and whispered in her ear, 'And remember, you're in charge of this one. Don't let Lounds get under your skin.'

She smiled up at him. 'Don't worry, boss. Once bitten twice shy, as the black widow spider said to her mate.'

'Have you any idea how much trouble you're in?' said DCI Lounds. 'Under the Misuse of Drugs Act 1971, for supplying a Class A Drug, you're looking at up to life imprisonment. Then there's manslaughter. Seven years, to life imprisonment. Always assuming you can persuade the jury it wasn't your intention to go round killing people willy-nilly.'

'Thank you, DCI Lounds,' said DS Stuart before the boy's solicitor could intervene. 'Mr Nelson is well aware of the gravity of his situation, aren't you, Patrick?'

The young man nodded his head. The effort made him wince with pain.

'I'm not sure that my client is well enough to continue with this interview,' said the duty solicitor.

'The police surgeon has given him a thorough examination, and begs to differ,' DS Stuart told her. 'We can take a break at any time, and if Patrick needs more pain relief he only has to ask. My impression was that he wanted to cooperate fully and speedily in helping us to prevent any further deaths. Isn't that right, Patrick?'

'Yes,' he replied, ' I do. 'But I want you to accept that I didn't know it was an illegal drug. That wasn't what I was told. And I didn't want to hurt anyone. Let alone kill them. You've got to believe me.'

There was desperation in his voice. He looked pitiful. From the outset he had shown nothing but remorse. Joanne Stuart had to fight not to let her sympathy for his plight deflect her from the job in hand.

'You've made that clear already,' she replied. 'And you'll be able to re-state it when you sign your statement at the end of this interview. Do you understand?'

'Yes,' he replied. 'But *he* said–'

'DCI Lounds was simply making sure that you understood what the consequences might be if you had intended any of this,' she told him. 'You've told us that you didn't. Now, it would be best if you just explained, in your own words, how it was you ended up here. Can you do that, Patrick?'

Behind the glass in the observation room Caton smiled. DS Stuart was conducting an exemplary interview, as he had known she would. She was managing to make it difficult for Lounds to play the bad cop role that came naturally to him, whilst reassuring the suspect, all without making the cardinal error of appearing to justify the boy's actions.

'Yes,' said the student.

He turned to the duty solicitor, who nodded her agreement.

'I was walking over to the library from the Student Union,' he began, 'when this guy stopped me.'

'So you were actually on the university campus?' said DS Stuart.

'That's right.'

'Good. Carry on, Patrick.'

'He asked if I was interested in making some money. He made some joke about it helping to pay off my student loan.'

'And you bloody well were!' said DCI Lounds.

Joanne Stuart placed her hand on his arm and squeezed hard.

'Of course you were, Patrick,' she said. 'Who wouldn't be? What happened then?'

'We sat down on one of the benches. He said he was with a firm that was market-testing a new product designed for anyone who wanted that bit of extra energy without having to drink buckets of coffee. He said it would help people to concentrate for longer. Great for studying, exams, clubbing. That's why they were targeting students.'

He paused and looked to his lawyer to see how he was doing. She nodded again.

'I said I didn't want to get involved with anything dodgy. He said it wasn't, it was straight up. He showed me some glossy leaflets about this firm. And he gave me a business card.'

'Have you still got one of those?' she asked.

'No,' he said. 'As soon as it happened … the girl … in the nightclub…'

'Mandy Morgan,' said Lounds. 'Her name was Mandy Morgan.'

The young man's eyes began to fill with tears.

Caton shook his head. 'Thank you, Dicky,' he said to the image in the windows. 'You prize prat.'

DS Stuart pushed the box of man-sized tissues across the table.

'It's alright, Patrick,' she said. 'Take your time.'

He wiped his eyes, blew his nose and crumpled up the tissue. He looked around for a wastepaper basket. Finding none he placed it on the tabletop.

'I went on the Internet to find the firm. It didn't

166

exist. I tried emailing the address on his business card. That was phoney too. I threw them away.'

DCI Lounds snorted. Caton knew how he felt. No chance now of getting any fingerprints, or DNA.

'I know it was stupid,' said the student, seeing their expressions. 'I panicked.'

'So you said yes, on the basis of that alone?' she asked.

'No,' he said. 'I'm not that stupid. I said how would I know that it was safe?'

'What did he say?'

'He took a packet out of his pocket, held one up for me to see, then placed it in his mouth and swallowed.'

'He dry-swallowed it?' said Lounds. 'You fell for that one?'

'No, I didn't,' he said. 'I made him open his mouth and show me. He said it wouldn't have made any difference because it would melt under your tongue.'

Lounds scowled.

'Then it was a substitute,' he said. 'Probably an aspirin. I don't blame him. You're giving me a headache.'

'What did he say you had to do?' said DS Stuart soldiering on.

'I had to go round the student bars and the clubs, explain what I was doing, and give people free samples.'

'More than one per person?'

He shook his head hard, and instantly regretted it.

'No, on no account more than one per person.'

'And then what?' said Lounds, leaning forward. 'Were you supposed to arrange to meet up with them again so they could give you feedback. *Can I ask you a few questions, madam, about your experience of our product? Ease of use? The highs and lows? Value for money?*' He hit the table with his fist. 'We may not have been to university, but we're not completely stupid.'

Joanne Stuart placed her hand on his arm again, and eased him back into his seat.

'It's a fair question, Patrick,' she said. 'How were you supposed to get feedback?'

'He said to leave that up to them. After the free handouts had been going on for a week or so they had a team of people who handle that on a random sample basis. He said there might even be an opportunity for me to join that team too.'

'What is it you're studying?' said Lounds. 'Economics? God help us!'

'How much were you being paid, Patrick?' said DS Stuart.

'A pound for every tab I managed to distribute,'

'How many were you given?

'Fifty at a time. One day at a time.'

'Christ,' said Lounds under his breath.

'How many do you think you managed to give out altogether?' said DS Stuart.

'About seventy. It was only my second day when that...Mandy, collapsed.'

'*Died*,' said Lounds. 'When she died.'

They watched him being led back to the holding cell.

'Poor beggar,' she said. 'Thinking it was a way of paying off his student debt fast so he could save for a flat when he left. Now he'll be thrown out of uni, go to prison, come out with a record. His career ruined before it's begun.'

'Serves him right!' exclaimed Dicky Lounds. 'It's not as if he's given us much to go on.' He read from his notes. '*Foreign, well dressed, in his forties. Possibly mixed race. Possibly Eastern European or Mediterranean.* What does that give us? French, Spanish, Italian,

Greek, Turkish, Russian, Romanian, Bulgarian?'

'It's something,' she said. 'The CCTV cameras around the university campus would be a good place to start. We can do that. Your team are better placed than anyone to narrow this down on the streets themselves.'

'I'll tell them that,' he said, getting to his feet. 'They'll be dead chuffed.'

'Incidentally, *I did*, as it happens,' she said.

'What?'

'Go to university.'

He grinned, turned, and opened the door.

'There you go then,' he said, as though it somehow proved a point.

'What now, Jo?' Caton asked as they made their way back to the Incident Room.

'Lounds will circulate the supplier's description to the Drugs Squad. I'll do the same Force wide, and to all of the pubs and bars in the PubWatch scheme. I'll also alert all three universities' Student Unions and security services. And I'll get Douggie Walters to see if there's anything approaching a match on the system.'

'What about Patrick Nelson?'

'I'll see if we can get him remanded in the morning. As much for his own safety as anything else. I don't think his solicitor is going to fight it. Then he can sit through hours of CCTV with DC Hulme until he manages to identify this guy.'

'DC Hulme's not going to be happy.'

She grinned.

'It's a thankless task, but someone's got to do it.'

Chapter 26

'How's it going?' said Kate. 'Your Italian escapade?'

Caton added another ladle of stock to the leek risotto, and carried on stirring.

'Frustrating, to be honest,' he said. 'I'm itching to do more, but strictly speaking this isn't my investigation. Mind you, my Italian is coming on. So is Umberto's English, come to that.'

'What about that silent sultry assistant he had with him in Venice? What was her name?'

She intended it to sound casual.

'Volpe. Sovrintendente Volpe.'

She reached up to the cupboard beside the cooker and took out two wine glasses.

'Does she have a first name?'

'Of course she does.' He stirred a little faster. 'Caterina. Caterina Volpe.'

She took the glasses over to the table, and set them down.

'How's she getting on? She didn't have a lot to say for herself as I remember.'

'She still doesn't. It's a problem really.'

She came back and stood at his side, watching him intently.

'How so?'

'It's not just the language issue. I have a feeling she understands a lot more than she's letting on. And I swear there's something going on between her and Umberto.'

'You're joking,' she said. 'He doesn't look like her type at all.'

'No, it's nothing like that, at least I don't think so. It's a work thing. As far as I can tell she doesn't seem to have much of a role, apart from following him round like a shadow.'

'Or a witness, or observer?' she said. 'Or maybe she's new to the job and he's mentoring her. And the language thing must be a hell of an obstacle for her. Just imagine if you were trailing round Italy on a case with Gordon Holmes in tow. He'd be climbing the wall if he couldn't throw in his threepen'orth every five minutes.'

'Fair point,' he said, filling another ladleful.

'Why don't we invite them over for a meal?' she said. 'The two of them.'

He turned to look at her, the ladle suspended in mid-air.

'Are you serious?'

'Of course I am. And if you spill that all over the cooker, you can clear it up yourself.'

He emptied the ladle into the risotto, and returned it to the saucepan.

'I know what you're up to,' he said as she walked over to the fridge. 'You want to size up the competition.'

'Don't flatter yourself.' She waved a bottle of Sauvignon Blanc in his direction. 'I'm just being neighbourly.'

She placed the wine in a cooler and took that to the table.

'Don't forget the parmesan crisps,' she said as she headed towards the bedroom. 'You put them in the oven ages ago.'

Caton cursed, stopped stirring and bent to open the oven door. He started to slide out the oven tray, yelped and let go. Hastily grabbing the oven glove he should have used in the first place, he placed the tray on the unlit rings, rushed to the sink and ran cold water over his fingertips.

'Everything alright?' Kate called from the bedroom.

'Fine!' he replied through gritted teeth.

He turned off the tap. The discs of parmesan were a perfect golden colour. The risotto, however, had begun to stick to the bottom of the pan. He hastily added a tiny bit of stock, and stirred until the rice came away. He took it off the light, sampled it, and added a twist of black pepper and some virgin olive oil, then mixed it all together with a gentle beating motion.

'It's ready,' he shouted as he took the bowls from the heating drawer.

Kate came out of the bedroom. She had slipped into the green comfy lounging pyjamas that were a perfect match for her rich auburn hair.

'Isn't it a bit early for comfies?' he said as he put her bowl on the place mat.

'It's never too early,' she retorted. She poured him a glass of the straw-coloured wine and some grape juice for herself. 'It marks the divide between work and home life.'

She placed the bottle back in the cooler.

'You might want to try it. Or are you worried Caterina might not approve when she and Umberto come to dinner?'

Caton couldn't tell if she was joking. There was a gleam in her eyes as she waited for his response, and a cheeky smile that gave absolutely nothing away. Winding him up like this was becoming a habit. He had only noticed it recently. He thought marriage was supposed to make a woman feel more secure, not less. Or was it something to do with her being pregnant? Either way, he had no idea how best to respond. In the end he just laughed it off, and sat down.

'Eat,' he said, 'or it'll go cold.'

Kate forked up some of the shiny risotto, broke off a piece of the parmesan crisp, which she placed on top of the rice, and then put it all in her mouth.

'Mmm,' she declared, licking her lips in a decidedly sensual manner.

The effect was nothing at all like Commissario Bonifati's customary utterance, reflected Caton. That had never led him to want to get straight into his own comfies, or Kate's for that matter.

'I take it it's alright then?' he said.

'It's delicious. Absolutely *fantastico, delicioso, buonissimo!*'

'Stop!' he spluttered.

He put his glass down, and wiped his mouth and chin with his napkin.

'Give me a rest; I get this all day at work at the moment.'

'From the delectable Caterina no doubt?' she pointed her fork accusingly.

Caton pushed his chair back and went into the wet room, closing the door after him.

She called after him. 'Come on, Tom, I was only joking!'

He ran the cold tap and splashed his face several times. He stared at his reflection in the mirror. His face was bright pink. From the heat of the stove and from embarrassment with himself. *You idiot*, he thought, *rising to the bait. She's only joking, and you've made it seem like she's hit a nerve.* He splashed his face again, wiped it with a towel and flushed the toilet for effect. He had one last look in the mirror. *She hasn't hit a nerve, has she?* The face staring back at him had no answer to give.

She was waiting for him. She looked concerned and a little chastened.

'Are you alright, Tom?'

'I just got something stuck in my throat,' he lied. 'I'm fine now.'

'If it was what I said, I was only teasing.'

'It wasn't.'

He sat down and forked up some risotto. It was surprising how quickly it had cooled down.

'I do trust you, you know,' she said, unwilling to let it go.

He put his fork down, reached across the table and took her hand.

'And I will never give you any reason not to. Now, can we please forget it?'

During the rest of the meal they discussed the way her PhD proposal had been received, Joanne Stuart's success in tracking down the source of the fatal drug supply, and whether they were going to spend their first Christmas together at home or with Kate's parents in Teddington. The latter might easily have become contentious, but the discussion was interrupted by the insistent tone of a Skype call on the computer.

'I'll clear this lot up and make us some decaf,' she said, pushing back her chair. 'You'd better take that. It's bound to be Harry.'

Chapter 27

'Hi, Dad!'

His son looked happy, and healthy. Light years from the way he had been when the two of them were plucked from Morecambe Bay just a couple of months before. But children were so much more resilient. Caton had endured a couple of flashbacks after the event, over several weeks. Harry had none. For him it was an amazing adventure. For Tom it had served to bring back to the surface the fact that he had survived, but that his parents had not.

'Hi, Harry,' he said. 'How are you doing? You look great.'

'I'm cool. How are you?'

'I'm cool too. How's school?'

The boy shrugged, and gave a lopsided grin.

'Okay, you know?'

'What are you now, Year 8?'

'Year 9!'

'Sorry, Year 9. We didn't have Years in my day. The class was named after the class teacher. What's your new teacher like?'

'He's pretty cool, except that he's a United supporter.'

Harry sat back in his chair and frowned to emphasise his disdain. Behind Harry's head Caton could see a large poster of the 2014–15 season Wigan football team.

'That was a great win you had over Maribo in the Europa League,' said Caton. 'I wish I could have been there with you.'

His little face lit up.

'It's was mega! Nick was awesome!'

'Nick?'

'Nick Powell! Come on, Dad, get with it.'

'Of course. He scored two, didn't he? Who scored the other one?'

'Ben Watson. Brilliant header. We could have had another six, easy.'

'It should boost their confidence for the League. Where are they now, mid-table?'

The frown returned. 'Fourteenth. But they've only got fifteen points. Burnley have thirty-two.'

'Never mind, son, we're only a quarter of the way into the season. There's a long way to go.'

Harry shrugged. 'S'pose.' His face brightened. 'Arsenal are showing your lot the way.'

Caton pretended indignation. 'We won yesterday. Now we're only three points adrift.'

'Yeah, but the Gunners are looking really good. The Blues have still got to prove they can be consistent. Play like a team, instead of a bunch of prima donnas.'

'Who told you that?' No pretence this time.

'Mr Walters. Our teacher.'

Caton laughed. 'What does he know? He supports the Reds.'

Harry's head turned away from the screen.

'Coming, Mum! Just saying goodnight to Dad.'

He turned back and looked straight at the webcam.

'Got to go, Dad.'

'Okay, son. Great talking to you. Say hello to your mum for me.'

Harry had already pushed back his chair and was

standing up. All Caton could see was the waistband of blue-and-white striped pyjama bottoms.

'Will do,' Harry replied. 'Night, Dad.'

His hand reached down towards the mouse.

'Stay safe, son,' Caton murmured to the empty screen.

He thought of Giovanni Richetti, floating head down in the Lagoon. Mandy Morgan, fighting for every breath before losing consciousness. Marvin Brown, leaking blood onto the rubber-tiled playground as the merry-go-round slowly spun. Just some of the youngsters whose deaths he had investigated. Taken before their lives had barely begun.

Guns N' Roses had it right. *Welcome To The Jungle.* There were too many people out there with an appetite for destruction. All police officers knew that, and feared for their own children. *But you can't be with them every minute of the day,* he told himself. *I can't even be with Harry more than once a week, if that.* In less than sixteen weeks he would have another child to worry about. What if it was a girl? Would he worry even more? Would that slowly create a divide between them? Her need for freedom, his endless warnings, rules and restrictions, interrogations and surveillance?

He quit Skype and stood up. There was no point in projecting. It would be on him before he knew it. He had every confidence that the joy this child would bring would far outweigh the burden of responsibility. *And you're not alone,* he reminded himself. *You have Kate to help you shoulder that.* The lovely Kate. Sensible, practical, dependable, optimistic, kind, thoughtful and beautiful.

The door opened. She popped her head around it.

'Oh good, you've finished,' she said. 'Because I've

just stacked the dishwasher, your coffee's going cold, and Downton Abbey's about to start. So I suggest you get your bum in here.' She raised her eyebrows and gave him that look. 'Now!'

He smiled to himself as she disappeared back into the lounge. Children? What was there to worry about? Kate would sort it. God help them.

They were about to retire to bed when the phone rang.

'Oh God, who's that?' exclaimed Kate.

There was no caller identity, just an 0161 number.

'I've no idea,' he said. 'But I'd better find out, just in case.'

She knew better than to protest. It was the nature of his work. It would have been the same if he was a hospital consultant. It went with the territory. She switched off the television standby and headed for the wet room.

Caton picked up.

'Hello?'

'Tom? It's me, Umberto.'

'What is it, Umberto? Have you any idea what time it is?'

'That is why I call you. You need to go to bed right now because we are getting up early in the morning.'

'Umberto, what are you talking about?'

'Agent Haigh has a European Arrest Warrant,' he replied, 'for someone we are interested in talking to. He will be calling on him in the morning. You and me, we are invited to join him.'

'Someone *we* are interested in talking to. Is that we as in *us*, or just you?'

'Ah,' he paused, long enough for Caton to realise that he was deciding how much to reveal. 'We, as in the *Polizia Di Stato*, and the *Direzione Investigativa Antimafia*.'

178

Caton sat down on the arm of the sofa.

'This is the real reason you're over here, isn't it?' he said. 'The Richetti murder is a sideshow as far as you're concerned.'

'No, Tom. You have it the wrong way round. I am here because of Richetti. Because I am already here, the DIA, they ask me to do this for them, that is all.'

Caton was not convinced, but there was no point in arguing.

'You don't need me though surely?' he said. 'Not if this isn't connected to the Richetti investigation.'

The reply surprised him.

'Maybe it is. We won't know unless we ask the question.'

It sounded to Caton like a fishing expedition. And a pretty random one at that. But his interest had been piqued.

'Where and when?' he said.

'Where, is maybe not good to say on this line,' Bonifati replied. 'But Agent Haigh will be in the hotel car park at 4.30 in the morning.'

'I'll be there,' said Caton. 'But this had better be good.'

'*Buono*, Tom,' the Italian detective replied. '*Molto Buono. Ci vediamo in mattinata.*'

'See you in the morning,' said Caton.

He placed the phone back in its cradle and sat there for a moment, replaying the conversation in his head.

He had known better than to scoff at Bonifati's paranoia about the phone line. After all, if they could listen in on Angela Merkel's phone conversation for ten years without anyone knowing, not to mention all those other Heads of State, how easy would it be?

Recent revelations had shown that the UK and the USA had monitored the telecommunications of both the Italian Government and major companies, with

179

the full knowledge of the Italian Secret Services under an information-sharing agreement. If *Direzione Investigativa Antimafia* or *Mafia* were among the standard search terms, the conversation they had just had might easily have been immediately relayed to the Italian Secret Services. Was it beyond the bounds of possibility that those organisations might themselves have been infiltrated by organised crime? By *Mafioso*? Of course it wasn't.

He stood up, took a deep breath, and prepared to face a more immediate challenge. His wife.

Chapter 28

'Where is Sovrintendente Caterina?' said Caton as he pulled out onto Oldham Road behind the second of the lead cars.

Behind him was a van carrying a search dog and his handler. Behind that, a Transit van containing a Tactical Aid search team.

Umberto chuckled. 'It is not fair to get her up so early. She needs her *sonno di bellezza*.'

'Beauty sleep.'

'Beauty sleep. And last night I asked her to spend today finding out what the *Agenzia Delle Entrate* has on *Signor* Salvatore *Turi* Borbone.' He caught Caton glancing at him and added, with a knowing smile, '*Lavoro importante*. Important work.'

He held out both hands, like a magician showing that they were empty.

'No reason for her to complain. Eh, Tom, you agree?'

Caton refused to be drawn. He had no intention of becoming part of whatever hidden agenda the commissario was pursuing. He concentrated on keeping up with the cars ahead of him.

It was pouring with rain. A major depression had come in from the south-west. Gusts approaching ninety miles an hour were battering the south coast, the Midlands and East Anglia. Even here, on the fringes of the storm, the wind was buffeting the car and bending trees in the fields on either side.

After half an hour the lead car signalled that it was leaving the motorway. Caton followed as it headed to the roundabout for the A6, and then turned north-west towards Chorley. In less than two minutes the convoy pulled into a lay-by nestling at the foot of the hill on which the town stood. Caton switched the engine off. He checked the time: 5.15. An hour and a half to go till dawn.

'What is this place?' said Bonifati.

'Blackrod,' Caton told him. 'Named for the coal seam it sits on. It's more of a big village than a town. Between five and six thousand people in all. Surrounded by farmland in the main. Yet close to the motorway. Not a bad place to lay low.'

Bonifati grunted. 'With a name like Alfredo Giambotta? It's like trying to hide in Mestre with a name like Tom Caton. You stick out like a Roman's nose.'

'That's not the name he's using.'

Caton consulted the notes Mal Haigh had sent to his tablet.

'Here he's known as Frederick Gladstone. Freddy to his friends. Not that he has many, apparently. He's been married to an English wife for seven years. They have two children. A boy age seven, and a girl age four.'

'Somebody had a sense of humour,' said Bonifati as though he hadn't been listening. 'When they come up with the family name.'

'Gladstone?'

'Giambotta! Do you know what a Giambotta is?'

'I have no idea.'

'It's what you call a stew. Not even a proper stew, with meat or fish. It's a vegetable stew. Peasant food.

Hah!'

'He's not the first Italian to settle here,' Caton told him. 'The Romans were here. This is a Roman road. They built a camp on the hill, which is why it's called Castle Hill.'

'Huh,' Bonifati replied. 'They send the Foreign Legions to places like this. The Gauls, the Greci, the Tedeschi. The Romans weren't so stupid to leave a beautiful city, good food, sunshine, to come to a wild, dark, wet, *ostile–*'

'Hostile.'

'Hostile place like this.'

'Like this must have been.'

The Italian chuckled. 'Who's talking history?'

'It's a nice place when the sun shines,' Caton retorted. 'Peter Kay lives here. So did Ryan Giggs, for a while.'

He switched on the ignition for a moment so that the wipers could clear the windscreen.

Malcolm Haigh had exited the second car, and was walking towards them. Caton switched off the wipers and lowered the window on his side. The man from the Organised Crime Directorate crouched. Drops of water dripped from the peak of his baseball cap and spattered the sill.

'It's just a mile from here,' he said. 'We go in quietly. Sidelights, no radio communication. The Firearms Team will lead, followed by me and my team. You two stay in the car until I give you the nod. Is that clear?'

'Fine by me,' Caton replied. 'It's your warrant.'

Umberto Bonifati placed his hand on the back of Caton's seat, and leaned forward.

'My warrant too,' he said. 'I would like to see his face when he opens the door.'

Haigh didn't bother to hide his irritation.

'You'll have to wait till we know it's safe.'

He stood up.

'You may as well come too, Caton,' he said. 'So long as you're prepared to trail through a farmyard in the pouring rain. It's your funeral.'

'I hope not,' said Caton, watching the agent walk back towards his car, leaning forward into the driving rain like a figure in a Lowry painting.

As they approached the stone pillars that marked the entrance to the drive, they slowed to five miles an hour. *Hillcroft Farm* said the slate sign on one of the pillars, barely visible in the rain and the overcast predawn light. *Beware. Dogs Running Free!* said the tatty white-painted notice on the other.

'I thought there'd be electric gates at the very least,' said Caton as the convoy crawled up the unmade drive.

'Gates say something to hide,' observed Bonifati. 'Better this way, I think.'

Twenty metres from the two-storey black-and-white stone farm building the lead car triggered security cameras. They were bathed in bright light. Caton was temporarily blinded. The brake lights up ahead glowed red, and rear tyres kicked up mud and stones. Dogs began to bark. Big dogs by the sound of it. Ones that resented being woken. Ones that had not yet had breakfast.

'So much for the element of surprise,' Caton muttered.

The doors on the two lead cars flew open. Six officers clad in body armour appeared. Three members of the Tactical Firearms Team headed for the front door, two more for the rear. Immediately behind the on-point trio came an officer carrying the Enforcer – a blue steel tube with a pad on the end capable of exerting three tonnes of force to problem locks. Behind him came Agent Malcolm Haigh, and a colleague.

Caton heard the rear door open.

'*Andiamo*!' shouted Umberto Bonifati as he ran after them.

Caton shook his head. 'As I recall,' he said to no one in particular, 'he asked us to wait in the car until it was safe.'

He reached behind his seat, and unhooked the Hi-Vis anorak hanging there. Umberto might not be bothered, but he for one wasn't going to take the risk of being shot at by a nervous rifleman. With some difficulty, he shrugged it on. Then he tugged the non-standard issue hood down over his forehead, and exited the car.

As though on cue, the rain had worsened. He could see the others clustered around the door. Lights had come on behind the curtains in several upper rooms. Someone was shouting, 'Open up! Police!' over and over again, attempting, and likely failing, to be heard above the wind and howling of the dogs.

He could see them on the other side of the courtyard straining at the chains that held them back. There were three of them. Large, muscular hounds with broad, flat heads, long muzzles and bared teeth. Their coats were reddish brown, with a distinctive ridge of raised hair running down the spine. Rhodesian Ridgebacks, aka the African Lion Hound. One of the police dog handlers owned one. He had always claimed they had a lovely temperament, and made great pets. Then he'd spoilt it all by adding that they were ferocious as a pack when hunting down a lion. These three looked like a pack to Caton. He just hoped that in his bright yellow anorak he didn't look too much like a lion.

A light went on in the hall. The officer with the

battering ram stepped back, his Enforcer hanging from one hand. The Firearms officers took up positions on either side of the door, their weapons raised.

'Armed police. Open up!' shouted the agent at Malcolm Haigh's side.

The baying of the dogs redoubled. Caton glanced over his shoulder. The Ridgebacks were straining so hard at their leashes that he feared the chains might snap before they choked themselves to death.

He heard the drawing of bolts. The door opened.

Chapter 29

Alice Gladstone was an attractive woman, despite the absence of make-up. Not the kind of beauty that would turn heads, but pretty. Dark-blonde shoulder-length hair, messed up by sleep, framed an oval face. Her features would have been perfectly symmetrical but for the slight misalignment of her nose; from a break, perhaps. Her hands grasped the hooded collars of a berry-red dressing gown trimmed in satin, clasping it tightly to her. Her feet were bare.

Behind her, on the staircase, stood a young boy in navy-blue pyjamas. He had a protective arm around a little girl in a pink hooded onesie. Her eyes were wide with bewilderment. She held a teddy bear in the crook of her left arm, and had a thumb in her mouth.

Caton was reminded of the famous nineteenth-century painting *When Did You Last See Your Father?* A Royalist family being questioned by Parliamentarians during the English Civil War.

Mrs Gladstone's tired eyes registered the uniforms, the weight of numbers, and the guns.

'What the hell do you want!?' she said, attempting indignation, whilst betraying panic. 'And put those guns away. Can't you see you're frightening my children?'

Malcolm Haigh placed one foot over the doorstep and moved forward, forcing her to retreat a pace into the hall.

'My name is Malcolm Haigh, of the Serious and Organised Crime Agency,' he said. 'These officers from the Greater Manchester Police are here to assist me in the execution of a European Arrest Warrant.'

'Arrest?' she said. 'Arrest of who?'

'Alfredo Patrizio Giambotta,' he told her.

Relief flooded her face.

'There you are then,' she said. 'That's it. You've got the wrong address. There's no one of that name living here.'

'That,' he said, 'remains to be seen. Now, I suggest that you take your children back to bed, and let your husband know that we are here.'

'I can't do that,' she replied, turning to wave her children to join her.

'Why not?' said Malcolm Haigh.

She scooped her daughter up in her arms and placed her free arm around her son's shoulders.

'Because he isn't here. But don't worry, when I've settled the children I'll text him and let him know. He'll want to talk to you, don't you worry. So will his lawyer.'

'Please don't do that, Mrs Gladstone,' the agent replied. 'Just tell me where your mobile phone is.'

She ignored him, and headed into what looked like a sitting room.

He turned to the only female member of the Search Team.

'Go with them,' he said. 'Make sure that no one leaves the room, and that none of them uses a phone or a tablet of any kind.'

'What if they want the loo?' she asked.

'Then you go with them and call for someone else to watch whoever stays behind. And you'd better get in there. I bet that little girl can send a text faster than we can.'

While the search team got to work, Caton and Bonifati did their own tour. The farmhouse was deceptively larger than it had appeared from the outside. An attached farm worker's cottage and a large barn had both been converted to extend the square footage.

The room into which Mrs Gladstone had taken the children was a massive open-plan space. It comprised a generous sitting area and a dining area with a table that would comfortably seat twelve. The focal point was an impressive inglenook fireplace with multi-fuel stove. Bi-fold wall-to-ceiling windows opened out onto what looked like a stone-flagged terrace.

It was possible to walk directly from the dining area into a stone-flagged farmhouse kitchen, complete with Rayburn range cooker, Belfast sink, fitted Fired Earth units, a polished marble-top island, and a six-seater table. Leading off from the kitchen was a walk-in pantry and wine store, a laundry room, and cloakroom with a toilet and shower.

They made their way back to the hallway, and up the stairs to a landing that branched left and right. This floor held four double bedrooms, three of which were en suite, and a large family bathroom with a free-standing Victorian bath. Each room was being systematically searched, with far more consideration than Caton had become accustomed to. He presumed that the European Search Warrant must have been far more specific, and proscribed, than might otherwise have been the case.

They headed back down to the sitting room where the children were curled up with their mother, watching CBeebies on a large flat-screen television. The female officer was seated on one of the dining chairs placed discreetly beyond their peripheral vision. Their mother deliberately avoided making eye contact with either Caton or Bonifati, which suited them both. There would be plenty of time for that later.

They crossed the room and passed through an open door into an even larger space, with a vaulted oak-beam ceiling and yet another inglenook fireplace. One half of the room was lined with books, and set up with sofas and armchairs like a snug-cum-library. The other half was a playroom for the children. Halogen spots picked out the original oil paintings and framed prints on those walls that were otherwise bare. A chandelier hung from the central beam. Two members of the search team were systematically removing books from the shelves into piles on the floor in case they might conceal a safe or hidden documents.

The commissario sucked air in between his teeth, and then exhaled noisily.

'Like an oyster,' he said. 'Outside, plain black shell; inside, *madreperla*.'

Caton knew what he was getting at. It seemed an odd way to keep a low profile. If he remembered rightly, the other two Mafia bosses who had been arrested in the UK within the past eighteen months had been living a far less conspicuous lifestyle. But then just how conspicuous was this place? Only those who got over the threshold would be aware of what lay behind the farmhouse's exterior. And living off a policeman's salary was hardly a reliable basis from which to make such a judgment on what constituted luxury.

They moved back to the sitting room in time to see Mal Haigh and his colleague coming in from the hallway.

'We need to see inside the outbuildings, Mrs Gladstone,' he said.

She looked over her shoulder, her face full of

contempt. She pulled her children closer.

'You'll find a large bunch of keys on a hook beside the fridge,' she said. 'Much good it will do you.'

'Thank you,' he replied. 'One other thing, is there a safe in the house? If there is, we'll find it, but it would save a lot of time and trouble if you could show me.'

Caton and Bonifati decided to follow the search team outside, as much out of curiosity as anything else, but also because it was becoming hot and uncomfortable inside.

The rain had slackened to a drizzle. As they crossed the yard, the dogs made a half-hearted attempt to warn them off, and then slunk back to the shelter of their kennels.

There were three stables. One of them was occupied by an ageing and apparently docile dapple grey horse. Next to it was a tack room. Beyond that was a barn containing a ride-on mower, a blue Quad bike, three mountain bikes, a child's tricycle and assorted garden furniture. Stacked on shelving were boxes of multi-pack toilet paper, tissues and detergents, and wine in wooden racks. On the floor were boxes of beer, lager and cider. In one corner was a large cabinet freezer filled with meat and fish, and a smaller one containing desserts, ready meals, pizza, bread and rolls.

Next door was a smaller barn full of garden tools and outdoor toys the children had almost certainly outgrown. On a pallet in the centre of the barn were six red LED stick lights that Caton took to be a large version of garden solar panel lights. On closer inspection he discovered that each of them was mounted on a 55cm-long black plastic mounting post with its own transformer box and wire cable attached.

The last building was a brick barn that had been

converted into a double garage. It contained a BMW X5 SUV, and a Porsche Cayenne. Had Gordon Holmes been here he would have known their worth to the penny. Caton had no idea, except that he doubted either of them would ever fall into his price range. Not unless they were twenty years old, with 200,000 miles on the clock.

Beside him Umberto clicked the roof of his mouth with his tongue. His expression told Caton that he was thinking exactly the same thing. Who'd be a policeman?

Suddenly, there was shout from somewhere beyond the barn. Out in the open ground they heard it again. The words were lost in the wind and rain. A torch was being waved to and fro. Then the wind dropped for a moment and they heard it clearly.

'Out here!'

Caton and Bonifati left the search team rifling through the outbuildings and headed across a paddock, through an open gate, and into a field. Eighty metres from the house, their trousers sodden, rain dripping from the ends of their noses, they came upon one of the Armed Response Team who had been sent to check the rear of the property.

'Look at this,' he said, pointing his torch at the ground and setting off at a steady pace. They followed.

When they arrived back at the point from which they had started it was clear that they had walked in a complete circle, and were standing on a concrete platform approximately forty-five feet in diameter. Too big for a trampoline. Too far from the house for a hot tub. Perfect for a helipad.

Caton looked back at the smaller of the barns.

'So that's what those lights are for,' he said.

Chapter 30

They stood dripping onto the doormat in the hall, watching the spectacle unfold before them.

Four members of the search team were queuing to come down the stairs. The first held a computer stack, the second an integrated MacBook, the third a printer, the fourth a pile of tablets. Alice Gladstone was at the foot of the stairs barring the way. Malcolm Haigh was at her side, trying to reason with her.

'Please,' she said. 'Not the iPad. It's my son's. It's got his homework on it.'

'Mrs Gladstone,' said the agent, placing his hand gently on her arm, 'you have to understand, the warrant…'

She shrugged him off, placed one hand on the newel post and the palm of the other on the wall.

'I don't give a toss for your warrant,' she said. 'This is stupid. It's petty. Freddy never goes anywhere near it. Why would he? As for the man you're looking for, I've told you, he doesn't exist.'

'Let her keep it,' said Umberto Bonifati.

The two of them turned their heads to look at him. There was relief and surprise in her expression, irritation in his.

The Italian detective shrugged.

'*Non ti preoccupare, Signor* Haigh' he said. 'I will accept responsibility.'

The agent shook his head and turned back to face her.

'Very well, Mrs Gladstone,' he said. 'But I expect your son to show us what is actually on there before you get to keep it.'

She stepped to one side and watched as the officers trooped past her. When the last one drew level with her she took the iPad from his pile and turned back towards the sitting room. Agent Haigh treated Bonifati to another stinging glance and followed her.

Caton studied his companion with renewed interest.

'I thought you were just along for the ride, Umberto,' he said. 'I had no idea you had this much influence.'

The commissario smiled inscrutably, slipped out of his sopping jacket, and hung it on one of the pegs beside the entrance door. Caton followed his lead. It was one thing to search her house for evidence, another to treat it with a complete lack of respect, although the trail of wet footprints across the wooden hallway and up the stairs suggested it was a little late for that. He wiped his feet for a final time, and followed his companion into the sitting room.

The children, watched over by the female officer, were glued to the television. Neither their mother nor the agents were in the room. The officer used her eyes to guide them to the kitchen, where they found them seated around the table.

In a pile in the centre was a stack of documents. Malcolm Haigh was sifting through them, listing them off as he did so. His colleague was keeping a record in a notebook. Stony-faced, Alice Gladstone sat opposite him with folded arms.

Unbidden, Bonifati sat down on the bench beside Malcolm Haigh. Rather than invade her personal space, Caton pulled up a stool from the breakfast bar.

'Passport in the name of Alice Gladstone,' the agent intoned. 'A joint will. Insurance – his, and hers. Two bonds, both in Mrs Gladstone's name. Two ISAs, one each. Two E111s. His and hers driving licences – paper *and* photo ID. Two NHS cards. Three cheque books, one in the company name, one joint, one hers.'

The agent picked up a blue plastic folder and speed-read the contents.

'Company incorporation document. A limited company registered as A. Gladstone Property Ltd. Two directors. Mrs Alice Gladstone holds seventy per cent of the shares, Mr Frederick Gladstone the remaining thirty per cent.'

He put the folder down and picked up a bundle of twenty-pound notes.

'I'll save you the trouble,' she said. 'There's five hundred pounds. It saves us having to keep going to cash machines. Freddy only just topped it up.'

Haigh put it down on the pile.

'I'll take your word for it,' he said. 'Not that we'll be taking it. You can keep all this, except for your husband's driving licences.'

'Don't do me any favours,' she replied. 'The more you take, the more our lawyers are going to sue you for.'

'Why,' he said, 'are all of your personal documents, such as your driving licence, locked in the safe?'

'Why do you think? Because like all men my husband is paranoid about them being stolen.'

He nodded, as though acknowledging the reasonableness of her assertion.

'I see you own the majority holding in your husband's property business. Why is that?'

The question took her by surprise. She sat back a little.

'Freddy said it was for tax reasons. I don't really understand it. The house is in my name too.' She saw the expression on their faces, and added, 'But we have a joint bank account. And Freddy runs the business.'

'When did your husband leave the house?' he asked, changing tack.

'Last night.'

'At what time did your husband leave?'

'Twenty minutes past ten.'

'That's very precise.'

'When your husband goes out late at night you tend to note the time. Worry if he'll be safe. And wonder how long it will be before you see him again.'

'His Porsche is still in the garage. How did he leave?'

'By helicopter.'

'Where has he gone?'

'I don't know. He had a phone call at around 9 o'clock last night. He said he had some urgent business to attend to, down south. He went and packed a case.'

'What else did he take with him?'

'I'm not sure. His laptop case. His document case.'

'Did this strike you as unusual?'

'Him going away on business? No. Late at night? Yes.'

'How often does he use the helicopter?'

'Maybe five or six times a year. That's all.'

'Do you know where the helicopter is based?'

'I have no idea.'

'What does your husband do, Mrs Gladstone? How does he earn the money for you to live like this?'

'Like this?' She looked genuinely puzzled.

'Two luxury cars in the garage. A helicopter to whisk him off whenever he needs to. A house that must be pushing a million pounds.'

'Only £825,000, according to Zoopla,' she retorted.

Only? thought Caton. The word spoke volumes for her aspirations, though he had to admit it was modest for a man reputed to be worth what they suspected. Still, factor in two families to support, and the need to keep a relatively low profile. It was probably about right.

'What does your husband do, Mrs Gladstone?' Haigh repeated.

'Property,' she said. 'He buys property and rents it out. Sometimes he'll buy a property, renovate it, and then sell it.'

'Where are these properties?'

'All over.'

'All over where?'

'The North. The Midlands. The South.'

'And abroad?'

'Yes.'

'Abroad where?'

'Spain. The Middle East. Cyprus.'

'Italy?' asked Bonifati.

She was clearly taken by surprise. She had barely been aware of his presence until now.

'Italy? No.'

'How can you be so sure?'

'He'd have said. And he never goes there. Only to these other places.'

The commissario raised his eyebrows.

'Mmm.' He scratched his chin. 'Does he tell you everything, Mrs Gladstone?'

'Yes.

'Are you sure?'

'Yes.'

She turned to Agent Haigh.

'Look, what is this all about? Whatever it is, there's some kind of mistake. There must be.'

He ignored her question.

'Did he say when he would be back, Mrs Gladstone?'

'No!'

Over the initial shock, she was now angry. Caton could tell that they were going to lose her anytime now. The shutters were going to come down.

'Does your husband ever go away for long periods at a time, Mrs Gladstone?'

Bonifati's tone made the question sound innocuous, but her head whipped round to face him. For all the fire in them, there were questions at the back of her eyes.

'That's it!' she said, folding her arms. 'I'm not answering any more of your stupid questions. Not without a lawyer. And I want you out of here, now.'

She stood, and pushed her chair back. It scraped across the tiled floor and set Caton's teeth on edge.

'Now I'm going to see my children.'

'There was something your husband didn't share with you,' said the Italian detective.

He placed a photograph on the table. With his index finger he slowly turned it to face her.

Despite herself, she leaned forward to study it.

As far as Caton could tell it was a family group, taken at some kind of celebration. A wedding, perhaps, or a christening. A man, a woman and four children. A boy and a girl in their late teens, and two girls somewhere between four and six years of age.

Bonifati pointed to each of the subjects in turn.

'This is Alfredo Giambotta,' he said. 'And this is his wife, Maria. They have been married for nineteen years, Mrs Gladstone.'

Alice Gladstone gasped. One hand flew to her mouth, the other gripped the table for support.

'These are their four children,' he continued in a

monotone. 'If you wish to know their names, I can tell you.'

He waited for it to sink in, and then dragged the photo back towards him, careful to ensure that the Giambotta family group continued to stare back at her.

'Your husband, Mrs Gladstone, is, among other things, a *bigamo*.'

'A bigamist,' Caton said helpfully.

Chapter 31

Bonifati's timing had been perfect. All thoughts of lawyers had fled out of the window, together with any inclination she may have had to protect her husband. Yet her husband was still how she thought of him. A liar, a cheat, a fraud, a bastard, yet still her husband. The father of her children. But from the instinctive way that she had responded, it seemed that whatever emotional connection there may have been was severed. Caton had the impression that deep down she had always suspected. Maybe not that he was a bigamist, and their marriage a sham, but that his business dealings were shady, and that he cheated on her with other women.

They waited until she had recovered from the shock of discovering that as the head of an organised crime clan, and an Italian one at that, the Ndrangheta originating in Calabria, he had been using their marriage, and by extension her children, as a cover to avoid arrest and prosecution. She was allowed to check that the children were happy watching the CBeebies channel, and to reassure them as best she could, before returning to the kitchen.

She was seated at the table, cradling a mug of coffee. Her face, that had previously flushed pink with indignation, was pale and drawn. Devoid of make-up she looked plain, ordinary, and lost. Nothing like the glamorous portrait over the fireplace in the lounge.

In front of her, on the table, was a copy of the European Arrest Warrant listing the grounds for the arrest of her husband, and the accompanying request for the seizure of potential evidence. It was a long list.

Participation in a criminal organisation, trafficking in human beings, illicit trafficking in narcotic drugs and psychotropic substances, corruption, fraud, laundering of the proceeds of crime, facilitation of unauthorised entry and residence, murder, grievous bodily injury, kidnapping, illegal restraint and hostage-taking, organised or armed robbery, racketeering and extortion, counterfeiting and piracy of products and the forgery of administrative documents.

Caton felt sorry for her, and for her children. She may have been stupid. Easily duped. At worst she may have subconsciously been party to a deception the nature of which she had not fully understood. But she was a victim, not a criminal. That much was clear.

'Did you really have no idea?' said Malcolm Haigh.

She slowly shook her head. 'No,' she whispered.

It was more reflection than an answer. As though replying to a question she had been asking herself over and over again.

'But his English must have been accented,' pressed the agent. 'His appearance is more Mediterranean than Caucasian. Surely you noticed that?'

It was gently put. He had no intention of badgering her. There was no need. They could all see that.

She clasped the mug tightly and looked up at him. She took a deep breath.

'He told me that his mother was Italian. His father English. He said that his father, who was a diplomat, had met his mother when he was stationed in Rome.'

'Did you never meet them?'

201

She shook her head.

'Not even when you were married?'

'He said they'd divorced ten years before we met. Then his father had a heart attack and died. His mother emigrated to America and remarried. He and she were now estranged.'

'How did you and your husband meet?' asked Umberto Bonifati.

'We met in Santa Maria, in Reggio Calabria. It's a seaside resort.'

Caton had never heard of it. The Italian detective nodded knowingly.

'I was on holiday with a girl friend,' she continued. 'Freddy...' His name turned sour in her mouth.

She took a sip of coffee.

'*He* was at another table in the restaurant where we were eating. He was having a drink with the owner of the restaurant. He looked over at us. Then the waiter brought us a bottle of champagne. "Compliments of *Signor* Gladstone," he said. When their meeting was over he asked if he could join us.'

She looked down at her mug.

'That's how it started.'

'Have you ever been back to Italy?' asked Haigh.

'No.'

'Not even to Santa Maria, where you met?'

'No.'

'Of course not,' said the Italian detective. 'Because Reggio Calabria is where Giambotta comes from. Where his other family live. In the capital, Catanzaro.'

The man from the Serious and Organised Crime Agency gave him a dirty look. Caton could see why. The less she knew at this stage, the better. A woman scorned. There was no telling what she might do.

202

Bonifati smiled, and shrugged. It was like water off a duck's back.

'So you see, he does go sometimes to Italy,' he said. 'But never for long. He flits in, he flits out. Like *un pipistrello*.'

He fluttered his hand in the air.

'A bat,' said Caton, earning a disapproving stare of his own.

Malcolm Haigh stood up and signalled for the two of them to follow him into the hall.

'Look,' he said, standing square-on to Bonifati, 'I let you come along, Commissario, because I was instructed to do so. But I understood that was for the sole purpose of observing us serving the warrant on behalf of your government. Do I need to remind you that you have no jurisdiction in this country, and consequently no right to question anyone, let alone someone not named in that warrant, about crimes that may or may not have been committed in this country, or your own?'

Bonifati steepled his fingertips in front of his chest, and began to shake them gently up and down. As he turned to face Caton, his hands slid down towards his waist.

'Long sentences, Tom,' he said. 'What is he saying?'

What Bonifati's hands were saying was far more eloquent. *I don't believe it. Why is he trying to bust my balls?*

Caton drew the index finger and thumb of his right hand across his lips.

'I think he wants you to keep it zipped, Umberto,' he said. 'Your mouth, that is.'

'Alright, you clowns,' said Agent Haigh, 'that's enough. Either you can it, or you're both out of here.'

The commissario raised his hand like a naughty boy in class.

'*Permesso*?' he said with exaggerated meekness.

'What!?' said Macolm Haigh, his face beginning to redden.

'Please,' said Bonifati, 'can Tom, who – correct me if I am wrong – does have jurisdiction here, ask a few simple questions on my behalf?'

'What about?'

'The murder of a British citizen in my country.'

'Richetti?'

'*Si.* We need to know if Mrs Gladstone ever heard the names of certain people we are interested in. If perhaps they might have visited her husband here?'

The agent looked puzzled.

'You think it may be connected in some way?'

The Italian shrugged. 'We don't ask, we don't find out.'

Bonifati started chuckling to himself.

'What?' said Caton.

'Can it,' he said. 'What does he think this is, Chicago in the Prohibition?'

Caton smiled. 'And he's Elliot Ness.'

'Those lights for the helicopter,' said the Italian.

'What about them?'

'If Giambotta left by helicopter, who put the lights back in the barn?'

It was a good question. One that had evaded Caton.

'His wife, presumably,' he replied.

'And left the children alone in the house?'

'It wouldn't have taken that long. And there are those dogs. If anyone had approached the house…'

'Mmm,' said Bonifati.

'At least he has some kind of conscience,' said Caton.

The Italian stopped and stared at him.

'What do you mean?'

'Giving her the majority shareholding. Putting the house in her name.'

Bonifati laughed, and started walking again.

'This company is what you call cover, that's all. Did you see the last year accounts?'

Caton had. The turnover was £2.6 million. From the buying, selling and renting of property. The net profit was £390,000, before tax. The tax would include capital gains as well as income tax. That would have put their net disposable income somewhere between one hundred, and one hundred and fifty thousand pounds. He could see where Umberto was coming from. It was not to be sneezed at, but hardly put them on the rich list.

'But the company assets are shown as £2.2 million,' he replied. 'All in the form of property.'

Bonifati shook his head. '*Come si dice*? Chickens' feed?'

'Chickenfeed.'

'Not enough to get your taxmen interested. They got a respectable firm of English accountants. Their taxes paid. Everything clean. In the open.'

Bonifati stopped and looked at him over the roof of the car.

'The real money, the big money, is somewhere else, Tom.   Other companies. Run for him, on his *instruzione* by members of his clan.'

'How do you know all this, Umberto? And why isn't there an officer of the *Direzione Investigativa Antimafia* here? Why you, not them?'

He shrugged. 'Who knows? Maybe they prefer to surprise him when he gets off the plane? Me, I just happen to be here already. I told you.'

He opened the door, and lowered himself into the passenger seat.

Caton looked back towards the farmhouse. Dawn

had broken, the rain had ceased, and the security lights had been turned off. The dogs were lying down watching members of the search team carrying sealed boxes from the house, and loading them into the boots of the two lead cars.

It reminded Caton of the original footage of Linslade Farm in the aftermath of the Great Train Robbery. Then, as now, the suspects had flown. The money had disappeared. An innocent woman, with young children, left to face the music.

He wondered if it would take as long to find Alfredo Giambotta, aka Freddy Gladstone. And if, like Ronnie Biggs, he would flee again, to live another secret life with yet another wife.

Above all, he wondered when Umberto Bonifati would tell him what was really going on.

Chapter 32

Umberto had asked to be dropped off at his hotel. Caton guessed that he wanted the freedom to make some phone calls without the possibility that he might be overheard, either by Caton himself, or by Caterina Volpe.

Caton lowered his window.

'Give me a call when you want picking up,' Caton said. 'If I'm free I'll pick you up myself, if not, I'll send a car.'

'*Perfetto,*' said Bonifati, turning to go.

Caton had come to realise that the commissario had developed a habit of retreating behind his native Italian whenever he wanted to avoid uncomfortable topics, or to formalise the conversation. Which amounted to the same thing. Not that it made it difficult for Caton to engage; it was more of a subtle signal. Conscious or otherwise. In this instance, Caton guessed that it was shorthand for: *Don't bother to ask me what I'll be doing because I'm not going to tell you.*

'What do you want me to tell Sovrintendente Volpe?' he called after him.

Bonifati stopped and turned.

'*Niente*, Tom, *niente di niente.*'

'Nothing at all?'

He sighed. 'Okay. That I am freshening up. That I'll explain when I see her. *Va bene?*'

'Alright, Umberto,' Caton replied. *'Va bene.'*

The Italian walked off towards the hotel entrance. As he reached the door, and without looking back, he raised his hand and waved, before disappearing into the building. Caton saw it as neither a friendly gesture nor a dismissal. It was just to let him know that he knew he was sitting there watching him. And that he knew what Caton was thinking.

Sovrintendente Volpe saw Caton enter the Incident Room and came straight over. He suspected that she had been waiting, and watching, for them to arrive.

'Chief Inspector Caton,' she said. *'Dov'è* Commissario Bonifati?'

'He told me,' Caton replied in Italian, 'to tell you that he was freshening up at your hotel. He'll phone when he's ready, and I'll go and get him.'

He could tell that she wasn't fooled. She took in his bedraggled hair and the spatters of dried mud on his trousers.

'Dove sei stato?' she said. *'Qui nessuno lo sa.'*

Where have you been? No one here seems to know.

Instinctively Caton replied in English.

'He said he'll tell you himself when he gets here, Sovrintendente.'

She gave a snort of disbelief and then quickly recovered. In the instant that she regained her composure, a flicker in her eyes told him that she knew he had caught her out. That he now knew her English was much better than he had been led to believe. That hadn't been his intention, at least not consciously, but it confirmed what he had come to suspect.

She did not bother to pretend otherwise, but turned on her heel and sashayed back to the desk that it seemed someone had allocated as her temporary base.

Heads turned to watch her pass. DC Hulme's and Douggie Wallace's among them. Caton was glad the Italian connection was but a temporary one. There were enough distractions as it was.

Half an hour later, and deep into a Monthly Activity Report, Caton was disturbed by a knock on his partition wall. Umberto Bonifati's grinning face appeared around the side of the panel opening.

'*Sorpreso*!' he exclaimed.

Caton was indeed surprised. He waved him in. Bonifati plonked down opposite him.

'Umberto, I told you to call me,' Caton said. 'How did you get here?'

'I walked. The rain is gone. It is a lovely day.'

It was true. The temperature had climbed to the mid-seventies, and there was barely a cloud in the sky.

'Has Sovrintendente Volpe seen you?' Caton asked.

The commissario leaned forward, and lowered his voice, pretending conspiracy.

'Your Ged tells me she is visiting *il gabinetto*.'

'Loo,' Caton told him. 'I hope, for your sake, she's in a better humour when she returns.'

Bonifati placed his hands behind his head and rocked back perilously in his chair.

'Not to worry, Tom, she will be fine.'

'Have you heard from Malcolm Haigh?' Caton asked.

'The bird is flown,' he replied.

'We know that. The question is, *where* has the bird flown to?'

Bonifati raised his hands, palm up, towards the ceiling.

'Air Traffic Control must know,' said Caton. 'They'll have had to file a flight plan. And a helicopter is not exactly a stealth plane, is it?'

'They did,' said Bonifati.

'Did what?'

'File a flight plan.'

Caton sat up.

'I thought no private helicopter flights are allowed at night.'

'They are not.'

The Italian fished a notebook from his pocket, found the page he was looking for, and slid it across the table. There was single line of text.

Eurocopter EC135, 135kph 6 seater, PAA

'What is this?' said Caton.

'A Private Helicopter Air Ambulance. It was requested at 21.15 hours last night. To take a patient with a heart condition to the John Radcliffe Hospital in Ox ford' He pronounced it as two separate words.

'Oxford?'

Bonifati nodded. 'The patient's name was Frederick Gladstone. The fee was paid immediately by electronic transfer.'

'Does he have a heart condition?'

'No. And *Signor* Haigh says the hospital in Oxford was not expecting him.'

'So what did he do? Just get out at the other end and walk away?'

Bonifati smiled. '*Esatto*. The helipad is on the ground. He said he could manage. He walked towards the entrance.'

'Then what?'

'Nobody knows. Why would they?'

Why Oxford? Caton launched Google Earth on his screen, with The John Radcliffe at its locus. Then he zoomed out and used the site ruler to calculate the distance between the farm and the helipad. One hundred and thirty-seven miles. Approximately two hundred and twenty kilometres. He tore off a sheet from his memo pad as Umberto Bonifati watched with an expression of faint amusement.

'According to his wife,' said Caton, 'he left at 10.20 p.m. Allowing for a slower night-time cruising speed, say one hundred kilometres per hour, it would take just over two hours.'

He looked up.

'He'd have got there about 12.30 a.m. in the morning.'

'12.18 a.m.,' said the Italian.

'You could have told me,' said Caton.

'You did not ask.'

Caton shook his head, and zoomed out a fraction from the hospital.

'The helipad is just a third of a mile from the A40,' he said. 'It's just six miles to the M40 motorway. Where was he going?'

He zoomed out again. If he had been warned about the raid and was leaving the country, there were a number of possibilities. Plenty of ferry ports on the south coast. But he'd be too early for the morning ferry. But then there was Heathrow Airport forty-six miles away, and just one hundred and twenty-five miles to the Channel Tunnel. At that time in the morning, motorway all the way, he'd have been at the Channel Terminal in well under two hours.

'What time did Mal Haigh send out the all-ports warning?' he said.

'*Non lo so*,' said Bonifati.

Neither did Caton, but it couldn't have been any earlier than about 5.30 a.m. when they discovered he had gone.

Caton Googled the Eurostar timetables. The first one in the morning was 3.27 a.m. The next one was 5.28 a.m. He could have been on either of them. Or on a plane. But if he had, then surely Mal Haigh would know by now. And why the subterfuge? Why hadn't he boarded a flight from Liverpool or Manchester?

'Were there no reports of him having boarded a flight, or the Eurostar?' he asked.

'*Qui?*' said Caterina Volpe from the doorway. '*Chi è andato su un aereo, o su un treno?*'

Caton pushed back his chair and stood up.

'Sovrintendente,' he said. 'Please excuse me. I have something to see to. Commissario Bonifati will explain.'

She stepped aside to let him pass.

Caton peered over the top of the partition. Caterina Volpe was sitting down beside her boss who, with one hand literally behind her back, was giving Caton the sign of the horns.

Chapter 33

Malcolm Haigh was not best pleased at having been disturbed.

'Egg all over our faces,' he said. 'The only question is, where did the leak come from? From them or from us?' He laughed down the line. 'You don't need to be psychic to know the answer to that one.'

'That phone call he received,' said Caton. 'If you know who that was from, you'll probably get your answer.'

'Only trouble is, we have no idea what mobile number he's using, and the caller probably used a pay-as-you-go throwaway phone. You know how it works, Tom.'

'You can still get them to analyse the traffic in and out of Blackrod.'

'We've got GCHQ onto that,' he replied. 'They'll give us something in time. Trouble is, we're not first on their waiting list. A European Arrest Warrant isn't up there with International Terrorism.'

'What's the stuff on his hard drives looking like?' said Caton, hoping to cheer him up.

'Wiped clean. Only he didn't have time for more than one pass of the erase software. Our guys will be able to recover most of it. It'll take time to analyse, but that's for the Italians to do. It was their warrant.'

'Does the Border Agency have any record of him having left?'

Caton heard him sigh.

'No one using the names Gladstone or Giambotta,' he said. 'There were two Italian businessmen, one accompanied by a woman, on the 5.28 Eurostar to Paris. One Italian, about the same age as our man, on the 5 a.m. Easy Jet flight from Gatwick to Amsterdam. After that it gets crazy. Between 5.30 a.m. and 7 a.m., thirty-seven Italian males left the country by Eurostar or from airports within an hour and a half drive of the John Radcliffe.'

'He could just as easily have used a false British passport,' Caton pointed out.

'True, but more problematic,' said Hulme wearily. 'We're trying to narrow it down by getting a list of anyone who booked their ticket at the last minute. Basically, between the time he got that phone call and the final check-in.'

'Then again,' said Caton, 'maybe he's still here. Just gone to ground somewhere else. He's managed to get away with it all these years. What's to say he doesn't have another wife somewhere down south?'

'And on that happy note,' said the agent, 'I'm off. Giambotta will have to wait for another day. Let's just hope they haven't screwed up with the other one.'

'Other one?' said Caton. 'What other one?'

'Hasn't Bonifati told you? They've sent us another warrant. Someone, as it happens, who's recently come to our attention, as well as theirs.'

'No, he didn't.'

'Well, you'd better ask him yourself then.'

'Don't worry,' said Caton, 'I will.'

'I was going to tell you, Tom,' said Bonifati, 'but you went off somewhere.'

It was a convenient lie, Caton decided. There was clearly another reason he was not willing to divulge.

'You can tell me now,' he said.

They were sitting, at the Italian detective's insistence, on the bench in front of the Fujitsu building. Bonifati was smoking; it was the excuse that he had used for them to step outside the confines of the Headquarters building.

'This one is more important,' he said. He stabbed the air with his cigarette. *'Molto più importante.'*

A centimetre portion of white ash dropped onto his trouser leg. He brushed it off as though swatting a fly.

'Un male bastardo, Tom.'

He raised the cigarette, inhaled deeply and then exhaled through his nose.

'Veramente terribile!'

'The Ndrangheta?' said Caton. 'Like Giambotta?'

Bonifati turned to face him.

'No, Tom. He is head of a Camorra clan, from Campania. From Napoli.'

'There's no connection between them then?'

The Italian laughed, took a final drag on his cigarette, threw the butt on the floor, and ground it beneath his heel.

'Ndrangheta, Camorra, they hate each other, and fear each other. They circle, like wild dogs, watching their backs.'

'And do you think this one may have had something to do with Guido Richetti's death?'

He shrugged. 'Like I say to Agent Haigh, who's to know? It's possible. But we don't ask…'

'We don't find out,' said Caton.

The Italian stood up. Caton joined him.

'Where and when is this one going to happen, Umberto?'

Bonifati stared back impassively. Behind those blue-grey eyes his brain was carrying out a risk assessment. Caton waited patiently.

'The SOCA team will be nearby,' he said at last. 'From 7 o'clock this evening. As soon as it is confirmed that he is there, the order will be given.'

'Whereabouts?'

'A place called Marple Ridge. You know it?'

Caton did. He had walked on the moors out that way with Kate. And before that, on his own.

'Are we invited?'

Bonifati spread his arms wide.

'*Naturalmente.*' Spoken as though anything else would have been unthinkable.

After this morning's debacle Caton could only conclude that his instincts had been right. Commissario Bonifati had a hell of a lot more influence than he liked to pretend.

'In which case I have to go home and get changed,' Caton told him. 'I smell like a wet dog.'

They started walking back towards the Divisional Headquarters.

'Will Sovrintendente Volpe be coming with us this time?'

'*Naturalmente.*'

It was not what Caton expected.

'Just one thing, Tom,' said the commissario, stopping and laying one hand on his arm. 'I have not told her yet.'

'I understand,' said Caton, not really understanding at all. 'I won't tell anyone else either. No one at all.'

Bonifati smiled. '*Bene,*' he said. '*Molto bene. E grazie,* Tom.'

They resumed their walk.

'Thank *you*, Umberto,' Caton replied.

'What for?'

'For trusting me.'

The Italian chuckled. 'Why would I not?'

Exactly what Caton had been wondering.

'In return, I'll do you a favour, and give you a warning,' he said.

Bonifati stopped in his tracks and, with apprehension, studied Caton's face.

'*Avvertimento*? *Che avvertimento*?'

Caton leaned closer, and lowered his voice.

'In England, dropping litter, including cigarette butts, is liable to an on-the-spot fine.'

Bonifati roared with laughter. He slapped Caton on the shoulder and then thumped the palm of his left hand with his fist to indicate mock rage.

'In *Italia* too!' he exclaimed. 'Is nowhere safe?'

Kate was home, marking assignments online.

'Tom!' she exclaimed. 'You look dreadful!'

'Thanks a bunch,' he said.

'Don't take those trousers off in the bedroom,' she ordered. 'Put them straight in the washing machine.'

He walked towards the kitchen.

'I'll just rinse them off and run them through the spin drier,' he said.

'You'll do no such thing!'

She came up behind him, waited until he'd taken the trousers off, and then seized hold of them.

Standing there in his underpants, he felt like a naughty little boy.

'It's only a flying visit,' he explained. 'I've got to go back.'

'Oh, Tom!' she said. 'You've already done over eleven hours. What is it this time?'

'Another European Arrest Warrant.'

She pulled a face. 'This is getting ridiculous. I'll be glad when Bonifati and his shadow have beggared off back to Venice, and you can concentrate on home-grown murder and rape.'

It didn't sound right coming from the lips of this lovely, kind and very pregnant woman. But he knew what she meant. And he agreed with her. It was beginning to get him down too. In a way he was starting to experience what Caterina Volpe must be feeling. Bonifati was acting like a puppet master, which made them what exactly? Marionettes? Dummies?

'At least get your head down for a couple of hours,' Kate pleaded. 'I'll make you something to eat when you wake up.'

'I can't,' he told her. 'I'm picking them up from the hotel in half an hour.'

She shook her head in disbelief.

'When are you going to eat? What did you have for lunch?'

Before he could think of a plausible lie, Caton's face had already betrayed him.

'Oh, Tom! For God's sake.'

'It's alright,' he assured her. 'The three of us are going for a meal first. A proper meal.'

She eyed the knives in the knife block.

'You'd better get out of here. And put some trousers on,' she said, 'before I do something I might regret.'

Chapter 34

He'd given them two options: Italian, or Spanish tapas. Caterina Volpe had been characteristically indifferent. Her boss had surprised him by pointing out that he could get plenty of proper Italian cooking at home. So they had ended up at Murillos, in the heart of Marple. It turned out to be an excellent choice. He and Umberto had gone for one of the set menus, with the standard weekday and evenings fifty per cent discount. Caterina Volpe had opted for a vegetarian menu. At £15 a head, it was a veritable feast.

'*Questo è fantastico!*' exclaimed Bonifati, twirling a piece of duck magret in orange sauce, one of twelve tapas set before the two of them. '*Sapori meravigliosi.*'

Even Caterina appeared to be enjoying her baked aubergines in tomato sauce. A dish that it would have been so easy to dismiss as inferior to the classic Italian version.

Caton forked the remaining slice of sirloin steak in peppercorn sauce, before it could fall into the clutches of the insatiable commissario.

'I'm glad you're enjoying it,' he said. 'There are not many places that start serving at 5 p.m. And certainly not ones of this quality.'

Umberto poured another glass of red wine, swirled it around in the candlelight, and drank half of it.

'A pity you are driving, Tom,' he said. 'This is also

molto buono.'

Bonifati had waited until his colleague was in the car before he told her where they were going, and why. Caton had watched in the rear-view mirror for her reaction. Her expression had remained impassive throughout. It confirmed two suspicions that had deepened over the past two days: the commissario did not trust his sovrintendente, and she was exceptionally good at hiding her feelings when it mattered most.

An hour later, they were ready to leave. Sated, and in Bonifati's case extremely cheery. He insisted on visiting the delicatessen area to sample the speciality cheeses and wafer-thin slices of Iberico and Serrano ham. He arrived at the table with a brown paper carrier bag stocked with Torta de Trujillo, Chorizo and an artisan loaf.

'For breakfast in my room,' he explained. 'I hope your boot is nice and cold, Tom.'

Caton had a flashback to Kate's expression when he'd told her that he was going out again. He flashed forward to the kind of reception he might expect on his return. He looked at his watch.

'Chat among yourselves' he said, and headed for the deli.

Five minutes later, he returned with a bag of his own, and a bottle of Rioja. Hopefully the contents of the bag would make all the difference. If not, at least he'd be able to drown his sorrows with the wine.

It was a four-minute stroll back to Memorial Park where he had left his car outside the library. The rest of the Arrest Team were parked up twenty metres away outside the police station. There were an extra two vans this time, Caton noticed. Did this mean that they were expecting resistance, or that there were many more exits to cover?

They put their bags in the boot and got in the car. Caton switched on his AirWave radio, and tuned into the channel they had been given. There was no traffic, just a clear indication that the channel was live. He pressed the transmit button.

'*Red Kites in place*,' he said. Ordinarily he would have found this use of code bizarre and unnecessary, but after last night he could understand why Haigh was taking no risks.

'*Eagle, Roger that*,' came the reply. '*Good of you to join us.*'

'*You're welcome*,' said Caton, ignoring the sarcasm.

He wound his seat back into a restful incline.

'I'd make yourselves comfortable too,' he told his passengers. 'We could be here for some time.'

'*Eagle to all Nests. The Cuckoo has returned. I repeat, the Cuckoo has returned.*'

Caton sat up, and began to lever his seat upright. He was having trouble getting used to the Boy Scout codes the agency insisted on using. Then again, maybe it was just Mal Haigh who felt the need to adopt them. At least with Gold, Silver and Bronze Commands you knew who the hell you were speaking to, instead of having to remember who was the Eagle, and who the Sparrow Hawk.

He could see in the rear-view mirror that Caterina Volpe was awake. Her colleague was flat out and snoring loudly. Caton shook him. Bonifati jerked awake.

'*Ma che cazzo!?*' he exclaimed, so violently that it didn't require translation.

He rubbed his eyes, levered himself upright, and stared accusingly at Caton.

'It's on, Umberto,' Caton said. 'The Cuckoo has returned.'

221

Engines started, and the lead car pulled away. Caton watched as the convoy passed them by. As they rounded the library, he tacked on at the end. They left the park and turned onto the A626. Almost immediately, just outside Marple Bridge, they turned right onto Longhurst Lane. A mile later, the convoy stopped alongside a hedged field between a farm and a row of detached houses.

Beyond a copse of trees he could see the odd car winding its way up Glossop Road. Three hundred metres to the south-west, hidden by a wood, lay Roman Bridge Lake. Quite apt, he reflected, given the two Italians in his car, and another that was their quarry. Very soon the sun would sink below the horizon in the west, and the moors would become a shadow against the night sky.

'I hope it's not another farm,' he said.

'*Almeno non pioveva,*' said Bonifati.

No, at least it wasn't raining. Turning up drenched and mud-spattered yet again would definitely have cancelled out whatever brownie points the bag of Spanish goodies might have earned him with Kate.

'I think, Umberto, that it's time you told me the name on the arrest warrant,' said Caton. 'And what he's wanted for.'

'*Anchio,*' said Caterina Volpe, leaning forward.

Me too.

So her boss still hadn't told her. Curiouser and curiouser, just like Alice in Wonderland.

'His name is Salvio Pistone,' said Bonifati. 'Among his associates he is known as *Il Carciofo.*'

'The Artichoke?' said Caton. 'Why so?'

He smiled. 'Because with the *carciofo* you can eat the leaves and the heart. *Signor* Pistone is said to have dined on the heart, liver and kidneys of several of his victims.'

'And did he?'

He replied with his characteristic shrug. 'Who knows? The source is reliable. One of his trusted lieutenants, whom he can no longer trust. Turned *pentito* to save himself.'

'An informant, will say anything to reduce his sentence, especially when it's likely to be life. How do you know that he's reliable?'

The smile broadened into a grin. 'Because, my dear Tom, he is why we are sitting right here, *in quest' auto.* He gave us Pistone's new name, and this address.'

'What is Pistone wanted for?' asked Caton.

Before the commissario could reply, his assistant asked him to translate. As Bonifati did so, Caton reflected that these requests were yet again becoming increasingly few and far between. When the commissario had finished, he turned his attention to Caton's question.

'Everything that was on the warrant for Giambotta, plus a little extra. *Lo smaltimento non autorizzato di rifiuti illegali.*'

He hammered on the car's fascia with the palm of his hand.

'*Bastardo!*'

The unauthorised disposal of illegal waste. Caton wasn't the least bit surprised. One of the most contentious and visible expressions of criminality across Italy, nowhere was it more evident than in the south. It was even suggested that the mountains of domestic waste in the streets of Naples were less the result of industrial disputes than the diversion of those workers to dump toxic industrial waste on the surrounding farmland.

If he remembered rightly, the head of one Camorra clan, and thirty-five of his associates, had been sentenced about five years ago for dumping millions of tonnes of such waste in lakes and quarries, on farmland, in caves, even behind a sports field. During the several trials, five people had been murdered, one of whom was a court interpreter.

The trade came to light when the cousin of the head of the clan was struck by remorse and became a *pentito*. A super informant. In addition to naming names, he provided details of the dumps, because he believed that if the waste was not removed and continued to seep into the water table, it would kill everyone living in the vicinity within twenty years. Caton had read that in the past twenty years, cancer rates in the towns surrounding the city of Naples had indeed risen by almost fifty per cent, and were accelerating.

'*Bastardo!*' Bonifati repeated. 'They dump around Venezia too,' he said.

'*Il Parco San Giuliano,*' said Caterina Volpe suddenly, surprising them both. '*Fuori Marghera.*'

'*Che avevo dimenticato,*' said Bonifati, striking his forehead with an open palm. '*Sono scorie nucleari!*'

Nuclear waste in a park outside Venice? Caton wondered how he would feel if he learned that criminal gangs had polluted the water that his son and unborn child would drink, the land on which their food was grown, the air they breathed. It was hardly surprising that the tide was beginning to turn against these gangs in Italy itself, forcing some of them to flee abroad.

The sound of the radio interrupted his thoughts.

'*Eagle to all nests. The hunt begins. I repeat, the hunt begins.*'

Caton shook his head in disbelief. The whole point of the TETRA system was that criminals could not listen in. Even if they had been able to, what message would they have taken from this nonsense? That a group of ornithologists were out doing a head count of endangered species? Or, more feasibly, that some villains close by, probably themselves, were about to be raided? He started the engine and watched as the sidelights of the other vehicles came on.

The first two vehicles set off. As soon as their tail lights had disappeared, the remainder of the convoy moved away. Caton slipped into gear, eased off the clutch and followed.

Chapter 35

This time there were no dogs. No mud. No barns. No helipad. Just a faux Georgian redbrick four-bedroom detached house behind a four-foot yew hedge. Security lights came on automatically as the lead car swung into the drive. The occupants of the second vehicle disembarked as soon as it came to a halt and split into two teams of three, one of which jogged left, the other right, to the rear of the building.

There was no room left for Caton to park in the drive, so he did so on the road outside. The three of them walked up the drive and waited, as agreed, behind one of the Tactical Aid Unit vans.

After waiting for over a minute, listening to the hammering on the door and shouted demands that someone open up, Caton decided to go and have a look for himself. Bonifati and Caterina Volpe followed close behind.

It was an appropriate moment. Agent Haigh had had enough. On his signal the Enforcer was swung in a tight arc, striking the door just below the mortice lock. The door shivered, and the faceplate broke through the plastic outer skin and became jammed.

They heard a woman scream. And then a torrent of invective.

'Stand away from the door,' shouted the leader of the Tactical Aid Team.

The officer twisted the ram until he was able to tug it free and take another swing. This time the door flew open. It hung at a drunken angle from the topmost hinge.

'Armed police!' shouted the first two riflemen as they burst into the hall, closely followed by a colleague.

The screaming intensified.

There were shouts from the rear of the property, urgent but indistinct.

The screams subsided.

They waited on the doorstep for the Firearms Incident Commander to give them permission to enter. After what seemed an age, he nodded to Malcolm Haigh.

'It's all clear,' he said. 'But there's no sign of the Cuckoo.'

Angela Benefico, née Travis, was standing in the lounge, her back to the mantelpiece above an unlit multi-fuel burner. On either side of her stood two members of the Armed Response Team, their weapons across their chests, angled towards the ceiling.

She was in her late forties, stocky and a little too masculine in looks to be considered attractive. Her layer-cut blonde hair, immaculate make-up and the shiny gold jacket over matching evening trousers would have more than made up for it, Caton thought, but for the crossed arms and the look of fierce defiance on her face.

'Going out are we, Mrs Benefico?' said Malcolm Haigh.

'What's it to you?' she replied.

'You've been shown the warrant,' he said, 'so don't mess me around. Where's your husband?'

'Out.'

'Out where?'

She shrugged. 'I don't know. On business.'

Her blue-grey eyes held his with that cold empty stare common to practised liars. What none of them seemed to realise was that it was the stare that was the giveaway.

'Funny that,' said Agent Haigh, 'because your husband was observed entering this house fifteen minutes ago. He was not observed leaving.'

'Funny that,' she said, 'because I've been here all evening, and I'm telling you he isn't here.' She smirked. 'Your observer must have been mistaken.'

'His car is in the drive.'

'I dropped him off in Manchester. He'll get a taxi back.'

'The engine of his car is still warm. The fan was still going when we arrived.'

'He asked me to let it run for a bit. The battery was getting low.'

'You've got an answer for everything, haven't you?' said Haigh.

She smirked again. 'I do my best. Now, why don't you all piss off?'

'This is your last chance, Angela,' he said. 'Where is he?'

'It's *Mrs Benefico* to you,' she said calmly. 'Now why don't you all bugger off, and while you're at it, send someone to fix that door before we sue the arse off you.'

She looked around at the sea of faces, as though committing them to memory.

'Come to think of it,' she said, 'we'll be doing that anyway.'

'Fair enough,' said Haigh.

He turned to the inspector in charge of the Tactical Aid Search Team.

'Let's have the dog in here.'

Caton watched her face. At the mention of the dog, the carefully constructed facade crumbled for an instant and was replaced by an expression of alarm. Just a flicker, but enough to signal that she had been lying. He was still here, somewhere.

They waited no more than a minute. Just enough time for one of the team to slip upstairs and return with a man's shirt taken from the laundry basket on the upstairs landing.

The dog was a Springer spaniel, white with patches of reddish brown. For a moment Caton thought it must be Roddy, the legendary King of the Kennels, famed for his work at Manchester Airport. Then he remembered reading that Roddy had been retired. The handler knelt and held the shirt out for the dog to sniff. Then she stood.

'Find!' she commanded, and he was off.

It took a little under five minutes. Caton thought it remarkable, given the hiding place. It was one of those houses where the space beneath the stairs had been boxed in. A door provided entry to what appeared to be a cloakroom and store. Anoraks hung from hooks on the inside wall, together with a cloth tube full of plastic throwaway supermarket bags. There was a small set of stepladders, an ironing board and a Dyson ball hoover. At the farthest end, where the roof sloped steeply, had stood a twelve-bottle wine rack full of wine. The wine rack had been removed and the loose strip of carpet lifted to reveal a wooden trapdoor set in the solid asphalt floor. A set of stone steps led downwards. The dog sat proudly beside the hole, a yellow ball clutched in its mouth.

The space was cleared, and Malcolm Haigh, the Firearms Commander and two of his men approached the trapdoor. Caton stood in the doorway watching.

'Armed police!' shouted Agent Haigh.

They listened to the words echo around the walls below.

'If you have a weapon, place it on the floor and kick it to the foot of these steps. If not, clasp your hands behind your head and walk towards the steps until I tell you to stop.'

They listened again. There was no response. Haigh wanted to go down himself, but the Incident Commander argued that it was out of the question. His men would go down first. When it was clear, then the agent could follow. It was decided.

Haigh gave the fugitive one more chance to show himself, and then a camera was lowered a foot or so into the cellar. They saw, on the tablet to which it was connected, a large room, half the size of the lounge in which they had stood, with a doorway at the far end. The room was empty.

The first of the riflemen descended the steps, followed closely by his colleague. Less than a minute later one of the riflemen appeared at the foot of the steps.

'It's clear down here,' he said. 'It's like a nuclear bomb shelter. There's another set of steps that leads up to an outhouse. He's left the trapdoor open that end, so he can't have got far.'

It took the dog five minutes to track him down. Now he was standing on the opposite side of the room to his wife, flanked by two more of the Armed Response officers.

'He was playing hide-and-seek in a wood on the other side of Knowle Road,' the handler told them. 'One of Jack's favourite games,' she said cheerfully, stroking the dog's head. 'Especially in the woods.'

'We searched the back thoroughly,' said one of the riflemen. 'Including the outhouse. He must still have been in the cellar at that point.'

'It's alright,' said Malcolm Haigh. 'Important thing is Mr Benefico has finally come home. Or should that be Mr Pistone?'

The husband and wife began to speak rapidly to each other in a dialect that Caton assumed must be the fabled Napoletano. The first consonant of many of the words was being doubled up. He had not the slightest chance of following any of it. He looked to the commissario for a clue. The slight shake of Bonifati's head told him not to ask.

'In English, please,' said the agent.

They ignored him. He let it run for another thirty seconds or so, and finally lost his patience.

'English!' he bellowed. 'Or the two of you will be taken into separate rooms.'

Caton thought that would have been the sensible thing to do from the start, but at least this had the desired effect. They both shut up.

'That's better,' said Haigh. 'Now, Mr Benefico, perhaps we can get this over with.'

Chapter 36

Caton studied the man standing before them. He was tall and thin, with a hawk-like profile. More Arab than Italian. More eagle than cuckoo. He tried to recall what Bonifati had told them in the car.

Salvio Pistone, 63 years of age. Aka Pietro Benefico. Peter the Beneficent. His wife, Angela Travis, was 47, and therefore sixteen years his junior. They met at a charity do in Stockport. She was selling raffle tickets. She had previously worked for a travel firm, and spoke enough Italian to get by. In the seven years they were married she had gained a working knowledge of the Neapolitan dialect and slang. And not just in the bedroom.

There were recordings in the possession of SOCO, the *Direzione Investigativa Antimafia*, and the Naples Flying Squad, of her conversing with Pistone's associates, clients and members of his clan with an air of authority that would place her squarely in the dock alongside her husband.

Here in Britain, he appeared to have kept his nose clean for the first five years, under the guise of co-director of an Italian textile factory supplying fabrics to the British clothing industry. Predominantly stretch fabrics for sportswear and underwear. The company was a legitimate operation, with an office in Manchester's Northern Quarter, close to Piccadilly

Station. His involvement in it was less clear, other than as a cover. In particular, it was strange that he had never travelled to Italy in the past seven years.

'My name is Pietro Benefico,' he insisted. 'I can prove it. I show you my passport, my *codice fiscale*.'

'Very well,' said Haigh with exaggerated patience. 'Where are they?'

'In the office,' he said.

He turned to his wife.

'Angela!' It was a command, not a question.

Not that she seemed the slightest bit bothered.

They waited in silence. She returned, and handed her husband his wallet and a passport. From his wallet he took out a plastic credit-card-sized card containing a unique sixteen alphanumeric digit code, and handed it together with his passport to Malcolm Haigh.

'They are both authentic,' he said.

His voice had a tone to it that Caton had heard a thousand times before. The firm, confident assurance of a guilty man playing the biggest bluff of his life, whilst knowing that it was already too late. The mere fact that he had hidden was proof enough.

Haigh handed them straight to Umberto Bonifati, who didn't even bother to look at them. Instead, he held them away from him with two fingers, as though not wishing to be contaminated by them.

'*Autentica*?' he said. '*Certo, che sono autentici. Ma onesto? Genuino*?' He laughed in mock amusement. '*Assolutamente no!*'

He opened his fingers and let the documents fall to the floor.

It was evident from the expressions on the faces of both Pistone and his wife that neither of them had realised there was an Italian speaker present. They glared at each other. If Caton could have put a word to that glance it would have contained just four letters.

'I'm sorry,' said Haigh. 'I forgot to introduce Commissario Bonifati of the *Polizia Di Stato*.'

Angela Benefico crossed herself and spat on the floor in front of the commissario.

'*llievace 'o mmale 'a tuorno,*' she hissed.

Bonifati smiled thinly. 'Deliver us from evil,' he said. 'In your case, I think it is a little late for that, *signora*, don't you?'

'Did you understand a word of what they were saying?' asked Caton.

The house had been thoroughly searched. Documents, software and hardware identified in the Search Warrant accompanying the European Arrest Warrant had been seized, boxed and labelled. Petro Pistone and Angela Benefico were in separate vans on their way back to Manchester for processing. Caton was following behind, with the two Italian detectives

Bonifati smiled. 'Of course. It's not so difficult when you've heard it spoken as often as I have. Even if you haven't, the average Italian will get the gist of it.'

'That's why you warned me not to ask,' said Caton.

He nodded. 'It is also why *Signor* Haigh allowed them to be in the same room together.'

'You knew they would try to get their story straight?'

'Not knew, Tom, hoped.'

'You cunning beggar.'

'Cunning?' said Bonifati. 'What is cunning?'

Caton hooked a finger beneath his left eye and pulled the eyelid down.

'*Furbo,*' he replied. 'Crafty, sly, tricky, shrewd, artful and cunning.'

The Italian laughed. '*Anche tu, penso.*'

You too, I think.

234

He raised both hands in the air.

'*Naturalmente*, Tom. We are policemen. It is what we do.'

Caton found it impossible to argue with that.

'So what else is there you haven't told me?' he said.

The commissario angled himself so that he could see Caton more clearly, and vice versa.

'*Niente*, my friend. Nothing at all.'

Caton glanced at him.

'Well,' Bonifati continued, 'hardly anything at all.'

He settled back in his seat.

'There was only one record of an Italian citizen by the name of Pietro Benefico. This person's *codice fiscale* – the fiscal code issued by the *Agenzia Delle Entrate*, the Italian revenue agency, to every Italian following registration of a birth, and used to identify them henceforth – matched that in the possession of Salvio Pistone, and was recorded in his passport. It was, like the rest of his story, a *falsificazione totale*.'

Caton nodded. 'A complete fabrication,' he said.

'*Si.* There was no such person.'

He turned to look over his shoulder at his colleague, who appeared to be dozing. He turned back, and lowered his voice to a whisper.

'Someone in the *Agenzia Delle Entrate* suspected of having created hundreds of these false identities is under observation. In time, that person will be arrested. Now is not the time.'

Caton understood that it would best serve the purpose of the authorities to track each new creation as it appeared, and let it lead them to yet another fugitive.

'Pistone has only recently come to our attention,' Bonifati continued. 'Thanks to the *pentito*.' He chuckled. 'You know the saying, Tom? Keep your friends close, your enemies closer?'

'*The Art of War*, Sun Tzu?'

The Italian detective shook his head and grinned.

'No,' he said. 'A common mistake. It was Don Corleone in The Godfather, Part Two.'

'I think you'll find it was also the title of one of the episodes of *Grand Theft Auto*,' said Caton.

Bonifati looked at him quizzically.

'You play *Grand Theft Auto*?'

'No! But one of the victims in my most recent investigation did.'

'Mmm,' said the Italian detective, who was wondering if Caton's denial had been a little too forceful.

'We have been looking for Pistone for more than six years. This *pentito* gave us the key. When your Serious and Organised Crime Organisation heard about the warrant, they contacted us.'

Caton glanced at him again. Something told him that he was still getting only half of the story.

'Why?' he said.

'Because it seems *Il Carciofo* got greedy. He began to involve himself in the supply of drugs into your country.'

'They know this for a fact, or did someone inform on him?'

'A little of each. They have enough to arrest them both, but they wanted to investigate a little further.'

'And?'

Bonifati shrugged enigmatically. 'He is wanted in Italy for many serious charges, including the murder of *competitori, pentiti, testimoni, magistrati, e procuratori*.'

That sounded to Caton like a cast-iron prior claim. Rivals, grasses, witnesses, magistrates and prosecutors. No wonder they wanted him back.

'But we are not unreasonable,' said Bonifati. 'We have agreed that you can question him for the maximum ninety-six hours, if your magistrates agree. Then, if you wish, you can charge him. But he must then come back with us.'

He laughed, more loudly than he had intended. In his rear-view mirror Caton could see Caterina Volpe stirring.

'You can have him back when we have finished with him,' said Bonifati. 'In another sixty years.'

He started laughing again.

His colleague was now sitting upright and rubbing sleep from her eyes.

'*Che c'è da ridere?*' she asked.

What's so funny?

Her boss told her.

'What about the wife?' said Caton.

'For now, *Signor* Haigh will question her, and then charge her,' he said. 'So long as we may have her when we need her. Who knows, she may be persuaded to become a *pentitio*.'

He chuckled, on and off, all the way back to Manchester.

Chapter 37

It was approaching midnight when Caton arrived home. Kate was still awake, sat up in bed reading on her Kindle.

'You shouldn't have waited up for me,' he said.

'Don't flatter yourself,' she replied. 'This one's got me intrigued, that's all.'

He sat on the edge of the bed and untied his shoelaces.

'What is it?'

'*Omertà*.'

He turned to look at her.

'Mario Puzo's final novel? What made you want to read that?'

She put the Kindle down on the duvet.

'Given your current escapade, I thought I'd give it a try. I enjoyed his other ones, especially *The Godfather* trilogy.'

He pulled off his socks, tucked one into the other, and tossed them over by the door.

'I hope you're not intending to leave them there,' she said.

He started to undo the buttons of his shirt.

'You know I'm not.'

He tugged the shirt over his head, crumpled it up, and threw it on top of the socks.

'So, what are you finding intriguing about this one?' he asked.

'That it's not in the same league as the others. It reads more like one of his non-fiction books. There's no pace or suspense.'

He stepped out of his trousers.

'Maybe it's because it was published after his death.'

She pulled a face. 'That's no excuse. He still wrote it himself.'

His underpants joined the pile by the door.

'You haven't been to the Y Club recently, have you?' she said.

He turned to face her.

'What are you trying to say?'

She smiled innocently.

'Nothing. It's just an observation.'

He picked up the pile of clothes and opened the door.

'You don't do *just* observations.'

She picked up the Kindle, and started reading again.

'Well I do now,' she said.

He dumped the clothes in the Ali Baba and put the food from the carrier bag in the fridge. The wine went in the wine rack. He would be relieved, he realised, when the baby arrived and Kate could start drinking again. Solitary drinking, in company, was not the same as sharing a bottle together. As for getting back to regular training, he promised himself that he would start the day after tomorrow. When he'd caught up on the sleep he'd missed.

The commissario and his sovrintendente spent the following two days at the regional SOCO headquarters. While they waited for the paperwork to be processed they sat in on Malcolm Haigh's interviews with Angela Benefico, assisting where appropriate, but primarily taking notes that might assist in the case against her husband.

'Not that we get very far,' he confided to Caton on his BlackBerry, late on the evening of the first day.

'What about The Artichoke?' said Caton, mindful that Bonifati's phone might not be as secure as his own, and feeling stupid in the process.

'Even worse,' he replied, 'like all of them, he thinks he is too big, too strong, too connected. But I can see in his eyes, deep down, that he knows we have him. Pistone's only hope is that he can bribe the *magistrati*, or more likely make the *pentiti* disappear.'

So much for secrecy, Caton reflected.

'Can he?' he said.

He sensed the Italian detective shrugging at the other end of the phone.

'Who knows? One of them, maybe. But not all of them. Believe me, Tom, they are queuing up to save themselves.'

'Rats on a sinking ship,' observed Caton.

'Rats?'

Caton explained.

'*Più appropriato*,' the Italian responded. 'Rats leaving ships bringed the *Peste Bubbonica* to Italy.'

'*Brought*, said Caton. And from there to the whole of the Western World.'

'*Esattamente*. What is it you English call the *peste*?'

'The Black Death.'

Bonifati rolled the words on his tongue. '*La Morta Nera*.'

'Or simply *The Plague*,' said Caton.

The commissario sighed.

'If only there was a *vaccinazione* against the *Mafioso*.'

'Or a pesticide,' said Caton.

Bonifati chuckled.

'How is your sovrintendente getting on?' Caton asked.

'Mmm,' came the reply.

'Is that good or bad?'

'*Nessuno dei due.*'

'Come on, Umberto, neither one nor the other, what kind of reply is that?'

'An honest one, *amico mio*. She listens, she makes suggestions, she writes.'

'I get the sense you're being a little hard on her,' Caton pressed.

'It is how we learn, being push-ed, is it not?'

He was beginning to sound like Hercule Poirot, but his reasoning was impossible to disagree with. It was how Caton had learned on the job. How he worked with his own team. Setting high standards. Having high expectations of them. He just hoped that they found him a great deal more encouraging than the commissario was with his assistant.

'Her English seems to be improving,' he said.

'Mmm,' Bonifati replied. 'So you noticed it too.'

It was a reflection, not a question. Caton could tell that this was not a topic he wanted to pursue.

'While the two of you are tied up with you know who, would you like me to dig a little deeper into the Richetti case?' he said. 'Or do you want me to wait till you're free to carry on with it?'

The commissario took his time considering his response.

'I am taking up a lot of your time,' he said at last. 'Do you have plenty to occupy you?'

'That's not a problem,' Caton reassured him. 'Although my paperwork is stacking up.'

'There you are then,' said the Italian. 'You do unstacking. Richetti can wait. He isn't going anywhere.'

Throughout the morning Caton worked through a stack of emails and paper-based updates, reminders and requests for information. Then he checked the case books of each of the three investigations being carried out by his team, including Joanne Stuart's.

'Patrick Nelson is on remand,' she told him. 'The search for the man who supplied him with the drugs that killed Mandy Mason is ongoing.'

'And?'

'We've distributed the e-fit to every pub and club in the city. It was also displayed at every shift briefing across GMP. Copies have been sent to individual officers' tablets. And it's on the front page of the Force newsletter.'

Caton had already seen it. Reading *Brief* was one the first things he did when he'd been away or out of circulation. It saved a lot of time trying to stay in the loop.

'You know how it is, boss,' she continued. 'In the absence of a name, it's going to be slow and methodical. You taught me that. Someone will recognise him, it's just a matter of time.'

'The trouble is,' he pointed out, 'with all this publicity, and what happened to Mandy, he's going to lie low. Maybe even move out of the area.'

'Well, it's been circulated nationwide too. And there haven't been any more fatalities.'

That was something at least, but Caton knew it wouldn't last. So long as there was profit to be made, and kids prepared to risk their lives for the promise of an hour or so of euphoria, of escape from whatever reality depressed them, there would be more deaths like Mandy Mason's.

'Has DCI Lounds stayed in touch?' he asked.

She grimaced. 'Only to let me know not to bother my pretty little head, because the Drugs Team would soon track him down.'

'At least he said *pretty*.'

'Actually, he didn't,' she said. 'That was artistic licence on my part. But he did call me *sweetheart*.' She grinned. 'Don't worry, boss, he'll get his comeuppance.'

Caton didn't doubt it. He grabbed a pastie and an apple from the canteen and took them back to the Incident Room. There were still several mind-numbing audit reports to complete, and the team's expense claims to sign off.

Every half hour or so he checked the time. It didn't help it to pass any quicker, quite the reverse. He was just wishing something, anything at all, would happen to give him an excuse to get out of there, when the phone rang.

'It's the Assistant Chief Constable, Crime,' Ged told him. 'It sounds urgent.'

'Caton!' said Martin Hadfield. 'Is that Italian still with you?'

'I take it you mean Commissario Bonifati, sir?'

'If that's his name. Is he still with you?'

'He's over at the SOCO/NCA regional office in Warrington. Following up on the execution of the European Arrest Warrant last night. He's interviewing the suspects, along with their own agents.'

'Bugger!' exclaimed the ACC. 'Well, tell him we need him over at Birch Services. Better still, you can pick him up and take him there.'

Caton was unsure which annoyed him most. Hadfield imagining that he could order a visiting member of a foreign force around, or that he saw his own chief inspector as part messenger boy, part chauffeur. Actually he did know; it was the latter that irritated the hell out of him.

'Commissario Bonifati is with us on attachment,' he replied coolly. 'He is actually investigating a case of his own. DCS Gates asked me to assist him.'

'Well, if you're assisting him, I can't see why he can't assist us.'

Caton imagined his blood pressure rising and his face going puce.

'Perhaps if you could tell me why you need him, I could help, sir?' he said more tactfully than the man deserved.

'Because there's a load of Italians trying to kill each other on the Birch Services!'

Now he was shouting down the phone. To be fair, Caton could see his point. He was already reaching for his jacket.

'I'll see what I can do, sir,' he said. 'In the meantime, I'll get up there myself.'

'What good will that do? Armed Response are already there. There's a Bronze Commander on the ground, and I'm Gold Commander.'

God help them, thought Caton.

'I speak Italian, sir,' he said.

'What? Oh, right. In that case you'd better get a move on. And don't forget to try and get this Benifetti up there too!'

'*Bonifati*,' said Caton, but the line was already dead.

He placed the handset back in its cradle and pushed back his chair. He was reminded of one of his aunt's favourite aphorisms: *Be careful what you wish for.*

Chapter 38

Lights flashing, siren wailing, Caton sped up the hard shoulder behind an ambulance and a paramedic car. All three lanes of the motorway were at a standstill.

According to the traffic on his AirWave radio, Hadfield's assessment had been overly optimistic. As far as Caton could make out there were already two dead and several wounded, including a police officer. Three cars were involved. One was on the Service Area itself, one was on the re-entry slip road; he wasn't sure about the other.

He had to slow down while the ambulance finally persuaded a couple of idiots to get out of the way who had decided to use the hard shoulder to jump the queue. Then he was able to drive into Birch Services itself.

It was chaos. The approach road was jammed up. He made his way slowly past the car park and was then able to speed up through the lorry park, from where he doubled back to what seemed to be the locus of the incident.

A silver Mercedes was embedded in the side of a parked Ford Taurus twenty metres from the entrance to the main concourse. Its windows were shattered. Two ambulances with their rear doors open were blocking the view of the hundreds of people gathered on the steps of the concourse trying to take photos and videos with their mobile phones. Uniformed officers and black-clad Tactical Aid officers were steadily pushing them back into the building. There seemed to be police cars and vans everywhere, their lights flashing wildly out of sync.

Caton parked up as directed. As he got out of the car he saw Umberto Bonifati waving at him from the passenger side of an unmarked car coming towards him. He waited for the car to stop, and the commissario to alight.

A uniformed sergeant approached them.

'DCI Caton?' he said.

'Yes,' he replied, 'and this is Commissario Bonifati. We're both expected.'

'Yes, sir. This way please.'

He led them to a white BMW TR3 that Caton recognised as a specially modified vehicle routinely used as a serious incident control, and pending the arrival of a mobile Comms Centre. The rear passenger doors were opened for them. One of the occupants got out. Caton and the commissario climbed in.

Commander Mike Jackson, Head of the Salford Division, was sitting in the front seat. He turned his head slightly as they entered, all the while keeping one eye on the head-up display in front of him, one ear tuned into his earpiece, the other into the open radio link with Gold Command.

'I am Bronze Commander, Tom,' he said, skipping the formalities. 'We're looking at a multiple shooting. Three cars involved in the original incident. The silver Mercedes in front of you had two up. According to witnesses, they were trying to flog high-end suits, allegedly left over from a major fashion show at GMex. One stayed in the car, the other one was approaching people. All of a sudden the one in the car yelled in Italian at his colleague, who ran to the car and got in. The car set off. Two black 4x4s, since identified as a Range Rover Evoque, and a Honda CRV…'

He broke off to listen to a message in his earpiece.

'*Roger that,*' he said. '*No offensive action. Wait on my instructions. I have a negotiator and interpreter with me now. Please confirm that you understand.*'

He listened to the reply, and then pressed a button on the console in front of him.

'*Roger that, Gold Command,*' he said. '*Both of them. With me now.*'

He sat back and continued where he had left off.

'They came tearing down the parking lane, scattering people as they came. The Mercedes had to slow at the end of the row because the Taurus suddenly pulled out in front of it. The Evoque pulled up behind it. The front passenger leaned out of the window and sprayed the Merc with what sounds like semi-automatic fire. The driver of the Merc must have slammed his foot on the accelerator, either in panic or as a reflex to being shot. His car jerked forward into the side of the Taurus. The two black 4x4s reversed at speed, and then sped off towards the exit.'

He stopped again to listen for a moment, then carried on.

'Two motorway patrol cars just happened to be parked up between the petrol pumps and the slip road. They heard the shots, saw the Evoque and the Honda tearing towards the exit, and decided to give chase. They came under fire. The driver of the Evoque must have panicked, because he misjudged his speed on re-entry to the motorway, swerved to avoid a truck and ended up halfway up the embankment. They're both still inside the vehicle. Both armed. We have them pinned down by armed officers. They're not going anywhere, but they present a continuing threat to the driver and passenger of the patrol car.'

He paused as he checked something on one of the screens, and then continued.

'The Honda is currently being pursued along the M62 by the other patrol car, which has been joined by two other cars. An Armed Response vehicle from West Yorkshire will join them this side of Leeds. The Honda is also being tracked, through the National Police Air Service, by our India 66 fixed-wing aircraft and West Yorkshire's X-Ray 99 helicopter. They won't get away, but we can't take any risks. We have to assume they are armed. Excuse me.'

He had a further conversation with Gold Command, and with the Armed Response Incident Commander. Then he came back to them.

'The driver of the Taurus took a stray bullet in the shoulder, and another in his back. He's critical, and on his way to Hope Hospital. The two in the Merc are both dead. The driver of the patrol car was shot in the thigh. A ricochet. He urgently needs to be extracted. He's our priority. That's why you're here.'

'You mentioned a negotiator?' said Caton.

Mike Jackson turned to look at him.

'That's you.'

'Me?'

He raised his eyebrows. 'You've done the course? You've acted as negotiator before?'

'Yes.'

'Then you're it. Gold Command has designated you negotiator. I understand you speak Italian?'

'Well, to an extent,' Caton replied.

'That'll do, especially since you've got Commissario Benefetti here with you.'

'*Bonifati*,' said Caton.

'You are Victor One, and he is Victor Two,' Jackson told him.

'Do you have names for either of the occupants of the Evoque?' asked Caton.

'No. The plates of both vehicles are false. They look like magnetic stick-over jobs. Probably switched over at the last moment specifically for this operation, otherwise they'd have been spotted by the motorway ANPR cameras. Gold Command has someone going through the footage from the gantry cameras, and I've got someone going through the Birch Services car park VCR to see if we can identify their original plates. If we get lucky we can get a handle on the registered keepers, and who's insured them. Providing they're not stolen.'

He didn't sound too hopeful.

'It's not a lot to go on,' said Caton. 'Are you certain they're both Italian?'

'According to a witness to the shooting, that's the language the passenger shouted to his driver in as they were reversing. Other than that, the only communication we've had is them shooting at the patrol cars, and a quick burst of automatic fire in the direction of the Armed Response vehicles when they arrived. That was ten minutes ago. Since then, nothing.'

He stopped to speak into his mouthpiece.

'Roger that, November Leader. They're on their way.'

He turned right round to get a good look at them both.

'You'd better get on with it,' he said. 'Is the commissario up to speed with this?'

'I understood much of what you said,' Bonifati replied. 'Detective Chief Inspector Caton will tell me what I need to know.'

The superintendent nodded. 'Right then. You'll find John stood by the boot. He'll mike you up, then someone will take you both down to the Armed

Response Incident Commander. Good luck.'

In the lee of the Service Station they were given bulletproof vests and helmets to put on. They were then taken on the back of two police motorcycles to the point where the re-entry slip road began.

The scene that greeted them was surreal. Normally at this time, the middle of rush hour, all six lanes on both carriageways would be packed with slow-moving traffic. Now they were empty. The only sound was the rustling of leaves on the bushes along the embankments, and the occasional murmur of voices on the radios.

Caton counted three Armed Response vehicles. The Command vehicle, an armoured Range Rover Vogue SUV, was parked diagonally across the slow entry lane onto the eastbound motorway lanes. Fifty metres ahead of it a Land Rover Defender was stationary in the outside lane. Thirty metres ahead of that, what looked like a BMW 5 Series saloon was parked across the centre lane.

Halfway up the embankment, opposite the Land Rover, the Evoque teetered at a seemingly impossible angle. Only a small shrub appeared to be preventing it from plunging back down the slope onto the hard shoulder barrier over which it had flipped before coming to rest.

The blue and yellow BMW motorway patrol car was stranded on the hard shoulder immediately below the suspect vehicle. From the way in which the car was leaning it looked as though both of the nearside tyres had been punctured. Crouched behind the offside wing, one officer appeared to be supporting a colleague lying flat on the ground beside him.

Caton and Bonifati were waved forward and ran in a crouch to the safety of the Range Rover. One Firearms officer ducked behind the front wing, while a second pulled open the rear door, motioned for them to get in, and then shut it behind them.

Chapter 39

'Welcome, gents,' said a serious voice from the front passenger seat. 'I'm DCI Watts, Armed Response Incident Commander. DS Mason, on your right, is keeping the log. I hope you bear that in mind.'

Caton and Bonifati both turned to acknowledge her. She nodded back.

'I'm afraid most of this is going to be in Italian,' Caton told her.

'I'm only logging the decisions and the reasoning behind them,' she reminded him. 'If you can make sure that's all in English it won't be a problem.'

'Our priority is to get an ambulance to that wounded officer,' Watts told him. 'He's taken a bullet through the flesh of his thigh. In and out. Missed his arteries, but he's in a lot of pain. We've tried talking to them, but all we've had in reply is what sounds like swear words, in what we assume is Italian.'

'What makes you think an ambulance would come under fire?' Caton asked.

'Because when the driver of the patrol car stood up and waved his handkerchief they shot at him too. He was lucky not to have been hit.'

Caton found it difficult to believe that anyone could manage to fire a semi-automatic rifle from such a precarious and unstable position. He craned forward to see.

The windows were tinted black and it was impossible to see the occupants, but he thought that the rear window was down a fraction – though he could be imagining it – and he could see something protruding from it.

'We think you're looking at a 9mm semi-automatic rifle,' Watts told him. 'Although going by the witness accounts, and the number and spread of cartridges in the car park, it sounds more like a machine gun.'

Caton turned to the commissario.

'Are you ready for this, Umberto?'

The Italian nodded. 'I have done this before,' he said grimly. 'Without benefit of an armour-ed car.'

'Good,' said Caton. 'DCI Watts will pass us a handset, which I will control. I would like you to interpret what I say and any response I get. If I want you to speak directly to them, we'll agree first what you are going to say. I need you to stick to what we agree. Is that clear?'

'*Perfettamente*,' Bonifati replied. 'For the *inchiesta*, when we mess up.'

'Inquiry,' Caton explained.

'You'd better *not* mess up,' said the Incident Commander.

'I have a question,' said Bonifati. 'How will we be able to hear what they say if our windows are closed?'

'The loudspeakers on these vehicles also operate as directional dynamic microphone receivers,' Watts told him. 'If there's too much wind noise I'll also lower the windows a fraction.' He unclipped the handset. 'You'll be alright,' he said. 'So long as you keep your head down.'

Caton hoped that he was joking.

Watts handed him the handset.

'This has been playing up,' he said, 'but we'll give it a try. India 99 is on its way. If all else fails we'll patch in to their *Skyshout.*'

'Give me a moment,' said Caton.

'No problem. While you're preparing, we're going to see how much closer we can get.'

He nodded to his driver, who started the engine. Slowly but surely the vehicle edged forward.

Caton knew that once the negotiations began he would have much less time to plan or reflect. He had to be clear about his strategy from the start. He closed his eyes and began to run through his mental checklist.

This was a hostage crisis. Not by intent, but the reality was that the injured officer and his colleague were to all intents and purposes hostages. The suspects may or may not be aware that they had a bargaining tool, but he had to assume that they would. It was also something he might be able to use himself.

The highest risk factor here was that the suspects had already set out to kill someone. They could not be certain that they hadn't succeeded. That was information he needed to use with care. There were two points of highest risk: the early stages, where they were at right now, with adrenalin running high, and where fear, panic and uncertainty rule; and the final stage of surrender, where the slightest mistake could spell carnage.

There would be three options swarming around in their heads: surrender, escape or suicide. How desperate they were depended on several factors. Firstly, how they perceived the police might respond. Could they trust them not to kill them anyway if they surrendered? Secondly, whether there were any cultural or personal reasons why these men would want to tough it out. Even to the point of being willing to die. Might they be more frightened of those who had contracted this killing, or were they really cowards hiding behind their weapons?

Experience and the textbooks told him that it was unlikely they were the type to consider murder suicides. Suicide by cop, as it was more commonly known. These were criminals, almost certainly psychopathic or sociopathic, but not suffering from a sudden episode of serious mental illness. Nevertheless, their behaviours would be largely unpredictable. And he could forget the Stockholm Syndrome. Empathy would be lost on these two.

The perimeter was secure, the scene controlled. The issue was how to get everyone out of this safely, and the suspects under arrest. The priorities were the wounded officer and his colleague, then the rest of the police officers, and last of all, the suspects.

There were three unacceptable solutions: that the suspects be allowed to leave with a hostage, that the suspects be offered their freedom, and that the suspects be killed or wounded, other than in self-defence.

The best, and frankly the only, solution was that an ambulance remove the wounded officer and his colleague safely, and the suspects surrender without further incident.

All that was self-evident. He was left with one decision about which he was less certain. Did he reveal that Umberto was a commissario of the *Polizia Di Stato*, or did he pretend that he was just an interpreter? Would they see the presence of an Italian law officer as an opportunity for extradition to a legal system with more opportunity for the prosecution to be undermined, or would they see it as a threat?

He took a deep breath and opened his eyes. They were now stationary again, just twenty-five metres from the suspects' Evoque.

'Umberto,' he said, 'I think it best if they believe that you are just an interpreter. *Di conseguenza, nessun litigio, nessuna analisi, nessun pressurizzazione. In realtà non commentare affatto.'*

Bonifati's shrug was noncommittal. He understood. That was all that mattered.

'Translation, please,' said DS Mason. 'For the record.'

'No arguing, no analysing, no pressurising. No comments at all,' Caton told her. 'Just an accurate translation.'

'Dead right,' muttered DCI Watts. 'Now, can we get on with it? There's one of our guys bleeding all over the tarmac.'

'I'm ready,' Caton said.

He raised the handset to his lips and pressed the button.

Chapter 40

'*This is Detective Chief Inspector Caton of the Greater Manchester Police. I am here to make sure that everybody stays safe. That includes you. I would like to discuss with you how we can do that.*'

Watts had been right. There was an initial squawk when he switched on, and feedback every time he replied. It was bad enough that the sound of his own voice, magnified in this way, never failed to surprise him, without this.

They waited for a response. It was evident that none was forthcoming.

'*I have an interpreter here with me if that would help?*' he said.

Still no reply.

'I'm going to say all that again,' he said to Commissario Bonifati. 'And I'd like you to repeat it in Italian. The same tone. Calm, neutral, yet firm.'

He raised the handset so that it was in a position where the two of them could take it in turns to lean in to speak. He retained control of the button.

'Here we go,' he said.

Bonifati's attempt was met with a stony silence. Caton leaned in and pressed the button.

'*Are you alright?*' he said. '*Is anyone injured? Do you need any medical attention?*'

He motioned for the Italian to repeat it.

There was still no response. He tried again.

'*We have a police officer who needs urgent medical attention.*'

This time Bonifati's words elicited a shout.

'*E chi se ne frega!*'

'Who gives a damn?' he translated.

'*Leccaculo!*'

The commissario raised his eyebrows.

'Go on,' said Caton.

'Arse licker.' Bonifati shrugged apologetically. 'Not exact, but close.'

'At least we know one of them is alright,' Caton observed.

And he now had an idea of his state of mind. This was false bravado, more accurately machismo. They knew how this was going to end, but at least they could pretend that was in their own hands.

'*There is no reason for anyone else to get hurt,*' he said. '*We just need to get our colleague to hospital. Then we can talk about how to get you to safety.*'

This time their response to Bonifati was much longer.

'They want you to move your vehicles away first,' he said. 'And they want a helicopter landed to take them away from here.'

'*Don't even think about it,*' said the Bronze Commander over the radio link.

'I wasn't going to,' said Caton, annoyed at the interruption. 'If I had, I would have discussed it with you first, sir.'

'*Of course you would, Victor One,*' Jackson replied in a conciliatory tone. '*Sorry, I was just talking to myself. You weren't meant to hear. Carry on.*'

Caton leaned in and pressed the button on the handset.

'*We can't do that, I'm afraid,*' he told the suspects.

'*Not until our colleague is safe and on his way to hospital.*'

Bonifati's translation was met with more invective.

'With a lady present,' he said, 'it would be difficult for me to say what they say.' He shrugged apologetically. 'But it involves your mother, your dog and certain parts of your body.'

'If I can just make an observation,' said DCI Watts.

'Of course,' said Caton.

'I know you'd normally try to play it cool and wear these bastards down,' said the Incident Commander, 'but until we get that guy to hospital we don't really know how bad he is. If you're prepared to call their bluff, I can guarantee they won't be able to stop you.'

'How can you do that?' said Caton.

'There's an Anti-Terrorist Response vehicle in the Vehicle Works shop in Openshaw for routine maintenance,' he said. 'It's bigger than an ambulance, and fully armoured. We could bring that up with a couple of paramedics inside, and get both those officers on-board and away in complete safety.'

It sounded to Caton like a genius solution. Something Gold and Silver Command should have come up with themselves.

'If we do that without their agreement,' he said, 'it could well provoke them to open fire.'

'I agree,' Watts replied. 'That's where your skill as a negotiator and my guys as shooters come in. All of our vehicles are armoured. Theirs isn't. It would be suicide if they opened fire. They must know that.'

'Only if you fired back,' said Caton.

The Incident Commander said nothing, and simply raised his eyebrows, and turned back to his screens.

Everyone saw the logic to it. While they waited, Caton, ably aided by Bonifati, tried, to no avail, to persuade the suspects to cooperate.

They knew from the driver of the patrol car that his

colleague's bleeding had been contained, and that whilst in a lot of pain, he appeared to be stable. There was no telling if and when shock might kick in. If that did happen, Caton knew they would have no choice but to force the issue.

While they were waiting, word came through that the second suspect vehicle – the Honda CRV – had finally been brought to a halt ten miles west of Goole. The driver and three passengers had surrendered without resistance.

Caton was not surprised. They had not discharged any weapons. At worst they would be looking at conspiracy to murder, and being accessories to murder. A clever barrister would argue that they had been told the intention was to warn off the opposition. The shooting had come as a complete surprise. The guns they had been carrying were for self-defence. In which case they'd probably go down for just seven years. It would all depend on the judge. Hopefully, he reflected, the Italian authorities could tie them into charges with much longer sentences. *For once, double jeopardy could work in our favour.*

It took twenty-five minutes before the call they had been waiting for came through.

'Bronze Command to November One,' came the call. *'Trojan Four, with paramedics, ready to roll. Please advise.'*

Caton put the handset down on the seat between them and adjusted his own mike.

'Roger that, Bronze Command,' he said. *'I need to let them know what is happening, and then I'll get back to you.'*

'Roger that, Victor One.'

The tension in the Land Rover was now palpable, not helped by the fact that there were five of them in this vehicle jammed full of equipment, all of them wearing body armour, and all of them hot and sweaty.

'This is November Leader to all units,' said the

Incident Commander into his personal radio. *'We have an AT Response Vehicle coming in, with a paramedic team on-board. They will extract Tango One and Tango Two. You will maintain position, keep eyes on the suspect vehicle and only fire on my command. Please Roger your understanding.'*

The responses came in turn.

'November One, Roger that.'

'November Three, Roger that.'

'November Five, Roger that.'

'November Seven, Roger that.'

'November Nine, Roger that.'

Five replies. That meant five marksmen, each accompanied by a buddy and a driver. Two pairs with the Land Rover Vogue, another with the BMW, plus the pair crouched down behind their own vehicle. If the suspects were stupid enough to open fire, Caton knew that they would not have the remotest chance of surviving. He picked up the handset and held it between them.

'I'm going to do this in three parts, Umberto,' he said.

The commissario nodded. 'I understand.'

Caton depressed the send button.

'We have a vehicle carrying medical staff, which is going to come alongside the police car in front of you. The injured person will be taken on-board.'

Bonifati repeated Caton's words. It was met with silence.

'If you have anyone in your vehicle,' Caton continued, *'that needs medical attention, the medical staff will treat them and take them to hospital. If you want this to happen, please tell us now.'*

They waited anxiously for a response to the Italian version. Again there was nothing but a little static and the heightened sound of the wind, which had strengthened as the evening drew on.

'*I have to warn you*,' Caton told them, '*that if this vehicle or any of the other vehicles come under fire, that fire will be returned.*'

This time there was a single shouted response.

'*Vaffanculo!*'

Bonifati did not translate it. Instead, he glanced at Caton and flicked his hand under his chin. Caton nodded grimly.

The Armed Response Incident Commander and his loggist both turned to look at them.

'I can guess,' said DCI Watts. 'But we need you to say it for the record.'

'He told you to get lost,' said the Italian detective.

Caton admired his chauvinist sensitivity, but knew that when it came to the record, euphemisms were not acceptable.

'What he actually said was, "Fuck off,"' he told them.

'That tells us nothing,' observed Watts. 'Will they start shooting, or won't they?'

'I don't think so,' Caton replied. 'If they were going to, I think they would have done so by now. This is bravado.'

He hoped he was right.

The radio burst into life.

'*Bronze Command, Victor One. Thank you. Our intentions have been made clear, as have the options open to them. The decision is made. Trojan Four is on the move. November Leader, you remain clear to take command if an armed response is required. Any such response to be proportionate, as laid down within the standard protocols. Please acknowledge.*'

DCI Watts nodded, as though the Bronze Commander was actually there with them.

'*November Leader to Bronze Command, understood.*

Trojan Four on the move. I am cleared to respond to any imminent threat to life.'

Caton sat back in his seat and listened to the Comms traffic between Bronze Command and the driver of the motorway patrol car, readying him for the arrival of the ATR. The display screens on the dashboard were obscured by DCI Watts, but in the wing mirror he could see the large black Trojan crawling towards them.

Looking as though a four-by-five-metre metal box had been welded to the front half of a Land Rover Defender, it had steel mesh gates over the windscreen, side windows, roof of the cab and the bonnet. Metal skirts prevented access to the underside of the vehicle. Originally developed for the streets of Northern Ireland during the Troubles, it was an awesome sight. As the sun began to dip below Saddleworth Moor, it took on the appearance of something out of an apocalyptic movie.

Then there was another sound, growing in intensity. Like a massive lawnmower. Instantly recognisable to the GMP officers as the Force helicopter, India 99. Caton looked out of his window, but was unable to see it. Judging by the images from its downlink visual pictures system on one of the screens, it must have been directly overhead.

'Tell them to back off,' said Caton. 'If there is any dialogue from the suspects, we'll never be able to hear them. Not to mention they could end up spooking the suspects and being shot at themselves.'

DCI Watts had arrived at the same conclusion and was already putting through the request. They heard the sound recede until it was merely an irritating buzz high above them.

'They're inviting us to patch through to AirShout,' he said. 'That would free us to use our microphone as a permanent receiver. Unless you've an objection, I propose to accept.'

'Go ahead,' Caton told him. 'Their speaker is a damn sight more powerful than ours.'

'More reliable, too,' Watts muttered. He pressed the open Comms button. '*Roger that, Police 151.*'

Anxiously they waited and watched as the Trojan rolled forward. What they assumed was the barrel of a rifle still protruded from the tiny gap at the top of the rear offside window of the Range Rover. It looked to Caton as though it was tracking the progress of the Trojan, but if so, the movement must have been be so slight that he could well have been imagining it.

They held their breath as the driver of the Trojan slowly turned the front wheels until the bonnet was pointing directly at the suspect vehicle, and the rear doors were alongside the boot of the stranded patrol car.

'So far so good,' said Caton, for no other reason than it relieved the tension a little. He wondered what it must feel like for the driver and his colleague, even behind bulletproof glass, staring down the barrel of that gun only metres away.

DCI Watts urgently spoke to his driver, who started the engine and inched the vehicle forward until they once more had a clear view of the Evoque. Then he spoke to Caton, without taking his eyes off the suspect vehicle.

'You'd better tell them again, Victor One,' he said. 'Just so there's no misunderstanding.'

Caton raised his handset.

'*If…*' he began.

The magnified sound of his own voice via the helicopter's AirShout speaker took him by surprise and stopped him in his tracks. He cleared his throat and began again.

'*If you have anyone in your vehicle that needs medical attention, please tell us now.*'

Bonifati repeated it. They waited. There was no reply.

'Right, November One,' said DCI Watts grimly, 'they've had their chance.'

Chapter 41

'*Please listen carefully,*' Caton said into the handset. '*The rear doors of the vehicle will open, and the injured officer will be taken on-board. Then the vehicle will leave. Do not take any action during this process that might provoke a response. Do you understand?*'

Whether they did or not they would never know. The commissario's translation fell on deaf ears.

'*Bronze Commander,*' said DCI Watts. '*Trojan Four may proceed. I repeat, Trojan Four may proceed.*'

'*Roger that, November One. Trojan Four, you may proceed.*'

'*All November units, stand by,*' said the Incident Commander. His voice was strong and calm, belying the weight of responsibility that he and his men carried.

The doors of the ATR swung open. Two Tactical Aid officers in black helmets and Kevlar suits vaulted over the sill. They helped down two other men, similarly clad, but with yellow and green jackets over their tops. On hands and knees they crawled in single file.

The first of the rescuers was less than a foot from the injured officer.

'*Eyes on! Wait! Wait! Wait!*' shouted the Incident Commander.

Caton's eyes darted to the suspect vehicle. The

266

driver's offside window was retracting. An arm emerged and gripped the exterior door handle. He held his breath as the door began to open. And then all hell broke loose.

'*November One, Target acquired!*'

'*November Three, Target acquired!*'

'*November Five, eyes on Target Two!*'

The responses came so fast they ran into each other.

'*All units, hold your fire,*' said DCI Watts. He half turned his head. 'Tell them not to move,' he said.

This was not a time for translations. Caton held the handset to Bonifati's lips.

'*Polizia armata*! *Resta dove sei*! *Non muoverti!*' thundered from the AirShout amplifier.

'Armed police. Stay where you are. Do not move,' Caton said for the record.

'The light's failing,' said Watts. 'We need the searchlight.'

'*Bronze Command to Police 151,*' came the immediate response. '*Light that car!*'

'*Roger that, Bronze Command.*'

A powerful beam of light struck the Range Rover Evoque. The driver let go of the door handle and covered his eyes. The vehicle swayed drunkenly, the shrub gave way and the Range Rover began to tumble over and over, down the embankment. It came to rest against the crash barrier, crushing it beneath its weight.

'*Units November One and Three, advance, assess and disarm,*' ordered the Incident Commander. '*November Two, eyes on, and cover.*'

They watched as the two Armed Response teams, including their own, emerged from behind their vehicles and raced forward. One pair crouched three metres from the bonnet, the other near the rear, weapons raised. They could hear them shouting commands.

'*Victor Two, tell them again,*' said Watts.

The commissario leaned into the handset.

'*Polizia armata! Resta dove sei! Non muoverti!*'

'And again,' said Watts.

'*Polizia armata! Resta dove sei! Non muoverti!*'

'The driver isn't going to be moving anytime soon,' Caton observed.

The Evoque was lying across the barrier on its offside. One arm protruded from beneath the sill of the driver's window, pinned against the barrier itself. From the ungainly angle at which it hung, the arm was broken.

The noise from the helicopter was louder now. The downdraft from the rotor blades flattened the grass and shrubs on the embankment.

'*Back off, Police 151!*' commanded Watts. '*Your downdraft is distracting my men.*'

Threatening to blow them over more like, thought Caton.

The nearside rear window appeared to have been smashed as the Range Rover careered down the slope. The two officers at the rear were pointing their weapons directly at it, shouting to be heard above the sound of the helicopter as it gained height behind them.

'Tell whoever's in the back of that car to raise his hands where we can see them,' said the Incident Commander.

Caton did just that, followed by Bonifati in Italian. Caton knew that this was the second most dangerous part of the operation. The moment of decision for the suspects. Surrounded and hopeless, did they surrender, or go down fighting? And there was going to be a millisecond of decision for those officers out there on the tarmac. One mistake, and they could die.

A different kind of mistake, and they faced internal investigation and potential disciplinary charges. Maybe even criminal ones. Either way, there would be trial by media. His admiration for them was boundless.

Out on the motorway, the shouting intensified. They watched as one hand emerged through the broken window, and then a second.

'Tell him to move slowly. Very slowly,' said DCI Watts.

Bonifati leaned forward, but saw that there was no need. He was already doing that in response to the commands from November One.

'Selective hearing,' observed Caton. 'Like most villains.'

The head emerged, and then the upper part of his torso. Caton leaned forward. The downward light from India 99 cast shadows beneath his eyes, accentuating the hollows of his cheeks. There were several gashes on his forehead and smears of blood down the side of his face. It was difficult to be sure, but Caton had the feeling he had seen this face before.

Slowly the suspect placed his hands on the side of the van, now effectively the roof. One of the officers, weapon raised, came forward and checked the inside of the van. Then he slung his weapon behind his back and secured the suspect's wrists behind his back with a single-looped cable tie.

'*This is November Two,*' he reported. '*We have two suspects. I repeat, two suspects. One secure, one conscious and disabled. Suspect claims three weapons in situ. Two are in sight.*'

'*Roger that, November Two,*' said the Incident Commander. '*Two suspects, one secure, one disabled. Three weapons, two in clear sight. All November units maintain positions.*' He switched channel. '*Bronze*

Command. I request emergency medical vehicle for man down; Tactical Aid support to remove Target One; and Emergency Fire support to extract Target Two.'

'Roger that, November One,' said the Bronze Commander. *'And well done.'*

'It's not over yet,' murmured DCI Watts. 'Not till the fat lady sings.'

Two Kevlar-kitted officers appeared from the rear of the Trojan and sprinted to the Range Rover Evoque. They gripped the suspect by the shoulders, and hauled him out of the van and down onto the hard shoulder. Unceremoniously they dragged him, feet trailing, to their vehicle. Arms reached down and hauled him inside.

An ambulance arrived at speed from the direction of Birch Services and pulled up beside the wounded officer, obscuring him from their view.

Close behind came a fire tender. While two armed officers trained their weapons on the remaining suspect, fire officers used air bags and cutting equipment to release him.

The same two Tactical Aid officers eventually pulled him free under the watchful eyes of two paramedics. Limping, he was helped to the Trojan and lifted gingerly on-board.

They watched as the paramedics climbed in, the rear doors were closed, and the Trojan set off towards Birch Services.

The commissario muttered something.

'What did he say?' asked DS Mason, her fingers poised to record his reply.

Caton smiled. 'He said "I don't know about them, but that thing frightened the shit out of me."'

Mason grinned at the Italian detective. 'Me too,' she said.

The Armed Response officers who had helped

them into the Range Rover approached carrying two of the weapons retrieved from the Evoque. He held one of them up for his boss to see before he placed it in an evidence bag.

'First one of these we've seen,' he said.

'What is it?' asked Caton.

'A standard 9mm .223 Remington semi-automatic rifle,' Watts told him. 'Fitted with a replacement Bump Stop recoil device.'

It looked, to all intents and purposes, like a cheap plastic stock and trigger.

'Appearances can be deceptive,' said November Two. 'This thing turns it into an automatic weapon. We've seen a video that shows it spraying bullets like a machine gun, ejecting the cartridges skywards as it fires.'

'I reckon that explains those cuts on Target two's forehead,' said his colleague, arriving at his side. 'Idiot must have forgotten about that.'

'The worst thing is, the US Bureau of Alcohol, Tobacco, Firearms and Explosives has declared it legal.'

'The worst thing is,' the Incident Commander corrected him, 'it's arrived on the streets of Manchester.'

Chapter 42

Predictably, a behind-the-scenes battle over custody, and who should have the opportunity to interview the suspects first, was immediately underway. The Chief Constable of Greater Manchester Police, Caton's boss, pointed out that the incident had taken place in one of his divisions, GMP had led the operation, and multiple shootings resulting in murder and wounding, including to one of his own officers, made it unquestionably his investigation.

The Director General-in-waiting of the National Crime Agency, in less than a fortnight effectively the most senior police officer in the United Kingdom, took a very different view. This was, he maintained, linked to the investigation currently underway, led by Malcolm Haigh, and belonged to the NCA's Organised Crime Division.

'I was led to understand that the men SOCA is questioning are subject to European Arrest Warrants,' said Robert Hampson, the Chief Constable.

'They are. But at least one of them has recently come to our attention as a person of interest,' the Director General replied.

'And do you have any proof that he *is* connected to the men we are holding?' asked the Chief Constable.

'We will, as soon as we've had an opportunity to question the suspects.'

'So that's a no then?'

The Director General sighed. The last thing he wanted was to have to ask the Home Secretary to intervene before he'd even officially taken up post.

'Look, Derek,' he said, 'I'm sure we can work this out. It might even become a model for how the Agency begins to work with regional forces.'

'I thought this had already been thrashed out with ACPO,' said the Chief Constable.

'So it has. The Association of Chief Police Officers agreed that wherever possible, primacy should be established before an operation takes place, and where that is not possible, mutually advantageous cooperation should be established as speedily as possible.'

'That was in principle. Practice is another matter entirely.'

'So let's explore the practice.'

'What are you suggesting?'

'GMP retain primacy over the murder investigation. We are given access to question these men with respect to their possible involvement in organised crime. We share all data.'

'We?'

'Come on, Bob,' said the Director General. 'You know what I mean. SOCA, which in two weeks' time will mean the NCA. You know very well it's virtually one and the same thing already. All the posts have been filled. Most of the staff are in situ.'

'You're talking about a joint investigation?'

'Exactly. You prepare the murder case for the CPS, we work on the organised crime aspects.'

'If there are any.'

'There will be.'

The Chief Constable leaned back in his chair and swivelled from side to side as he thought through the ramifications.

'Go on then,' he said. 'So long as we lead, and you remember you owe me one.'

Which was how Caton found himself, at 10 o'clock that evening, in one of the conference rooms in the interview suite, listening to Chief Superintendent Gates, who had been appointed as Senior Investigating Officer, and Agent Simon Levi, Head Designate of the NCA Organised Crime Command, his old adversary from the Okowu-Bello case. The debrief concluded, they were trying to reach agreement on the interview strategy.

Also in the room were the Bronze Commander, DCI Watts, the Armed Response Incident Commander, someone from the CPS Caton hadn't met before, and Umberto Bonifati.

'That's not going to work,' Helen Gates was saying. 'We have them bang to rights on the murders of the driver and passenger of the Mercedes. Also the wounding of the driver of the Taurus, and of the motorway patrol officer. We have their weapons, the cartridges, CCTV from the Motorway Services, and eyewitness accounts. I need to take them through that stage by stage.'

'You know it's just going to be *No comment*,' said Levi.

'I don't care,' she replied. 'If it is, so be it.'

'My point is,' he persisted, 'you don't even know who they are. Or who the dead men are. You don't have a motive.'

'They had the means and the opportunity,' she said. 'And they did it. The motive can wait.'

'I can get you that,' he said.

'I don't doubt you can,' she replied. 'In the fullness of time. Right now, I don't need a motive. I just need them to reply to the charges and get them processed.'

'This could be the start of something bigger,' said Levi. 'A turf war. Or worse. Don't tell me you're not interested in that?'

Caton had never been a fan, but he knew he was right about this. He could see that DCS Gates knew it too.

She sucked her lip.

'You'd have to have something more than a hunch,' she said. 'Otherwise all you'd get would be *No comment.*'

Touché, thought Caton. *Fifteen all.* He studied Levi's face. His expression told him that that was all the agent had, a hunch.

Beside him Umberto Bonifati raised his hand. DCS Gates looked at him in surprise.

'Yes?' she said.

'Commissario Bonifati,' he said, conscious that at least one person in the room didn't know who he was. 'I believe that Agent Levi may be correct.'

Now he had their full attention

'Go on, Commissario,' she said.

'The men you have in custody,' he said, 'they are from Calabria.'

She raised her eyebrows. 'How can you be sure?'

'From their speech. The way they spoke.'

'But they only said a few words,' DCI Watts pointed out.

The commissario waggled his head. 'Detective Chief Inspector Caton took me down the…'

He looked to Caton to complete his sentence.

'The custody suite,' said Caton. 'Where they were being processed. I thought it might turn something up.'

Helen Gates allowed the hint of a smile, and raised her eyebrows in silent appreciation of his initiative.

'And did it, Commissario?' she said.

Bonifati smiled in return. 'It did,' he said, clearly enjoying himself. 'They didn't see me there behind them. If they had, they would have had no idea who I was. They spoke to each other in Italian. All of it with the accent of Calabria. Some of it in dialect more difficult to follow.'

'What did you overhear?' said an impatient Simon Levi.

Several of them gave him withering glances. *Like water off a duck's back*, thought Caton.

'*Principalmente*,' Bonifati replied. 'They blame each other for the mess they are in. But one of them, the tall one with the red hair, he tells them to keep quiet. Say nothing. Or else, "*Il Carciofo, egli taglierà le palle, e li spingere su per il culo!*"'

He showed no inclination to provide a translation.

The Detective Chief Superintendent looked directly at Caton and raised one eyebrow in that disconcerting way she had.

'*Il Carciofo* will cut off your balls, and shove them up your arse,' said Caton helpfully.

'*Il Carciofo*?' said Helen Gates. 'Who the hell is *Il Carciofo*?'

'The man we arrested in Marple yesterday, on a European Arrest Warrant,' said Mal Haigh.

'The man we are currently holding for questioning in Warrington,' said Simon Levi triumphantly. 'You do know what this means?'

'Enlighten us, do,' said Helen Gates through gritted teeth.

'They are Ndrangheta,' he said. '*Mafioso*, from Calabria.' He positively beamed. 'We have our connection. What's more, we've got you a motive.'

'I think you'll find,' said Caton, before the agent could get completely carried away, 'that Commissario Bonifati made that connection.'

Before Levi could respond, Umberto raised his hand again.

'I also believe,' he said, 'that the two dead men were from Campania. Most likely Napoli.'

'You heard the dead speak?' scoffed Simon Levi.

'*Che stronzo*,' muttered Bonifati.

'What a power that would be,' said Caton.

Although sorely tempted, he saw no mileage in providing verbatim Umberto's actual response, which had been far more appropriate – *What an arsehole*.

'Their appearance and their clothes,' said the Commissario, 'it speaks of Naples.'

He sensed the agent about to protest yet again and pushed his hand, palm up, out in front of him, stopping Levi in his tracks. Then he reached down to the folder in front of Caton, identical to others around the table, selected a photograph and held it up with a magician's flourish.

'Also,' he said, 'this face I have seen before. In a file in Milano belonging to the *Direzione Investigativa Antimafia*. His name is Giuseppe Giambotta. *Nipote*…'

'Nephew,' whispered Caton, as transfixed by this revelation as everyone else in the room.

'Nephew,' the Italian detective continued, 'of Alfredo Patrizio Giambotta, also known as Frederick Gladstone.'

He looked around the table, enjoying the surprise and rapt attention on the faces of his audience.

'He is *Mafiosa*. A member of the Giambotta clan. Camorra.'

Then he shrugged, as though it was nothing at all, returned the photograph and sat back in his chair.

'It seems your Arrest Warrants may have stirred a hornet's nest, Commissario Bonifati,' said Helen Gates.

The subtext was clear from her expression and the frosty tone of her voice.

Judging by the expression on the Italian detective's face, Caton wondered if that might be what Bonifati had been hoping for along.

'All the more reason why the NCA needs to interview these men,' said Agent Levi. 'Do you really want a Mafia-style gang war erupting across this region? Maybe even nationwide?'

'It would seem that it already has,' DCS Gates replied. 'Erupted in this region.'

She pretended to look through the file in front of her. Caton knew that she was collecting her thoughts. She looked up.

'This is what I propose. All four of these men have been arrested on suspicion of murder, conspiracy to murder, wounding with intent, causing grievous bodily harm and possession of firearms. GMP officers will begin by questioning them in relation to those offences. I welcome the assistance of NCA agents in the preparation of the interview strategies, and I have invited you to *observe* the interviews. When we have finished, the suspects will then be charged and remanded in custody.'

She glanced at the man from the Crown Prosecution Service, who nodded in agreement. No magistrate was going to agree bail on charges as serious as these.

'Whilst on remand, all of the suspects will be available for questioning by you and your colleagues, Mr Levi, in relation to their involvement in organised crime. Given the snail-like pace with which the legal justice system moves, you should have at least six months to do so. We'll run our separate investigations in parallel, and share any information that may have a bearing on each other's investigation.'

Given that a GMP officer had been wounded, Levi knew that it was the best he would get. He reluctantly nodded his assent.

Helen Gates turned her attention to Umberto Bonifati.

'Commissario,' she said. 'Thank you for your assistance thus far.'

She managed to make it sound more like an admonition than a compliment.

'For reasons of continuity and transparency we will, from now on, be employing our own interpreter in relation to this investigation. I am sure you understand.'

Bonifati did. As did Caton. It was shorthand for, *You've caused us enough trouble already. The sooner you bugger off to your own country the better.*

'This will free you and DCI Caton to continue your own investigation into the unrelated murder of Mr Richetti,' she said.

Caton was no longer sure if it was unrelated. Everything to do with Umberto Bonifati perplexed him.

'Operation Tortoise, ma'am,' he reminded her.

She raised one eyebrow. 'Tortoise? I hope that doesn't prove prophetic. I can't spare you much longer.'

Out of the corner of his eye Caton could see Simon Levi smirking. Ever since the computer had thrown up this randomly generated name he and his team had had to suffer this childish banter. It was beginning to wear thin. Worse still, he had started to worry that they might be right. Operation Tortoise was going nowhere fast.

Chapter 43

'Thank God for that!'

She adjusted the screen to white on black, and prepared to pick up where she had left off.

'You get back to working eight-hour days, with time off for good behaviour at the weekends, and I can look forward to a good night's sleep without you coming in at all hours.'

'Amen to that,' Caton replied as he slipped into bed beside her. 'I've had enough excitement for one week.'

He took his book from the bedside table and opened it at the COPS bookmark. He held the bookmark in his fingers for a moment. He had forgotten that he had signed up to the *Run to Remember* charity initiative. Two miles a day, for 125 days, starting at the beginning of December. In aid of two linked charities: Care Of Police Survivors, and the North-West Police Benevolent Fund and Victim Support. It wasn't entirely altruistic, he reflected. Like Gordon Holmes had pointed out, you never knew when you or those closest to you might need their help.

He looked at his heavily pregnant wife sat beside him. Heaven forbid that she and their unborn child would ever qualify for such support. Or Harry, come to that. The day she had told him that they were having a child together he had made himself a solemn promise that he would do everything in his power to avoid putting his life at unnecessary risk.

He smiled grimly. In this job, it was a meaningless promise. Risk assessment was all very well, but at the end of the day you could only control the things you could control. Sometimes that was about heart rather than head. Did you jump into the water to save a child from drowning, or wait for emergency services to arrive too late? That was an easy one: he had jumped. But the psychopath police hater with a gun, the knife-carrying drug-crazed idiot, the cornered criminal desperate to escape? Every police officer knew that was about fate. You were either lucky or you weren't.

She turned, and saw the look on his face.

'Tom, what is it?' she said.

'Nothing,' he lied.

She put her Kindle down and placed a hand over his.

'Is it your investigation?' she said. 'Operation Tortoise?'

'No jokes, please,' he said.

'Shall I tell you what I think?' she snuggled closer. 'You can forget all that Mafia nonsense; there'll be a woman involved somewhere. There always is.'

He put his own book down, kissed her on her forehead and drew her closer.

'That's what I love about you,' he replied. 'You have this amazing ability to simplify the complicated, and complicate the simple.'

She laughed. 'It's called being a woman,' she said.

He was about to reply, but she punched his arm lightly with her fist.

'And before you utter a word, just remember I'm entitled to say that because I *am* one.'

He slipped his right arm around her waist and cupped her breast with his free hand.

'I can't argue with that,' he said.

Caton was in early the next morning. He had to write up his account of his own role in the previous evening's dramatic operation, and that of the Italian detective. That done, he went over to the workstation dedicated to the investigation Joanne Stuart was heading up, officially known as Operation Juniper. He was not surprised to see DS Carter already at his desk, but it was a pleasant surprise to find DC Hulme in situ too.

'Morning, Nick, Jimmy,' he said.

'Morning, boss,' said Nick Carter. 'Didn't see you come in.'

'That's because you were here before us, weren't you, boss?' said DC Hulme without looking up.

'How did you know?' Carter, turned to look at him.

The young DC looked up, leaned back in his chair, and grinned.

'I know it's hard to believe, but I have this finely tuned sixth sense.'

'Really?' said DS Carter. 'Well, I'd never have guessed.'

Hulme ignored the jibe, bent forward and began typing on his keyboard.

'I also happened to clock that DCI Caton's car was in the car park,' he said. 'It wasn't hard. I'm a detective, you see. It's what I do. Observe, record, deduce.'

DS Carter merely shook his head and stood up.

'Sounds like you were in the thick of it last night, boss,' he said. 'Two dead, two wounded, including one of ours. Mafia gang war comes to Manchester. Blimey! Who'd have thought?'

'Who said anything about a Mafia connection?' said Caton.

Carter moved the plastic box that contained his

lunch ,and picked up the paper hidden beneath it. He handed it to Caton.

'The M.E.N. And we all know they're never wrong.'

Caton looked at the Manchester Evening News headline. Carter had quoted it verbatim. It was above a dramatic photo of the incident in the car park that had sparked it all off. A stretcher bearing the injured driver of the Taurus was being carried towards an ambulance. The bodies of the two dead victims were clearly visible in the crashed Mercedes, but their faces had been deliberately blurred.

'There are more photos on the inside pages, Carter told him. 'And hundreds more on people's Facebook pages. There are even videos on YouTube that must have been taken within seconds of the shooting. I bet Scenes of Crime will want to get their hands on them.'

Caton read the lead article. Not surprisingly the byline belonged to Larry Hymer, with whom he still had an ambiguous relationship. They both needed each other. Neither of them trusted each other, and they were both right not to do so. At least this time Hymer had stuck to the facts. Judging by the headline, however, they could look forward to a few days of colourful speculation.

He handed the paper back.

'Thanks, Nick.'

He pulled a chair across from one of the other desks and bade his DS sit down.

'Tell me,' he said. 'How's Juniper coming along?'

The Detective Sergeant grimaced. 'Slow, boss. Very slow. Don't get me wrong, Jo is doing a great job, but we've only that e-fit to go on, and so far we've drawn a blank.'

Caton was glad that Carter had overcome his disappointment that Joanne Stuart had passed her

Inspector's Board first and was now leading this investigation. It must have been hard for him. And it would have been easy for him to put it down to positive discrimination; not that the Force was into that in an overt way. He was about to congratulate Carter on the way he'd taken it when it hit him. *We've only that e-fit to go on, and so far we've drawn a blank.*

He swivelled his chair round and stared at the photographs on the board behind him. He leapt to his feet so fast that Jimmy Hulme stopped typing and looked up to see what had happened.

Caton strode over to the board and stood there for a moment. The door to the Major Incident Room opened, and Joanne Stuart walked in.

'Good timing, Detective Inspector,' he said. 'I've something for you.'

He passed her a photograph.

'Well?' he said. 'What do you think?'

She held the photo at arm's length, then brought it up close again. Then she looked at the e-fit up on the board for the fourth time.

'I see what you mean,' she said, trying hard not to let the excitement she was feeling show. 'It's definitely close.'

'Close!' exclaimed DC Hulme. 'It's like he was sat there in front of them when they put that together.'

'And DC Hulme knows what he's talking about,' said Nick Carter. 'He has a Master's in Observation. He's a detective, apparently.'

'Right,' she said, ignoring them both. 'Boss, how fast do you think we can get a VIPER set up?'

Caton had been there when the Home Office Minister had first announced trial Video Identification Parades back in 2002 at Longsight Police Station. Since then the technology had advanced. Tens of thousands of hours of police time and hundreds of thousands of pounds had been saved.

'We'll already have the video that was taken of him when he was charged,' he told her. 'It just depends on whether or not there are enough men of his age, build and ethnicity in the system.'

'Mixed race, French, Spanish, Italian, Greek, Turkish, Russian, Romanian or Bulgarian,' she said. 'Should be a doddle.' Her voice had lost a little of its excitement.

'There are over sixty thousand images in there,' Caton reassured her. 'More than enough.'

'Right,' she said. 'Jimmy, I want you to get a copy of this man's video. Let DS Carter know as soon as it's on our system. Then I want you to ask Mr Wallace to enter our suspect's image into PROMAT. Nick, I want you to bring Patrick Nelson in as soon as you've got the nod from DS Hulme. Is that clear?'

'Yes, boss!' they chimed as they headed back to their desks.

'Looks like you've got it covered, Jo,' said Caton.

'Thanks to you, boss.'

'Sheer fluke,' he told her. 'If anything, I should have realised last night.'

'Can't have been easy,' she said, 'under those circumstances.'

She was right, of course. What with the lights and the noise from the helicopter, all the shouting, and the guns. Tension running high. But later that night, sitting with the folder in front of him with the man's face staring back at him, he should have clocked it then.

'They still don't have a name for him,' he told her.

'No matter, I can charge him if Nelson picks him out. I'll put him down on the charge sheet as Number 6.'

'Number 6?'

'*The Prisoner*,' she said. 'Patrick McGoohan.'

'You're too young to have seen that. I barely remember it myself.'

'They did a mini-series repeat three years ago. You must have missed it.'

Caton shook his head. He was already thinking about what Simon Levi's reaction was going to be when he heard the news that his suspect was already wanted for supplying a poisonous substance that had resulted in the death of a young woman.

'Well, whatever he's called,' he told her, 'if you want to interview him you're going to have to join the queue.'

Chapter 44

Much to his surprise, Umberto and Caterina were already in the little office space they shared for the Richetti investigation.

The first thing to catch Caton's eye was a cute little aluminium Espresso maker sitting on a black base that looked like a skirt. It had pride of place on a small coffee table that had also appeared out of the blue.

The two Italian detectives were seated opposite each other, both clutching a white porcelain coffee cup. The commissario waved expansively towards the remaining seat.

'Tom, come and join us,' he said. He saw Caton eyeing the Espresso machine. 'Nice, eh? Bialetti Easy Caffè. Three cups. Your timing is good.'

Caton lifted the lid. He was right, it was still warm, and there seemed to be just enough left for him. As he poured the thick, dark liquid into the remaining cup, he noticed the character depicted on the side of the pot and repeated on the base next to the brand name. It was of a short thickset man, with striped trousers, black jacket and bow tie. The neck and face formed a single triangle. The Inspector Clouseau-like figure had a pork-pie hat on his head, and his right hand and index finger were raised straight up into the air. It could easily have been a cartoon image of Commissario Bonifati.

He smiled to himself, and went to sit between them.

'Where did you get it from?' he asked.

'Expenses,' Bonifati declared. '*Un elemento essenziale. E' impossibile lavorare senza una tazza di caffè corretta.*'

His colleague nodded vigorously. Finally they had found something they could agree on. It was indeed impossible to work without a proper cup of coffee. Every Italian knew that. Caton wondered if Bonifati had a bottle of grappa concealed about his person.

'No, Umberto,' he said. 'I meant where from? '*Da dove?*'

The Italian grinned. 'From Amazon. Where else?'

'You had it delivered here?'

'No, to the hotel.' He lifted his cup in salute. 'Ah, the power of the Internet.'

'And the cups and saucers?'

'The hotel. *Un prestito.*'

Caton raised his eyebrows. 'They lent them to you?'

Bonifati shrugged apologetically. 'Remind me to return them when we leave,' he replied. 'I would not wish to have a friend embarrass-ed.'

Caton had to smile. *Stolen property discovered at Police Headquarters.* Larry Hymer would have a field day with that.

'I have been telling Caterina about the events of yesterday,' Umberto told him. 'She was sorry to have missed the excitement.'

First name terms again, Caton noticed. The man still seemed to blow hot and cold with his colleague.

'Your friends at the *Direzione Investigativa Antimafia* must be pleased,' said Caton, watching to see his response.

'I imagine so,' he replied. 'But the fact that they have committed these serious crimes in your country will be a complication they had not planned for.'

'Nevertheless,' Caton pressed, 'to have so many of your countrymen, apparently engaged in organised crime, arrested in addition to the two men they sought … that must be a real bonus.'

Bonifati made a play of translating for his colleague. Caton was not altogether sure that he needed to, although her expression also gave nothing away. He had to turn his head to see her face. In yet another moment of paranoia he wondered if the seating arrangement had been deliberate, preventing him from seeing them both at the same time. A ploy he had used himself on occasion.

'Time will tell,' the commissario said enigmatically.

He drained his cup and placed it down on the saucer. He looked up.

'Time will tell,' he repeated.

'Well, I've some more news for you,' Caton told him, 'that might interest them as well.'

He brought them up to date with the latest developments involving the man suspected of the shootings, and his likely connection with Joanne Stuart's investigation, Operation Juniper.

'Drugs,' said Bonifati thoughtfully. 'Mafia, Camorra, Ndrangheta; they are all involv-ed in drugs. Heroin and cannabis in from Turkey, cocaine in from South America, out across the rest of Europe. There are *laboratori* in Calabria making *cristallo metadone*, and designing new drugs.'

'So they could be manufacturing it down there, and distributing it here,' said Caton. 'But why distribute it themselves? Why not just sell it on to our own drug dealers?'

'Good question,' said Bonifati. 'Maybe they hope

to cut out the man in the middle?'

'The middle man,' said Caton. 'That would more than double their earnings.'

'But bring them to your attention. Something their bosses have been trying to avoid for a long time. How can they hope to clean their money, and hide their *fuggitivi,* in a place where they do this kind of business?'

The commissario was right. It was careless. Worse than careless, it was stupid. But at least it had brought it out into the open. Shone a light on activities that Mal Haigh had admitted were low down on the list of priorities the NCA's Organised Crime Command was about to inherit. Not any more.

'About Giovanni Richetti,' he said. 'I've been having a think. It's something Kate said last night.'

Bonifati looked surprised.

'Your wife? You discuss these things with your wife?'

'Kate is an investigative profiler,' Caton told him. 'She lectures in Investigative Psychology at the university.'

'*Psicologia investigativa*!?' exclaimed Bonifati. '*La bella* Kate, *un investigatore psicologico*? *Non è possibile!*'

Both of the Italian detectives looked at him with a mixture of surprise and admiration.

'She's interviewed more serial killers than I have,' Caton told them. 'And seen as many bodies in the morgue.'

'This makes for interesting bedtimes?' said Bonifati with a smirk.

Caton shook his head. 'Not in the way you think. Seriously, she said something that got me thinking.'

Bonifati held his palms up in yet another impenetrable gesture.

'Okay,' he said, 'we are listening. What did Kate say?'

'There'll be a woman involved somewhere. There always is.'

Umberto and Caterina looked at each other. He translated. She shrugged. He shrugged. They both looked back at Caton.

'Don't you see?' he said. 'Richetti's new girlfriend. Why is it that nobody knows who she is? Why the mystery? What did he have to hide?'

Chapter 45

They began by revisiting Richetti Limited, in Ancoats. Despite the fact that they had little or no progress to report, they were received far better than the first time they had been there. It was as though resignation was beginning to replace the shock and anger that had been so evident before.

They were all there. The father, Franco, and his wife Elena seemed the most resigned of all. They looked weary and worn down by it all. His brother Roberto and his wife Liona came to sit beside them. Liona held Elena's hands in hers. The only two who seemed to have retained some of the passionate desire for justice and revenge were, paradoxically, the oldest and the youngest of them all: Mari Richetti, the grandmother, and the victim's brother, Guido.

'Girlfriends!' hissed the grandmother. 'What do girlfriends have to do with it? You think they overpowered Giovanni, trussed him up like a turkey, tied heavy sacks to him and threw him in the sea?'

'Nonna!' exclaimed her grandson.

'It's alright, Guido,' said his father. 'Your nonna is just upset.'

The grandson turned to face the three police officers sitting in a row like starlings on a telegraph line.

'She is right, though,' he said. 'I think you should

tell us why you keep asking about my brother's girlfriends.'

'I could repeat what I told you last time,' said Caton, 'that we have to explore every avenue. And we do. But the reality is, that at this moment in time there is nothing to suggest why your brother was murdered.'

'Nothing?'

'Not one shred of evidence.'

'As to motive,' added Umberto Bonifati, 'we do have some forensic evidence, but we have no suspects to match that evidence to. To arrive at suspects, we need motive.'

'So you're saying what?' the young man said. 'The motive was jealousy?'

'Not necessarily,' Caton replied. 'That can't be ruled out, but there could be other explanations.'

'Sometimes we share secrets with lovers that we do not share even with our family,' said the commissario.

'I told you before,' Guido Richetti replied. 'My brother did not have those kinds of relationships.'

'You also said something about a mutual friend having been dumped by his girlfriend,' Caton reminded him. 'You and your brother were laughing about it on your way to the airport.'

He looked surprised. 'So? What does that have to do with anything?'

'Is it possible that Giovanni could have been the reason that she dumped her boyfriend?'

The young man began to laugh and shake his head from side to side. They waited for him to stop.

'I'm sorry, Mama,' he said when he'd caught his breath and registered the surprise and disapproval on his parents' faces. 'But if you'd seen her… She was not Giovanni's type at all.'

Caton flipped through his notebook until he found

the page he was looking for.

'You told us that your brother liked to *play the field*,' he said.

'Marta Bronski belongs in a zoo, not a field,' he retorted.

'Guido!' said his father sternly.

He held up his hand in surrender.

'Okay,' he said. 'I'll give you the details of the last girlfriend Giovanni had, whose name I knew. But that was months before he was killed. You want to try his workmates. Maybe he told them who he was seeing.'

They managed to track down the girl whose name the brother had provided. She was still at her place of work, a clothes shop in King Street West. The three of them filled the tiny office space in the basement. Caterina Volpe had volunteered to stay upstairs, looking at the clothes.

'Who? Guido?' she said. 'Oh yeah, him. We were in a club in town. Don't remember which. I was half pissed at the time. Good-looking guy. Bit too smooth. Too sure of himself. Real arm candy, though. And amazing in bed. Didn't last long, though.' She looked faintly disappointed.

'What happened?' said Caton.

She gave him a flirtatious smile. 'What, in bed? You cheeky devil.'

Bonifati found it amusing. Caton did not.

'How did he finish?' he said in his most authoritative-sounding voice.

'He buggered off, didn't he? No explanation. Just failed to turn up for a date. Blew me off.' She shrugged. 'I should have known it was coming. Typical of his sort.'

'What sort is that?' said Caton.

'Serial shaggers,' she said without emotion. 'Must

of had commitment lobotomies, the lot of them.' She smiled ruefully. 'Mind you, that's just about every bloke you come across these days.'

They had no problem dragging the sovrintendente away from the clothes rails. Her expression suggested that English tastes lagged some way behind.

'Well, that was a waste of time,' said Caton.

'Not completely,' Umberto Bonifati replied. 'I learned a new English phrase.'

He shared it with his colleague, who pouted and then muttered something back.

'I didn't get that,' said Caton.

The commissario grinned. '*Signorina* Volpe says she thought it was only Italian men who were male chauvinistic pigs.'

'Next stop, Italian Magical Tours,' said Caton, looking at his watch. 'It's only a three-minute walk to Bridge Street. Let's hope we have better luck there.'

'Mr Santagata is out. He had a meeting at the bank,' Teresa Borbone, the office manager and fellow director, told them.

'In which case, perhaps we could have a word with you, and then with your colleague?' said Caton.

She looked surprised.

'I can't think of anything I haven't already told you,' she said, 'but if it'll help, of course you can.'

She turned to her colleague.

'I'll go first, Janice. Are you okay minding the shop?'

'Of course,' she replied, without taking her eyes from the screen in front of her.

They followed Teresa Borbone to the back office where they had previously interviewed her boss. She took his chair and invited them to sit down. Then she scanned their faces, hoping for a clue.

'It's about Giovanni's girlfriends,' Caton began. 'We wondered if you could tell us about any of them?'

Her face relaxed into a smile. She sat back in the chair and folded her arms, but not, Caton decided, in a defensive way.

'That's easy,' she replied. 'We knew everything and nothing.'

'We?'

'Janice and me. He saw himself as something of a lothario.' She frowned briefly. 'Or should that be Casanova? Probably both. He'd come in every Monday morning full of his latest conquest. It was funny at first, but then it got to be downright depressing.'

'Depressing? In what way?'

She puffed her cheeks, and then let it all out like a sigh.

'The way he talked about them. Like they were meat. Easy meat. As far as we could tell he wasn't interested in having proper relationships, only casual sex.'

She shook her head.

'Janice was quite taken with him at first. She'd have gone out with him at the drop of a hat if he'd tried it on. But Arturo would have put a stop to it. He made it clear whenever he appointed new staff that office romances were off limits.'

'Did he? Try it on?'

'No. He didn't need to, he had plenty of other fish to fry.'

She shook her head again.

'That should be *birds to roast*. That's what he used to say. Anyway, once she realised what he was really like she lost interest. Listening to him bragging became boring. And to tell the truth, it was all a bit distasteful. Seedy, is the word I would have used.'

'Did any of his girlfriends ever come here?' Caton asked.

She raised her eyebrows and her forehead furrowed.

'Here? To the office? Absolu…'

Her voice trailed off as she recalled something.

'There was one girl. Just the once. It was rather unpleasant.'

She was clearly reluctant to talk about it, but the three of them just sat there waiting for her to explain.

'She seemed like such a nice girl. Late teens, early twenties. Very pretty, in a wanna-be-a-celebrity sort of way.'

'Did you get her name?'

'No, not at first. Janice was dealing with her. She said she was looking for a holiday in Italy for her and five of her girl friends. I remember Janice telling her that we don't accommodate hen parties, but she said that was okay, they wanted something more cultural.'

'Giovanni Richetti?' the commissario said, showing his growing impatience.

'I'm getting to that,' she replied, giving him a cold, hard stare.

Then she composed herself.

'Anyway, Janice was going through the brochures with her when Giovanni walked in. She turned and smiled at him, said something like, "Hello, lover boy. Surprised to see me?" He froze on the spot. I've never seen anyone look so embarrassed. Like he'd been cornered. Which in a way I suppose he had.'

'What happened?' said Caton, as curious as the rest of them to find out.

'He was lost for words at first. Then he said, "Let's go outside, Angie, and talk about this." That's when she stood up. But instead of going outside, she reached into her replica Prada tote and pulled out a small transparent bag full of dog poo. Calm as you like, she untied the knot, held the bottom of the bag and threw the contents at him as he retreated down the office. "That's what you are!" she shouted. "A nasty piece of shit!"'

The commissario appeared to be taking great delight in the simultaneous translation he was giving his sovrintendente. It distracted Teresa Borbone. She stopped. Caton urged her to continue.

'I grabbed her arm,' she said, 'and pushed her down the stairs.' She saw the look on their faces and hastily added, 'No, not like that. I had hold of her all the way down, and she was holding onto the handrail. She kept screaming at him, even when she was out on the pavement. I had to close the window so we couldn't hear.'

'What did Mr Santagata say?' said Caton.

'He wasn't here, thank God. By the time he got back, I'd made Giovanni clear it all up. Then I sent him home to get changed, and told him not to come back till the following day. I also told him I'd cover his back with Arturo, but if it ever happened again that was the end of him.'

'Why not sack him on the spot?'

She shook her head. 'Employment law. Verbal warning, followed by a written warning. It was her that had committed gross misconduct, not him. But he was on notice. And it never happened again.'

'When was this?'

'Over a year ago.'

'And you never saw her again?'

'No. Thank God.' She smiled. 'Though to be honest, if I had, I'd have probably shaken her hand. It took some guts, and I've no doubt he had it coming.'

'What about more recent girlfriends?' said Caton.

She pursed her lips. 'Not really. He'd gone quiet in

that respect over the past few months. It's odd now I come to think about. No mention of women. No bragging. Just work. Not like him at all really.'

She pushed back her chair.

'Now I'll go and fetch Janice. Can I get you a drink while I'm at it?'

While they were waiting, Caton had a call on his BlackBerry. It was one of the staff manning the reception desk at the Headquarters building.

'A car has arrived,' said the receptionist, 'to take Mr Bonifati to the NCA regional headquarters.'

'Just a moment,' said Caton.

He handed Bonifati the phone.

'*Dimmi,*' he said. Confronted with a confused silence, he said, 'Tell me.'

'Apparently, three officers have arrived from...' He struggled bravely with the words. 'The *Dir-ez-ione Investi-gat-iva Antimafia.*'

'Officers? What kind of officers?' demanded Bonifati.

'A *Primo Diri-gente* from the *Poliz-ia di Stato,* a *Colonello* from the...'

'*Carabinieri,*' supplied Bonifati.

'And a Ten-en...'

'*Tenente Colonello.*'

'That's it,' said the hapless receptionist. 'From the...'

'*Guardia Finanza!*' said Bonifati, having run out of patience.

He turned to Caton.

'Where are we?'

Caton took the phone and told him.

'We'll have someone watch for the car to arrive,' he said. 'Tell the driver to put his hazard warning lights on, and Commissario Bonifati will come straight down.'

'You see,' said Bonifati, 'the DIA consists of three organisations, none of which trust each other. So, every time it's three officers. Hah!'

'Which is why we now have a National Crime Agency,' said Caton. 'Only that's going to have to work with all the regional police forces, MI5, MI6 and GCHQ. I'll let you know when it's cracked the *working together* conundrum. But don't hold your breath.'

'I suggest that *Signorina* Volpe stay with you,' said Bonifati. 'Four Italians will be more than enough for Agents Levi and Haigh to cope with.'

He repeated his decision in Italian for Caterina, but it was clear from her expression that the translation was redundant. For the very first time, Caton noticed, she did not bother to protest.

Chapter 46

'I don't know,' said Janice. 'It's ... it's ... difficult.'

She was fiddling with a cheap ring on the index finger of her right hand. A sterling silver band with silver wings on either side of a ruby-style heart. Over the past ten minutes she had verified everything that Teresa Borbone had told them. There had been something in her manner that told Caton she was holding back. He had told her so. Appealed to her better nature, the need to help them get justice for Giovanni and bring closure for his family. Then he had piled the pressure on. Finally, this crack had appeared in her defences.

'In what way is it difficult, Janice?' said Caton.

'This is where I work. I like it here.' She looked directly at him, pleading with her eyes and voice. 'I don't want to get the sack.'

They both knew that now she had revealed there was something, there would be no going back. He could see it in her eyes. Deep down she wanted to tell him. Needed to tell him. Whatever it was had been eating away at her ever since the news of his death, and the manner of it, had reached her.

'I'll see that doesn't happen,' he said, hoping, not for the first time, that it was a promise he could keep. 'Nobody need know what you tell us in here.'

She tried to read the expression on his face, gave

up, and stared past him into the main body of the office. Seeing that Teresa Borbone had her back to her and her eyes on a monitor screen, and that their boss had still not returned, she took a deep breath and began.

'It's probably nothing.'

'Let us be the judge of that, Janice,' he told her as gently as he could.

'It's Caterina, you see.'

'Caterina?'

'Mr Santagata's daughter.'

Caterina Volpe nudged Caton surreptitiously with her elbow.

'What about her?'

'Well, ever since he started here she'd be making eyes at him. Not surprising really, with him being so good looking, and her being so young.'

Caterina Volpe nudged him again.

'How young?' asked Caton.

She thought about it.

'She'd have been fourteen when he started here.'

'And now?'

'Seventeen. Eighteen next month.'

Eleven years younger than the victim.

'How did Giovanni respond to all this attention?' he asked.

'She wasn't here that often. Only when her dad brought her in during the school holidays. He treated her like a kid sister, really. Always making jokes, joshing around with her. I don't think he was even flattered, with her being so young, and him used to the attention of women a lot older.'

'You said *at first*. How did their relationship change?'

She frowned, and became defensive.

'I never said there was a relationship. Not a proper

one. I'm not saying that.'

'It's alright, Janice,' he said, desperate to retain her cooperation. 'I didn't put that very well. I meant their behaviour towards each other. How did that change?'

Her expression softened. 'She started to grow up. She became less silly and more composed, and confident. And she began to fill out. I could see he'd noticed. So could she. You could see it in the way they began looking at each other.'

'What way was that?'

'Flirtatious. And recently it was as though they shared a secret. Sometimes I would catch them whispering to each other.'

'Surely her father noticed?'

She shook her head. 'No. They never behaved like that in front of him, or Teresa. They knew better. His precious little daughter and Giovanni the Casanova? No way! He'd have gone ballistic.'

'How were they in the weeks leading up to Giovanni's trip to Italy?'

She looked thoughtful, as though trying to remember the specifics.

'That's the funny thing,' she said. 'A few weeks before Giovanni disappeared, she stopped coming into the shop; and we haven't seen her at all since. And what's more, I don't think I've heard Mr Santagata mention her at all in all that time. And I can tell you that *is* unusual.'

They got nothing more from her; she was growing more and more anxious about the likely return of Arturo Santagata.

'You won't tell him I told you, will you?' she pleaded as she headed for the door.

'I don't think there's any need for us to mention you at all,' Caton assured her.

Secretly he knew that if they ever found a

connection between her evidence and what happened to the Richetti boy there was no way he could avoid mentioning her testimony. But they were a long way from making such a connection.

'Thank you,' she said.

She was reaching for the door handle when she suddenly paused.

'Something else that's funny,' she said, as though it had only just occurred to her. 'We haven't seen her brother either.'

Caton decided to wait in the coffee shop opposite for Arturo Santagata to return. It would give them a chance to plan their strategy uninterrupted. It also meant that he could get to know Caterina Volpe a little better, and she could enjoy a half-decent cup of coffee.

'*Cosa pensi*?' he asked.

What do you think?

She smiled, deciding at last to drop the pretence. 'We try in English, if it is okay?'

He smiled back. 'Of course it's okay. Let's see how it goes. So, what do you think?'

She blew the froth of her cappuccino to one side of the cup, and licked it up. It reminded Caton of a cat with a saucer of milk. She took a sip of coffee and then put the cup down. Her eyes locked onto his. He found it unsettling.

'She said the girl, *la figlia di Santagata*, was gone. *Suo fratello* also?'

'That's right, his daughter and his son.'

'Two week before Guido Richetti was murdered?'

'Yes. The daughter, anyway.'

She shook her head. Her eyes never left his. Her hair swayed from side to side. The effect was almost hypnotic.

'This is not *una coincidenza*.'

'No,' he agreed. 'I don't believe it is.'

Her jacket was over the back of her chair. She wore an abstract black-and-white print shirt that fitted like a glove, except where it flared over the top of tight black trousers that he knew were tucked into knee-length boots. She began to play with one of the buttons of her shirt with the fingers of her left hand as she lifted the cup and took another sip. Her eyes never left his.

It was Caton's business to read body language, but he didn't need to go on a training course to understand exactly what was going on here.

She put the cup down again.

'I did not believe him, Santagata,' she said. '*Dall'inizio.*'

From the beginning? Caton was surprised. It was true that the man had seemed edgy, but his concern for the Richetti family's loss had seemed genuine.

'*I suoi occhi*, his eyes,' she said, pointing to her own. 'They are *ingannevole, ambigua.*'

'Shifty,' he said, wondering if the same could be said of hers. At this moment it was impossible to tell. 'What do you think was going on, Caterina?' he asked.

Her pupils dilated at his use of her given name. She smiled.

'*Romeo e Giulietta,*' she replied.

Her fingers strayed from the button, traced the outline of her breast and slid down towards her waist.

It was so obviously artful that it should have been funny. To his surprise and discomfort, Caton found that his body had a mind of its own. He tore his eyes away and looked out of the window. He was relieved to find that fate had come to his aid. Crossing the road and heading for Magical Italian Tours was Arturo Santagata.

He drained his cup and pointed to hers.

'Drink up,' he told her. 'He's back.'

Chapter 47

Janice had her head buried in a brochure when they walked in. She did not look up. They could see that he was in his office with Teresa Borbone, standing with his back to them, still wearing his donkey jacket.

'No doubt she's filling him in,' said Caton.

Caterina Volpe looked understandably confused.

'Telling him about us. *La nostra visita.*'

She nodded that she had understood.

When Caton knocked, Santagata turned. Through the glass they saw his expression change from surprise to anxiety. He quickly recovered, and opened the door.

'Chief Inspector,' he said, as though pleased to see him. 'Teresa was telling me that you had called. Please come in.'

When they were seated, he took his place behind the desk.

'Perhaps Miss Borbone can get you a drink?' he said.

'Thank you,' Caton replied, 'but we've just had a coffee across the road.'

His eyes flickered. So they had been waiting for him to return.

'Thank you, Teresa,' he said. 'I'll be fine.'

He waited until the door had closed behind her.

Then he smiled, nervously.

'So, how can I help you?'

'Actually, it's your daughter we're interested in,' said Caton.

The directness of the question threw him completely, as Caton had hoped it might. He was flustered, almost stuttering over the words. His face paled.

'My daughter?'

It was interesting, Caton noted, that he had not asked what they thought she had to do with all this. Perhaps that was because he already knew.

'That's right, your daughter. We were hoping to ask her a few questions about Giovanni. How he seemed to her shortly before he disappeared. If he had mentioned any of his girlfriends to her.'

Santagata edged back in his chair, holding the arms as though to steady himself.

'How would she know? She hardly knew him.'

'Really?' said Caton, watching him closely.

Letting the silence work its magic. Watching him squirm like a bug under a microscope. Watching him trying to decide if a response was expected. If anything he said might betray him. Wondering how much they already knew.

'Where is your daughter?' said Caton when the silence finally became oppressive.

'In Italy,' he replied. 'Staying with her nonna. To improve her Italian. She's fine.'

One question, three answers, Caton reflected. That was something that liars did, give you too much information as though the weight of it might convince you.

'I'd like to speak with her. Do you have her number?'

'It's no good,' Santagata replied. 'She left, as always, in a rush. She forgot to take her mobile phone with her.' He read the disbelief in Caton's expression and hastily added, 'I can give you her nonna's apartment number.'

'Thank you,' said Caton.

He waited as Santagata tore a piece of paper from his memo pad. His hand shook as he scrawled the number. It was his right hand, Caton noted. He held out the note for the policeman to take. Caton reached out to take it, but instead of doing so he stared into the man's eyes as he spoke.

'Where does she live, her nonna?'

The pupils of his eyes contracted.

'In Venice.'

'And where is her brother?'

Beads of sweat appeared at his temples. His eyes darted downwards to the right. He was having an internal dialogue. Deciding whether or not to lie. Now they flicked up to the right. The truth had won out.

'Also in Venice.'

Caton took the number and placed it in his inside breast pocket.

'Really?' he said. 'And what is he doing there?'

His eyes darted up to the left. Caton waited for the lie.

'The work that Giovanni had been doing when he was murdered. Trying to rebuild our reputation.'

'I didn't realise that you had a son, or a daughter.'

'You didn't ask.'

Eyes left.

'It wasn't relevant.'

Once again, Caton let the silence linger.

'I would like your son's mobile number too,' he said. 'Unless of course he has also forgotten to take it with him?'

Reluctantly, Santagata wrote out the second number and handed it over.

'Is he staying at his nonna's?' Caton asked.

Eyes up to the left.

'I don't think so.'

'So where do you think he's staying?'

Eyes left.

'I'm … not sure. At one of the hotels we use, perhaps. They sometimes let us stay a few nights without charging us.' He attempted a smile. 'Perks of the trade.'

'I told you,' she said. 'He is *un bugiardo*. A liar.'

'You did,' he agreed. 'And you were right.'

They were sitting a few doors down from Italian Magical Tours in the Bridge gastro pub, he with a Virgin Mary, she with a Camparinette.

'What is that?' he asked.

'*Due misure di gin, una misura di Campari, una misura Martini,*' she replied.

Two parts gin, one part Campari, one part Martini. It sounded like a drink that Kate would enjoy. Except that he'd have to explain where he'd come across it.

She raised the glass to her lips.

'Probably best if you waited,' he told her. 'Until you've spoken to the grandmother.'

She frowned, and lowered the glass.

'Me? *Perche* me?'

Caton found it amusing that she was beginning to speak a combination of both languages. Something he had been guilty of when he was first learning Italian. He wondered if there was a name for it, like Franglais. *Italese*, perhaps?

'It's unlikely that the nonna's English will be that good,' he explained. 'It will sound more formal, more *ufficiale*, if it comes from you.'

He handed her the number.

She nodded thoughtfully, took the number and

reached into her bag for her mobile phone. She entered the number and paused, before pressing CALL. She looked straight into his eyes.

'You trust me to do this? To ask the question?'

'The questions,' he corrected her. 'Yes, of course I do.'

She smiled, and pressed the green icon. While they waited for a response, she increased the volume so that he could hear the conversation. Caton leaned closer, his head only inches from hers. He could smell a perfume he had not noticed before.

'*Pronto?*' said a woman's voice. She sounded wary.

Caterina Volpe introduced herself, and checked that she was speaking with Rosetta Santagata. She did not say at first why she was calling. Caton thought it a smart move. The woman's response confirmed it. Instead of asking why a detective of the Venice Questura was ringing her, from the United Kingdom, she merely asked how she could help her.

The sovrintendente told her only that she needed to speak with her granddaughter, Laura, who she understood was staying with her.

Another smart move, since the girl's grandmother did not ask who had given her that information. Instead, she simply said that Laura was not in. Her voice was harder now, as though she had drawn strength from somewhere. Caton wondered if someone else was listening in at her end.

Caterina Volpe asked her to save and make a note of her number, and get her daughter to ring her back as soon as she returned. Then she asked, in a very off-hand manner, if Laura's brother, Rafaelle, was also staying there, at his nonna's.

The response was adamant. He was not staying there, and she had no idea where he was. She hadn't seen him in months. If he was in Venice, it was news to her.

An over-reaction, Caton thought, with more information than had been requested. He nudged the Italian detective sergeant with his elbow, scribbled in the air and silently formed the word *address* with his lips.

She nodded her understanding and requested Rosetta Santagata's address. It was reluctantly provided. Caterina Volpe repeated it slowly for Caton to write down. Then she repeated her request for the granddaughter to return her call, and rang off.

'*Come ho fatto?*' she asked.

How did I do?

'Very well, Caterina,' he told her. 'Very well indeed.'

'Tell Commissario Bonifati,' she said. 'It will be a nice surprise for him.'

Her smile was ironic.

Chapter 48

'Sovrintendente Volpe rang the nonna three times last night,' Bonifati told him. 'And again this morning. No reply. No answerphone.'

He had reverted to sovrintendente, Caton reflected. Despite the fact that Caterina Volpe was in the room fixing the three of them espressos.

'She doesn't want to answer our questions,' he said.

'Evidently.'

'Why don't I try this time? She won't recognise my number.'

'But she will see it is from the United Kingdom.'

'If it doesn't work, you could ask your colleagues to call at the apartment and find out what's going on.'

Bonifati smiled expansively. 'I will *command* my colleagues to call on her,' he said.

Caton noticed his assistant's grimace as she placed their coffees on the table in front of them. She went back for her own, and then came to join them.

Simultaneously the Italian detectives raised their cups, sniffed the aroma of the contents and took a sip, pursed their lips and jiggled their heads from side to side to indicate that it was just acceptable.

It might almost have been rehearsed. Caton smiled to himself as he dialled the number.

The three of them waited. Eventually, he shook his head and ended the call.

'*Non è stato possibile collegarsi,*' he told them.

It was not possible to connect you.

The commissario picked up his own mobile from the table where it lay in readiness. He waved it theatrically in the air.

'She don't wanna talk to me? She gonna talk to my friends!'

'Don Corleone?' asked Caton. '*The Godfather*?'

'No,' said Caterina Volpe. 'Umberto Bonifati.' She made speech marks with her fingers. '*Il Buffone Veneziano.*'

The Venetian Buffoon.

The expressions on their faces told him that she had heard it many times before, as had he her riposte. Their relationship still confused him. It was, he supposed, a little like his with Gordon Holmes.

Bonifati dialled. Almost immediately he was through to the commissariato. Caton listened in quiet amusement as Umberto struggled to make his request understood.

No, he didn't want them to question the woman. Just to find out if the granddaughter was there. If so, to insist that she either ring his mobile number, or accompany them to the commissariato. On what pretext? Who gave a damn? Just make one up. Obstructing a police investigation, that would do. If she was not there? Find out where she is, and see if the brother is there. What brother? *Her* brother, you idiot!

It reminded Caton of the battle that Camilleri's Inspector Montalbano had to understand, and to be understood, every time he met with the confused yet likeable Catarella.

There was no police launch available? So take the *vaporetto*, Bonifati told whoever was at the end of the line.

Caton brought the map up in his head. Having

been to the police station on Fondamenta San Lorenzo, he knew that it was three hundred yards, give or take, to the San Zaccaria *vaporetto* stop. Then just three stops to Redentore on the Guidecca. And another three hundred metres on foot through the *calle* to the apartment block they had been given as Rosetta Santagata's address. About a mile in total. In Manchester, less than a minute by car, or twenty on foot. Closer to forty minutes in Venice. Longer in winter. Longer still when the Aqua Alta tides flooded the city.

'*Madre di Dio, Fallo! Fallo!*'

Mother of God. Just do it!

Had the commissario been holding a handset, Caton had no doubt he would have slammed it back into its cradle. As it was, he waved his cellphone in a circle above his head before striking his temple with the palm of his hand. Then he took a deep breath and placed the phone gently down on the tabletop.

'Antonello?' said Caterina Volpe.

Her boss nodded.

She shook her head in sympathy. 'Antonello Morisini,' she said.

Their expressions said it all. Every police station had one, it would seem.

'Now we wait,' said Bonifati.

He drained his cup and pushed it across the coffee table towards his colleague.

'*Facciamo un altra,*' he told her.

To his surprise, she smiled sweetly, stood up, said, '*Buona idea,*' picked up her bag and left the room.

The three of them had finished their second cup of coffee. The commissario had made a point of waiting for his sovrintendente to return from the restroom. He finally gave up, admitted defeat and made them himself. Caton suspected that she had waited outside the door, listening for the sound of the cups tinkling on the saucers before coming back in. They had run out of things to say, and the tension mounted. It was close to an hour before Bonifati's phone rang.

'*Pronto!*' he said.

This time there was no two-way conversation. The commissario listened intently. When he ended the call he looked puzzled, and then thoughtful.

'The girl is not there,' he told them. 'Neither is her brother. But their clothes are. The nonna was … *ansioso e sfuggente.*'

Caton nodded. 'Anxious and evasive. What did the grandmother say about where they were?'

'That they had gone out. She did not know where. She did not know when they would be back.'

'What do your colleagues think is going on?'

He shrugged. 'They have no idea, but they are sure that there is something seriously wrong. I told them to leave, but to set a watch on the apartment.'

He pushed back his chair and stood up.

'The sovrintendente and I are going back to see for ourselves,' he said. 'It would be helpful, Tom, if you came with us.'

Detective Chief Superintendent Gates was only too happy to agree. Gordon Holmes was back. Joanne Stuart was on top of Operation Juniper. Things were relatively quiet. And you never knew when you might need the help of the Italian police.

Caton suspected that she just wanted to be sure that the commissario and his sovrintendente actually got on the plane and did not return.

Kate was far less happy as she watched him pack. 'Why do you have to go?' she asked. 'It's their investigation. It always was.'

'But we're talking about two British citizens,' he retorted. 'Three, if you count the victim.'

'But you don't even know if anything's happened to them.'

'We can't assume that it hasn't. Or they may just be trying to avoid us.'

She pulled a face. 'Come on, Tom. You don't seriously suspect them of having had anything to do with Richetti's murder?'

He closed the lid and took hold of her hand.

'I have no idea what's going on, Kate. Not for certain. But you saw Giovanni Richetti's body in that *riello*. How do you think we'd feel if these two ended up like that, and I'd done nothing to try and stop it?'

She eased her hand away.

'That's not fair, Tom, and you know it. It's emotional blackmail. You're not the only person who can do this. If you were ill, or had food poisoning or something, somebody else would have to go. What about Gordon? He's back, isn't he?'

He locked the case and, to show his resolve, started to put the identification straps on.

'Have you any idea how long it's taken to establish this relationship with Umberto?' he said.

'And with Caterina,' she said. 'Let's not forget the lovely Caterina!'

'Not that again!' he protested. 'What is it with you and the sovrintendente?'

'It's no good using her rank instead of her name, that's not going to convince me.'

Suddenly, they were standing facing each other. The bed lay between them like no-man's-land.

'Convince you of what?'

'That I can trust her,' she said. 'Because I don't!'

'Well neither do I!' he shouted. 'The issue here isn't

about her, it's about me. Whether you trust me.'

To his surprise, she burst into tears and ran into the lounge.

Caton sat on the bed, head in hands, and tried to make sense of it all. This wasn't like Kate at all. This was someone else. Someone he didn't know. It wasn't just about her being pregnant, surely? Maybe it had all been too much. Finding out about the baby. Planning the wedding. He and Harry nearly not making it. The honeymoon interrupted by the discovery of the body. Then the succession of late nights and early mornings, most of them in the company of the very attractive Caterina Volpe. Kate looking in the mirror and seeing her own shape changing dramatically, and not for the better. He thought it made her more beautiful. Not just the way her skin had softened and her eyes seemed darker, but what it represented. This was their baby she was carrying. He loved her for it all the more. The question was, how to convince her of that fact.

He need not have bothered. It turned out that Kate had never really doubted him. It was about their being apart again so soon. She had been trying to find a more powerful, less selfish reason for wanting him to stay. Now she was full of guilt and remorse. Practically pleading with him to go. The result was that when he left it was him that was consumed with feelings of guilt, which only a very special present from Duty Free was going to assuage.

Chapter 49

Caton was surprised to discover that Rosetta Santagata's apartment was just one block away from the one that he and Kate had shared before they moved across the Lagoon to the San Clemente Palace. It too was on the top floor of three, in a modern white-stone block.

There were two officers waiting for them. A *Vice Sovrintendente*, whom Bonifati identified as the hapless Antonello Morisini, and a very young female *Assistente Capo* called Alessandra da Vigonovo. There was no question of them speaking anything other than Italian. Caton kept up as best he could.

'She is far worse than before,' Morisini told his boss. 'She hasn't slept. She cries all the time.'

'What has she told you?' said Bonifati.

He shrugged. 'Nothing. Just that the girl has gone. She's frightened for her.'

Caton spotted the expression on the face of his female colleague. Raised eyebrows, and a twisted mouth. Bonifati saw it too.

'What about you, *da Vigonovo*?' he asked. 'Can you think of anything worth mentioning?'

The AC nodded tentatively.

'She is worried about her grandson, too. He's called Rafaelle. He went after his sister and has not returned or contacted her in any way. And...'

She paused, to see if Morisini might take the cue and provide the information himself. There was little sign of it. He seemed as interested as the rest of them.

'Go on,' said the commissario.

'She says that the reason she is frightened is that her granddaughter is pregnant.'

Bonifati exchanged glances with Caton. The implications were glaringly obvious. Caton noticed that Caterina Volpe, standing beside her boss, had paled.

'Where is she?' said the commissario. 'The grandmother.'

Rosetta Santagata was sitting at a marble-top table in the surprisingly spacious lounge. Behind her, a balcony opened up onto the Lagoon. She was twisting a table napkin in her hands and every so often dabbing with it at her eyes. When they entered the room, she looked up expectantly.

Caton placed her in her early seventies. She was tall and gaunt, with sharp features. Just like her son, Arturo. Her grey hair was swept back in a bun. She had fierce, intelligent eyes, reddened by constant crying. Her face fell when she registered that the officers were alone.

'Signora, my name is Commissario Umberto Bonifati,' he began. 'These are my colleagues.'

'I know who you are,' she said.

'Really?' He looked surprised. 'From where do you know me?'

She pointed to the wide-screen television on the facing wall.

'From that. And from the newspapers.' She stared straight at him. 'Have you found them? Laura and Rafaelle?'

She did not strike Caton as being distraught. Perhaps that was a phase she had passed through.

Instead, he sensed an iron resolve. This was not a woman to cross.

Bonifati pulled out a chair from the table and sat down facing her.

'No, *Signora* Santagata, I am afraid that we have not. Nor are we likely to without your help.'

She dabbed her eyes.

'I have already told your people everything I know.'

'So I understand,' he replied coolly. 'Though I also heard that it took you a long time to do so.'

It was almost as though he had slapped her face. She jerked upright, her back ramrod straight. Her posture defensive aggressive.

'What are you saying?' she said.

Bonifati shrugged. 'That the time for playing games is past, Signora. The longer we spend chasing shadows, the less hope there is that we will find your grandchildren alive.'

It was so self-evident that she did not try to protest. Instead, she placed her hands on the table, as though providing a support for what she was about to do.

'What do you want to know?' she said.

'The truth,' he said. 'From the beginning.'

She took a deep breath. 'My son rang me. He said we had a situation. My granddaughter Laura had got mixed up with a boy, and he had got her pregnant. He was not worthy of her. But love had made her blind. So he was sending her to stay with me so that I could convince her of the mistake she was making, and help arrange for her to resolve the issue.'

'*Una interruzione volontaria di gravidanza?*' said Bonifati, wishing to be clear.

A voluntary interruption of a pregnancy. An abortion.

She nodded, reluctantly.

'Is abortion legal in Italy?' Caton whispered to Caterina Volpe.

The commissario answered for her.

'Yes, Chief Inspector. It has been legal since 1978. Providing it is accomplished within ninety days of conception. In this case, because of her age, her father's consent would have been required.'

He turned back to address the grandmother.

'Have you managed to convince your granddaughter, *signora*?'

She looked down at her hands, and slowly shook her head.

'And how many weeks gone is she?'

'Eleven.'

'Another reason, then, that we should find her quickly.'

Rosetta Santagata spat out the words. 'You bastard! You think that is why I want her back? So that I can kill my great-grandchild? I just want my Laura back, safe and sound.'

Morisini was about to respond, but the commissario stayed him with one imperious hand raised in the air.

'It's alright,' he said. 'Signora Santagata is understandably upset.'

He lowered his hand.

'Signora,' he said, 'did Laura come willingly to stay with you?'

She wiped a trace of spittle from her lips before replying.

'No.'

'So how did your son make sure that she arrived here safely?'

She paused. Caton could tell that she was carefully choosing her words.

'He sent Rafaelle to look after her.'

Bonifati's eyebrows rose. 'Look after her? Or keep an eye on her?'

'Both, I suppose.'

'Mmm,' he responded. 'He seems not to have managed either.'

'That's not fair!' she protested. 'It was not his fault. He had some important business to conduct for Arturo. Laura only went as far as the Co-Op.'

She looked at each of them in turn, trying to find someone who would understand.

'It's nearby, on Calle Corte Grande. Only two minutes away.'

It was, Caton reflected, where he and Kate had shopped. Less than a quarter of a mile, most of it in plain sight. More like five minutes each way.

'I waited twenty minutes,' she continued. 'When she did not return, I went to look for her. They told me she had been there. She had left with her shopping some time ago.'

'What did you do, Signora?'

'I hurried back here and rang Rafaelle. He told me not to worry. To tell no one and do nothing. He would look for her and bring her home.'

She had started to lose her composure. Her body sagged and tears were beginning to well up in the corners of her eyes. She raised the napkin and began to dab at them.

'After almost an hour he came back. He said that one of the people he asked, a neighbour in the next apartment block, told him that he had seen a young girl who appeared to have collapsed being tended by two paramedics by the bridge on the Calle Scuola. She was lifted into a water ambulance by two male paramedics.'

'What did you do, *signora*?'

She gave him a withering look.

'What do you think we did? We rang the Ospedale Saints Giovanni e Paolo. There was no record of a woman matching her description having been brought in. Then we rang the new Ospedale in Mestre without success. It was just after that that Rafaelle received a phone call on his mobile.'

The commissario raised his hand again.

'One moment!' he said. 'This is the second time that you have mentioned him having a phone. Why is it that whenever we tried to ring the number his father gave us, we could not be connected?'

She looked sheepish.

'He has another phone. A number he gives only to family and friends.'

Bonifati nodded. 'So, he receives a phone call.'

'He went out onto the veranda to take it. When he came back in he looked pale. I asked him what was the matter. He said that he had to go out. He was going to get Laura. He said I was not to worry, and I must tell no one. Especially not the police.'

Once more she sought understanding in their faces. She found only pity. Her eyes welled up.

'When was this?' asked the commissario. 'The phone call.'

'Perhaps an hour before your man here came to the apartment yesterday.'

'Yesterday morning?'

'Yes.'

He shook his head. 'Did Laura have her mobile phone here in Venice?' he asked.

'Yes,' she sobbed.

'Did she have it when she was taken?'

'She always carried it with her. She was always texting. She had been waiting for someone to call her for weeks.'

Caton and Caterina Volpe exchanged glances. That would have been the victim, her lover, Giovanni. Had they not told her that he was dead?

'Do you have her number?'

'I don't remember it.'

'Has she ever rung you from that phone?'

'Yes. Whenever she goes out. She only goes to her cousins' on Calle Nuova, and to the Co-Op. She rings to say she has arrived, and when she is on her way back. I insist.'

'Then it will be on your phone. Her brother's, too. Please write down the number of the phone he uses.'

He signalled to Morisini to give her his notebook and biro.

'Does your grandson have a car?'

'He has one on the mainland that he and Giovanni Richetti used when they were over here on business. It is garaged in Mestre.'

'Is it a hire car?'

'Arturo bought it for them, second-hand.'

'What is the car's registration?'

She shook her head. 'I have no idea.' Her eyes brightened a little. 'But Rafaelle will know. And Arturo.'

Caton and all four of the Italian police officers stared at her in amazement. It was clear that she had no idea the Richetti boy was dead. They had kept it from her, lest she might tell her granddaughter.

The commissario pushed back his chair and stood up.

'Thank you, *signora*,' he said. 'Now we are getting somewhere. I promise you we will do our best to find Laura and Rafaelle.'

The honesty of his promise, and the stark reality that it represented, were not lost on her. She buried her head in her hands, and her shoulders began to heave as the sobbing intensified.

Bonifati gestured for the young *Assistente Capo*, Alessandra da Vigonovo, to stay with her, and led the others out onto the landing.

Caton heard him mutter under his breath as he followed them out.

'*Meglio tardi che mai.*'

Better late than never.

Chapter 50

'Morisini,' said the commissario. 'I want you to organise a door-to-door of all the neighbouring apartments until you have the name of the neighbour who spoke to Rafaelle. We need a description of those two paramedics.'

'The mobile phone numbers,' said Caterina Volpe. 'We need to set up a trace on both of them.'

'I'll arrange that,' he told her. 'I have a contact in the Information and External Security Agency. If we have to wait for a warrant, we'll still be waiting tomorrow.'

'The car, then,' she said, 'it must be registered to one or other of them. There'll be the insurance, too.'

'Do it,' he said.

'If Arturo Santagata bought it for them to use, he must have the details,' said Caton. 'Why don't I ring him?'

'Good idea,' said Bonifati.

'I'm surprised he's not flown out here himself,' Caton said. 'Perhaps he's scared of what might be waiting for him.'

He was definitely scared of something. He sounded even more distraught than his mother when Caton told him what they knew so far. He claimed to know nothing about their disappearance. Caton only half believed him.

'What did you think had happened when your mother told you that she had gone?' Caton asked.

'That she had run away.'

'Why would she do that?'

'Because of the baby. Because she wanted to keep it.'

'The baby you neglected to tell us about?'

There was a telling silence at the other end of the line.'

'I didn't...'

'Think it was relevant?' guessed Caton. 'It seems there have been a lot of things you didn't think were relevant.'

Santagata had no reply to that.

'I'll tell you something else that's relevant,' Caton said. 'The make and number of the car you bought for your sons. The one that is garaged in Mestre.'

Bonifati had just finished arranging for the details of the Fiat Bravo to be sent as an urgent stop-on-sight to all *Carbinieri* and *Polizia di Stato* units, when the news came in.

'An *ambulanza* was reported stolen from outside the hospital at 9.30 yesterday morning,' he told them. 'Thanks to the incredible efficiency of our Vigili Urbani, it was discovered moored at the Passo Campalto Marina, just to the East of Mestre, at 10 o'clock this morning. It had been abandon-ed.'

Over twenty-four hours to locate a missing ambulance? Caton was unsurprised by the note of sarcasm in the commissario's voice.

'The *Carabinieri Polizia Scientifica* have just finished examining it. If they thought it was a... What do you call it? A *giro di gioia*?'

'A joyride,' Caton told him.

'If they thought that, imagine how little trouble

327

they took.'

They heard the sound of heavy feet slapping their way up the stone steps. An overweight and panting Vice Sovrintendente Morisini appeared on the landing. They waited for him to recover his breath.

'Marcello Molare,' he said at last. '*Una dentista.*'

'Molare? A dentist?' said Bonifati. 'Really?'

Morisini nodded enthusiastically. 'Really, Commissario.'

'What about him?' asked Bonifati.

'He's the witness. What saw the kidnappers.'

'Did he describe them?'

'Yes. A big man. Maybe one hundred and eighty-three centimetres tall. Heavy build. Black curly hair. The other one, short, but muscled. Maybe one hundred and sixty-five centimetres. He couldn't see his hair. He was wearing a black bob hat.'

'A black bob hat? How did he know they were paramedics?'

'They were wearing white shirts and black trousers.'

'That's it? White shirts and black trousers, and he instantly knew they were paramedics?'

'They had an *ambulanza*. It was moored in the *rio* immediately behind his apartment block.'

'How old were they?'

He shrugged, just like his boss was wont to do.

'He isn't sure. Between twenty-five and forty-five.'

'What about their faces?'

Another shrug. 'He didn't really notice them. He was looking at the girl. He was concerned for her.'

The commissario raised his hands in one of his familiar gestures. This time it neither looked nor sounded like a blessing.

'Two males, one tall, one short, black trousers, white shirts, aged between twenty and forty. *E 'incredibile!*'

'In the company of an *ambulanza*,' the hapless Morisini reminded him.

His boss shook his head. 'Not any more,' he said.

It was almost exactly nine kilometres to the Passo Compalto Marina. With the siren blasting, it took them just under twenty minutes. A hair-raising trip on which they had cut across the bows of a cruise ship seven storeys high, and almost swamped a procession of gondolas. At one point the launch turned so quickly that Caterina Volpe lost her balance and cannoned into Caton's chest. Instinctively he threw his arms around her and leaned forward to stop the two of them falling overboard.

He could feel the swell of her breasts, the heat of her body, and her soft hair against his cheek. There was that same scent, of fragrant rose and lavender. He held her just a fraction too long. She placed her hands on his arms, eased herself free and brushed her jacket straight.

Caton looked away and found Umberto Bonifati staring at him, a huge grin on his face.

'*Acqua di Parma*,' said the commissario. 'Her favourite.'

Both she and Caton blushed. She with anger, he with embarrassment. It came as a relief when the launch pulled in behind the ambulance and moored up.

The ambulance was a sleek yellow motor launch with a red stripe down the side, emblazoned with *Ambulanza, Venezia Emergenzia, 118*. No wonder Umberto had been scathing about the time it had taken to locate it.

A carabinieri marshal was sitting in a green Mitsubishi jeep, waiting for the Scene of Crime officers to return following an intervention from Bonifati's superiors. He was bored, and less than sympathetic.

'It's less than two minutes from here to the A27,' he told them. 'After that they've got motorways in all directions. They could have been in Slovenia, Austria or Switzerland before tea time.'

'There was supposed to be a car waiting for me here,' the commissario told him. 'Please tell me this isn't it?'

'Down the end of the marina,' the marshal replied with a backward jerk of his thumb. 'You must know someone, that's all I can say.'

The three of them started walking in the direction he had indicated. *It's all very well*, Caton was thinking, *but if they had no idea where the kidnappers had gone, what was the point of coming here?*

Fifty metres ahead of them was a blue and white Alfa Romeo 159, with red stripes and *Carabinieri* on the side and bonnet in large white letters. The driver was sitting on the bonnet smoking a cigarette. He saw them coming and, in a leisurely manner, stood up, stubbed the cigarette out under his heel, and placed his cap on his head. As they approached, he threw a lazy salute, and opened one of the rear doors, smiling at Caterina Volpe as he did so. It was almost as though her superior and Caton were invisible.

'*Carabinieri sanguinosi!*' Bonifati muttered.

'Where to?' asked the driver once they had strapped themselves in.

'Can you pick up *Polizia di Stato* communications?' asked the commissario.

'If I tune into them,' came the reply.

'Well why don't you do just that,' said Bonifati. 'Then we wait.'

He turned to Caton sitting in the back seat alongside the sovrintendente.

And then, as though having read Caton's thoughts,

he said. 'I have … *un'intuizione.*'
A hunch.

Chapter 51

They had been sitting there for almost half an hour. Even with intermittent air conditioning, it was becoming uncomfortably hot. Where Caterina Volpe's perfume had previously been entrancing, it was now cloying. The close proximity of her body, one of her thighs resting against his, was another reason Caton felt an urge to get out of the car. If only he could think of an excuse.

Then came the breakthrough. The IMIE from Laura Santagata's mobile phone. The global positioning coordinates were coming through.

'Where is it?' said Bonifati.

Caton and Caterina Volpe both craned forward between the front seats to look at the satellite map on the fascia display.

'It's in the forests north of Treviso,' said the driver.

'How far?' asked the commissario.

'About fifty kilometres as the birds fly.'

'We're not birds. How far in this?'

He punched the coordinates into his satellite navigation system.

'Sixty-two,' he replied. He read the journey time. 'One hour twenty-five minutes.'

'In this, with the siren going?' said Bonifati.

The driver grinned and turned on the ignition.

'Half that,' he said.

They sped along dual carriageway roads with flat farmland on either side. Caton had one hand on the handle above his side window, the other on the top of the seat in front. He had never suffered from travel sickness, but there was a first time for everything.

As they approached the town of Montebelluna, the road became busier. On either side were industrial estates, and an increasing number of trucks to overtake. Beyond the town, wooded slopes rose steeply ahead of them.

Please tell me we're not going up there, Caton silently prayed. The car turned left onto a single carriageway, and picked up speed. His relief was temporary. Four kilometres later, they turned right at a crossroads on the far side of the hills and headed east. To their left, in the distance, were the mountains of Trentino Alto-Adige and the Southern Tyrol, to their right, those same wooded slopes they had approached from the other side. After less than five minutes, the driver indicated right onto a narrow road, and headed into the hills.

They travelled along a narrow valley, and then, without warning, began to climb. The road twisted and turned as it ascended. Much of the time they were enclosed by pollarded birch trees growing right up to the edge of the asphalt. Occasionally there were glimpses of blue sky. Dappled shade coloured the surface of the road purple. Under different circumstances it would, he thought, have been beautiful. Unfortunately, the driver seemed intent on keeping his promise. Caton and Sovrintendente Volpe clung on for grim death.

'Wait!' shouted Caton suddenly.

The driver slammed on his brakes bringing the car to a standstill broadside across the road.

'*Che diavolo*!?' shouted the commissario.

'Back there,' said Caton. 'Off the road, on a track. There's a car. A red one. I think it's a Fiat Bravo. Isn't that what Rafaelle Santagata would have been driving?'

'Which side of the road?' said Bonifati.

'Our side.'

The commissario told the driver to back up. Grumbling, he did as he was asked.

'There!' said Caton. 'Right there.'

It was twenty yards up the narrow track. A six-year-old red Fiat Bravo bearing the licence plate Arturo Santagata had given him. The driver's door was open. There was no one inside.

Caton took a deep breath and pushed the Fiat badge in the centre of the boot. The boot swung open. It too was empty.

'We have a choice,' he said. 'We can follow this track and see where it leads, or carry on to the place where his sister's mobile phone is supposed to be.'

'We go there first, and come back here if we find nothing,' Bonifati proposed.

'I agree,' said Caton.

They piled back into the Alfa Romeo.

It turned out to have been the right choice. One kilometre further on they reached a roadblock manned by Carabinieri. More accurately, a large blue Carabinieri van positioned across the road.

A sombre-looking trooper spoke to their driver and then checked their identification.

The trooper frowned when Caton showed him his warrant card.

'He's with me,' the commissario said. 'What's going on here anyway?'

The trooper shrugged. 'I've only been here five minutes myself,' he said. 'But from what I gather, it's bad. You find out for yourselves. But you can't take the car. Orders. You'll have to go on foot.'

After less than a hundred metres, the trees on either side thinned out. Ahead they could see a number of Carabinieri vehicles parked up. Two vans, a jeep, a motorcycle and an Alfa Romeo that was a twin to their own. Caton's heart sank. It had all the hallmarks of a murder scene.

They were stopped twice more before a trooper led them off the road and along a short track towards some farm buildings.

'What is this place?' asked the commissario.

'*Una fattoria Cinghiale,*' he replied.

A wild boar farm. Caton's chest tightened. It felt as though a giant bear was trying to squeeze the breath from him. He stopped and took a deep breath.

Sensing that something was wrong, the commissario stopped, turned, saw Caton standing there hunched over and hurried back.

'Tom. Are you alright? What's the matter?' he said.

Caton took another breath and let it out slowly.

'It's alright,' he said, straightening up. 'I felt sick there for a moment. It must have been the car.'

'Mmm,' said Bonifati. 'He drove like a maniac.'

They carried on until they reached an open space around which were four buildings. One looked like a single-storey farmhouse, one like a large barn. The other two had chimney-like tubes sticking vertically out of corrugated steel roofs. They looked to Caton like factory units. There were close to a dozen Carabinieri standing in two groups. Their voices were hushed. The atmosphere sombre.

A senior officer came to meet them.

'You must be Commissario Bonifati,' he said. 'I am Colonello Romano.'

He was a tall and imposing figure, more so in his uniform.

Bonifati introduced Caton and Caterina Volpe.

'I'm afraid the men you are looking for have left,' said the colonel.

'What about the boy and the girl?' asked the commissario. 'Are they here?'

'We think so,' the colonel replied. Seeing their reaction and realising what he had said, he hastily added, 'That is to say, the girl is. The boy, we are not sure about. Come, I'll show you.'

He led them to the farmhouse. Lying on well-worn sofa, her body covered by a blanket, a cushion beneath her head, was a young woman. A female officer seated on a chair watched over her. Three other Carabinieri sprang to attention as their colonel entered the room.

'We found her in the kitchen,' he said. 'She was tied to a chair, but otherwise unhurt. What injuries she has are not visible. She was completely traumatised. Too shocked to speak to us. We had to give her an injection. To sedate her.'

He registered the expression on Caton's face.

'Please tell him that we are a paramilitary organisation, Commissario,' he said. 'My men served in Afghanistan. They are trained in battlefield first aid. We carry medical supplies with us.'

'I speak Italian, Colonel,' Caton told him. 'Not that well, but well enough. Thank you for the courtesy of an explanation.'

The Carabinieri inclined his head in acknowledgement.

'Excuse my presumption,' he said.

'What about the boy, her brother?' Bonifati asked impatiently.

The colonel glanced at the sleeping girl.

'Not here,' he said. 'Outside.'

He took them first to the barn, where they had to stay behind a ribbon of yellow tape strung out between portable metal posts a metre inside the door. The barn was full of bales of hay and sacks of feed. There were also pieces of discarded steel kitchen units along one wall. In the centre of the barn was a metal chair. Beside it were coiled loops of rope and three distinct piles of clothes. The floor stank of urine and faces.

'Over here we found a single spent cartridge,' said the colonel.

He pointed to a spot a metre behind the chair and to the right. A small triangle of card marked the spot. It could as easily have been a major incident scene Caton reflected.

Colonel Romano led them outside and past one of the other buildings.

'This one is where they slaughter them,' he said. 'The wild boar, that is. The other one is where they process the meat into salami, prosciutto, mortadella, steaks and so on.'

They rounded the corner of the building and were confronted by a bizarre sight. In a large compound, surrounded by a five-foot-high fence made up of steel strands, were a dozen or so wild boar, covered in thick grey-brown hair, grubbing in what looked like a completely barren and desolate landscape of earth and stone. Beyond the fence corrugated metal tunnels, each several metres long, were scattered across the clearing as far as the edge of the woods a hundred metres away. Out there were too many wild boar for Caton to count.

In any case, his mind was elsewhere. He watched the animals watching him with their tiny yet frighteningly intelligent eyes. They sniffed the air with their snouts, as though scenting for food.

'Don't worry,' said the colonel. 'They're harmless, providing you don't provoke them. And anyway, I'm armed.'

I'm not, Caton reflected.

Behind the factory unit there was a smaller building, like a barn, with three sides and a roof. It held a large pen. Two troopers stood guard, their backs to the pen. They parted as their colonel approached. In the pen were seven large wild boar.

'I am waiting for an expert to come and move these animals,' he said. 'Then our forensics team can have a proper look. But so far we have counted five long bones, femur and humerus by the looks of it, and the remains of three crushed shaven skulls. Their contents have been completely devoured, along with everything else.'

Caton was so absorbed by the horror of it all that he failed to notice her slip away. It was only when he heard her retching behind the barn that he realised she was no longer there.

'Don't worry,' the colonel called out to her. 'You're not the first, and I doubt you'll be the last.'

Caton and the commissario watched as the ambulance carrying Laura Santagata departed. Caterina Volpe was sitting in the Alfa Romeo, her head in her hands, the door open, just in case.

'I suppose Laura will recover in time,' said Caton. 'But there's no telling what the shock may have done to her unborn child.'

Behind them the *Polizia Scientifica* were already at work.

'It looks like they shot one of them before he was thrown in that pen,' said Bonifati. 'Let's hope for her sake it was Rafaelle.'

'Presumably they used her to lure him up here, then forced him to tell them who he'd got to kill the Richetti boy,' said Caton. 'They probably wouldn't have needed to torture him, just threaten to throw his sister in with the wild boar.'

'That would do it for me,' said Bonifati. 'If I had a sister.'

'Given that they smashed his mobile phone, why did they leave hers on the kitchen table?' Caton wondered. 'They must have known you'd put a trace on it.'

'Because they wanted us to find this place. What they had done,' Bonifati told him. 'Now this is how the Mafia do it. A proper Mafia signature!'

Chapter 52

'I'm picking them up at 11,' he told her across the breakfast table.

'Them?' Kate's eyebrows rose, the tone of her voice incredulous. '*She's* coming with him?'

'Yes.'

'So he hasn't confronted her with it yet?'

'Seems not.'

She had a bite of toast, and chewed it thoughtfully. When she had finished, she had a sip of juice. She put the glass down.

'I was right about her.'

She was trying not to show it, but a hint of triumph came through.

'For all the wrong reasons,' he said.

'I was still right. I never trusted her.'

'Nor, it seems, did Umberto.'

'When did you know?'

Caton drained his cup of tea.

'Not until Mal Haigh confirmed it. I suspected from the start that there was something going on. Umberto never trusted her with anything important. So when he did, there had to be a reason for it.'

'So why did he bring her with him in the first place?'

'According to Mal, Umberto Bonifati's presence

here in Manchester had less to do with the Richetti case than with drawing out the *Mafiosi* in the north-west of England. And to test out his suspicion that Caterina Volpe was leaking information to the Sicilian Mafia. Including, he surmised, their suspicion that Rafaelle Santagata had been involved in the Richetti murder.'

'My God!' she said. 'That means that his blood and that of Richetti's killers is on her hands.'

Caton nodded. And Bonifati's too, perhaps.

'If Umberto is right.'

Over the past two weeks there had been times when he could almost see and smell that pen, and hear the sound of Caterina Volpe retching. There were other, even more horrific images of what must have come before. The ones that woke him in the dead of night. He wondered how much more they haunted the sovrintendente's dreams.

'It's just as well you didn't bring them here to dinner,' said Kate.

She stood, and picked up her cereal bowl and empty glass.

'That was the reason, wasn't it, your suspicions about her?'

'Of course,' he said, lying through his teeth.

Caton sat in Arrivals waiting for their plane to land. The commissario and the sovrintendente were coming back to formally interview Arturo Santagata. He had been so terrified of further retribution being visited on him that he had not had the guts to fly out to Italy to be with his daughter.

When Caton broke the news to him he had collapsed. Now he was a broken man. Hardly surprising, given that not only had he lost his son in the most terrible circumstances, but also that now she knew the truth, his daughter was all but lost to him. When she was released from hospital she had gone to stay with her cousin until she had the baby, which she was determined to raise on her own.

Caton was convinced that Santagata had been the unwitting victim of his son's decision to hire amateurs to teach the Richetti boy a lesson. Having gone too far, they had tried to cover up their mistake by making it look like a Mafia killing. Everything that followed stemmed from that.

Except, of course, that none of this had anything to do with the Arrest Warrants. Other than the fact that Bonifati's connection with those, and the Richetti case, had led others to believe that it did. And to wreak a terrible revenge.

He saw Bonifati first, with Caterina Volpe following close behind. He rose to greet them.

She said that she needed to visit the ladies' restroom. Caton suggested he get them all an espresso while they waited.

'Caterina,' said Caton when she was out of earshot. 'are you absolutely sure about her, Umberto?'

Bonifati took a sip of espresso, grimaced and pushed it away.

'Like me,' he said, 'she has a phone for official purposes, and a personal phone. But she also has a pre-paid phone provided by the Mafia. That was the one she used the last time she claimed she was going to the restroom.'

'How do you know?' said Caton.

The commissario smiled paternally, as though a child had asked the question.

'Because our Secret Service is listening in to suspected Mafia calls on a continuous basis. After the Arrest Warrants had been served there were many calls to, and from, the UK.'

Of course, it was a stupid question. Thanks to Wikipedia, everyone knew that GCHQ exchanged information regularly with the Italian Secret Service.

'One of the calls,' the Italian detective continued, 'came from your Headquarters, at precisely the time Sovrintendente Volpe left to visit the ladies' restroom.'

'But why did she ring?'

'To send a warning that the police were going to the apartment.' He shrugged. 'But it was unnecessary. They had already taken the girl.'

'How did the Mafia know she was there, and that she had been involved with Santagata?'

'Because there was another call to that number, from another pre-paid phone, the night before.'

'After we had learned from Arturo about the daughter, and her brother, and that they were staying in Venice.'

'And where do you think the call came from Tom?'

'The vicinity of your hotel?'

'Exactly.'

At that moment he saw the sovrintendente approaching. Bonifati's face lit up, as though delighted to see her.

'Caterina,' he said, standing up. 'We are leaving. As soon as I can, I am going to get us a proper coffee.'

The following morning, Caton was still finding it difficult to concentrate. One question nagged at him. Had Umberto been playing her all along? Had she always been the commissario's unwitting accomplice. For how long had she been a pawn in the much wider game? He doubted that he would ever know. Either way, everyone else but him seemed happy.

The NCA had been handed a media coup tailor-made for their launch into the public consciousness, gained a foothold into two Mafia groups in the region, achieved the arrest and deportation of two Mafia bosses, and gained information and an arrest related to the supply of dangerous drugs poised to flood the city.

As for Bonifati, the killers of Richetti, and the man who had hired them, had received the roughest kind of justice. But that still left those who had commissioned their deaths, and those who had carried them out. Furthermore, someone had provided the details of the whereabouts of both Pistone and Giambotta, and quite probably set their acolytes against each other with such dramatic consequences. He had a hunch that he knew who that someone was.

Salvatore Borbone appeared completely at ease.

'It seems to me, Mr Caton,' he said, 'that you should be very happy. Two wicked men will finally be sent back where they belong to be punished for their crimes. Their organisations here in the north-west have been weakened. Justice has been done for the Richetti boy.'

'I understand that you are extremely well connected, Mr Borbone,' said Caton. 'I imagine that very little goes on in the Italian heritage community here in the north-west without you knowing about it?'

His use of the word *connected* had elicited the hint of a smile. Borbone was self-evidently confident in the security of his business dealings, to the point of smugness. He reminded Caton of others whose paths he had crossed who had yet to find their defences breached, their criminality exposed; men like Dimitri Izmailov and Ying Zheng Xiong. The kind of men for whom the National Crime Agency had been created. Caton earnestly hoped that the NCA would succeed where others had failed. He hoped that one day he would be there to see that smile wiped from their faces.

Borbone waved a languid hand in humble acknowledgement of Caton's assessment.

'Success in any sphere of life broadens one's pool of acquaintances,' he said. 'I imagine the same is true for you?' His smile faded. 'You must have many informants: snouts, grasses, snitches, squealers? Why do they call them squealers, I wonder? I have always associated that word with pigs.'

Caton ignored the taunt, and the accompanying message that Borbone knew where this conversation was heading.

'When did you discover that Giovanni Richetti was courting Arturo's daughter?' he asked.

He studied Borbone's face as the man decided how to respond. How much of the truth to share. How much this policeman really knew, as opposed to merely suspected. His expression softened. The smugness returned.

'Arturo came to see me,' he said, 'several months ago. He told me that the Richetti boy had seduced his daughter. That they had been seeing each other behind his back. That she was pregnant. He was distraught.'

'He wanted your advice?'

'I was his friend, as well as his business associate.'

'What did you tell him?'

'I *told* him nothing. I said these infatuations soon resolve themselves in the hard light of day. I suggested that he send the girl to stay with the grandmother in Italy. That she be persuaded to abort the child. That he not be hasty in relation to the boy.'

He smiled knowingly, man to man.

'You will know how young people respond to

being told no. It strengthens their resolve. I suggested that while the two of them were apart he might put temptation in the boy's path. Especially when he was in Italy.'

'A honey trap?'

'A few photographs, that's all. Enough to show the girl what kind of man he was.'

'But Giovanni Richetti insisted on trying to see her, and her brother decided to teach him a lesson?'

Borbone raised both hands in a gesture that reminded him of Umberto.

'You would have to ask the brother,' he said. He shrugged. 'But of course that is impossible.'

Caton kept his face deadpan.

'When Giovanni Richetti's body was found, did Arturo Santagata contact you?' he asked.

'He came to see me. This time he was even more distraught. He was worried that the murder would be laid at his door. He wanted me to try to find out who had done it.'

'Why you?'

Borbone shrugged. 'Like you said, I have contacts.'

'And did you find out?'

His eyebrows rose. Through his voice and his expression he simulated disappointment.

'Detective Chief Inspector, would I hide something like that from the police? If I had found out I would have told him, and he would have told you, and you would have told Commissario Bonifati.'

He shook his head gently.

'No. Nobody knew anything. They were amateurs. Sometimes amateurs are the hardest to find. You must know that? Not known to the police. Not known to law breakers.' He smiled. 'Not known to squealers.'

'Which is why they had to abduct his brother

346

Rafaelle, and torture him to get their names. Who would want to do that?' said Caton. 'Not his father. Not the Richettis. They didn't have a clue what was going on. So who?'

Caton only needed him to confirm what he already suspected. Not because they would ever be able to prove it, or to use this as testimony, but to satisfy his own professional curiosity.

Borbone clasped his hands together in his lap and entwined his fingers. He took his time replying.

'Ask yourself, Mr Caton, other than the death of the Richetti boy itself, what consequences did the murder have?'

'It brought Commissario Bonifati and his colleague to Manchester.'

'But they didn't come just to investigate Richetti's murder, did they?'

'He also had two arrest warrants on unrelated matters.'

Borbone nodded sagely. 'And who did those they arrested think had tipped off the police as to their whereabouts?'

It was beginning to feel to Caton like a Socratic dialogue, with the master leading him stage by stage to an inevitable conclusion. No, not to a conclusion. To the final imponderable.

'Each other?' he said.

Borbone shook his head, as though disappointed in his pupil.

'Only at first,' he said. 'Until someone pointed out that it had all begun with the discovery of a body on an island in Venice.'

Caton knew that Richetti's murder had had nothing to do with the warrants. That had been down to the *pentiti* Bonifati had told him about, and whoever had disclosed their whereabouts here in the UK. It was the more established traditional Mafia in the United Kingdom that had the most to gain from their arrest and extradition. From removal of the competition.

Nor was it certain that either the Camorra or the Ndrangheta had abducted and killed Rafaelle and the hired killers. It could just have easily been the Sicilian Mafia making a point. *This is what happens to those who try to bring the police to our door.* Was this a clever attempt by Borbone to muddy the waters further?

'Someone?' said Caton.

'So I am told.'

'And you have no idea who this someone is?'

This time Borbone's smile was sympathetic. 'Some things we will never know. I realise it is disappointing, but that's how life is.'

He stood up, signalling that the conversation was over. When they reached the front door, he paused.

'Sometimes, Detective Chief Inspector,' he said, 'it is safer that we do not know.'

Chapter 53

'You can't win them all,' said Holmes. 'But at least justice has been done.'

They had a table in the window of Albert's Shed, looking out at the former lock keeper's house on the opposite bank of the canal. It was a farewell meal for their Italian colleagues.

'Gordon is right, of course,' said Bonifati. 'One of the bones from the farm belonged to a young man who worked as a *scavatore di tombe* on San Michele Island.'

'A gravedigger?' guessed Caton.

'He had history with the *Polizia*. Street robbery, assault, what I think you call grievous bodily harm. He came out of prison six months ago. He and his brother went missing immediately after the girl was snatched.'

'Gravedigger?' said Holmes. 'So he was doing a spot of moonlighting the night he disposed of Giovanni Richetti.'

'Moonlighting?' said Caterina Volpe.

'Working outside of his job, on his own account,' Caton explained in Italian.

Bonifati chuckled. 'Blame the City Council,' he said. 'They have just passed a law allowing residents to scatter the ashes of their departed in certain places in the Lagoon. Fifty euros a time. Putting a lot of people out of business. Maybe Emilio was one of them.'

'So the brother asked around,' said Caton. 'Came up with these two amateurs with a family funeral gondola – which is presumably why nobody took any notice of them – and decided to make it look like a Mafia killing.'

'Their undoing,' said Holmes. 'And your case closed, Umberto, unless we can convince the CPS to charge the father as an accessory.'

He drained his glass and reached for the bottle.

'And pigs'll fly.'

He caught sight of Caton staring at him reproachfully. Two days ago Arturo Santagata had received a package through his letter box. It contained a small vacuum pack of thinly sliced wild boar prosciutto. Whatever state he had been in before, he was now a total wreck.

'Whoops! Faux pas,' said Holmes. 'Sorry.'

'Will you catch their killers, Umberto?' asked Caton.

The commissario swirled his wine around in his glass, and waited for it to settle.

'Eventually,' he said. 'The CCTV from the hospital did not cover the *ambulanza*. But in time they will be arrested for something else, and there will be a match to evidence they left at the farm. More likely, a *pentito* will give them to us.'

'*Pentito*?' said Holmes.

'A government informer,' Bonifati explained.

Holmes nodded. 'A grass.'

Caterina Volpe speared some pasta and twirled it on her fork.

'*Uomo morto che cammina,*' she muttered.

'Dead man walking,' Caton translated.

'Not necessarily,' Bonifati told them. 'These days

they run like rats from a sewer to tell us names and dates. We have a joke: *ci sono più pentiti che mafiosi.*' He smiled to himself. 'There are more *pentiti* than *Mafiosi.*'

They left the hustle and bustle of Albert's Shed behind and strolled along the towpath towards the Beetham Tower. Gordon Holmes and Caterina Volpe strolled ahead. Bonifati transferred to the pocket of his coat the copy of *Caminada, The Crime Buster* that Caton had given him as a reminder of his time in Manchester.

'May I ask you a question, Umberto?' said Caton.

The Italian detective, sensing the import of the question, studied Caton for a moment before he replied.

'It is always possible to ask.'

Caton pressed on regardless.

'All the time we've been together,' he said, 'whenever you've talked about the *Mafioso*, and what your law enforcement agencies are doing to combat them, you've used the word *we*, not *they*?'

'That is a question?'

Caton stopped walking, forcing his companion to do the same.

'*Keep your friends close,*' he quoted. 'That's what you said, Umberto. I had hoped that you thought of me as a friend. A trusted friend.'

The commissario looked out across the canal and pursed his lips. When he turned back, his lips had curled into a gentle smile.

'*Scusa,*' he said. 'Forgive me, Tom. You are right. In my world it is easy to forget who is friend and who is not. Let us just say that from time to time I do a little work for the *Direzione Investigativa Antimafia*. Not all of my colleagues know of this.'

'Not all?' said Caton.

He shrugged apologetically. '*Nessuno.*'

'None of them? Not even your superiors?'

Bonifati thrust his hands into his pockets and started walking again.

'*Loro?*' he muttered. '*Meno di tutti.*'

Them, least of all.

There was a full moon almost identical to the one they had shared on that fateful night at the San Clemente Palace. This time it was a lighter blue, in a sky where the stars were hidden by the glow of the city. Bonifati followed Caton's gaze to the canalside apartments, lit like jewels against the silhouettes of the darkened office blocks.

'*É bello,*' he said. 'But it is not Venice.'

'It's the same moon,' Caton observed.

'It is sad, do you not think, this moon?'

'Melancholic,' Caton agreed.

Bonifati nodded sagely. '*Melancólico.*'

The commissario stared at the backs of their two colleagues as they disappeared into the shadows beneath a bridge.

'*Ancora, getta una piccola luce nel buio,*' he muttered.

Caton did a rough translation in his head. *Yet it sheds a little light into the dark.* Something like that. It was a familiar phrase. One that he could not quite place.

They walked on for a while, watching the moonlight shimmer on the canal and the reflected street lights dance where the breeze ruffled the surface.

Without warning, Caton stopped and touched the commissario lightly on the arm. In unspoken agreement they waited until they judged their colleagues to be out of earshot.

'What will happen to Caterina?' Caton asked quietly.

'Her work will be restricted. She will be fed...' He

struggled to find the word, and gave up. '*Basura.*'

Caton shook his head and raised his eyebrows.

He tried again. '*Dis-informazione?*'

Caton smiled, and nodded. 'Dis-information.'

'In time, she will be questioned.'

'And then?'

Bonifati shrugged. 'Who knows? If she was frightened into this. Her family threatened. Maybe she resigns.'

'If not?'

'The *Procura della Repubblica* must decide. Will making it public be good, or bad, for the *Polizia* and the *Questore?*'

He held out his hands palm upwards, and lifted each in turn.

'Look how we weed out corruption? Or, the *Polizia* still cannot be trusted?'

He shrugged his shoulders and thrust his hands deep into his pockets.

Caton thought about Dave Woods, the former disgraced detective constable. He wondered what he was doing now, and if his wife, the architect of his downfall, had left him.

'Either way,' he said, 'what a waste of a career, and of a life.'

'We make our choices,' Bonifati replied.

An empty lager can lay by his foot on the towpath. He nudged it with the toe of his shoe into the canal.

They watched it float, waiting for the water to discover the hole where the ring pull had been. Slowly it began to fill. Just when it seemed that it might settle there, in suspended animation, it slid silently beneath the surface and descended into the inky depths. A cloud passed across the moon, deepening the darkness as though a light had been extinguished.

Slowly they turned and set off again, each lost in his own imaginings.

Epilogue

A fortnight later, a parcel arrived for Caton at the apartment. It contained a copy, in Italian, of *The Art of War* by Sun Tzu. It was based on the Lionel Giles 1910 translation.

Umberto had written on the flyleaf.

Per il mio buon amico Tom. Con gratitudine, e con ricordi felici. Perdona il mio sotterfugio. Per noi, e un modo di vivere.
Cordiali saluti alla bella Kate.
Umberto

One sentence had been underlined: *Forgive my subterfuge. For us it is a way of life.*

There was a post-it note marking a page. Caton turned to that page and found two more yellow stickers, marking the beginning and end of a passage. He began to read, translating as he went.

"It is the business of a general to be quiet and thus ensure secrecy; upright and just, and thus maintain order. He must be able to mystify his officers and men by false reports and appearances, and thus keep them in total ignorance. By altering his arrangements and changing his plans, he keeps the enemy without definite knowledge. By shifting his camp and taking circuitous routes, he prevents the enemy from anticipating his purpose."

Caton smiled. Poor Umberto. It must be a hell of a way to have to live and work. And then he remembered the disgraced Dave Woods. Perhaps it was not so different here, merely a question of scale. Furthermore, it was exactly how so many of the most successful organised criminals operated. Know thine enemy indeed. But keep them close? He shut the book and placed it on the coffee table.

That was never going to happen.

Acknowledgements

Nica Cardinal, for checking my Italian text. And Sarah Cheeseman, my proof-reader. Any mistakes that remain are mine alone.

As ever, Suzie Tatnell at Commercial Campaigns, for book blocking the paperback version. Mike Atherton of Dragonfruit design for his superb cover design.

The hundreds of sources that I consulted about the Italian *Mafiosa* in its many forms, including its presence in the United Kingdom in the modern day are too numerous to list, but I thank all of those authors and investigative reporters for making their work available, and for the rich and fascinating resource that it represents. And finally, Google Earth, which helped me to ensure that my memories from very many visits to the glorious city and islands of Venice had not been clouded by time or sentiment.

The Author

Bill Rogers has written nine crime thriller novels to date – all of them based in and around the City of Manchester. His first novel *The Cleansing* received the ePublishing Consortium Writers Award 2011, and was short listed for the Long Barn Books Debut Novel Award. His Fourth novel, *A Trace of Blood, reached* the semi-final of the Amazon Breakthrough Novel Award in 2009.

Bill has also written *Breakfast at Katsouris,* an anthology of short crime stories, and a novel for teens, young adults and adults, called *The Cave.* He lives in Greater Manchester where he has spent his entire adult life.

www.billrogers.co.uk
www.catonbooks.com

List of DCI Tom series titles in order

The Cleansing
The Head Case
The Tiger's Cave
A Fatal Intervention
A Trace of Blood
Bluebell Hollow
The Frozen Contract
Backwash
A Venetian Moon
All of his books are available as paperbacks
from bookshops, or on Amazon,
and as Amazon Kindle EBooks

Lightning Source UK Ltd.
Milton Keynes UK
UKOW02f1301051116
286918UK00023B/238/P